BURNING INTUITION

MAKENZI FISK

MISCHIEVOUS BOOKS
2015

MW00906370

Copyright © 2015 Makenzi Fisk

Mischievous Books
www.mischievousbooks.com

All rights reserved. No part of this publication may be reproduced, distributed, or transmitted in any form or by any means, including photocopying, recording, or other electronic or mechanical methods, without the prior written permission of the publisher, except in the case of brief quotations embodied in critical reviews and certain other noncommercial uses permitted by copyright law.

First Mischievous Books Edition 2015
Cover Design: Makenzi Fisk
ISBN: 978-0-9938087-4-6

ACKNOWLEDGMENTS

Stacey, my love, you never doubted.
I couldn't have done it without your support.

Wahnita, you have so many talents. May you realize them.
Thank you for your help with names and ideas.

Tracey, thank you for your friendship and guidance.

Thank you, readers, for entrusting me with your time.

DEDICATION

For all those who think they can't,
just get up and do something.

CHAPTER 1

"Relax your shoulders. Now inhale. Bring your chin down. Head up and exhale." The bare-chested yoga instructor sat before the class, cross-legged in baggy white trousers.

Allie closed her eyes and obediently followed his directions. Her shoulders sank but the insistent buzz in her brain resisted. The new lady beside her wore too much perfume.

"Inhale. Keep your head down."

Allie drew in a lungful of the nauseating odor. Who would wear such a cloying scent? She opened an eye and peeked sideways. The woman looked normal enough, despite her penchant for inexpensive plastic jewelry.

"Bring your chin down more. Now push your head back and—" He stopped mid-sentence and shot Allie a dark look. "Focus!" Waves of energy pulsed in her direction.

She snapped her head forward. Where was the regular instructor? Tamara radiated utter tranquility. This man did not. If he was permanent, she might have to find a different class.

"Now exhale."

Allie breathed out. Muscles knotted and joints kinked everywhere. What was wrong with her? She hadn't been able to sustain attention on anything for such a long time and now her body suffered for it.

"Mommy. I need to go to the bathroom." A little girl in a princess dress crept toward the lady with the perfume.

"Shhh." The lady's pink bracelet clinked when she held a finger to her lips. She was a mom. That explained the bracelet and the perfume. Gifts from her daughter. "Only a few more minutes. Go wait in the lobby."

White spots fluttered behind Allie's closed lids. *I wonder if I ever made a bracelet like that for my mama?*

"Inhale. Fill your lungs."

"Now!" The girl's face reddened. "And you said I could have a cookie."

"Exhale. Head up. One. Two. Three… Would you please tend to that child?"

A titter of amusement flitted across the room when the princess's mom grabbed her mat and hurried out.

The room blurred and Allie blinked her eyes. When she was six, she too had been a willful child.

"No Mama, I don't want a sandwich." My stubby finger points out the window to the familiar golden arches. "I want that."

"Shhh, Allie." Mama's eyes frown at me in the rear-view mirror. "Stop kicking."

"No. No. NO." My pink glittery boots pummel the back of Mama's seat. "I want the toy!" The car swerves left, then right. A blue van glides past my window. The buzzing in my head won't go away. It makes me angry. Mama doesn't care about me. She just cares about making sure that her car is ahead of all the others. I pound my fist against the foggy glass when the people in the van look over. Everyone can see how upset I am.

"I cut your cheese into squares, just how you like it."

"I don't want cheese." The big yellow sign I yearn for has passed and the agony of loss overwhelms my six-year-old brain. "I need the toy." That will make my head feel better. Sparks fizzle when I close my eyes. Something's coming. Mama knows it too. She is rubbing her forehead.

I grind my knuckles into my brows. It hurts. I want Mama to make me feel better but she's busy driving. I pull back my legs and kick the seat as hard as I can. "No!"

"Allie! Stop that right now." Mama turns to me and her face is not angry any more. She's frightened. She turns back and a dark shape veers onto the road in front of us. A truck. A big one. It's too close. "Ohhh," she sighs.

"Mama!"

We slide sideways and the truck's black tires are at my window. I'm upside down, my body snapped tight into my booster seat. I focus on my pink boots while the road spins. For a moment, everything stops. The air is so thick I can't breathe. Mama's red hair is frozen in motion, wild ends tangled into angel wings. I stare with awe.

I wake in the car. My chest hurts. The sparks behind my eyes are gone. Outside, people are yelling. Blue and red lights flash everywhere.

"Hey, little one. Are you okay?" A strange man with a mustache looms through the foggy fist marks on my window. He pulls at the handle and then breaks the glass to release me from my seat. When he picks me up, his coat is rough against my cheek. He smells like smoke.

I'm carried away. Away from Mama.

"I'm sorry!" I sob into the man's dark coat.

"Miss, are you ill?" The yoga instructor bent over Allie, his expression a mixture of annoyance and worry.

"I'm fine." She sat up and covered her face with her hand. When had she curled up on her side like that? Oh my God! She had zoned out. In public.

"Are you sure?"

Allie rolled up her mat and jumped to her feet. "I guess I was too relaxed," she fibbed. "I must have fallen asleep."

"Uh huh." The instructor shook his head.

Her cheeks warmed at whispers behind them.

"Let's call it a day, ladies." He clapped his hands in dismissal and the whispers were swallowed up by the simultaneous rustling of twenty yoga mats.

Allie grabbed hers and dashed to the parking lot. Alone in her Jeep, she wiped beads of sweat from her forehead and let her hair loose from its ponytail. She was trying so hard.

Her hand on the wheel grounded her. Her foot on the gas was control. Allie took a breath and straightened in her seat. She rammed the shifter into gear and squealed out of the lot. She didn't stop until she reached home.

Erin's truck wasn't in the driveway but that wasn't unusual. A police officer's hours were erratic. Allie turned off the engine and stared at the house. It would be quiet, the cat asleep somewhere. There would be echoes of her previous life where furry canine feet skittered just inside the door. Those were gone now. Her seatbelt was suddenly tight. She unsnapped it but the uncomfortable pressure remained.

She plucked her cell phone from her bag and dialed the numbers she knew by heart since she was a child. Her foster mom answered on the second ring and she choked back a sob.

"Allie? Sweetheart, is that you?"

"Yeah." Her voice cracked. "I was just calling to say hi…"

"What's wrong?"

There was no fooling Judy, the pragmatic woman who had raised her since her mother's death. "I'm having a hard day."

"Flashbacks? Nightmares? Premonitions?" Judy knew all of Allie's quirks and still loved her.

"I zoned out in the middle of a yoga class. Thinking about the car accident and… and about Mama."

"It wasn't your fault."

"I know," Allie sniffed.

"Sometimes things happen. No matter what you do, you can't change the outcome."

"You mean fate."

"Some call it that."

"Well, fate does not like *me*. I'm a mess. I can't concentrate on anything and I can't keep it together." When tears threatened, Allie rifled through her bag and found the package of tissues beside her Swiss Army knife. One thing Judy had taught her was to be prepared. She wiped her tears and blew her nose.

"Are you getting enough sleep? Eating right? You're not drinking *alcohol* are you?"

"No, mom." Allie rolled her eyes. A half-grin tugged at the corner of her mouth. "I'm not *completely* insane."

"Are you and Erin okay?"

"I… I think so." Her relationship with Erin was just fine, wasn't it? There hadn't been any disagreements, but things hadn't been quite the same since last year.

"I like that girl. She's good for you, sweetie."

"I know." Allie extended each tool in the knife and examined it. She'd never had cause to use the toothpick thing. Perhaps someday she'd be stranded somewhere with no dental floss and she could rejoice. She smiled and slid it back into its notch. Judy's calm presence on the other end of the line already made her feel better.

"I think you two have some unfinished business. You're stuck. There's no going back and you can't go forward until it's resolved. Talk to Erin. The two of you need to find something you can do about *that girl.*" Judy couldn't even say Lily's name.

Her foster mom always said she'd heard it all, but no story had disturbed her like the one Allie told her last year. The story of a child who manipulated adults. Professionals even. A child? Arson and murder? It was beyond comprehension.

Allie nodded. Through the tears, through the emotion, Judy had homed in on the crux. She was right. They were stuck. She was holding on to the past. She couldn't change the fact that she'd lost her mother, nor what had happened with Lily. But there was a future. She and Erin needed to talk.

Allie raised her hand when Officer Chris Zimmerman pulled up in his police cruiser. The passenger door flew open and Erin lurched onto the sidewalk. Zimmerman hurried around to guide her. Was she drunk?

"Judy, Mom, I need to go." Allie gathered up her bag and got out of the Jeep.

"Bye. Remember Marcel and I love you… and make sure you tell Erin how you feel."

"I'll *definitely* tell her." She stuffed the phone into her bag and met Erin on the step.

"Hi Baby. I hope your night was better than mine." Erin pulled herself up the stairs by the rail and fished in her pocket. "I can't seem to find my keys."

The odor of liquor stung Allie's nostrils when she opened the door. "You've been drinking."

"A bit." Erin forced a smile and waved off her best friend. "I'm good, buddy. I'll see you at work tomorrow."

"You should take a day off, girl." Zimmerman nodded to Allie and backed down the stairs to his car.

Erin hobbled through the doorway and headed for the sofa. Murky clouds churned around her. She plunked one running shoe on the coffee table and eased the other beside it.

Allie sat across from her and waited.

Erin's strained smile disappeared and she stared at the ceiling. "I twisted my ankle at a break and enter and the suspect got away. I'm losing it. I can feel it. He was right there. Right in front of me, but I couldn't catch him."

"Can I get you some ice?"

"Naw, I wasted the last part of my shift with my foot in a bucket.

5

The Emerg doc said that was all I could do for a sprain. After work, the guys bought me a few beers. Z-man thought it best that he drive me home."

"Did the doctor tell you how long to stay off that ankle?"

"I don't need time off, if that's what you're asking. I'm sure the desk officer wants some fresh air. I can swap with him." Erin sat up. "I was awake all night but you're the one who looks tired."

"I zoned out in yoga class," Allie blurted. "In front of everyone. I'm sure you'll hear all about it at the grocery store."

"What a pair we are," Erin snorted. "Maybe we need a vacation."

"Judy thinks we're stuck."

Erin eyed her. "Whaddyamean?"

"We can't move forward until we resolve what happened with Lily."

"Aw, you're not suggesting a stuffy old counselor?"

Allie's eyes widened. "God, no. We just need to figure out if there's something we can do."

"Fair enough." Erin wedged a pillow under her ankle. "I'm sure I can get time off. But you know this means I'll have to talk to Derek."

CHAPTER 2

It was like the high school cafeteria all over again, but this time Derek was not king. This time he swam at the bottom of the pond, and the big fish up top were hungry. Something was up. He could smell it in the sour odor of the men around him.

Sweating under his inmate's uniform of denim shirt and jeans, he nonchalantly slid his empty tray onto the conveyor and sauntered past the guard's pod. He kept his eyes on the floor and his limbs loose but anxiety writhed in his gut. Two more doors. Make that two doors and one stairwell before he was safely back in his cell.

The first door hummed. He nodded at the security camera and passed. *Best to keep your polite face on when dealing with the guard.* You'd hate for his finger to stall on the button at the wrong moment. The absence of cameras in the stairwells made him nervous. He bounded up the steps two at a time. At the top door, he pushed the buzzer but heard no answering hum. What happened to the guard? He thumbed it again. Laying his cheek against the reinforced safety glass, he peeked as far as he could around the corner to the next guard station. He couldn't see a damn thing.

The bottom door hummed and two sets of soft-soled inmate shoes entered the stairwell. Sweat soaked his armpits. He pressed the buzzer twice more. Footsteps pounded up the stairs behind him and he turned to face his attackers.

Ethan Lewis and a giant tattooed man stopped two steps down. Derek backed up to the steel door. He waved a hand in front of the window and Ethan snorted. He'd arrested Ethan years ago for nearly killing his wife. In here, everything was personal.

"Ain't nobody coming today, pig." He tilted his head sideways and glared at Derek with his good eye. Fine scars knotted the opposite side of his face.

"It doesn't have to go down like this, Ethan." Head-on, Derek faced the man in charge of this duo.

At six foot five, Ethan's henchman towered over them. Recruited as today's muscle, he punched his fist into his palm. A cartoon bad guy.

Derek flicked his eyes to the giant, and back to Ethan. He alerted to the way Ethan held his hand at his belt line.

"Don't call me that." Ethan's body tensed, shoulders cockeyed like a sidewinder. "My name's Badger."

"Okay, Badger." He held up both palms and kept the big guy in his peripheral vision.

"We ain't in back alley Morley Falls no more. No more badge. No more gun. You're nothin' in here."

"Yeah, nothin'," the giant parroted, bobbing his head. His long dark braid swung behind him. "A bitch pig already kicked your ass. Now yer gonna find out what a couple of real men can do to you."

Derek shifted his weight and bent his knees slightly. Steel glinted in Badger's hand when he came at him. The big man dove for his ribs at the same time. Derek was ready, ducking the worst of the force and coming up behind. He grabbed hold of the giant's braid and used it to slam his head onto the top step. His skull bounced like a jackhammer on concrete.

Lights out. One down, one to go.

Badger sucked air through his teeth and his nostrils flared. Without a downward glance at his fallen partner, he lunged. Derek dodged and a sliver of sharp steel flashed inches from his face. He pivoted and kicked his assailant hard in the knee. There was a loud pop. Badger crumpled, a marionette with clipped strings. He groaned and clutched at his deformed leg.

Derek glanced down at him. He'd likely suffered a torn anterior cruciate ligament. Not many fully recovered from that kind of soft tissue injury. He'd be able to predict the weather with that knee in a few years.

Before he'd wound up on the wrong side of the bars, Derek had used the same knee-popping move on a dirt bag named Randy

Walker. He'd caught Randy a block from a break-in at four in the morning, a trail of cash and cheap jewelry in his wake. At a skinny five-foot-five, Randy was no match for the policeman and he knew it. He'd dropped the loot and put up his hands.

It had been a tough week. Derek's wife had been bitchy. He'd been sleeping on the sofa in the police lounge. He really didn't feel like chasing the dirt bag all over town if he bolted. He had raised his size eleven boot and crushed Randy's knee.

Of course, that's not the statement he'd given to the PD's Internal Investigations Unit when Randy's parents filed an official complaint. Randy Walker had resisted arrest. The force was necessary and reasonable. Derek had seen the medical reports. Over and over. He could spell the name of that ligament in his sleep. Randy would walk with a limp forever. It had taken a year of internal investigation, and a sizable bribe, before it all went away.

In here, men played by a different set of rules. There would be no complaint against him, and no investigation. If you failed while taking a run at another inmate, you didn't go whining to the guards afterwards. You took your lumps and didn't squeal or you were the next target.

Derek bent and picked up the weapon. He slid the homemade shiv into a fold in his cuff and jabbed the buzzer one last time. It hummed. He stepped through the door and strutted past a clearly surprised guard and into his cell.

Once his door clanged shut he sank onto his cot. The practiced sneer slid from his lips. His head throbbed. Sweat drenched his shirt from neck to waist. If the other inmates didn't kill him, the stress would.

He flung the sturdy rubberized pillow to one end of his bunk and pulled up his legs. Someone with a sense of humor had named this place as if it were a country club. Oak Park Heights. He'd survived nearly a year in Minnesota's only Level Five maximum-security prison. It had taken this long to get out of the Protective Custody Unit where he might as well have had a target on his forehead.

Take aim boys, I'm in PC with the child molesters and the rats.

He threw his pillow against the cinderblock wall. After he'd signed the PC Waiver he'd finally walked among the men in general population. Word spreads fast inside prison when a high value target is in sight. There would always be someone coming for him but the

9

first time he'd stepped onto the grass in the exercise yard under the clear blue sky, he'd decided it was all worth it. The isolated PC Unit, with its tiny fenced exercise pad, had been unbearable.

He unfolded the shiv from his sleeve and examined it. Someone had broken the blade from a disposable razor and melted it into the handle of a toothbrush. Simple but deadly. He scratched the scar at his thigh where he'd nearly bled to death his first week inside and counted how many times he'd been attacked. Five times in one year. His nose had healed crooked after the second assault, but he'd learned more each time.

By now, he could feel the attitude change in the other inmates and knew when someone was coming for him. This was the first time he'd been aware of collusion by a guard. He made a mental note to find out which guard was involved. He had fifty years to serve, plenty of time for payback.

He rubbed his finger where his ring had been. The tan line was gone. It hadn't taken long for his wife to file for divorce. Was it right after his arrest? She'd wanted an excuse and had finally found it. She got the house, his Mustang, his new boat. Everything.

His daughter had been sent away without a chance to say goodbye. He'd never hurt his own child. Who'd made her say that he had? He smoothed the creases from a pencil sketch she'd given him before this had all started. Well, she hadn't actually *given* it to him. He'd found it crumpled on the seat in his car after he'd dropped her off one day. He'd snatched it up as if she'd drawn it just for him.

It was a picture of a little house in the woods. A house with a picket fence. He brought the drawing closer. It looked a bit like the Johnson house. The one where he'd investigated a fire. He turned it over and read the back. The word NEXT was scrawled in pencil.

Why would she...?

He folded it in half and put it on the shelf. No. His kid had nothing to do with that old woman's death.

He wanted his daughter back, and he wanted to find her mother. Tiffany, the love of his life since high school, had disappeared years ago without so much as a note. The child had gone to live with her grandfather and rumors had swirled. Rumors that amounted to smoke. Tiffany had vanished.

Now he had no one. His entire family had disowned him. The only ones who still talked about him were those mysterious acquaintances that kept popping up on talk shows. He didn't recognize most of those people but now everyone was an expert on his life. They didn't know a thing. Everything he'd loved, he'd lost.

Derek turned the shiv over in his hands. The weapon was crudely built but the razor was securely attached to its hilt. It would cause major damage. He angled the blade at the inside of his wrist, its cold point sharp against his skin. What was he doing? That was a pussy way to go. He held it to his throat. How long did it take the average man to bleed out?

No hesitation buddy, just finish it.

"Inmate Peterson." A voice boomed through the intercom. "You have a visitor." The lock hummed and his cell door slid open.

Lily! Was she back? Had she come to visit? Derek shoved the contraband into his sleeve and hurried to his feet. He slid his hands through the slot in the metal door and waited. Seconds later, a guard approached and snapped cuffs around his wrists. The door opened and the guard positioned himself behind Derek to the right, in escort position. They made their way through the maze of hallways.

"Who's here to see me?" The only visitors he'd had in the past year were lawyers and his now-ex wife. He hadn't had a single visitor in over two months. "Is it my daughter?" He turned halfway to the guard.

"Eyes forward, inmate."

Derek snapped back around. He knew better than that. *Don't make the guard nervous.* "Is my daughter here?"

"They said it's some cute blonde. Didn't say who."

His heart leapt. She was here. The weight of the shiv suddenly became onerous. He bent to sneeze and dropped it by his foot. The guard took a step away and he covered the weapon with his shoe. When the guard motioned him forward, he straightened and coughed, simultaneously toeing the shiv into the crease where floor met wall. With his attention on the inmate's hands, the guard missed it. The next person who passed might spot it, but Derek would be gone.

They continued to the visitor's cubicles. When he'd last been here, he'd been served divorce papers. This time would be different. Lily had come to see him. Derek shuffled around the stool and sat. He held up his wrists. The guard snapped his cuffs on a chain secured to the floor and exited.

* * *

A uniformed prison guard held open the heavy door and Erin Ericsson stepped into the no-contact visitor's room. Derek bolted upright on the other side of the unbreakable glass partition. His movement strained the chain that tethered him.

"Remain seated for the duration of the visit, inmate." A guard's voice boomed over the intercom. Derek sat but the startled look remained. He'd lost weight and his fair skin was gray.

Erin settled on the cheap plastic chair and inched closer. The entire room was painted a dull institution brown, enough to make even those with the sunniest dispositions contemplate the darker side of life. She plunked her notepad onto the narrow ledge that served as a counter and picked up the phone receiver wired to the wall. The mouthpiece looked sticky. She grimaced and rubbed it against her sleeve before she brought it to her mouth. It didn't touch her lips.

Derek's eyes went to the closed door behind Erin. His pupils constricted and his gaze reluctantly settled on her. He reached over and yanked his receiver from its bracket.

"Da fuck you want?"

"Only a year and already you sound like one of them."

He glared at her and rapped the receiver against the wall. A painful squeal burst from Erin's earpiece and she wrenched it away. *What a juvenile trick.*

"Damage to institution equipment will result in the termination of your visit." The bored guard sounded as if he was reading off a cue card. Erin couldn't see him, but the omnipotent being presided over everything.

Derek held up his hands in submission to the round-eyed security camera and slouched in his seat. Handcuffed at the wrists, he could only raise his hands to his waist, but the gesture was unmistakable. She suddenly understood his posturing. Everything that happened in prison was noted, and remembered. Prison gossip was worse than station house gossip and they both knew how *that* worked. Now that he had established his tough guy persona, and disdain for his police visitor, he was done showboating.

"Ah, same old Derek," Erin mocked. "Always happy to see me."

He pressed the phone to his ear. "What are you doing here?"

12

His voice was raspier than she remembered and a shiver of guilt niggled her. The last time she'd been this close to him, she'd been crushing his windpipe. She might have killed him if her girlfriend Allie hadn't intervened. The snappy retort withered on her tongue and she stared at his Adam's apple. It was off-center. Was she responsible for that?

"What the hell, Erin?" He met her gaze, eyes flat and cold. A shark.

She took a deep breath. "I need your help."

He reeled back in his chair and let out a harsh laugh. "Are you out of your mind? After what you did to me? You are unbelievable."

She focused on an imaginary spot on the counter and drummed her pen on the ledge. "I know about Lily."

There was a spark in his flat green eyes and he brought his face closer. His angry breath steamed a fuzzy semi circle below a red sign that warned him not to touch the glass. "What do you know?"

"I know she's your daughter."

The spark winked out. Everyone with a television had heard about the cop gone bad. The cop who'd abducted his own kid. Everyone knew he'd confessed to burning a woman to death, poisoning a man, and almost killing a second woman. Every man in prison knew he had been taken down by a diminutive female officer. Everyone knew he would rot in jail until he was ninety-two. But Erin knew more.

"You couldn't have killed Dolores Johnson. And you didn't poison Gunther Schmidt."

"I don't kill old ladies." The spark flickered again, but he was wary. "And I'd never hurt the old man. We were friends."

"You didn't try to kill Gina Braun either," Erin said. "Maybe you wished you had."

His eyes narrowed and the corner of his lip lifted. "What do you want?"

"I told you. I need your help."

"Why the hell should I help you?" His ropy forearms tensed when he clenched his fists.

"Because you want to protect your daughter and you want to find her mother."

Derek's sneer drooped.

"Because you don't want to spend your life in jail for something you didn't do." Erin laid her pen against her notepad.

13

"Nobody else believes me." He rubbed a scraped knuckle against his unshaven chin. "There is not a single man in here who admits he did the crime. You know how it is. We're all innocent, right?"

"Your case is different."

"I ain't no choirboy." His gaze flicked to the spot between her elbow and shoulder.

She touched her bicep. The scar beneath her sleeve was still pink where his knife had cut through skin and muscle. She'd fought back. She'd mangled his vocal chords and half-drowned him. Then she'd arrested him.

"Why did you confess to all those crimes?"

"I had my reasons. It was a mistake."

"A helluva mistake, Derek." Nobody confessed by mistake. Was protecting his kid really worth all this? Aside from the phone and her chair, the room was completely empty. A lone bulb affixed to the ceiling was encased in plastic. The rest of the prison would be an extension of this. Sparse. Industrial. Depressing.

"Now we both know the only crime I'm guilty of is *that*." He jutted his jaw at her arm.

That, and threatening her with his pistol. Not to mention beating her senseless with a chunk of driftwood. Had he gotten what he deserved? "I think she's doing it again." Erin averted her eyes from his throat.

A crease formed at the corner of his mouth. To his credit, he didn't denigrate her by pretending he didn't know what she was talking about.

"Lily's gone to live with Gunther's nephew and his wife."

Derek grunted.

"Gunther's in no shape to parent anyone. When I last saw him, he couldn't even walk. They're telling him to sell his place and move into assisted living."

Derek's complexion took on a lighter shade of gray. "He'll never do it. He'll die alone at his own house before he lets them force him into a nursing home."

"There are nice retirement villages. He could be mostly independent."

"Drool slobbering down his chin? Gunther won't let that happen."

They'd skirted the issue long enough. She steered them back on topic. "Lily is in Winnipeg with Albert and Barbara Schmidt. She just tried to kill Barb."

His body froze. "How?"

"It sounds the same as what happened to Dolores Johnson. Gas explosion."

His head dipped in deference. He'd been lazy when he'd ruled that case accidental.

"Did anyone tell you we found fingerprints at that crime scene?"

"Fingerprints." He leaned forward. You can't get fingerprints off ash."

"Someone had been watching the house from a spot outside the fence, near the bog."

"Yeah, right."

"It was definitely an observation post, with flattened grass and a couple of stashed beer cans. I brought those in as evidence."

"You were busy behind my back, I see." He tensed his jaw.

"Kathy in Ident found fingerprints from a young woman or child. Lily was watching the house."

"That's a stretch." The chain rattled when he tried unsuccessfully to cross his arms. He laid his hands in his lap.

"Lily knew what kind of car Dolores drove. She'd been watching her. I think she did it."

"You got a vendetta against my family, Ericsson?"

"She's going to keep doing it, Derek. Open your eyes. This time the fire crew rescued Mrs. Schmidt. She's in the hospital with severe burns."

He shifted uncomfortably.

"The newspaper reported that a female teen," Erin air-quoted, "that's got to be Lily, escaped unharmed."

"No! Lily's only a little girl." He frowned at his knuckles as if he was counting on invisible fingers. "She just turned thirteen," he said slowly. "I guess she is a teenager now."

"Did you miss the part where a home was destroyed and a woman is in the hospital?"

"No, I didn't miss that." He sighed and his shoulders sagged. "It's just that... well, she's my daughter. I always wanted kids but that wasn't in Karen's life plan." He steadied his gaze on Erin. "It can't do any more damage now to tell you this, but I didn't even know I had a kid until a few years ago. When Tiffany finally told me, the news blew me right out of the water. I figured she got pregnant in high school by some other guy but the first time I saw Lily I knew she was my blood."

His voice wavered. "Tiffany was always there for me and understood that I wasn't ready to be a father at the age of seventeen. I was too selfish. Even after I married Karen, I still saw Tiff on the side sometimes. Being with Karen made me lonely."

Erin felt the skin around her eyes tighten in judgment.

Derek looked at the floor. "I was going to leave my wife and marry Tiffany, swear to God. I gave her a ring and everything. I can't believe, after all that, she left. It sounds stupid, but I thought we were soul mates."

"Lily killed Dolores. She tried to kill her grandfather and Gina. Is it possible she was also responsible for her mother's disappearance?"

"She's just a kid. She's all I've got left." His eyes hardened.

"I'm going to stop her, Derek. I'm going to Winnipeg."

"Nooo!" He howled like a feral animal and lurched forward. His forehead collided with the glass and a bright red crescent welted above his eyebrow. "Leave her alone." He lunged again and the chain that tethered his wrists jerked taut.

"Inmate. Remain seated!" The guard's voice crackled over the intercom. The steel door behind Derek opened and two uniformed men entered. Derek didn't even look up. He drove his shoulder into the belly of the first guard within range. Chained to the floor, the blow lost its force and was easily deflected. Both guards leaned their weight onto him and flattened him. Derek pawed at them from the side but they overpowered him. Two more guards appeared in the doorway with a flat Velcro-strapped board.

On her feet, Erin turned at a hand on her elbow.

"This visit has been terminated. Please follow me."

It was not a request. A guard led her away. "You're the cop that arrested him right?"

She nodded.

He whistled. "You must have enjoyed seeing that."

She didn't respond.

"They're gonna board him until he cools off. It don't hurt but it's not fun."

Erin could visualize a pissed-off Derek strapped to a wooden plank until he calmed. That might take a while. She looked up and her frown reflected back at her from the convex mirror mounted at the corner of the hall.

"He don't usually give us trouble," the guard volunteered, "but I heard he had a rough day. A couple other inmates tried to take him out in the stairwell and we seized a shiv in the hallway a while ago. I'd put the two incidents together." He grinned. Gossip was prison entertainment. "He's tougher than he looks. The two guys who attacked him are in the medical wing."

Derek's bellows followed them to the lobby. The guard shrugged and buzzed the last door.

"Have a nice day," he said. The guy at the fast food restaurant had told her exactly the same thing this morning when she'd paid for her breakfast sandwich.

It was not a nice day for Derek and it would be the last day of his daughter's undeserved freedom when Erin caught up to her.

CHAPTER 3

Socked feet propped on the Tacoma's dash, Allie thumbed to the next page in her e-book while she waited. She focused on the screen and blocked out everything but the words until a vivid story built. It muted the omnipresent drone of intrusive thoughts. She sighed in relief.

In the story, Pearl was about to fall for the wrong girl. The words the author had chosen were sheer deliciousness. Allie tucked her knees into her chest and turned another page. Would she make this huge mistake?

No Pearl. Don't do it. Ruth is way better for you.

The story was sappy, the characters fantastical, but she loved the way she could never guess what they would do. Reading was so much easier than being around actual people. Real people had conflicting emotions and energy to absorb. It was hard to block it all out. Gosh, it made her tired. This particular story was so entertaining, and *spicy*, that it offered her a welcome reprieve.

Above the digital book, she spotted her girlfriend's exit from the prison and hurried to finish the paragraph. When she closed it, everything she'd blocked assaulted her senses.

Erin wrenched open the driver's door and Allie cringed at the jagged spikes of negative energy that intruded. Anger, fear and despair permeated every crevice of the truck's cab.

"It went that well, eh?" Allie put her tablet away.

Erin twisted the key in the ignition and the engine caught. "Let's just say Derek is not having a good day."

"I know." The shoes Allie had tossed to the floor had somehow made their way under the seat and she contorted her legs to wiggle into them.

Erin regarded her with a slight smile. "Right now the sunlight is reflecting into your eyes and the cute little green flecks are absolutely on fire."

"You don't want to talk about it, do you?"

Erin looked out to the parking lot. "Tell me."

"It felt like his life was in danger, right before we arrived." Allie had tuned in to Derek's energy. Focusing on the story made it easier to block out the rest of the world. Still, the world seeped in.

Erin looked over, and a wrinkle formed between her eyebrows.

"He's safe for now, but he's furious."

Erin shook her head. "I guess I don't need to tell you the rest. You already figured out that he wasn't helpful."

"He's afraid."

"Afraid? That's not how I would have described him." Erin's hands gripped the wheel. "He would have taken my head off if he wasn't handcuffed to the floor. He can be a jerk, but I've never seen him so volatile. Did I do that to him?"

"His actions were not your fault." Allie turned in her seat to face Erin. "He did this to himself."

Erin pushed the shifter into drive. "I nearly killed him. Who's the one with control issues now?" She put her foot on the gas pedal and the truck lurched forward. "I damaged his vocal chords. The guy sounds like a bullfrog."

"But he might have shot you. And don't forget the knife."

Erin nodded. "He deserves jail time, but he shouldn't go down for crimes he didn't commit."

"Forgive me if I don't understand your sympathy for him right now."

"He brought it on himself. It's the part where I lost control that still bothers me." Her voice softened. "You saved us both."

"We're here for each other." Allie paused. "I'm sure you've made the right decision. Besides, it's only a temporary leave of absence. Time away from work could be a good thing for you." She glanced over at Erin who stared at the road. "Well, I took the day off to keep you company, so let's make a real outing of it, shall we?" The truth was that staying home alone still tortured Allie. Wrong-Way Rachel slept most of the day, as cats do. She was wonderful, but a feline's company was on its own terms. Allie missed the unconditional love of her dog. Every day she missed Fuzzy Fiona's presence. The sound of toenails clicking on hardwood echoed in her memory. When she put out her hand to touch soft fur, the memory faded to the grave marker and rock cairn along the river. Fiona, there would never be another like her.

"All right. We should take advantage of the lovely weather." Erin slowed when they neared the businesses near the St. Croix River.

Allie forced a smile.

Erin pointed to a parking lot off Water Street. "Let's go have lunch at that café." She turned the wheel and found a spot in the shade. "Afterward we can check out the famous Stillwater Lift Bridge."

They held hands while they walked to the restaurant and a spiky-haired young man asked them twice if they really wanted to sit on the patio.

"Of course, it's a beautiful day," Erin told him.

He shook his head and hustled them to a table outside with a view of construction barricades between the end of the parking lot and the river.

"Somehow I imagined this being more romantic." Allie plucked her napkin from the table and dropped it into her lap. She ordered the poached salmon and steamed vegetables, along with a glass of ice water. Erin ordered a cheeseburger, fries, and a beer from the local brewing company.

Allie shook her head. Erin's metabolism was so fast that she would burn off every last calorie with an hour and a half of fidgeting. Allie needed to work harder to keep in shape. She hit the gym at least five days a week, six if she was stressed. A side benefit was that working out was better than reading. When she focused on exercise, the intruding thoughts blurred.

"I didn't notice the construction from where we parked." Erin offered up her lopsided grin when a front loader's bucket screeched against concrete. "We can escape this noise after lunch and walk across the bridge."

"I'd like that."

"Did you know it was built in the 1930s? Cables keep snapping and the downtime is horrendous. They say it's obsolete. As soon as the new bridge is built, they'll convert this one for pedestrians. The lift will still operate to allow water traffic."

Allie smiled indulgently. "Thank you, tour guide. Did you read a brochure or something?" This trip to town, the insistence on patio seats, Erin's knowledge of the local landmarks, she had planned this whole outing.

The loader turned and scraped gravel in a different direction. Erin raised her voice above the screech. "Believe it or not, I searched up the most romantic lunch spots in Stillwater before we came. They had a blurb on the historic bridge, but there was no mention that half the waterfront was under construction."

"Well, I suppose everyone for a block radius has discovered if they have any loose fillings." Allie grinned. She dug into her meal, eager to finish and get away from the loud machinery.

Erin crumpled her napkin. "Why don't we skip the dessert menu and go someplace quieter?"

Their stroll along the river was refreshing. They walked past the white gazebo, and across the lift bridge. A historic tour bus emptied tourists onto the trail and they hurried to keep ahead of the crowd. At the boat dock, they considered taking a paddleboat cruise, but the next one wasn't until dinner.

Allie glanced at her watch. She'd hoped to be back home by then. There would be a lot of catching up for the day off. Her heightened job demands were directly proportional to the toxic atmosphere in the office. The company was downsizing, if that was the correct term for firing half its staff. She might be next unless she quit first.

A woman stepped onto the path ahead. Beside her, a young child held the leash of an energetic golden retriever.

"Look." Erin pointed and quickened her pace. "That dog is gorgeous. Let's catch up and maybe they'll let us pet her."

An image of the rock cairn that covered Fuzzy Fiona's grave flashed into Allie's mind. *I'm not ready. I can't. I just can't.* She turned abruptly and peered out at the bridge. "We should go across again." As fast as she could, she walked the opposite direction.

"What's wrong, Baby? Are you getting one of your premonitions?" Erin jogged on her stiff ankle to keep up with Allie.

"No, it's not that." How could she explain the scar on her heart that ached whenever she thought of Fiona? She studied the steel

21

cables that supported the ancient bridge with more interest than she felt.

Calm down, that's just a dog. It's not your dog.

She took a deep breath and the painful knot in her chest began to unwind.

"You're missing Fiona aren't you?" Erin squeezed her elbow.

Warmth pulsated through Allie's body and centered in the middle of her chest. *Who was the intuitive one now?* Erin might not have intuition, but she had no trouble reading her.

"Let's go home." Erin held out her hand.

Allie intertwined her fingers in Erin's for the walk back. She'd never had another girlfriend who was so comfortable with herself. Erin never cared if anyone noticed or if they frowned. The knot in Allie's chest unwound a few more turns.

They skirted the barricades on their way to the truck. It had started out as a nice break, but virtual storm clouds gathered around Erin. It was only a matter of time before she voiced her concerns.

"I'm going after Lily," Erin blurted once they reached the main highway.

"I know."

"I contacted Albert Schmidt. He told me his wife is being released from the hospital this week."

"You didn't tell him about the girl?"

"I lied." Erin's cheek twitched. "I said I was the admin assistant from Lily's old school, sending out her records. He told me she's doing great, making all kinds of friends. I didn't believe that for a second. He also mentioned that Barb was in an accident and would be in hospital for a few more days. Then I got the name of the school wrong and the conversation went sideways." She was a terrible liar, and that was another thing that Allie loved about her. "He got suspicious and said Lily warned him about people out to get her. I can imagine the lies she concocted. Albert hung up on me."

"He won't help us when we get to Winnipeg," Allie said.

"Us?" Erin's eyebrows shot up.

"I told you, we're in this together." She'd already arranged a place to stay in Winnipeg but she'd tell Erin all about that later. "Besides, you need me."

"I do need you. I won't have my trusty sidekick Z-man to back me up on this case." She tickled Allie's palm.

"You and Z-man were a pretty good team. I doubt I can measure up."

"You have skills." Erin smirked. "I sure hope your surveillance skills are better than his. He does not have a sneaky bone in his body and stakeouts with him are painful. I love that guy but every single thing he does is loud. I swear you can hear him chew gum two blocks away."

"You're exaggerating." Allie raised an eyebrow. Chris Zimmerman had been Erin's best friend and colleague for years. In another life he must have been a southern gentleman. Every time she'd spoken to him, he'd been like a bashful teenager. He'd even called her ma'am once and she'd burst out laughing. He'd shuffled his huge feet and blushed from ear to ear. He was adorable.

"Nope." Erin retorted. "I talked to him on the phone before we left. He's worried about some guy in a red sports car prowling the alley behind his mom's house. He tries to keep an eye on the place when he's working nights but the guy sees him coming a mile away and takes off. Z-man hasn't even been able to get a license plate number. He's really worried about her safety."

Allie squinted out the windshield and the road blurred. Nothing about this story felt threatening. Exciting maybe. "I don't sense that she's in danger."

"That's the weird thing. He says his mom's ignoring the whole thing. She doesn't seem worried at all. In fact, every time he brings it up, she changes the subject."

"A security camera is a bad idea."

"How did you know he was going to?" Erin rolled her eyes. "Of course, you just *know* things. Well, if it was my mom, I'd get her a ninety-pound Rottweiler."

"The next time you talk to him, tell him not to worry so much about his mom, okay?"

"He won't take my word for it. Do I tell him that I heard it from my psychic?"

"Don't be ridiculous. I'm not psychic. If I was, I'd buy lottery tickets and we'd go to the Bahamas."

Erin tilted her head back and laughed.

"And remind him that it's time to tell his mom he's dating Gina."

"I can't imagine the sheer volume of stuff you know." Erin shook her head. "You're such a beautiful puzzle."

CHAPTER 4

Frances Anne Hopkins Junior High is an ugly brick building on a boring street. Some colorblind loser chose the paint. The front doors are Barney the Dinosaur purple. Everything else is puke yellow. Yellow tile, yellow walls and yellow lockers. Yellow must have been on sale when they built this place.

A huge painting of a voyageur canoe hangs on the wall in the main entrance. Who cares about history? Not me. The only time is right now.

Lily wuz here. With a fat black marker I add my scribble to the graffiti on the painting.

Late again, I need a stupid pass to get into math class. I aim the toe of my shoe at the raised edge of a loose tile on my way to the office. It snaps off. I chase the wedge down the hall, kicking it every time I catch up. School is a waste of time, but it's better than sitting home watching daytime TV.

Home. I smirk. There is no home. I've been staying with Albert at a crappy motel since what he calls *the incident*. Barb pissed me off for the last time and now half their kitchen is ash. The rest of the house stinks like smoke and everything's ruined.

Someone boarded up the doors but I can still get in through an unlocked basement window. I don't go very often because it smells like burnt garbage, and my clothes reek all day. I can't get the stink out of my nose for a long time. I skipped my last class yesterday to go get my knife. That's all I missed from that place.

Maybe I'm a nomad. Maybe there's a time limit for how long I stay in one place. I sure hope we aren't in the motel forever. Even with all the movie channels, it can get boring.

When I get to the office, I pull my hood off before the receptionist gives me a lecture. She's on the phone and waves me to a seat. Sure, I don't give a crap if I'm another five minutes late. I sit in the plastic chair and put my hand in my pocket to turn my knife over in my fingers.

My minion, the man who called himself my father, stole mine. This one is better. I found it in a drawer at Albert and Barb's house. As soon as I saw it, I knew it should be mine, so I took it. No one ever mentioned it so I guess I was right.

The first night, I sat up and practiced until I could flick the blade open with one hand, in case I ever needed to. When I had that down, I faced the mirror in the bathroom and pulled down my jeans. I always heard so much about this at school. I ran the blade across my thigh and there was a brief flash of pain. I looked at the blood for a minute and wiped it off with my finger. *Nah, not my thing.* I'd pulled up my jeans and put the knife away.

It was truly mine now. A relationship forged by blood. At least that's what they would have called it in the Viking movie I watched last night.

The receptionist is still blabbing on the phone when a new girl walks in with her mom. New girl sits beside me, and smoothes her perfect slacks over perfectly shaped thighs. She looks like she stepped out of a teen fashion poster. Her mom stands at the counter, timid as a field mouse, and clears her throat a couple of times. The receptionist doesn't look up. Mom sits beside her daughter and all three of us wait until she's done her very important call and notices us.

"This must be Nina." I'm totally ignored while the receptionist goes ga-ga over the new girl. "What pretty hair you have, and what a sweet smile."

Blah, blah, blah. I grind the heel of my shoe on the floor.

Finally she addresses me. "Lily, you and Nina are in the same home room. Why don't you show her the way while I talk to her mom?"

I glance down at my worn jeans, gray hoodie and favorite ratty shoes. *Do I look like I wanna make nice-nice with the fashion princess?*

She hands me my late pass and shoos us out the door. As soon as

I leave the office I pull my hood back up over my hair and Nina follows me, a meek clone of her mother.

The receptionist is right. Nina is pretty. Not the clown-makeup, big-boobs kind of pretty the boys around here seem to like, but real American apple pie pretty. She peeks over while we're walking and gives me a shy smile. I get the impression that she prefers to be invisible to adults.

I drop my cigarettes on purpose and she immediately bends to pick them up. When she hands the pack to me, I notice her shoulder-length brown hair, and the sprinkle of tiny freckles across her nose. For a second, her green eyes meet mine. She catches her breath and her pupils dilate. I curve one corner of my mouth up and she looks away. A trace of interest prickles deep in my brain. Maybe she's not a stupid pretty girl. Maybe.

Nina sits a row over from me at the back of math class. The boys twist their necks to salivate over the fresh meat and the girls turn their catty eyes to her. Notes pass down the aisles and they whisper. I cross my arms over my chest and stare down each one of them. *I saw her first.*

I can already tell Nina is smart. She's way ahead of me but that might have more to do with how often I show up in class. She lends me a pencil and graph paper. As usual, I haven't brought anything with me. I was expecting a sharpened-at-one-end pencil, but she's given me a mechanical pencil. Not a cheap one from the dollar store either. It's one of the good ones that don't break the first time you poke it into a crack in your desk.

She leans over to help me and her shampoo smells nice, like laundry detergent and soap. I give her a real smile this time and she blushes pink as a wild rose petal when she tells me to keep the pencil.

After class, a couple of boys approach Nina. She twitches and puts her head down so I step between them and they back off. Everyone clears a path for us when I walk Nina to her next class. I'm a badass panther. No one messes with me. Not since I showed my blade to the girls in the locker room. You know how girls gossip. I didn't need to show anyone else.

One year in this school and things have changed a lot for me. Barb walked me to school on my first few days, like a moron in Kindergarten. When I told her to lay off, she kept trying to get me ready like a baby. I don't need anyone doing that for me. I've been pretty much taking care of myself for years. I'll go to school on the days I feel like it. Teachers don't care. It's not like they're gonna flunk me. No one fails any more, no matter how bad they do.

The first few months I kept my head down and watched to see how things worked. Seems every place has its own unwritten rules. I learned to ignore the boys because they're not interested in me and they're stupid. The girls were my biggest obstacle.

I tried. I really tried to get them to like me. I tried to fit into the popular crowd. I tried to fit in with the ones that hung out after school. I smiled at all the right moments. I laughed at their stupid jokes and even wore the stupid outfits Barb bought me.

Sooner or later, I'd say something and they'd all stop and stare. 'You skinned a squirrel?' The whole herd of them would move away like I suddenly had cooties. After that, I never quite fit in. I don't care. They're idiots anyways.

Nina is different. She's smarter than them. She's almost as smart as me. I drop her off at Social Studies class and she talks me into going inside with her. She's nervous, she says. I go in and sit beside her even though this is my least favorite class. Math is easy compared to Societies of the Past. They're all dead. Isn't it obvious that they were losers? What could we possibly learn from them? I walk Nina to the rest of her classes and wait outside with her after school until her mom comes.

"Don't you live close enough to walk home?" I ask her.

"We're staying in a townhouse until we get a place."

"Do you have a dad?"

"Uh, he lives somewhere else." She studies her pink fingernails.

There's something she's not telling me.

"I'm in a motel with my uncle right now." Albert isn't exactly my uncle. He's my grandfather's brother's son. What does that make him? I never had enough relatives to want to puzzle that out. Uncle is close enough for me. I didn't even know he existed until I had to move in with him.

It's not like my grandfather and I had a lot of meaningful conversations. It was more like, 'This is how you bait the hook', or 'Back up the truck so I can load the boat trailer'. It usually ended with 'Dummkopf, you're doing it wrong!' I didn't expect that old buzzard to live and I can't believe that he'd ever want to talk to me again. He knows by now that my dad wasn't the one that poisoned his beer.

A dented red minivan pulls up in front of the school and the front tire bounces over the curb with a loud screech of steel against concrete. I bet that rim won't last long. Everyone notices and Nina's whole body shivers.

Interesting.

Her mom sits behind the steering wheel and her face is red and puffy. She's been crying all day. Her hair is flat in the back with that slept-on look.

I stand up from the concrete planter and Nina touches my forearm. I flinch. I don't like to be touched. She catches my eye and gives her head a tiny shake. She grabs her backpack and runs to the car. I shrug and turn away. She wants to get the hell out of here so everyone will stop staring. I know what that's like.

When they're gone I walk back to the motel. Albert is still at work and Barb will be in the hospital for another day or two. She says I scare the crap out of her. I'm not supposed to visit, but that's not what I told the cops who investigated the fire. I told them we all got along great. They are the best guardians ever and I'm happy I moved to Winnipeg.

Then I said that Barb gets confused sometimes and that old gas stove always worried me. The two of them together made me downright nervous. The firemen looked at each other and I walked away, satisfied.

Barb made it easy to convince the cops. The pill I put in her tea made her sound addle-brained. She made no sense at all when they asked her what happened. *Thank you to the lady at the mall who had them in her purse.* I scored fifty bucks and a bottle of sleeping tablets the day I grabbed that bag.

I throw my math homework into the cheap metal trashcan and open the fridge in the kitchenette. There's no beer. In the cupboard I find fruit snacks. Albert must think I'm a baby. Just like Barb. They're both clueless.

It's quiet in here, just the way I like it. I curl up on the pullout sofa. There's nothing good on TV so I open the door to the bedroom and go through the drawers. There's gotta be cash somewhere. Everyone hides money, don't they? I find a twenty-dollar bill in the pocket of Albert's pants in the laundry basket. I can usually count on a few coins, but twenty bucks is a bonanza.

I hold it up to the light and the yellow bulb shines through the transparent plastic section. Canadian money is pretty cool, I gotta admit. You can tell what you have right away, just by the color. It doesn't fold properly so I bend it in half and jam it into my jeans pocket. It's Friday night and I've decided I'm going out as soon as it gets dark. I want to figure out where Nina lives.

A block from the motel is a bar where construction guys drink all afternoon. I don't know why they're not out fixing roads in this city. There are enough potholes to keep them working all summer but here they sit getting drunk. This seems like a good spot to find a car and I try the doors one by one.

In the city, most people lock their doors and finding a key under the mat is not as easy as in Morley Falls. Today is my lucky day and there's an open door with a key in the ignition. It's a beat-up construction truck with a club cab, littered with squashed coffee cups and a mound of smelly old blankets on the rear seat. I don't care as long as it's got an automatic transmission and it starts. I'm not so good with standards.

I gun the engine and take the back alley to the main road to avoid streetlights. Even with my hood up, sometimes people turn their heads when they notice how young I am. I don't want to get pulled over by the cops. I got stopped once back home but my minion came and took care of it. He can't do that for me from jail. I cross Portage Avenue and get back onto a side road.

I've been driving for about twenty minutes when I pass a sign covered in graffiti. You can't even read it. It's all row houses for blocks and it might have been an okay place twenty years ago. Now everything looks busted. Peeling paint, sagging fences, dirty cars, and a helluva lot of trash on the street. Gangs have scribbled, scratched or spray-painted everything.

A boy on a BMX bike grabs his crotch when I cruise past and his buddies laugh. They probably did half the graffiti around here, trying to copy the big boys. The kid who grabbed his crotch pedals fast to catch up to my back bumper. He thinks he's cool to coast along with me so I jerk the steering wheel and he slams into a parked car. There's a lot of swearing and yelling when his buddies crowd around him to haul him back to his feet. He kicks his bike. Now I'm the one who's laughing.

A red van is parked cockeyed in front of a house at the end of the next block. I pull a U-turn and come back. *That's it.* That's the same dent and gouged rim I saw bouncing over the curb in front of the school. It sits right in front of an end unit where a TV glows blue through open curtains. Someone is watching Dora the Explorer. Couldn't be Nina.

I'm surprised when she stands up with a little kid in her arms. The kid laughs when Nina twirls her around. I'd never imagined she'd have a younger sister. She's way nicer than me. I'd never watch Dora for anyone. I pull my hood around my face and idle the truck across the street.

After a while her mom comes in and she's as red-faced as she was this afternoon. She's yelling. I can't make out any words but I can tell that what her mom says upsets Nina. I push the shifter into park and slide out of the truck.

With a palm-sized rock in my hand, I duck behind a hedge along the sidewalk. Years of practice pay off when I pitch the rock at the center of the window. It crashes like a gunshot and cracks spider out from the hole. Mom jumps straight up and Nina hauls the kid off. I bet she's locked herself in her bedroom by now. She's smart. She'll stay there until it's safe.

The lights go out and her Mom squints out the side window into the dark. I make out the shape of her head through the screen from where I'm crouched. If I can see her, she might see me. I sprint across the road and into the truck, jam it into gear and chirp the tires. A couple of blocks away, I slow to the speed limit and whoop like a savage.

"What the hell is goin' on?"

The reflection of a squirming mound of smelly blankets in the rear-view mirror almost makes me pile the truck into the back of a Volkswagen. I yank the steering wheel straight in time to avoid its back bumper.

A bearded guy with checkered shirt and bleary eyes looms up to stare at me in the rear-view mirror. "Who the fuck are you? Where is Charlie?" He puts his hands on my seat back. I pound the gas and he's thrown backward.

I need to get out. Before he can find his balance, I brake hard and he bashes his face into the back of my headrest. Now he's really pissed. He'll kill me if he gets his paws on me.

I screech to a stop and leap out the door. The truck rolls, picks up speed down the hill and smashes into a concrete bus bench. Tossed forward, the construction worker's big boots are in the air. I'm halfway down the block before he shoves the door open and lurches onto the road, rubbing his hairy face. In five minutes he might wonder if he drove there himself.

I stop running three blocks later. I'm winded. My heart pounds in my ears and I have to bend and hold my knees. City sidewalks kick my ass like the backwoods trails never did. I'm out of shape and I hate it. I could trot for hours back home, but not here. Have I been sitting around too much?

When I catch my breath, I tilt my head back and look at the sky. I can't make out a single damn star under these streetlights, but they buzz like bugs mating in the swamp. That makes me feel more at home. Blood rushes in my veins. The surprise of the freaked out construction guy gave me more of a rush than throwing the rock at Nina's mom.

She better leave Nina alone.

CHAPTER 5

"Hey asshole!" The inmate's muted voice crept from the adjacent cell.

Derek Peterson didn't move from the edge of his bunk and kept his feet planted on the floor. After another attempt on his life, he'd been transferred back to the protective custody wing. The loneliness ate at him worse than last time. He focused on the muscle car magazine he'd borrowed from the prison's library cart. He'd already read it front to back twice but it was a distraction from the mouthy dirt bag next door who'd been taunting him since breakfast.

"Badger gonna kill you."

Badger, a.k.a. Ethan Lewis, had been gunning for him since Derek had popped his knee out in the stairwell. He walked with a cane now. Most guys would have backed off, but not Ethan. It made him more determined than ever to recover his jailhouse reputation. He needed to kill Derek to do that.

"He gonna stick a shiv right in your throat."

Derek didn't rise to the bait. He tried to relax his tense shoulders and loosen his jaw. How did anyone survive the chronic stress in here? It was worse than being in uniform on the street. Worse than staying constantly alert and always looking over your shoulder. At least out there, you weren't trapped in a six by eight concrete cubicle. Out there, you could plan your attack, or escape.

"We gonna watch your blood make a swimmin' pool on the floor. Then we gonna party."

That got Derek to his feet, fists balled tight, but he was smart enough to keep his mouth shut. The rat next door didn't need to know he'd riled him. It was only a matter of time before someone got to him in here. If it wasn't Ethan Lewis, there were a dozen more waiting in line to take out a cop.

Derek picked up the photo of his daughter and sat on the edge of the thin mattress. Eight years old in the picture, Lily straddled a shiny bicycle and beamed up at the camera. Sunlight backlit her blonde hair with angelic radiance. He cradled it in his rough hands and a half smile cracked his dry lips.

Tiffany had given him the photo when she'd first told him the girl was his daughter. He knew instantly that it was true. He could see himself in her pale green eyes, fair skin and hair. There was something more, something about the way she stared directly into the camera's lens. It was compelling and unnerving at the same time.

He'd tried to be a father to her, hadn't he? He'd been a standup guy when he'd talked to her grandfather and together the two men came to a gentlemen's agreement. Every month since, Derek drove out to Gunther's place by the river. He left a check in the shed for his daughter's care and a six-pack of beer in the fridge for Gunther. He didn't know many other men who would take on this kind of responsibility. He really was a decent guy.

At first he tried to be Lily's friend, her confidante, then her father. She didn't buy it and she never listened to him, except when she feigned interest long enough to ask for money. She could sure put on a pathetic face, and she was relentless. Nothing could keep her from what she wanted.

When he saw her wandering town at night, he always gave her a ride home so she didn't have to walk through the woods. There were bears and wolves out there, not to mention the risk of getting lost. That would be scary for a young girl, wouldn't it? He squinted at the picture and the intense eyes stared back. Maybe not.

There was more to Lily than the cheerful smile she produced for pictures. She'd used that same smile on him but it vanished as soon as he gave in. The weirdest thing about her was the way she talked to him, like he was her servant or something. Minion? What kind of kid called her dad that? He'd heard disrespectful teens call their parents by first name, but this? He was no father of the year, but even he knew this was unusual.

At first he'd thought it was in jest and he tried to treat it as a private joke, something special they shared, like a man calling his wife his 'old lady' in front of his drinking buddies. It was all for fun, wasn't it? After a while, the joke grew stale but Lily kept at it. He finally realized that she truly regarded him not as a father but more as a man who would do whatever she asked. He set the picture back on the desk. It was true, he would.

He unfolded the pencil sketch Lily had left in his car. Why did it look so much like Dolores Johnson's house? Why had Lily scrawled the word *NEXT* on the back? Had she been casing the place? Did she have something to do with the gas explosion? Was his kid really responsible for all the things Erin said?

He'd been so eager to protect her. He'd operated on pure gut reaction when he'd confessed and hadn't considered all the angles. He rubbed tired eyes with coarse fingers. All this ruminating was getting to him. He re-folded the drawing and placed it beside Lily's photo.

Think about the facts, just the facts, man.

Okay.

He thought back to the night he'd picked Lily up from the Stop 'N Go. The kid was damn lucky that Gina, the manager, hadn't insisted on pressing charges. He'd given Lily a short lecture about shoplifting, which she'd ignored, and a ride straight home. She'd used those pathetic eyes and talked him into giving her a cigarette.

She was a kid. What was she doing smoking?

Well, it was better that she got cigarettes from him than by stealing. He'd discovered later that she'd lifted his lighter while she was at it. He wasn't entirely surprised. What else was she capable of?

He'd dropped her off at Gunther's place and there was the flicker of a TV in the living room. Gunther was probably up watching the game. Lily would have gone in and watched it with him.

Come to think of it, she hadn't entered the house when he'd dropped her off. His Norman Rockwell vision of a young girl watching a ball game with her kindly grandfather crumbled. She had gone directly to the shed. It would have been so easy for her to wait for him to leave and then head straight back to town. Lily was determined when she got something in her sights.

He didn't want to allow himself to remember the fleeting glimpse he'd had of a kid ducking behind a fence by the Stop 'N Go. He'd seen her in his rear-view mirror later when he was on his way to the bar. The skinny girl in the gray hoodie. She could have lit that fire. She must have. He didn't like loudmouth interfering Gina any better than he had in high school but he'd never hurt her. It was Lily.

No!

This was his daughter. His little girl. He was not thinking straight. It must be the claustrophobia of the cinderblock walls closing in on him. He got to his feet. Three steps to the door, turn, three steps back. He pivoted on his heel and walked to the door again. With hands flat against the glass, he bashed his forehead into the steel frame. The newly healed cut split open and a trickle of blood ran down the side of his nose.

He flashed back to the last time he'd hurt himself. He'd taken a run at the safety glass separating him from Erin Ericsson. The guards had terminated the visit. He'd lain face down, strapped to that board longer than he cared remember, so angry his entire body shook. Murderous thoughts intruded. They hadn't let him up until he'd been a sniveling wreck. He sank onto the bed and put his head in his hands.

There had to be something the girl had not told him. In his bones, he felt she held the key to finding Tiffany. They would be together as a family some day. Tiffany had his heart and Lily had his blood. That was what life was all about, wasn't it? If his daughter was in trouble, he needed to help her but he couldn't do that from here. He had to get out, before she did something she could never come back from. Then he'd never find Tiffany.

Lily was his connection to Tiffany, but Erin was his connection to Lily. Within a matter of days, Erin would be in Winnipeg. She was a bulldog once she got her teeth into something. She would find Lily. As much as he hated to admit it, he needed Erin's help, but she was the one woman immune to his masculine charm. How would he possibly get her on his side?

Derek jumped like a startled rodent when the lunch cart rattled up in front of his cell door. How the hell had it snuck up on him? He did his best to look unruffled when the inmate worker slid a plastic-covered tray through the slit in his door.

"Ethan says to enjoy your lunch," the worker sniggered. He shot a glance over his shoulder and scurried off to the next cell.

Derek waited until he could no longer hear the rattling and got up to retrieve his food. He flipped off the plastic cover and held the tray at eye-level. The sandwich with crisp lettuce and a pickle hanging out the side looked innocent enough. He poked a finger at the apple and it rolled harmlessly over to the piece of plastic-wrapped cheese. What did he expect? An apple bomb? He was being ridiculous.

He picked up the sandwich and lifted the top slice of whole grain bread. A bright red tomato nestled on top of a generous leaf of fresh lettuce. Tiny water droplets still clung to the edges. The toppings had been as neatly arranged as a magazine ad, not at all the kind of sandwich he'd expected in prison. His stomach rumbled. It had been hours since he'd suspiciously sifted through this morning's oatmeal. He was starving.

Prizing up the lettuce, he checked underneath and dipped the tip of his finger into the chicken salad. It tasted amazing. He immediately took an oversize bite, sighing in relief as he chewed. This was the best sandwich ever.

On his third bite, he found it. The pain in his tooth shot right to his jaw and he spat out the half-chewed mouthful. A rusted nail and a shred of tissue paper jutted from the layer of mayonnaise. At least he hoped it was tissue paper. His gut told him it was probably toilet paper. Nausea stung the back of his throat.

He left the rest of his lunch on the tray and slid it back by the door. Ethan had connections in the kitchen. If he couldn't jab a shiv between his ribs, he planned to starve him to death. Derek needed to get out.

CHAPTER 6

"Have you seen the cat carrier?" Allie held the squirming feline like a football under one arm and closed the closet slider with the other.

"In the basement, on the shelf by the washing machine," Erin called through the open front door. "I already packed her vet records." She stowed the last suitcase in the bed of her truck and shut the tailgate.

Allie trundled downstairs, retrieved the carrier and loaded the indignant cat. Wrong-Way Rachel let out a perturbed yowl and curled into the back corner, swishing her tail over her nose. "It's okay buttercup," Allie crooned. "You'll like Winnipeg, and you'll like Ciara. She's nice to kitties." She set the cat carrier by the front door.

"Are you coming?" Erin called.

Allie took one last walk through the house to make sure she hadn't forgotten anything important. Erin had been grabbing bags and loading them into the truck faster than she could bring them. Now she wasn't certain what she'd packed and what she hadn't.

In the kitchen, she stopped and stared at Fiona's water dish on the floor. It had remained undisturbed in that corner since she'd lost the dog last year. Even Erin mopped a circle around it. She bent for the dish and held it to her chest until flashes of memory seeped into her mind.

Fiona's timid nose on the back of her knee when she walked. Soft brown eyes, blind to the world but so insightful to Allie's emotions. Her unconditional love of all creatures but fear of so many human things. Fearfulness turned to fierce loyalty when wolves had threatened Allie. Wolves that had ultimately torn away Fiona's very life.

Horrific images from that night in the woods revolved in Allie's mind until the dish trembled in her hands. She dropped it like a hot coal into the trash bin and backed out of the room.

"Coming!" She hurried out to the driveway with the carrier and slid it onto the front seat.

Erin was already sitting in the truck, safety belt on, tapping her knuckles on the wheel.

"I did a last check of the house." She turned her tears to the window.

"I miss her too, Baby." Erin reached for her hand.

"I'm ready." Allie opened the wire door and smoothed Wrong-Way Rachel's ruffled fur. She noticed the deep furrow between Erin's brows. "I guess you can't get away from here fast enough either."

Erin shrugged and backed out the driveway. "You know why I didn't get the transfer to Forensics? Some of the guys in admin were buddies with Derek and they didn't take too kindly to the way he went down. It's a case of the Old Boys Club at the station."

"You're not angry with Bert, I mean Striker, are you?" Darn that silly Muppet nickname. She wished Erin had never mentioned it. Even though it suited the dark-haired, fuzzy-browed man, she'd be mortified if it slipped out in front of him.

"I know Bert's a good guy. I don't really begrudge him the Forensics transfer, but I was sure I was more qualified."

"You promised not to call him that."

"I did promise, but he took my job, so I figure that nullifies my verbal contract with you and..."

Allie raised an eyebrow.

Erin's facetious words stalled in her throat.

"You have to acknowledge that you're being penalized for the way you investigated Derek Peterson. You kind of made up your own rules and you're lucky you didn't get sacked altogether."

"Nobody else was going to stop him. We thought he was abducting Lily, remember?"

"Officer Chris Zimmerman was on your side. So was Officer Striker."

"You're right. I dragged Z-man and Bert into it with me." Erin shot a sideways glance at Allie. "Sorry, I meant *Officer Striker*." She sighed. "I didn't follow protocol, and that leaves everyone wondering if I'm a liability to the department. The constant negative media attention this case generated was the kicker. When I asked for a leave, I got the impression that they hoped I'd walk out the door and never come back."

"It was all over the news for weeks," Allie said. The newspapers sure liked their dramatic names. "I could barely go out without someone begging to know how you caught Derek Peterson, the Morley Falls Monster."

"I hated when they called me The Raging Ranger," Erin spat. "That's not even remotely accurate. Can't the hack reporters tell a ranger from a police officer? Every time I heard them bring up the whole deal about excessive force, I wanted to scream. Internal Investigation cleared me. It was justified."

"No one who knows you believes what they said on the talk shows. I think six months leave will be good for you. You've rarely been outside Minnesota."

"Cities are stressful. The sheer number of traffic lights makes me dizzy."

"You seemed fine with it when we first met in Toronto." Allie gave her a wink.

"I was utterly distracted by you."

Her touch sent quivers of excitement up Allie's spine. "I think this trip will be good for me too. I need to meet potential clients who headquarter out of Winnipeg. It's better to set these things up in person."

The skin at the corner of Erin's eyes pinched.

"Don't worry, Honey. I'm the boss of my own consulting business now, with all the perks. I can work anywhere I want and we'll have more time together."

Erin looked unconvinced.

"Remember that everything is done online? My office is wherever I happen to be. I'm so glad I quit that terrible job. I felt like it was sucking my soul. Now I have my first big deal and I really don't want to blow it by looking like an amateur."

"I worry that this means—"

"I'm not going anywhere, but I need to travel for client meetings once in a while. You can come whenever you want. We're together now, aren't we? We'll make a vacation of it."

"When? In between your meetings and my chasing the psychotic monster-child?"

"That's harsh." Allie frowned. Erin's anger prickled between them. Mixed with the anger was something else. Fear? Insecurity? She could only guess.

"You can't deny that Lily *is* a killer."

"Yes, but there's a child in there somewhere."

"Beats me where you get your unwavering faith in humanity."

Two hours later, Erin's shoulders straightened when they reached the sign for the town of Stillwater. "I can't believe Derek said he wanted to talk. I'm a bit nervous. Last time he lost it and they boarded him. Prison life must be excruciating if he wants to risk a repeat of that fiasco." She pulled into the parking lot of Oak Park Heights Prison and found a spot of shade under the canopy of a large tree.

"I told you he wanted to talk," Allie said. "He only needed more time. Be mindful of how protective he is toward his daughter and he will talk to you today. I'm sure of it."

Erin gave her a lopsided grin and hopped out of the truck.

Allie watched her walk across the parking lot and enter the big door before she pulled her tablet from her bag and released the cat from her carrier.

Rachel disappeared under the seat and Allie kicked off her shoes. She stretched socked feet onto the dashboard and opened the e-book she'd downloaded. Today's story was a ridiculous tale of mutiny on the high seas and a lady pirate who falls for her buxom cabin girl. The more outlandish and unexpected the story line, the better she could avoid uninvited thoughts. Sappho's Boundless Seas was perfect for today.

By the second paragraph, the ominous cloud of emotion emanating from the prison retreated to a corner of her mind and she relaxed. The cat finished her exploration and snuggled onto Allie's lap.

* * *

Erin passed through the security gate and was led to a visiting booth. She took a seat and nodded at the glass lens of the camera on the wall. Eyes everywhere. It was enough to make one paranoid.

She looked at her watch and thumped her heel on the concrete floor. She was eager to get back to Allie and get on the road, but her curiosity over Derek's sudden turnabout was irresistible.

Ten minutes passed before the opposite door opened and Derek entered the inmate side. He averted his gaze and perched uncomfortably on the stool. The guard secured his cuffs and clunked the door shut when he exited.

Erin was chagrined to see the former police officer, eyes on the floor, flinch at the sudden noise. The only other time she'd seen him like this was when he was in grade ten, and she in eight. In playoffs he'd missed a critical pass and was blindsided by an opposing football player. Winded, he'd gasped for air. His teammates had ignored him. Game over, scoreboard mocking them, they'd left the field and silently filed past. One teammate had the gall to slap him in the back of the helmet as if the loss was a direct result of his incapacitation. Today, she saw the return of that cowed boy.

Slowly, he raised his eyes and she knew the shock of his appearance registered on her face. She tried not to let her shock turn to pity, but there it was. His red-rimmed eyes sank into his eye sockets, dark against the pallid color of his face. There was a certain looseness to his skin that alarmed her, like a terminal patient who has lost all hope of recovery. The two regarded each other for a long moment. Words failed her.

"Hey," she said finally, arranging her hands on her lap.

He sighed and his shoulders slumped like a deflated ball.

Erin fidgeted in her seat. This was not going as she'd expected. She'd been prepared for a repeat of their last meeting, where Derek had come at her with the fury of a threatened bear. This was not the man she knew.

"Derek, you look like hell."

He twitched as if he'd been slapped.

"What's happening to you in here?" She leaned forward in her seat.

Elbows on knees, he laid his stubbly chin on his hands. "I can't do this." Raspy words faded to a whisper.

"You can't do the time?"

"Yeah, that." He straightened and smoothed the front of his denim shirt. "And..."

Erin held her breath. Once again Allie was right.

"You're right about my kid," he stated in a clear voice. "She's the one who burned the Stop 'N Go." He skipped the part about the attempted murder of Gina Braun.

Erin sat back and kept her face neutral. She didn't want to interrupt him.

"I should have told you this when—" He clipped off his words and eyed her cautiously. "When I was arrested."

The corner of Erin's eyelid tightened. Couldn't he face the reality that she'd been the one who'd taken him down? He'd fought. He'd lost. She stared at the broken man. If that's how he chose to remember the epic battle they'd had, so be it.

"After Gina caught Lily shoplifting, I heard the call on my radio. I drove over as fast as I could to talk her out of charging my kid."

Erin pursed her lips. She wasn't about to lecture him now.

"I dropped Lily off at home that night but she threatened to hurt Gina."

"Threatened? How?"

"She told me she would make Gina pay. She would get even. I didn't imagine she was serious. I laughed about it and told her Gina had been a pain in my ass since high school. She said she would get even for the both of us."

"Do you remember her exact words?" Erin reached for her notebook. This was new information. She subtly scratched his comments onto the lined paper without taking her eyes from his.

"Something like, 'She's going down, sucker. She's gonna fry'." He raised cuffed wrists and covered his mouth in a belated attempt to stop the words. Moist droplets seeded the corners of his eyes.

"Why are you telling me this now?"

"She's done things. Awful things." He swiped at an eye before the tear breached. "I know you. You'll find her and you'll send her up for a long time. She might even get hurt."

Erin narrowed her eyes and nodded. "Only if she—"

"But she's just a kid. My kid." The tear welled again and dashed down his cheek before he could stop it. "She had a rough start, but she still has a chance. She just needs a little help. She can get better. I don't want her hurt. Do you promise?"

"I would never willingly hurt a kid." Erin met his eye. "I'm going to stop her but I promise to do my best to make sure no one hurts her."

He nodded.

"What else do you know?"

"After I dropped her off, I know she didn't stay home. I saw her in town later. Pretty close to the Stop 'N Go." He took a deep breath and his chest sank when he exhaled. "She ducked behind a fence when she saw my car, but it was her."

"So, she had motive, she had opportunity. But what about means? What makes you think she's capable of arson?"

"Fire is her thing. It's always been her thing. Yeah, she does lots of shit she shouldn't do, but starting fires is her favorite. I can't even count how many lighters she's stolen from me." He met Erin's eyes. "Old Gunther has been putting out fires since he took her in. Remember the outhouse behind the shed?"

"That was a classic. A three-holer in three different sizes. Nice enough for the Shah of Iran. It must have been a hundred years old."

"Gone," he said in a monotone. "She burnt it down right after she moved in. Remember the canopy he built over the dock for his boats?"

"Burnt too?"

"Yup." He nodded. "Gunther told me she nearly burned the house down a million times. Kept him hopping with the bucket of water he kept by the old wood stove. He said he tried to teach her properly so she'd stop burning his house and do it right."

"How do you do arson right?"

Muscles rippled at the point of his jaw.

You idiot. He's trying to cooperate. She closed her mouth and waited.

Finally the skin around his eyes relaxed. "Why do you need to make everything so hard?"

Erin shrugged.

"I meant that he taught her to use fire properly, like for getting rid of trash in the burning barrel, not destroying shit for fun. After that, she kept the fires off the property, but I don't think she stopped altogether."

Erin raised her eyebrows in a question.

"She never liked her sixth grade teacher, Ms. Barker. Remember that her garage mysteriously burned down a couple of years ago? I'm pretty sure that was Lily. I saw her wandering around that night and gave her a ride home. I thought it was weird that she smelled like gasoline but she said it was turpentine from cleaning paintbrushes. Said she volunteered for an after-school project."

He wrinkled his nose. "Contrary to what she thinks, I'm not stupid. I can smell the difference between turpentine and gasoline. Besides, that kid never did a school project she wasn't forced to do. It's time to pull my head out of the sand. She really likes fire. This is her M.O."

Erin leaned close to the Plexiglas window between them. She believed him, but a lot of others wouldn't. "They're going to say you're making this up to get out of jail."

"Damn sure, I want out of here, but you know I'm telling the truth."

"Bizarre as it sounds, I believe you. And I'm sorry," Erin blurted, "about your throat." She held two fingers to her own. "I crossed a line. I shouldn't have gone all ape-shit on you. You were down, that was enough. I knew better." The tremendous weight she carried began to ease.

"I thought everyone was out to get my kid and I needed to protect her. I see more clearly now." His face flushed. "I ain't proud of how it went down either."

"We both lost our minds," Erin said magnanimously. She took up her notepad. "Tell me everything you can about Lily. What motivates her?"

* * *

Allie uncrossed her ankles and pulled her feet off the dash of Erin's truck. The cat squeaked at the abrupt posture change. She'd reached the end of her chapter and the prison's oppressive emotions crowded in on her again. This time, it was not only the overwhelming despair she felt. There was hope. A tiny ribbon of optimism shone through the dark clouds.

Erin had connected with Derek and he was cooperating. Erin was good. When she wasn't being a hothead.

CHAPTER 7

I wait outside school Monday morning. Rain drips off my hoodie and I try to keep my cigarette dry with my cupped hand. Nina is late. I haven't seen her since I threw the rock at her mom's window Friday night. What if she never comes back? That would suck. I take one last drag and blow a perfect smoke ring in the air, the way Minion showed me the first time he let me smoke with him.

Homeroom with Ms. Henderson is almost over. I shake my head. That teacher has a face like a goat. She's also one of those do-gooders who spends way too much time poking her nose in other people's business. I steer clear of homeroom if I can help it.

With an expert flick, I ditch the glowing cigarette butt in the planter and walk to the entrance. A car door thumps behind me and a red van zooms past in my peripheral vision. *Nina!*

Head down, feet heavy, Nina joins me. On her first day in school, she'd looked like she'd be comfortable in a teen fashion magazine. Today, she looks rumpled, tired, and her backpack hangs from her shoulder as if it's filled with rocks.

"You made it." I dazzle her with my best smile and Nina's frown lifts.

"My mom slept in."

A knight in shining armor, I snatch the backpack from her sagging shoulder and she's too tired to complain. It is as heavy as it looks and I struggle to pretend it's no big deal. She must have every single textbook in here. She follows me to the office where I make up a lie to get our late passes.

In Social Studies, I hand the passes to the teacher and saunter past to save Nina a seat in the back. With their noses wrinkled, the girls whisper between the rows and the boys watch with interest. Even when she's got bags under her eyes, she's the cutest girl in school. I stare down the boys so they don't get any ideas.

She sits beside me, a mouse in a room full of cats, and lays her head on the desk. For the first time in my life, I try to listen to the teacher. And I take notes. Usually I scribble but today I make perfect loops and precise strokes. Nina is too tired to pay attention so I'll give them to her after school.

At lunchtime, I squat beside her locker while she puts away her things. Neither of us brought a lunch or have any money so it's pointless to go to the cafeteria. She shuts the door and sits beside me and I let her lean on me a little. I don't like being touched, but I try my best suck it up. I can smell her shampoo but she's too close and I wriggle to give myself an inch to breathe. My agitation subsides. Maybe it's not so bad. Nina looks up at me but I have no idea what she wants. She's hungry? She's happy? Angry? What?

"Thank you for being nice to me," she says finally.

That's it? That one wasn't even on my radar.

"I'm always nice," I lie. I'm never nice. I hate nice. Nice means you're a sheep. I'm no sheep. I'm a badass panther. Sheep fear me. I smile at her again. Her face turns pink, and she looks at her fingernails.

"I'm having trouble concentrating today," she says.

I know what that means. "Me too. Let's get out of here and do something fun." I stand and she gets up right after me but I can tell she's never skipped school before. She has no idea what to do. I take the lead and ditch my backpack in my locker. She follows me right out the front door like a duckling following its momma. As soon as we're off school property I pull out my pack and hand her a cigarette. She shakes her head so I stare at her hard until she takes it.

"Go ahead. It's not going to kill you," I say, like every bad guy in every movie.

"I don't... I've never..." Her fingers tremble and I catch the cigarette before she drops it. When we reach the alley, I hand it back to her and she takes it again, pinkie finger out like the Queen of England with her teacup.

"It's not a friggin' joint." I take her hand and readjust it so she's not a total dork. When I touch her, she sucks in a breath and her eyes dilate like a drug addict. I look directly into them. My lips curve upward when her freckles dissolve right into her bright red cheeks. I like this kind of control. She breathes out hard through her nose. Now I'm sure. She's attracted to me.

I lean in close so she can feel my breath on her neck and hold my lighter to the end of her cigarette. She breathes so quick I wonder if she might pass out. I back off a step and she relaxes. I tell her to suck air in all the way to her lungs and she obeys.

"This is awful!" Nina bends over coughing and her face is what my mom used to call green around the gills. She's going to barf. I take her half-smoked cigarette and finish it for her. The pink comes back in her cheeks.

"Yeah, I did that too, the first time I tried it." I smoke the cigarette to the filter and toss it, still burning, into an open trashcan.

She starts to go after it. "What if it starts a fire?"

I shrug. "It's only garbage."

She peeks into the can like a good little citizen.

I pull her by the arm. "Let's go get some lunch." That gets her attention and makes me wonder how long it's been since she ate. It's time to teach her how to get a meal around here.

Outside the corner store, I pause and smooth Nina's hair. She has to look good. Predictably, her face flushes when I get close. In Morley Falls, I did what I wanted and there was no one around to catch me. Here, people are everywhere. I've had to adjust my technique.

"All you gotta do is go in, grab a Coke, and go to the counter."

She bites her bottom lip. "I told you I don't have any money."

"Don't worry, all you have to do is stand there and make a big deal about looking in your pocket for the cash. Say you had a twenty but someone musta stole it or something."

She's not convinced.

"You don't have to do anything at all. Just stand there like a good little girl and take your time. Check all your pockets real slow, and then say how sorry you are. Leave the Coke and walk out of the store."

"Really? Is that it?"

"I got this."

She puts her hand on the door handle.

"And don't look at me. Pretend you don't know me." I enter a few seconds later and scurry down the furthest aisle from the checkout. There's pre-cut fresh fruit and vegetables in the refrigerated section. Veggie sticks. She looks like a girl who cares about what she eats so I slide a package of baby carrots into the back of my waistband.

Nina is nervous and she moves too fast. I barely have time to grab two sandwiches before I hear her say she's really sorry about having no money. She heads for the door and I shove a Coke into my sleeve. The plastic-wrapped sandwiches in my pockets crinkle every time I move. I cough like I have the plague to cover up the telltale noise.

The checkout guy looks at the security monitor and I realize he might have seen me take the soda. I stuff a chocolate bar into the front of my pants. Time's up. I head for the door but he's coming around the counter to intercept me so I run for it. His hands tug the back of my jacket. I twist and his fingers tear free. Fast on my feet, I'm out the door and down the block before he hits the sidewalk.

Nina runs like a terrified deer right beside me. She's surprisingly fast, or is that the fear? The checkout guy is no runner and he gives up after a few steps. He puts his hands on his knees and wheezes. When he goes back inside I know the cops will be here soon. I keep running until we're a couple of blocks away. We turn a corner and I slow to a walk. Nina slows with me. Like wheels on the same car, we're in sync.

She looks like she's just gotten off a roller coaster, a mixture of relief and excitement. She laughs and grabs my hand. I step sideways and reclaim it. I meet her eyes and it's like looking into my own. Hers are only a shade darker than mine and it almost makes me dizzy. Her lips move but she doesn't say a word. I pretend that I just needed my hand back so I could tuck hair behind my ears and I give her a big happy smile. Her ears turn red and she looks at my mouth.

Wait 'til she sees what I got her. I'm as proud as a mighty hunter with a good kill. Maybe I should do it up right and treat her to a movie with dinner. I take her back to the motel and she silently follows me inside. She'd follow me anywhere.

I've enjoyed having the place to myself during the day when Albert's at work. That could all be over tomorrow. Barb's getting out of the hospital. She says she won't stay here. I think she means she won't stay here *with me*. Tomorrow everything might change again and I don't know where I'll be so I might as well enjoy the place while I can.

I'm suddenly aware that Nina is looking at me. Was I daydreaming? As if I was building up the suspense for my big reveal I empty the loot from my pockets. I shake the Coke out of my sleeve.

"You stole all that?" Her eyebrows arch.

I produce the carrot sticks from the back of my pants and her face softens. "Just in case you're a vegetarian."

"I'm not a vegetarian." She takes the package from me. "But I like carrots."

"And for dessert…" I whip out the chocolate bar like a waiter in a fancy restaurant, not like I've ever seen one in real life. "Kit Kat." I love Canadian chocolate bars. "You can have the soda. I only had time to get one." I hand it to her and she sets it on the table in the kitchenette.

"I don't mind sharing." She sits uneasily on the chair and I bounce onto the pullout sofa. "Action? Comedy? Chick flick?" I hold up the remote.

"What about school?" She puts down her carrots.

"You've never smoked before, and I bet you've never skipped a day of school in your life."

"Um, no."

"First time for everything." I settle into the soft cushions. "Come on over. It's way more comfy than that chair."

Her chest rises and falls. She slides onto the furthest edge of the sofa, leaning away from me.

"How about Bruce Willis?" I hit the channel button and bypass all the stupid porn. "It's Die Hard Monday. They play all the Die Hard movies back to back."

She shrugs and shakes her head at the same time. I can't figure out what that means so I go with the shrug and choose Die Harder. She doesn't argue.

An hour later, we've eaten every last crumb of food and she's conked out, stretched half the length of the sofa bed. I'm squashed to the other end. She fell asleep hard, like she hadn't slept in a month. I leave her be as long as I can and then nudge her with my toe. We need to get back before the bell rings and her mom arrives. Rule number one of ditching school is not to get caught.

"What?" Nina bolts off the couch like I woke her with an air horn. I step in front of her before she blasts out the door.

"Whoa, slow down! We have time." The movie credits are rolling and the next one will start soon. For some weird reason, I don't mind missing it.

She rubs her face with her hands. Near the door, she slides her shoes on and fidgets. It's weird. She steps toward me and stares at my mouth again.

"Come on, you're so slow." I brush past her and head out to the street.

She's quiet for a whole block, probably still trying to wake up from her nap. "If she's drinking again, she'll be late." Nina bends and tears a weed from a crack in the sidewalk. "I don't want to go home, but my sister…"

This is the most she's ever told me about her family. "You have a sister?" As if I didn't already know. I saw them together through the window.

"She needs me to look out for her." Nina runs ahead and I have to work to catch up.

"Isn't that your mom's job?"

"My mom's an alcoholic. Everyone knows."

"Is it her that's been hitting you?" It's a wild guess. I watch a lot of movies and she has that look.

"No one's been hitting me." She walks ahead of me and her feet stomp on the pavement.

"Take it easy, I won't tell."

"It's not my mom! She just drinks too much." She whirls around with her tiny fists clenched. With her lips pulled back from her teeth like that, she looks intense.

"So…" I'm calm as a cat. "It's your dad."

She pulls back like I punched her. Her mouth quivers. "No."

"He doesn't *hit* you, does he?" I touch her arm and somehow this doesn't bother me. Maybe I need to be in charge.

"I can't tell." Her eyes fill with tears and she hugs herself with both arms.

"Bastard!" I hiss through my teeth. He's got no business messing with her. She's mine now.

"Oh my God!" She pulls away. "Don't tell—"

"I ain't gonna tell anyone." I touch her arm again and she sobs deep in her throat.

"No one else knows."

"I promise I won't tell."

She hugs me hard around the waist. The squeeze comes so fast that I have no time to react. A dark shadow recoils in my gut. She lets me go right away but the damage is done. I feel weaker, like I lost a piece of myself in the exchange.

Her mom's red van pulls up in front of the school as we scoot beside the building. We saunter out a moment later so she can tell her mom we came out a side door. Before she runs to the car, she turns and stares into my eyes. Is she trying to tell me something, or is this her goodbye? It's intense and I want to break contact but I force myself to stare back.

"I had fun." She hurries to the car and her mom shouts at her about her backpack, which she left in her locker. Before they drive off, Nina puts her head down and turns back into a mouse.

CHAPTER 8

I have a lot of time on my hands. Since Barb got out of the hospital she's been staying somewhere else. Albert has to work so he can't take her for her treatments and he's a cranky bastard. Today, he complained about paying for an extra week at the motel. What's his problem? I like it here. There's a ton of TV channels and someone picks up my junk every single day.

If you ask me, Barb's making too much of a big deal about this whole burn treatment thing. Why doesn't she put a Band-Aid or something on it and shut up? I burned my hand once and it wasn't the end of the world. I wrapped it in a wet tea towel for a couple of hours and I didn't even get a blister. I learned not to stand in the fumes when I was lighting gasoline so it was a win-win for me.

The big city is not quite what I imagined before I moved here. Winnipeg. Winter-peg they call it when it's friggin' forty-below and the freezing wind howls in from the prairies. I'd rather be in Minnesota, where the woods protect me. Where I know every square inch of my bog.

The only thing this place has going for it is Nina. She helps me with my homework every day. Well, actually she *does* my homework, and my social studies teacher smiled at me when I handed it in for the first time. I like that she's so smart. Finally there is someone in my league and I try to give her my full attention when we hang out. Last weekend I taught her how to smoke a cigarette properly and blow smoke rings. She didn't cough or anything.

Scoring beer around here is way harder than back home. I could take it from the Stop 'N Go, but here you have to be eighteen just to go *look* at beer. At the corner of the liquor store, I hang around like I'm waiting for my dad or something. The sun's going down and it's a warm night so the parking lot is busy. That might be a problem for some, but not me. I'm invisible.

After about twenty minutes I flick my cigarette onto the sidewalk. I've all but made up my mind to leave empty-handed when the Fates smile down on me. A woman with too much makeup pulls up in a dented twenty-year-old Chevy car. Dressed in a skanky black mesh tank top and jean shorts half up her butt-cheeks, she's left her car running with the air conditioning cranked.

Should I steal it and forget about the beer? I take too long to make up my mind and she's back out with a six-pack of wine coolers. What a lightweight. She puts them behind the seat and runs back in for something she forgot.

I'm at the car before she's out of sight and aim directly for the six-pack on the floor. As soon as my hand touches the bottles, a tiny foot boxes me in the ear and I notice a kid in her car seat. She was partly covered by a blanket and I didn't even see her until she kicked me. With great big googly eyes gawking at me, she flaps her chubby arms and starts to pitch a fit.

"What's-a-matter? You want one?"

She freezes, mouth still open, like she can't believe the scary monster spoke to her. I sneak a peek through the front windshield. Her mom is at the checkout with a bottle of something so I better hurry.

"You must be thirsty." I hunch behind the seat and twist the cap off a bottle. When I hold it out, the kid grabs it between her fat little fists. A monkey at the zoo.

"Ain't got no a sippy cup so don't spill it."

She tilts it back and gushes it down her face. It runs down her ducky shirt and I snort when she cries. "Oh, don't be a baby. It's your own fault."

I leave her bawling and disappear into the alley. I don't have to wait for her skanky mom's reaction. I can see it in my head, and it's funny. The last five wine coolers clink in their cardboard carrier all the way to Nina's house. *Totally worth it.*

Nina is waiting for me in our spot at the park. She raises her hand and her face breaks out in a huge smile when she sees me coming. I slow down so I don't look too eager but I can't wait to show her what I got. She doesn't like beer but I bet she will like these. She has more sophisticated taste than me.

After her first cooler, she giggles. She can't stop and I've never seen her so happy. I like when I can make her happy so I give her another one and she sucks it down like it's a soda. Then it gets weird.

She sits close to me under the tree and I know for damn sure she's aware that the back of her hand is touching mine. It's like battery acid on my skin and I yank it back. By now, she knows I don't like to be touched. Why is she touching me?

"I'm sorry," she says. "I forgot." Big fat teardrops well up and she reminds me of that kid in the back of the car. "It must be the drink. I feel strange."

"I think you got a buzz on."

"A buzz. Bzzz." She leans against the tree and away from me, giving me room to breathe. "That is such a funny word. Who thought that up?"

Is she kidding? Is she really drunk after only two coolers? I hold the label up and squint at the alcohol content in the streetlights. "Is this your first time?"

Her face flushes deep red. She rolls her empty bottle into the grass and leans toward me, breath like dragon fire on my neck. "First time." She grins like the possessed doll in that horror movie and flops her head on my shoulder. This totally violates my *don't touch me* rule and she knows it. I scoot out of reach.

"You wanna do something fun?" I need to change the subject before she makes me lose my mind.

"Yes." Her eyes shine like wet rocks. Somehow she's too close again. I scramble to my feet and pull her up with me. I don't know why it doesn't bug me to touch other people but I absolutely hate when they touch me.

"Come on!"

She's not very coordinated but that's because of the alcohol. She had two coolers and I sucked back the other three. Unlike her, I don't feel a thing. No, that's not true. I feel happy. Hanging out with Nina makes me happy, except when she gets too close. I let her hang onto the back of my shirt while we sneak down the alley. Her laughing is starting to annoy me. She's so loud she'll get attention for sure. Beside a big metal dumpster, I motion her down and she squats obediently. This is the Nina I like better.

Along the row of houses, I slip around fences and try the knobs on each garage door. At the end of the block I hit the jackpot, a swimming pool in the backyard and no lights on. Looks like fun.

I go back to fetch Nina and find her lying in the weeds like a drunk hobo. The water will do her some good. I help her to her feet and she trails behind me to the house with the pool. She looks worse than the first time I let her smoke a cigarette. I'm afraid she'll barf so I keep her at arms' length when I hoist her over the fence. She lands on the other side with a loud *oomph!*

I climb over, quick as a cat, join her on the lawn and there it is. The pool. The moon reflects in wavy patterns across the surface of the water and I can't think of a better gift for Nina. I'm damn well proud of myself but she doesn't look very appreciative. In fact, she doesn't seem to notice at all.

I grab her chin and point her face toward the pool and she sees it but she's still not impressed. I can't believe I went to all this trouble. I'm considering leaving her here and going home when she gets up and walks over to it.

"It's all right. This is my uncle's house," I lie.

She yanks off her shoes and rolls up her pants. I do the same. With feet dangling in the water, this is more of what I had in mind. Nina looks less like she wants to throw up. She treats me with a sad smile. I don't want her to be sad. That's no fun. I want her to be happy.

"As long as I can remember, my dad said he would buy us a house with a swimming pool." Her face darkens and she suddenly looks angry, or sad. Something is wrong.

"That sounds… nice." The words are stupid, but what else can I say to someone who tells me about something good with a mad look on her face?

"Yeah, it *sounds* nice." She kicks her foot and water splashes up her leg. "He used to make a lot of promises."

I don't get what she's upset about. Don't everyone's parents make up fairy tale shit for their kids? My mom did. We were going to Disneyland. We were going to move into a beautiful mansion. New car, blah blah blah. It never happened and after a while I stopped getting sucked into her fantasy world.

When mom took me for a picnic and told me she stopped doing

drugs, I knew it was only temporary. Then she took it too far. She said she was going to marry my father and we'd all live happily ever after. That was a goddamn lie. He would never leave Mrs. Perfect in the perfect house at the other end of town. Parents lie. That's why my mom ended up at the bottom of the bog.

Nina is still splashing water like she's doing the flutter kick from the pool deck and I block her with my leg. She stops instantly and slumps over like she will plunge right in. That's when it dawns on me. This has got nothing to do with parents lying. It's something more. I stare in her eyes and she meets mine for a long moment.

Her nostrils flare. "My dad is a monster. My mom is a pathetic drunk. That's why we left. That's why we're hiding." She opens her eyes so wide I can see the whites all the way around and it looks freaky. "He beats the crap out of my mom. He nearly killed her once but she won't report him."

"He tried to kill her? How?" Details, I want details. Does her dad measure up to mine?

"I can't tell anyone."

"Oh, seriously. This is me you're talking to. *My* dad is in prison for kidnapping me and almost killing a cop."

Her mouth drops. "Really?"

"Yup." I lean back on my hands. "That's why I'm here in witness protection. They moved me from Minnesota so he can't find me when he gets out. He's a dangerous felon. Look it up."

Nina takes a breath.

"Tell me."

"She almost caught him… He was in my room…" Nina tilts her head back and the moonlight glistens in her eyes. "My mom interrupted him and he pretended he was only tucking me in. She told him to get out and let me go to sleep. He said he was just being a good dad and she shouldn't be so suspicious. He beat her so bad that I had to call the ambulance. I didn't want to get my mom in trouble. I lied to the cops but I don't think they believed that my mom fell down the stairs. They said they couldn't arrest him if my mom wouldn't testify. She was in the hospital for three days. That's why we had to run."

"So, your dad made you have sex with him."

"What? I didn't say that!" Nina pulls her feet from the pool, a terrified mouse.

"Yeah, ya kinda did."

"I didn't mean to." Face ghostly white against the sky, she leaps to her feet. "If he finds out I told..."

"Ah, don't worry about it. You know I won't tell. That crap happened to me too." The lies come so easily, I don't even have to stop to think about them.

"Really?" She crouches beside me.

"Swear to God." I pat the pool edge and she sits down again. "We're best friends right? I'd never lie to you."

"He can't possibly be my real dad anyway. My real dad wouldn't do that. I dream about him sometimes."

"Who?"

"My *real* dad. He's a famous news anchor or something. My mom always acts weird when she sees this one guy on TV and my fake dad gets jealous. That's probably why."

"My mom's famous too." I can't let her get above me. "She's in Hollywood but she's between jobs right now."

"Oh." She looks down at the water and I think she must realize that the story she made up about the news guy can't be true.

"Yeah, my mom's got tons of money," I tell her. "She's going to come get me soon." I wish that was true but my mom is dead and she's never coming.

All this talk has Nina sobered up. She's not quite herself yet but I think we had a valuable bonding moment. I give her shoulder a push and it startles her. She whips her head up and catches my eye, then pokes me with two fingers. I flinch, but only a little.

"I think you're afraid of girls," she says, and gives me a harder nudge.

"Shut up." In a way, she's not wrong but I hate when boys touch me too. I shove her hard and she tumbles right into the pool, clothes and all. She comes up laughing and grabs me by the leg. There is no way she's strong enough to pull me in. I smirk at her and rock my weight back on my arms.

I'm still smirking when she hauls my ass into the pool with her. Never in a million years did I think she could do it. She's way stronger than I thought. She should have kicked her pervert dad's ass when he tried to touch her. Why didn't she?

We're splashing in the pool and she's shoving my head underwater when the yard light comes on. Two gray-haired heads pop up behind the screen door. Someone is home after all. One of them is on the phone and I bet the cops are on the other end.

I'm half-drowned before Nina notices we're lit up like Christmas. She beats me out of the pool and we shinny like two otters over the fence. Bare toes on gravel, shoes in our hands, we laugh all the way to the park.

With our backs to the tree, we slide down the trunk until we're sitting in the same spot we left earlier. She sighs and leans toward me, then checks herself and veers away. "I like you."

"I... uh... I like you too." My heart shrivels. She is not going there.

"No, I mean, I *like* you."

She did. What do I say? Do I tell her the truth? Neither gender does it for me? I don't mind other people sometimes, but I really only need myself. Or is it different with Nina?

"Oh, look! A shooting star." I point at the sky.

Nina looks up and I'm off the hook. There never was a shooting star but she will spend the next five minutes looking.

"There. It was there." I aim my finger at an imaginary spot. "Maybe there will be another one." Now we can talk about something else. "I used to see the Northern Lights back home."

"We don't see them here in the city." Her gaze on the sky, she slinks down onto her back. "What time is it?"

"I dunno. I'm not wearing a watch. Check your cell phone."

"You know I don't have a cell."

It's a joke between us that we're the only ones in our entire school without cell phones. It seems to bother her but I don't care. Who would I text anyway? There's only Nina.

Realization hits her and she smacks me on the shoulder with the back of her hand. I narrow my eyes. This new Nina wants to talk about stupid shit and thinks she can smack me. It's like the grade four boys who punch girls they like. From now on, her drink limit is one.

"It's probably after ten." I take a guess, based on the position of the moon.

"I have to go!" She jumps to her feet like she's been sitting on an anthill. "My mom has to work at ten and I'm supposed to babysit my sister!"

She runs off without saying goodbye. Nina has been babysitting her sister since her mom got the night shift job cleaning offices and I hate that she always has to go home early. I lie back in the grass and search the sky for my favorite constellations. When the mosquitoes find me I walk back to the motel.

CHAPTER 9

"There it is!" Allie pulled her hand out of the cat carrier and latched the door. Wrong-Way Rachel immediately meowed.

"Canadian border ten miles." Erin read the road sign as they passed. She rolled up her window and ran a hand through her hair to smooth each strand back into place.

"You've been quiet a long time."

"My ankle feels naked." Erin tugged up her pant leg as if to prove this fact. "I miss my off-duty piece already."

"I'm sorry you don't get to carry your precious gun in Canada." Allie wasn't sorry. Not really. The only part she was sorry about was that it made Erin uncomfortable.

"It's just a pistol." Erin frowned. "It's not like I want to carry a bazooka down the street."

"Maybe you'll find that you don't really need to rely on your *pistol* so much north of the border." She'd gotten used to the gun on Erin's hip when she was in uniform but the concealed off-duty holster made her nervous. She hadn't grown up with guns and had only seen them on TV. Americans were so different in subtle ways.

"Are you going to tell me about your visit at the prison? You've hardly said a word." Allie squinted in the oblique light that angled through the clouds. In the visual distortion, Erin's usual radiance was etched with a crosshatch of darker energy. Did she have something on her mind, or was there a storm coming? Maybe she and Derek had not found common ground. Maybe something bad had happened. "Will you tell me about it? Your emotions are so intense that I'm getting concerned."

Erin smiled at her and the darkness eased. "Oh, Baby," she said. "I didn't mean to worry you." She reached over and took Allie's hand.

As if plugged into a conduit, warm energy flowed through her and she sighed in relief.

"Derek had a lot to say when he started talking. Some of it might be helpful. I've been lost in thought trying to puzzle out how we're going to stop that kid."

"What can you tell me?" Allie asked.

Erin smirked. "This is not covert ops. There are no secrets between us. I'll tell you everything I remember. We're in this together, aren't we?"

Allie's chest tickled. That smirk always melted her and Erin knew it. "I already sensed that Derek is in trouble. He's very motivated to get out of there. He's loyal to his daughter, God knows why, and he desperately wants to find her mom."

Eyebrows raised, Erin nodded.

"He wants to help Lily. I feel like he thinks she can be saved and he doesn't want you to hurt her."

"You make me sound like I'm the bad guy."

"No, Honey. I only mean that he's afraid Lily has gotten herself in too deep and might give you no other choice."

"There are always other choices," Erin said flatly. "It seems like you sensed all the important big-picture stuff we talked about."

"Can you fill in the details?"

"Well, he doesn't quite understand why I'm going after her, since she's a kid and would probably never stand trial."

Allie was pretty sure Derek hadn't said it quite like that. The words *so damn gung-ho* resonated through her mind, and she had a distinct sense of his indignation.

"I told him that it wasn't about convicting her. It was about stopping her. I understood his loyalty to his daughter more when he told me about Lily's mom."

As if eavesdropping on the past conversation, Derek's anguish swept over Allie. He'd certainly felt strongly about Lily's mom.

"Let me preface this next part by telling you that it was a bit weird for me to be sitting in a prison talking to a macho guy about feelings."

Allie grinned and squeezed her hand. Erin protested too much. She was actually pretty in touch with her feelings but she didn't like to admit it.

"Derek feels guilty that he didn't help Tiffany get off drugs."

That was it. Tiffany. The name had been on the tip of Allie's tongue for the past half hour.

"He should have helped her when she'd asked. He thought it was fun to smoke a joint with her in high school but after she had the baby, she smoked more. Eventually, she turned to crack."

That was when Derek distanced himself from her. He saw a different future.

"That was when Derek distanced himself from her." Like instant replay, Erin's words echoed the ones that had run through Allie's mind. "He wanted to be a police officer. He stopped taking Tiffany's calls and they drifted in separate directions."

Allie listened to Erin's words and her mind flashed unfocused images. *A teenage mother passed out on the couch while the baby cried. Gunther holding Lily's small hand at his wife's graveside.*

"He said he tried to help Tiffany by paying her as an informant. He wanted her to use the money to get clean. When her mom died of cancer, it was a wake-up call. She got her life under control and finally told him about Lily. He promised to leave his wife and be a father. They would be a family. He proposed and she accepted. She was going to take their daughter for a picnic and tell her all about their new life. He never heard from her again. He worked so hard to find the woman he loved, did his best to be a dad, but he failed."

Allie tried to conjure up an image of Tiffany's face. *Where is she now?* Every time she focused on the name, the image of Lily overwhelmed Allie, obliterating her train of thought. It was a mental block she couldn't get past.

"He knew Lily was different, right from the beginning. He thought that if only he spent more time with her…"

"She treated him like a pawn," Allie finished.

Erin nodded. "He told me that she called him her minion."

"That's a strange way for a child to talk to an adult."

"Lily's an unusual girl, but she's no longer just a child. Derek has had a lot of time to think about that in prison."

Allie remembered the moment when Derek had realized his daughter needed to be stopped. His feelings had surged through the prison's parking lot like an emotional tsunami. Even the distraction of her romance novel couldn't shield her from the force.

"Derek told me he remembered seeing her in town on the night of the fire at Gina's store. He took her home, but she went right back to town. He thinks she wanted to get revenge."

Allie didn't interrupt Erin. There was more she had to say.

"He also said he caught Lily poisoning her grandfather."

"He caught her? Why didn't he stop her?"

"He didn't understand what she was doing at the time. He'd driven to Gunther's place to drop off his monthly child support payment. No one was at the house so he checked the shed. He saw Lily through the window. She was using a pair of pliers to crimp the cap back onto a Budweiser. There was an old brown bottle on the workbench. When he went inside, she hid that bottle from him. He asked her what she was doing and she said she was just getting her grandpa a beer."

"That sounds more than suspicious to me."

"The thing was, Gunther wasn't even around." Erin exhaled. "Derek says that, in retrospect, he should have known that she was up to something but he didn't want to accept that fact until now. He knows she's accelerating. She needs to stop before it's too late and someone dies."

"Someone already *has* died." As if on cue, the dark clouds opened and great droplets of rain splashed the windshield. Ahead, a torrential downpour made it appear that the water literally bounced off the asphalt.

Erin slowed when she caught up with a semi-trailer. Their windshield was coated with the spatter from its rear mud flaps. "He's not totally convinced that Lily killed Dolores Johnson. He thinks it must have been an accident or mistake." She stomped the gas pedal to the floor and overtook the semi, buffeted by watery wave.

Allie grimaced when the truck was rocked by the gust. Erin was so competitive. Would it kill her to back off and follow the semi a while longer? Finally in their own lane, they could see the road ahead. Almost deserted today, there had not been an oncoming car for at least five minutes.

Erin continued talking as if her truck had not just nearly been pummeled off the highway. "The fingerprints on those beer cans behind the house weren't exactly definitive proof of murder."

"And you kind of bent the rules with that evidence."

Up ahead, a bright yellow sign on Interstate Highway 29 announced LAST EXIT BEFORE CANADA.

"Thank you for reminding me of yet another of my screw-ups." Erin withdrew her hand from Allie's and massaged her temple. "I got Kathy, who happens to be my favorite forensic tech, in the loon shit. They denied her the course she deserved."

"She wouldn't have done it if she didn't want to. She doesn't hold any grudges."

"I feel like crap. I second-guess every single thing I do now. Maybe time will heal that, and maybe they'll all forget—"

"Erin. Pull over!" Allie squeezed her palms against her eyes as a white-hot flash blinded her. Like a strobe light in a sleazy nightclub, fragments of images came. Shadows, a pair of animal eyes on the road, squealing tires, screaming faces, and the inertia of hurtling through space. Finally, bone-jarring impact and then... nothing.

Erin braked hard and their bodies were thrown against their seat belts. She pulled the truck onto the shoulder right before the road narrowed for the Pembina River Bridge. The tires vibrated over rumble strips and Rachel let out a disturbed yowl.

"Go there." Allie clutched the cat's carrier to her chest and pointed to a trail of tire marks in the knee-deep grass.

"Good thing I have four-wheel drive." Erin gunned the engine and followed the tracks until they reached a set of downed fence posts tangled with barbed wire. The tracks passed through them and disappeared into the brush along the river.

Allie set the carrier on the floor and stared out her window. There was a flicker of consciousness out there. She unsnapped her seatbelt and shoved her door open.

"Not without me, you don't!" Erin jumped out right behind her and they followed the muddy trail. Pouring rain soaked them to the skin, obscuring their vision. Erin shook her head like a dog and water sprayed in all directions.

Allie smoothed back her ponytail and twisted it into a knot at the base of her neck. She was guided by her internal navigation system. *Go there.* Ankle deep in muck, she slicked water from her eyes with her fingers and followed fresh gouges in the ground. *Through here.* She scrambled into an opening in the bushes. Jagged branches splayed outward and Allie pushed her way through. Erin swore behind her.

"Here!" Allie called out. A minivan was partly submerged in the river with the passenger side underwater. The top half was scraped from end to end, buckling the metal near the slider. Covered in mud, it was not easily visible from the road. Not in this downpour.

"Oh no!" Erin slid like an otter down the riverbank, splashed through the muck, and crawled onto the van.

Allie waded in after her. It was so cold. Her teeth chattered before she reached her thighs. She pulled at the damaged sliding door but it wouldn't budge.

Erin tried the front and released a deluge of muddy water when it gaped open. An elderly man was slumped in the driver's seat, confined by his safety belt. "Sir! Can you hear me? Is there anyone else in the car?" Erin probed the unconscious man's throat with her fingers and released his seat belt.

"He might be hurt. He'll freeze here." Someone else was in the van. Someone frightened, so frightened and alone. The only way in was through the open driver's door. *No time. There is no time.* "Hurry. I *need* to check the back."

"Give me half a minute." Erin slid an arm under the driver's shoulders and pulled.

The man looked heavy. *There is no more time.* Allie hurried to the rear door and pulled at the handle. It was locked. Frigid water rushed around her, raising rough goose bumps on her skin. The cold stiffened her joints.

Panic reverberated through her skull, but it was not her own. Tiny handprints marked fogged side windows. The dark tint prevented her from seeing inside. There was a cry.

"A child! There's a child!" *Break the window.* She waded to the bank and seized a hefty rock. She brought it down hard and smashed the glass from the rear window frame. It fell away like a shiny marbled sheet, held together by its laminated tint.

There he was, a child no older than four or five, white-faced and panic-stricken, struggling to escape his booster seat. The river surged around his shoulders and he floundered to keep his head above water.

Allie crawled through the window, over the seat and wedged herself beside him. "I'm going to help you." Crouched chest-deep, she tore at the booster seat's unfamiliar clasp with cold fingers.

The boy whimpered. His eyes rolled upward. *Was he in shock?* Perhaps he was thinking of a happier place.

"The driver's alive but I can't wake him. I dragged him onshore." Erin crawled across the empty front seat. Adrenaline burst from her like electricity. "Is there anyone else?"

The minivan rocked and water sloshed from one side to the other. Would it roll over in the river's current? Allie spread her feet like Erin had taught her to balance a canoe. It stabilized.

"A kid." Erin was ablaze with strength. "Is he conscious?" Emergencies were her drug.

Allie was so cold her teeth ached. "This child is freezing. I can't get the belt off." Her fingertips were numb.

"I'll look for something to cut—"

"My knife is in my pocket. Help me. I can't feel my fingers." Allie's foster mom, the most practical woman she'd ever known, had given her the Swiss Army knife. At this moment, its value was incalculable. If she could only get it.

Erin wiggled over the seat and retrieved the knife. With her thumbnail, she slid open the first blade and handed it over. The serrated saw was the perfect tool and Allie plunged it underwater. She worked the strap from the inside out. One more stroke should do it.

The knife slipped from her hand. "My knife!" She ducked under and scrabbled blindly along the seat. She connected with Erin's fingers in the dark but they both came up empty.

"It's gone."

Allie grabbed the seat belt and wrapped her fingers around it. "Pull!"

Erin's hands joined hers, and with the strength of two, they tore the remaining shreds of seatbelt.

The boy floated free and Allie scooped him to her chest. She stumbled toward the open driver's door and the van rocked violently. Water surged higher. She leapt out and held him above water. He was already too cold. Chilled to her marrow, her numb limbs foundered.

Erin put an arm around Allie's shoulders and lent her strength. Together, they made their way across the river and up the muddy bank. They collapsed beside the elderly driver.

The man's body heat radiated through his soaked clothing. His chest rose and fell with each shallow breath. His energy was there, but he desperately needed something. *Insulin? Sugar?* What medical emergency was he having that rendered him unconscious?

Allie curled against him to share body heat. She tucked the child under her shirt. The boy's skin was cold. He was so weak that she feared it was too late.

"Is the kid alive?" Worry lines furrowed Erin's brow. The boy was nearly the same age as her nephew.

"Yes, but he's very cold."

Erin knelt beside the unconscious man and pressed two fingers to his carotid artery. "Sir! Sir! Can you open your eyes?" She turned to Allie. "His pulse is stronger than before but he won't wake. I'll go call 9-1-1. I'll be right back."

Allie pictured the green sign right before the bridge. "Tell them we're at the bridge crossing the Pembina River."

Erin squared her shoulders, turned and dashed through the wet grass.

Allie tucked her arms around the boy and hugged him close until he began to shiver. That was a good sign. As did every kid at her summer camp, she'd learned that for someone suffering hypothermia, the lack of shivering was scarier. She brought her knees up and surrounded him with all the warmth she had.

He whimpered and she stroked his cheek when he opened his eyes.

"Grandpa," he whispered.

"Your grandpa's sick, but help is coming. Here snuggle closer." The boy tucked his face into her armpit, a baby bird under its mother's wing.

Erin was back in minutes, her cell phone pressed tight to her ear. She knelt beside the driver and read the lettering on his bracelet. "Diabetic! It says he's diabetic. Yes, he has a pulse. No, he's not conscious." She flung the jacket she'd retrieved from the truck over him and tucked it tight. From her pocket she withdrew a square of shiny foil and quickly unfolded it several times until it expanded into a thermal blanket.

"Ahhh," Allie sighed when Erin wrapped it around her and the boy.

"Ambulance is ten or fifteen minutes away. They are coming lights and sirens." Erin huddled in and wrapped her arms around both of them. Together, they generated an orb of heat.

Allie's head jerked upright when the sirens approached. "I'm not letting go. You need to guide them here."

Erin leapt to her feet and bounded up the hill. A red-faced young trooper and two seasoned paramedics followed her back.

"You have the child?" The first medic addressed Allie, still wound tight in the foil.

She nodded and opened the blanket wide enough for him to see.

"Any signs of trauma?"

"None that we could tell. He was still strapped in his car seat."

He bent for a quick vital check and stepped back. "Good. Keep him warm." He turned to the man on the ground. One medic held C-spine while the other rolled the unconscious driver onto a plastic board. They strapped him in and hauled him out to the waiting ambulance.

Awkward in his crisp new uniform, the trooper tipped his hat to the two women and strode to the river's edge. Already his shirt lapels wilted in the rain. He peered down at his shiny boots, sighed, and stepped into the muddy water. He scraped muck from the van's license plate, wiped his hand on a trouser leg and took out his notebook.

The first medic returned with a warming blanket and motioned to Allie. She reluctantly uncurled herself from the child. His cheeks had regained a light pink glow and he cried when she let him go.

I need to protect the baby. She followed the medic to the ambulance where flashing lights reflected from every wet surface. *The baby boy is in danger.* She blinked hard. But this was not a baby. This child would be fine. Allie squeezed her hands into fists and stepped aside.

"Don't worry," the medic told her. "You did great." Child in his arms, he hopped in the back where his other patient lay on the stretcher. "The boy's color is good and his body temperature is almost back to normal. Kids are resilient. He'll be fine." He pulled one rear door shut and paused. "His grandpa's doing better too. No sign of injury. His sugars were out of whack but we'll fix him up. They were both very lucky you two found them when you did. A few more minutes in that cold water and—" He slammed the door and the ambulance pulled away.

Lump in her throat, she stood in the rain until the lights disappeared.

Erin joined her at the truck. "Are they going to be okay?"

Allie grabbed her and held tight. The boy was going to be okay. The medic said so. Why was she absolutely bereft? Why did she feel like, somewhere, a baby boy still needed help?

"Aren't they okay?" Erin held her at arm's length.

"It must be the adrenaline." She pulled away and wiped her eyes. Rain ran down her face to replace the tears.

"Yeah, coming down from that can be hard. Some guys get muscle shakes afterward."

"Let's get going." Allie tucked her hair behind her ears and looked down at her clothing. "We're going to have to pull over at that last rest station to change before we try to cross the border. We look like swamp rats."

Erin grinned and opened the door for her. "I gave the trooper a statement. He'll contact us if he needs any more information."

Fifteen minutes in the rest stop washroom transformed them and they tied their muddy clothing into a plastic bag. Allie swabbed her running shoes with a paper towel. "All my socks are at the bottom of my suitcase. I guess I'll just have to deal with soggy feet."

Erin finger-combed her hair into place and regarded Allie with interest. "You're amazingly calm in an emergency, Baby."

"What were you expecting? Did you think I would break down into a simpering puddle and make you do everything?"

"No, I just thought maybe all the stuff in your head might interfere—"

Allie raised an eyebrow.

"—Or something." Erin attempted a smile but it only reached one side. "Not that you're—"

"It doesn't work like that." Allie wrung water from her ponytail. "When there's stuff going on that's immediate, I don't really have time to think. I just act. Sometimes, it's like I'm guided, but I don't sit there and cogitate on every single thing. The times I really have to focus to block things out are when I'm sitting quietly without distraction."

"Like meditation."

"Or yoga." Allie was a self-professed yoga-holic. It was a challenge to focus both her muscles and her mind.

Erin shrugged. "I think I could know you for a hundred years and still have more to learn." They walked out to the truck and headed north once more.

"Here we are!" Allie patted Erin's knee and winked when they passed Canadian Customs. "Did you know that Canada nationally legalized same-sex marriage more than a decade ago? Maybe we should get hitched while we're here."

Erin's lips tightened and an uncomfortable spike of energy jolted through Allie's fingers. She'd touched a nerve. She loved Erin completely, but did Erin feel the same way about her?

CHAPTER 10

"We're nearly at the house." Allie prodded the cat back into her carrier and shut the door. Rachel grumbled.

"Are you absolutely sure it's okay for us to stay at your friend's house?" Erin turned the truck off Pembina Highway.

Allie gave her a sideways glance. "You're asking me this *now?*"

Erin shrugged.

"Of course it's okay. Don't be shy. Ciara has been my friend since university. She's tons of fun and you'll love her." Allie poked a finger through the wires in the cage door to stroke the cat's ear. "You'll love her too, sweetie," she assured Rachel. "Ciara likes kitties."

Erin slowed to squint at the street signs as they passed. "She lives by the river?"

"I thought you might be pleased about that." Allie smiled. "There's the turnoff!"

They eased onto a tree-lined street. High fences on their right separated residences from the road. Erin kept her attention on the left, where stately homes backed onto the river. Her head swung around at each private drive to each oversize lot. Allie pointed to a house on the right and Erin's excitement waned.

In stark contrast to the opulence of the riverfront homes, the older bungalow shrank back from the street as if hiding from its affluent neighbors. An untended yard in front of weather-beaten siding suggested decades of neglect.

Allie skipped to the top of the concrete steps and rang the doorbell.

71

Erin followed, cat carrier in hand. She avoided the exposed steel mesh jutting out of the third tread, nearly lost her balance and was forced to grab the rusted rail. The carrier banged against the siding and Wrong-Way Rachel yowled her disapproval. Erin yanked her hand back and wiped multicolored paint chips on her thigh. "I need a tetanus shot," she muttered.

"It will be okay, Honey." Allie rolled her eyes when Erin jammed her contaminated hand in her pocket. "It's not that bad." Heaven forbid she touch something dirty with no immediate access to soap and water. Allie rang the doorbell again.

"You should try her cell." Erin looked at her watch.

"I would, if she had one." As long as Allie had known her, Ciara had practically lived off the grid. Right now she was probably on a park bench writing notes longhand, oblivious to the time. She often went months without a working phone.

"I guess we've got some time to kill and a cat can only hold her bladder so long." Erin released Rachel from her carrier and Allie helped her manipulate the struggling furry body into a harness.

Unaccustomed to confinement, the cat lay flat. Her indignation was clear when she beetle-walked to the dried-out flowerbed. Allie shook her head. It would take her a while to calm enough to pee in a strange garden.

"What the heck is wrong with her? Did I hurt her when I bumped the cage?" On the balls of her feet, Erin looked ready to sprint for the closest veterinarian.

Allie laughed. "No, she's not hurt. She's just not used to being in a harness. She feels oppressed."

Wrong-Way Rachel flopped to her side, alligator-rolled and hopelessly twisted herself in the leash. Allie knelt to free her.

"Should I get her litter box from the truck?" Erin shot a hopeful glance at the neglected flower bed.

"She needs time to get used to the new place. Let's let her explore for a few minutes." She finished unwrapping the leash and set the cat down. Like broken springs, Rachel's legs folded until her belly settled on the ground. "Really? Is this how you've decided to use your semi-freedom?"

Allie left the cat to her own devices and lay flat on her back in the middle of the lawn. She pointed to a fluffy cloud that had morphed into a wild animal. "It's a galloping giraffe."

Beside her, Erin stretched out and held an imaginary sword. "It looks like a knight saving a beautiful maiden."

"Now it's a horse."

"Dragon."

"Poodle. In a tutu."

Erin sat up and frowned down at her. "Now you're messing with me." She clasped Allie's hands and pinned her to the ground.

Laughing, Allie struggled half-heartedly and waited until Erin kissed her. When their lips sizzled with first contact, she flipped Erin onto her back and held her between muscular thighs.

"Fine!" Erin giggled. "It's a poodle in a tutu!"

Allie leaned down and kissed her back. There was no resistance this time and their energy flowed together until warmth reached her toes. Erin's touch was like no other. She saw a future unfold. She yearned for years of comfort and warmth together with this woman.

"Excuse me, ladies. Are you going to traumatize my neighbors on your first day here?"

Allie rolled out of Erin's arms and rose to her feet. Ciara grabbed her in a bear hug and Allie squeezed back with the same intensity, and then held her at arms' length. Her old friend looked fit and happy; a flash of the mischievous free spirit she knew still shone in her eyes. "You look fantastic!"

"This must be the one." Ciara towered over Erin and appraised her with bright hazel eyes.

Allie shook her head. Her friend was checking out her girlfriend. Above black combat boots, Ciara's pastel patterned dress waved in the breeze. With her dark shoulder length hair, she was a walking specimen of feminine power. Ever since their university days, Ciara had been critical of Allie's love interests. The weak-hearted found her mere presence intimidating.

"I'm *definitely* the one." Erin stood and groped for Allie's hand. "You didn't tell me she was British," she whispered from the side of her mouth.

"Didn't think it mattered." Allie squeezed her hand in reassurance. She had long-since ceased to notice her friend's accent and it had never occurred to her to mention it. Ciara was just Ciara. Besides, the strength of her accent came and went depending on her mood, and how much she'd had to drink.

"Well, it doesn't, but…" Erin left the rest to Allie's intuition.

Allie gave her a half-smile. Was Erin worried that she'd neglected to mention other things? Was she worried about a romantic connection? That would be ridiculous!

"And this must be the legendary Wrong-Way Rachel!" Ciara lay flat in the grass, nose-to-nose with the now-relaxed cat.

Rachel's eyes widened at the approach of the stranger, but she stubbornly held her ground.

"Who's a good kitty?" Ciara cooed, scratching her behind the ear. "You are!"

As if hypnotized, the cat slowly rolled to her back and allowed access to her underbelly.

Erin tilted her eyebrows at the brilliant Japanese-style tattoos covering Ciara's entire left arm. Sleeved-out they called it.

"She may look fierce," Allie whispered. "But all cats adore her." She squeezed Erin's hand again. "You will too."

After a few minutes of kitty love, Ciara got to her feet, pulling the fluffy cat into her arms. "Sorry I am late. I was working on my thesis in the park."

Allie grinned. She'd been right. She took the cat from her and untangled the leash again. Rachel struggled for freedom.

Ciara retrieved her bicycle from the end of the driveway. A throwback from decades past, the pink urban cruiser even had a flowered basket mounted in front of the handlebars. She rolled the bike to the rear of the house, propped it against a tree, and scooped her notebook from the basket."

"Don't use the front steps." She led them to the rear porch. "They're treacherous and that door sticks. I always use the back." She turned the unlocked knob and Erin raised her eyebrows. "The lock doesn't work properly," Ciara said, "so I don't bother with it. Last time I did, I had to squeeze in through the upstairs bathroom window."

Allie followed her line of sight to the tiny window above the porch overhang. It was anyone's guess how she'd managed to get up there. Knowing Ciara, she'd balanced with one foot on her bicycle and the other on the rickety rail.

"I ripped this fabulous dress that day!" She smoothed a neatly sewn patch on the hem.

"Aren't you concerned about a break and enter?" Erin examined the knob.

"Nah. If anyone wants my junk, they can have it." She clutched her notebook to her breast. "Except this. My entire Master's thesis is in here."

Erin shot Allie a look when they filed into a dingy kitchen. A stack of unwashed dishes and a month's worth of mail greeted them. Tidiness had never been Ciara's strong suit. It wasn't that she was unclean, but housekeeping was not high on her priority list. When Erin winced at the dirty pot on the stove, Allie reassured her with a hand on her elbow. Once the kitchen was cleaned, Erin would relax.

"If my feet could talk, they would be screaming right now." Ciara unlaced her heavy boots and stretched bare toes on the dusty floor. Allie did the same and the two grinned like compatriots. Ciara led them down the hall to their room.

"You can put your things in here." She flung open the door to a dining room that had been converted to a surprisingly spacious sleeping area. "I need to run out to do an errand but I'll be back later. Make yourselves comfortable."

Round-eyed, Erin closed the door to face Allie. "We can stay in a motel."

"Oh come on, Honey." Allie set the cat on the bed and opened the curtains to release a plume of fine dust. "We haven't budgeted for a motel stay. You're on leave and I haven't billed any new clients yet. We need to be careful."

"We can put it on our credit card." Erin coughed and rubbed her eyes. The cat hopped off the bed and patrolled the perimeter of the room. "Look, even Rachel is not so sure about this place."

Hands on hips, Allie was about to remind Erin that she was not a wimp but paused at her desperate tone. "Give it a chance. It'll be fun." Flakes of paint rained down from the protesting windowsill when she forced it open. "We'll help Ciara tidy up. She loves when I take over and clean the house. When we're done, it'll be nice."

She pressed herself against Erin's body and wrapped her in her arms. Their energy blended, blue, or perhaps turquoise. If she had to attribute a color to this feeling of harmony they had, that would be it.

"Okay," Erin purred. "You know this place is stretching it, but I'd do anything for you, Baby."

"It'll be like a pre-wedding honeymoon."

Erin froze. Their mingled energy cooled to a darker indigo.

Allie bit her lip. Why did that theme keep popping up? Wasn't their current relationship enough? Did she really want to get legally married?

Erin turned away. "Uh, let's go find the cleaning supplies and we can get started first thing in the morning."

CHAPTER 11

Erin rubbed her eyes. She hadn't slept well on the unfamiliar mattress in Ciara's extra bedroom. Somehow, between Allie's nightmares and her own worries, she'd managed to get a few hours, but she was still tired.

She stacked a box on top of the shoe rack. She'd simply raked the pile of mail from the kitchen table and dumped it inside. Now Ciara could ignore her bills as long as she wanted and they would all be here when she decided to pay them.

She put down her screwdriver and stared at the bare counter. Where had they gone? They were here a few seconds ago. She was sure of it. She bent and checked under the cabinets. There was no sign of the two screws she planned to use to replace the handle on the silverware drawer. They couldn't have disappeared into thin air. She checked her pockets and then turned in a circle, scanning the floor. She stared at the silver handle in her palm. The screws must have fallen somewhere. Was she losing her mind?

She whirled around at a muffled thump, just in time to see the bottom cabinet door bounce against its frame and it dawned on her. Wrong-Way Rachel, her favorite feline arch-villain was playing tricks on her again.

Erin took one silent step, laid the handle on the counter and crouched by the door. She flung it open.

"There you are!" A box of breakfast cereal and two jars of peanut butter stared back. Where was that sneaky cat? On her haunches, Erin duck-walked to the next cabinet and did the same. No cat there either. Tiny hairs prickled the back of her scalp. She checked all the cabinets without success.

A crash behind her raised the tiny hairs upright. There was the handle on the floor. It had to be Rachel. There was no other explanation, was there?

Stealthy movement in the dinner plate cabinet got her attention and she eased open the door. A telltale tuft of Persian cat hair nestled on the top plate. Rachel had been in here. Erin thrust her hand into the cupboard, past the plates and around the wine glasses. In the rear corner, hidden from view by the stacks of dishes, was a cutout in the wood. She poked her fingers through and cool air wafted past. In the bottom cupboard, she found the same.

At some time in the home's renovation history, workers had removed ductwork and neglected to patch the wall. This secret passage allowed a sneaky feline access to the top and bottom cupboards through the abandoned holes. Wrong-Way Rachel was adept at opening cabinet doors and was probably enjoying her new spelunking adventure.

"Give me back my screws, you rascal." Erin knocked on the cabinet door closest to the most recent scrabbling noise. She was rewarded with silence. The cat knew she was on to her. A moment later, a screw ricocheted off the counter and she looked up to a set of unapologetic yellow eyes. On top of the cabinet, Rachel licked the back of her single front paw. Apparently, the cutout in the wall extended that far.

"One? Is that all I get?" The cat stretched full length, her purr rumbling in satisfaction. "No catnip for you today, missy." Erin opened the junk drawer at the end of the counter and searched for another screw. At this rate, it might take all summer to fix everything in this old house.

Her head pounded. Ciara was gone and Allie had just left for a yoga class. She headed for the sofa. Now would be a good time to take advantage of the quiet. She'd have a quick nap and finish cleaning when Allie got back.

Erin discovered that the living room sofa was a divine spot to nap. It had just the right combination of softness and structure. By the time her girlfriend breezed in the door from her class, she was rejuvenated. Back to her old self.

"I found these for you. That upstairs bathroom is scary." Erin kissed Allie's cheek and handed her a pair of rubber gloves.

"Is it that bad?" Allie winced.

"Don't worry, there aren't any spiders."

Allie rolled her eyes. "I'm not afraid of spiders. Just monsters." She jogged up the stairs. Where did she get her energy?

Erin attacked the rest of the kitchen. When she finished, she sat back and assessed her work. Under the pile of pizza boxes and unopened envelopes, she'd been flabbergasted to uncover an antique table. What a shame to hide such a unique piece. She ran her fingers over the grain of the hand-rubbed wood finish. Stunning, really.

She sat in an equally amazing chair to admire the sheen on the scrubbed countertop and gleaming stove. The time on its digital clock glowed in red.

She sprang to her feet. It was nearly five o'clock! She'd promised to meet Barb Schmidt at a coffee shop at five-thirty and hadn't yet figured out how to get there. All she knew was that it was miles from here. She poked at the screen on her iPhone and huffed in frustration.

"Allie!" she called up the stairs. "Can you spare a minute?"

"What's wrong?" Allie's voice sounded muffled, like she literally had her head in the bathtub while she scrubbed it.

"I need to meet Mrs. Schmidt in half an hour and I can't figure out the GPS. Can you tell it to do what I want?" Erin vaulted up the stairs.

In the bathroom, Allie's face was flushed and her hair in disarray. Yellow rubber gloves extended to her elbows.

Erin took in her soap streaked jeans and soaked T-shirt clinging to her shapely waist. She had certainly been putting elbow grease into her work. "You look gorgeous, Baby!"

"Why do you tell me these things at the weirdest moments?" She snapped off a glove and took the phone from Erin. Seconds later, she handed it back. "You enter the address first, and *then* click Navigate. Not the other way around."

"You're my favorite tech-head, and the cutest."

"Are you sure you want to go on your own? I can get cleaned up in—"

"Um, I think you need a shower before you go anywhere." Erin stroked hair from Allie's face and kissed her on the eyebrow.

"Besides, Barbara Schmidt is freaking out and we shouldn't overwhelm her. She sounded paranoid when I talked to her on the phone."

"Maybe she's got a point. She was nearly killed, wasn't she?"

"True, but she's afraid that Lily is constantly stalking her. I wonder if her imagination has gotten the better of her. Lily's only a kid, not a super spy."

"Please remember that I have a conference with my new clients tomorrow. Don't make me show up on Ciara's bicycle with my presentation in the flowery basket."

"I promise I won't go to any clandestine meetings when you need the truck, and I'll even wash it for you before you go." Why was Allie having pre-meeting jitters? Didn't she already know the outcome?

Allie turned at a crashing noise in the bathroom. "Rachel!"

Erin grinned as she made her way out the door. The cat was probably knocking breakable stuff off counters, settling in by doing some feline housekeeping.

The drive to the coffee shop was shorter than she'd expected and Erin arrived early. She parked across the road and walked to the building, noting the adjacent paved alley with light industrial businesses on one side and older residences on the other. The shop had a half dozen tables and stools against a window counter with a view of the street. Two young men turned as she walked in and she nodded politely when they greeted her with friendly smiles. A couple at a corner table was too engrossed in conversation to notice her.

Erin looked over the handwritten menu, and the pierced and tattooed barista. Unaccustomed to the variety of personal expression in a big city, she couldn't tell if she was a he, or he was a she. Both? Neither? She finally decided that it really didn't matter and focused back on the menu.

Moose Juice, Winnipegger Bacon 'n Egger, and the Windy City Smoothie made her smile. The Bacon 'n Egger actually sounded pretty good. She might have to bring Allie here for breakfast. She dismissed the plethora of specialty drinks and ordered a nice dark roast. A good strong cup of coffee would clear the dust from her throat and perk up her tired brain.

She settled into a corner spot at the window counter where it would be easy to keep an eye on customers and watch for anyone coming from the street or alley. Her first sip of coffee convinced her that this would be a regular drive. Ciara didn't seem to have a basic coffee pot, let alone a fancy Italian cappuccino machine. Erin would have to fend for herself. She swished the last of her coffee and checked if the barista was busy. Another one would be nice.

A dark green sedan emerged from the alley and cruised past the window. Erin straightened up, coffee mug poised halfway between table and lips as a middle-aged woman with large sunglasses turned her face to the building. The woman looked in her rear-view mirror and then yanked her car to the curb. She swiveled her head to both side view mirrors before exiting. With one last glance over her shoulder, she gingerly eased her waistband away from her skin and walked stiff-legged into the coffee shop. She darted straight for Erin, the only woman sitting alone.

"It's you, isn't it?" She slid onto a stool and shielded her face from the window. Twisted cords of healed flesh knotted the back of her reddened hand. At her throat, melted skin like bloody wax dripped from her jaw until it disappeared into the neckline of her shirt. Erin's eyes lingered on her hand and the woman pulled her sleeve over to conceal the scars.

"Nice to meet you, Mrs. Schmidt." Erin rose and stuck out her hand, careful not to stare.

Barb flinched. "I know I look ghoulish," she ducked her head. "I'm sorry if my appearance scares you."

Erin decided to ignore this. "Do you want a coffee?" She sat back down and put her hand on her coffee mug.

Barb shook her head. "No, there's no time."

Erin forced herself to focus on Barb's face. She could barely see through the lenses but, eyes puffy, Barb looked like she hadn't slept in weeks.

"She might find me." Her lips pursed and she tilted the dark glasses to peek around the room. "Is it safe here?"

"You're safe." Erin leaned away from her. Was she always nuts, or did Lily do this?

"I must be careful. She follows me everywhere. She's trying to kill me."

"Tell me what happened." Erin took out her notebook. Telling her story might keep her from spiraling into madness this very minute.

Barb regarded the notebook for a moment and took a breath. "You're a fish out of water, aren't you?"

"What do you mean?"

Barb looked out the window, then back. "Well, you're not even a police officer here, are you? What can you possibly do to help me?"

"I can work with local police who have the authority to act." Erin omitted the fact that Winnipeg Police Service had been less than willing to take her seriously when she'd contacted them. Even north of the border, last year's police scandal in Minnesota was fodder for gossip. "And I have a personal interest in the case."

One of Barb's scarred eyebrows lifted. The hair would forever be missing from the outer half. "She got to you too, didn't she?" She took off her sunglasses. Her eyes were red. "Lily is a wicked girl. Evil. Maybe even the devil." Her chest heaved.

Pen poised in the air, Erin kept her face neutral. "Please, tell me what happened. Tell it like you are describing the action, play-by-play."

"Well, you know we went to pick up Gunther's granddaughter in Morley Falls last year. She was family after all. We couldn't leave the child there on her own after he took ill. Especially after what the poor thing went through, with her sinful father and all that."

Erin didn't have the heart to tell her that the story of Lily's abduction and abuse by her father was the child's fabrication to hide her own sins.

"She looked so innocent, so…" she searched for the right word, "…so *vulnerable*." Her eyes narrowed and scarred brows puckered. "But that little demon was probably *born* spitting venom."

"Mrs. Schmidt."

Barb's expression smoothed and she straightened her shoulders. "I'm sorry." She readjusted her shirt sleeve. "You just wanted the facts."

Erin nodded.

"She seemed so sweet, at first. We saw how she didn't fit in with the other kids and Albert knew she was a bit different right from the get-go, but he really took to her. She helped with the dishes and kept her room tidy and went to bed on time. I made her lunch and walked her to school every day, so she would feel safe and loved." Her voice wavered and she stared directly at Erin. "She never really was unsafe in Morley Falls, was she?"

Erin tilted her head slightly. How much should she tell Barb? How much could she handle?

"She is the one who made Gunther sick, isn't she?" Barb frowned.

"Let's concentrate on what happened to you."

"I'll take that as a yes. You wouldn't have driven all the way up here, otherwise." Barb adjusted herself on the seat and pulled her blouse away from tender skin. "After a few months, she changed. It was like it was too much trouble to pretend to be nice and she let her real self show. I was walking her to school one morning, like I always did, and she turned to me and told me to stop making her 'stupid sandwiches'. It was a slap in the face! I put a lot of effort into making those nutritious lunches. Can you imagine that was what started it all?"

"I'm sure her attitude had nothing to do with your lunches."

"I couldn't believe the change in her! She was like a different person." She balled up a reddened fist and released it. "I told her in no uncertain terms that she was never to speak to me like that. I was only trying to help. She looked me straight in the eye and told me to F off! Can you imagine the language? She said she didn't need anyone taking care of her."

While Barb talked, Erin scribbled notes. She filled two pages before Barb paused and patted her forehead with a napkin.

"I told her that we would see what Albert had to say about all of this, and she had the audacity at that moment to ask me for twenty dollars. I turned around and left her standing there right in front of the school." She folded and arranged the napkin on the counter. "That's when it got bad."

She unfolded the napkin and laid it flat. "Lily only did it when Albert wasn't home so he thought I was making it all up. He thought I didn't want to be a sixty-year-old parent to a teenager. I did *not* make up anything!"

"What did she do?" Erin redirected.

Barb's face flushed crimson. "*What did she do?* I'll tell you what that awful girl did to me." She picked the napkin up and tore it in half. "First, she started with little things, like moving items around in the house so I couldn't find them. My car keys, my purse, even my underpants for heaven's sake! Some things I found hidden in strange places and some I never saw again. Once I found my grandmother's necklace in the toilet. Albert complained that I kept putting the coffee in the oven and he thought I was getting Old Timer's Disease. He wouldn't believe me when I told him the girl was playing mean tricks on me. She was always so sweet to him!"

So far, this merely sounded like the work of a mischievous or upset child. How did it progress from hiding an elderly woman's panties to attempted murder?

"I didn't trust that girl. Not one bit, and I told her so. I told her that if she didn't like the hospitality we were showing her at our home, she was welcome to find another. I said maybe I could ask the social workers to find her a new place to live."

Erin raised her eyebrows. "What did she think of that idea?" Considering Lily's experience with Child Protective Services, it couldn't have gone over well.

"She looked at me with such hate that I felt afraid. Afraid of what she might do." Fear crept into Barb's sleep-deprived eyes. She fidgeted with the torn napkin and then crumpled the pieces into a ball. She tucked the ball into her purse and brushed tiny shreds of paper from the counter.

Erin watched the entire process with fascination. It was interesting to see the things people fixated on when they struggled with upsetting emotions. She laid a gentle hand over Barb's. "What did she do?"

Barb's pupils constricted. "Albert was at work. He gets more money for night shift, you know." She stared into the distance. "Ever since that girl moved in, I've had trouble sleeping. That night, Lily was acting particularly unusual."

"Unusual? How?"

"Well, she was usually surly and mean to me but that night she acted kind. She made me a cup of tea before bed and I honestly thought the tides had turned, that she was over her angry phase." Barb planted a foot hard on the floor. "I should have known better. After I drank that tea, I felt groggy. I couldn't keep my eyes open. I went to bed early and completely conked out. Sometime during the night, the smoke woke me. Evil black smoke coming under my bedroom door. I put on my dressing gown and tried to get out but I couldn't. The doorknob was tied from the outside. I could open the door a crack but I couldn't get out. All I could see was smoke but I could hear strange noises, like laughing or giggling."

She shuddered. "I screamed as loud as I could, but no one came.

Through the crack I swear I could see someone jumping up and down like a maniac at the end of the hall. It looked like Lily but she was acting like a crazy person. Then she was gone. I fought to untie the rope but my arms were burning and I had to shut the door."

Barb told the story in a monotone, as she had probably already told it many times before today. "I opened the window. It was too far. I was afraid to jump. Besides, I knew Lily was out there somewhere and I certainly didn't want her to be the one that found me lying helpless with a broken leg."

"Is that where the firefighters found you?" Erin already knew the rest of the story. Luckily, someone reported the smoke. First responders had rescued Barb from her second floor bedroom. No one had mentioned a rope on the doorknob. Had it burned off before their arrival?

Covered in soot, Lily had been located a block away. She'd told police that Barb often left the stove on because she abused her sleep medication. She boasted that she had heroically attempted a rescue but the intense heat forced her out. The presence of Triazolam in Barb's Tox screen at the hospital seemed to confirm Lily's claim and the whole incident was written off as a tragic accident caused by negligence.

"That story that girl told isn't true," Barb blurted. "I've never taken a sleeping pill in my life! She tried to kill me." Eyes darting from Erin to window to door, her agitation could easily be mistaken for mental instability.

"I believe you."

"I miss my husband." Barb twisted the ring on her finger. "I don't like that he's got to stay in that motel with *her*. She's destroyed our home, and now she's ruining our marriage. We've never been apart this long before. At least Albert promised not to tell anyone where I am." Barb's eyes flicked back to Erin and she exhaled. "She's filling his head with her poisonous words so who knows what she'll talk him into. Sleeping pills, the nerve! Even Albert doesn't really believe me. He doesn't think she's following me."

"I do. I'm going to help—"

"There she is!" Barb jammed her sunglasses back on and sprang to her feet. She ducked behind Erin and pointed out the window. "She's hiding by my car! Oh my God! She's found me!"

Erin leaned to the window and scanned the street. It looked

deserted, Barb's car still exactly where she'd parked it. The other patrons in the coffee shop watched the spectacle with amusement. "Mrs. Schmidt," she said calmly. Palm out, she motioned for Barb to sit back down. "Maybe it's time you thought about seeing a counselor—"

"There!" Barb squealed and Erin turned her head in time to see the peak of a gray hoodie slip out of sight behind the car.

Erin reacted on instinct, bolting to the door in one fluid motion. "Wait here." She dashed across the street to the sedan. "Lily!"

A slight figure darted from the car and sprinted away.

Erin pursued, her feet pounding only yards behind. Lily was quicker. She had never met a girl who could run so fast. She was losing ground.

At the next intersection, the hooded figure narrowly missed a car turning left and easily vaulted over a low wrought-iron fence, arrowhead points scraping at pant legs.

Erin stopped to avoid colliding with the car and vaulted the fence with less athletic grace. *Am I losing my edge?* Already a half-block behind, her lungs burned and she pushed herself to keep up.

Ahead, her quarry veered to the left and she lost sight. By the time she reached the alley, it was empty. She bent, hands on knees, to catch her breath. She kept her eyes on the alley for any sudden movement.

Three houses away, a dog's surprised bark alerted her and she crept outside the gate. The dog took on a frantic tone. Someone's terrier or shih-tzu was becoming protective of its territory and it was a matter of time before the dog drove off the intruder. All Erin had to do was be quiet, be patient, and wait.

On cue, the gate eased open and the thin figure in the hoodie backed cautiously out. Right in front, a fluffy white mixed-breed asserted all twenty pounds of her fury with gnashing teeth and frenzied barking.

Thank you Miss Fuzzy Pants.

Erin kicked the gate closed and pulled the hood over the suspect's face, bringing her target to the ground.

Miss Fuzzy Pants quieted and Erin saw a brown eye peeking at the action through a crack in the fence. "Good doggie," Erin murmured and the dog responded with an angry yelp. Erin was a stranger too.

Below her, Lily struggled against the knee Erin pressed between her shoulder blades. Solid muscle rippled under her hoodie. What kind of young girl had such physical power at the age of thirteen? She eased the pressure and allowed Lily to turn over.

"I didn't do it!" The male voice stunned Erin and she backed away. "Who are you? Undercover cop or what?" A young man pulled his twisted hood from his face and rose to his feet. She reeled back against the fence. That explained a lot.

Around twenty years old, he had the scarcest shadow of stubble across his chin and unkempt brown hair. He was also much taller than Lily. No wonder he could run so fast. How could she have mistaken him for her?

"I was just *looking* at the car. I wasn't breaking into it or nothing! It wasn't me."

So, that was it. He was only some random petty criminal pilfering valuables from unlocked cars. She glanced at a tear in the leg of his pants where a trickle of blood dripped onto the top of his running shoe. Miss Fluffy Pants had punished him for intruding on her property.

"I'm going to let you off with a warning this time." Erin placed her hands on her hips. She had no authority to arrest anyone outside her own jurisdiction, but he didn't need to know her back-story. "If I catch you around here again…"

He was halfway down the alley before she finished her sentence and Erin hurried back to the coffee shop.

Barb's green car was gone.

CHAPTER 12

School's out for summer and I can sleep in every damn day if I want. I wiggle my toes out from under the blanket to give them some air. My jagged nails catch on the sheets. I gave them a try with my knife yesterday and I would have to rate that a fail.

The sun through the blinds makes a triangle of light on the pile of dirty clothes in the corner. Back home, I could always guess the time by the position of the sun in the sky.

"Eleven," I say out loud and twist around to the clock radio. The red digits read 11:08. I'm that good.

It's a cushy life here but Albert sulks all the time. I can't believe he misses his nosy wife. *Good riddance!* With Barb gone, I can enjoy my life. He should do the same but all he does is work and sleep. I hardly ever see him. I snatch up the twenty-dollar bill he left on the table.

I've been bored since Nina was grounded. She stayed out late with me and made her mom late for work. Now she won't sneak out, no matter how stupid I tell her she is. She has two more days of torture, but I know she's going stir crazy and I can talk her into it. I'll let her trim my nails. She loves doing shit like that.

I roll over and fish my shorts off the back of the chair. As I step out of bed, I slide my legs in and I'm on my way. At home, I ran barefoot every summer but not here in the city. There is too much broken glass and I learned that the hard way. I twist my feet into a pair of worn flip-flops and head out. On the way, I finger comb my wild hair and tuck it behind my ears.

At the convenience store, I grab a bag of chips and two sodas. I consider my footwear choice and decide to pay for them today. If I had to make a run for it, and the cashier chased me, I'd wipe out on my face. The checkout guy rings in my purchases and then I get lucky. Another customer distracts him. I can't resist. I pocket the closest roll of candy from the shelf.

There's a strange white van in Nina's driveway with decals that read A-1 Electrical. Half a dozen crumpled beer cans and papers are scattered across the floor. Nothing worth breaking in for. I veer around the rusty bumper and skip up on the back step. Her mom must be having some work done. That house is a piece of crap.

At the door, I rap twice with my knuckles. *Where's Nina?* After a minute I go to the front and peek through the window. Duct tape crisscrosses the hole from my rock. The TV is on really loud in the living room but there are no people. I knock on the glass and the whole pane shakes as if it will shatter. I back off and head to the rear.

Always on night shift, Nina's mom sleeps during the day but not today. Today her window is wide open, curtains blowing sideways in the breeze. I stop dead in my flip-flops when I hear a man's low voice coming from inside.

"Come on, sweetcakes."

"Not again. I told you if you ever—" Nina's mom's voice shakes like a kid in the principal's office. I lean under the window.

"Aw sweetcakes, I had time to think about what I done wrong. All this time apart made me a better man. I promise—"

"You promise. *You promise.* You always break your promises!"

I strain to hear his pleading voice when it deepens. "You're so purty. You done something new to your hair?"

"I can't. No more. I have to think of the girls."

"Didn't they tell you what a good daddy I been? Little girls need their daddies."

Hate churns my gut. This is no random electrician trying to get into her pants. This is Nina's father! Is her mom going to swallow that crap? I should jump in there and stick my knife in his throat.

There is no more talk, only bed squeaks and sucking noises. Ugh, she's letting him! I'm only a few feet away from where Nina's parents are doing the nasty. I push away from the wall and bail out of there before I barf.

Around the back corner of the house, I toss a few pebbles at the window and Nina's head pops up like the critter in the Whac-A-Mole arcade game. She slides it open.

"You know I can't come out today," she whispers. Her sister's head pops up beside her. Puffy-eyed, they've both been crying. Here the two of them are, holed up like rodents while their parents have disgusting sex in the next room.

"Sneak out." I know the cure for Nina's sad face. "Come on. We'll have some fun."

"Shhh!" She pushes her sister away from the window. One mole down, like the game. "You'll get me in trouble."

"Don't be a pussy. I promise you'll have fun." I mean it. It'll be more fun than listening to her parents' grunts and groans. "You'll be back before they notice."

"No." Nina's brows crowd puffy eyes.

"Chicken."

"I am not." She wipes her eyes with the back of her fist.

"Scared."

"I can't leave my sister," she hisses through the open window. "Someone has to be responsible around here."

"Pussy." Nina is easy. All I have to do is get her angry and she will do what I want. She sure hates being called a pussy. "Bring Beth with you." Her eyebrows lift, clearing away frown lines.

"Wait out front." She disappears from the window. I bob my head and gangsta walk to the road. Works every time.

A minute later, Nina emerges from the side door, her little sister in tow. Beth is wearing her pink Little Pony shoes and Dora the Explorer backpack. Nina has on checkered shorts and a sleeveless shirt. They're dressed for shopping but I hate the mall.

"Let's go to the water park," I say when we're a block away from their house. It is hot and, around here, every kid loves going to the concrete water park. The one with the brightly painted flowers, spritzing fountains and buckets that dump water. The parents leave their purses and bags over by the picnic tables and I usually can score a few bucks whenever I go.

"I don't have my bathing suit," Beth announces like a spoiled princess so I give her the sassy face right back. "I want an iced coffee."

"You're only four!" Nina holds out a stern index finger. "Four-year olds don't drink coffee."

"Daddy said he would buy me one if I rode on his leg like a pony."

Blood drains from Nina's face. "You didn't do it, did you?"

"No, mommy made us move away and I never got to." Beth stomps her pink shoe. "Daddy said it would be fun."

Nina looks dizzy so I step in and grab the strap on Beth's backpack. I drag her until her feet catch up. "Let's go for a ride instead. It'll be way more fun."

Nina heaves a grateful sigh and follows.

A half block from the pub where the construction workers drink their afternoons away, I tell them to wait. Nina crumples into the shade, taking her little sister with her.

"I'll be back in a few minutes. Then we'll have fun."

Nina folds her arms around her sister and buries her head in her shoulder.

I take the long way around, so I can come up to the parking lot from the alley. It is packed today. The men are all inside to escape the heat. That means some loser will leave his truck running to keep the air conditioning on. They always stay longer than they plan and that makes for easy pickings.

It takes a few minutes to find my ride, since there are two to consider. Finally, I choose a dusty Chrysler with a sunroof and a half tank of gas, enough for an afternoon of entertainment.

I shift into drive and squeeze through a gap in the cars, heading back down the lane. Nina jumps when I honk the horn but Beth stands and gives me a happy wave.

Nina freezes on the sidewalk when I hit the power button to roll down the window. "Where did you—?"

"Come on." I lean over, pull the handle and shove the passenger door open.

"Yay!" Beth hops in, climbs over the seat and buckles up in back as if she does this every day.

"Whose—?" Nina is still frozen so I give her a prod.

"Well, your sister is all ready. Maybe we'll go without you." I reach for the door.

"Come on Neeeeena!" Beth sings out. Her short legs flutter kick the back of my seat and I elbow it, hard. She stops.

Nina meets my eyes, and then slides in. She pulls on her seat belt, stares at mine.

"Fine." Even though I don't see the point, I buckle up too. "Let's go get a Slurpee!" I holler. Beth squeals in delight. I squawk the tires when I take off and she screams like she's on a carnival ride.

I park a block away from the 7-11 and we walk to the store, Beth suspended like a pink Yo-Yo trick between us. Inside, Nina pretends she doesn't want anything but her sister sure does. The bossy brat gives me step-by-step instructions to mix her swamp water Slurpee. Cherry, lemonade, blue raspberry - in that exact order, so that the layers are equal. Then she wants a curlicue of cola on the very top. I narrow my eyes at her. They are both watching so I have to pay with what's left of Albert's twenty.

We load the kid into the car with her drink and cruise the back alleys real slow so she can count trashcans. Nina looks over at me and a hint of smile curves the corner of her lips. I make sure I brush her fingers when I hand her a beer from my pack.

It's my science experiment. It never ceases to amaze me how something so simple can make her pupils dilate like a junkie. She clutches the can in both hands and takes a polite sip but I know she will ask me to finish it. I grin at my power and she smiles back. I pop the tab on the second one for myself.

I enjoy driving, especially a big boat like this old Chrysler. In this, I'm a shark hunting the back streets for Barb's car. It's only a matter of time before she comes up for air and I can finish what I started.

"Is that beer?" In the back seat, Beth the brat has noticed. "Daddy says no beer for kids." She giggles. "Except one time he let me have a sip after he hugged me really hard on his lap. I'm glad Daddy is back."

Nina's face pinches. I hate when she's like this. This kid in the back will ruin our whole day with all the talk of their dad.

"If I had money, I would take her and run away," she hisses. Fists clenched around her beer, she takes a long swallow and her nose wrinkles. She still can't stand the taste.

I think about her problem for a minute. "I know how you can get rid of him."

Her head snaps around on her neck and she stares at me. "What?"

I wonder if she didn't hear me the first time so I say it louder. "I know how to get rid of him, for good."

Nina's eyes swivel to the kid in the back seat, who is not paying attention. "You're not talking about—"

She's not ready. My great idea is out of the question for now. I need a more subtle approach. "I mean, I know how to get money from him *and* get him to leave you alone."

"Are you suggesting blackmail?"

"Black, green, red. Get the mail!" Beth chimes in from the back.

"Shhh!" Nina holds a finger to her lips. "Let's talk later." She likes the idea, I can tell. This could be a way for us both to get some extra cash. She turns around and puts on her happy face for her sister. "Let's go to the water park!"

"I don't have my bathing—"

"Let's go in our clothes this time. Lots of kids do, and we'll be dry by the time we get home. Mom won't know."

Frowning, Beth considers this for a moment. The excitement proves too much to handle and she smiles. "Okay. Like daddy says, it will be our little secret."

When Nina turns her face back around, I see murderous anger in her eyes. Maybe my idea is not out of the question. When she gets mad, she'll do anything I ask.

I pull the car into the lane opposite the big concrete and plastic water park. Beth runs across the road without looking and Nina yells after her but the kid is too fast, and too excited, to pay attention.

The park is full of soaking wet, screaming children and Beth blends right in. She skips over the spritzers and dashes past suspended water buckets seconds before they spill over.

There are no unattended purses so I veer away from the swooping gulls at the picnic tables and choose a spot outside the concrete perimeter. Nina sits on the grass beside me. Her stiff posture tells me she's still upset. She's going to be cranky and destroy my whole day if I don't fix this.

"Will you clip my toenails?" I kick off one flip-flop and waggle my toes at her. "I tried but you see how that turned out."

"What?" It's as if I asked her to walk on the moon.

"I know you have trimmers somewhere." I poke at her pocket. She fusses over her nails all the time and sometimes even carries fingernail polish, as if she'd be stuck on a desert island any moment with bad nails. "I'll tell you my idea if you do it."

"Fine." Her eyes darken as if a cloud blocked the sun. "Go rinse your feet first. They smell like old man, and they're dirty." She grins at me, but her eyebrows keep their frown. I don't know what that means, but I'm getting my nails trimmed, so what do I care? Albert is stinky. At least I get that.

I chase Beth through the sprinkler for a few minutes to wash the old man stink off. She shrieks when I make monster noises and then backs into a picnic table.

"Stop!" She holds her hand out like a school crossing guard.

I growl and dig my fingers into her ribs, to prove that stop signs won't work on me. A gull zips between us with someone's stolen french fry in his beak and I jerk my body out of his path. Birds have always freaked me out.

"That hurt!" The brat puts her hands on her hips and glares at me. "You're supposed to stop when I say stop!"

"I was only tickling you."

"You're doing it mean!"

I make a scary face and show her my teeth before I back off. It's the friggin' gulls I really want to escape from. Someone left their spilled fries all over that picnic table and the birds are swarming like piranhas.

I rejoin Nina on the grass, one foot in the air to advertise clean toes. She produces a nail clipper from the pocket of her shorts, I knew she had it, and takes my heel in her hand. My skin crawls but I don't dare move or she'll clip off my toe.

"I hate my father so much that sometimes I think about cutting." She does a quick visual check on Beth who has her butt positioned over a spritzer, squealing loud enough to break eardrums.

"Random." I quip, but she's not amused with my sarcasm.

"I'm serious. I hate him." She twists the tiny attached file sideways from the nail clipper.

"What are you gonna do?" I laugh. "Scratch yourself to death?"

She pivots the file back in and throws it on my lap. "Finish your toes yourself."

"Hey, j.k." I say, and then clarify. "Just kidding. Wow, who peed in your cereal this morning?"

"My mom always takes him back. Every. Single. Time." She takes the clipper back and finishes my nails. The last one is crooked but I let it go. "You *know* what he did to me. Now he's after my baby sister."

Beth is not really a baby any more. She's a spoiled little shit. I'm pretty sure if I say that out loud I'll piss Nina off so I roll onto my belly beside her. "Leave it to me. I'll make him stop."

"How?"

I don't like the way she's looking down at me so I get up and look her in the eye. "I'll take care of it, don't worry."

The skin around her mouth tightens.

"And don't cut yourself. That's stupid." I mean it. Cutting is for pussies. I came to that conclusion after I tried it with my knife. I still have the scar on my thigh. What was the point? Why hurt yourself when what you really want to do is hurt someone else? I'm a problem solver. It's one of my better qualities.

Nina needs to understand how much better it feels after you get rid of your problems. I mentally tick off the ones I'm proud to have solved. One, my mother's screaming face sinking into the bog. Two, the meddling church lady blown to hell on her back porch. I snicker. Three, nosy Gina at the Stop 'N Go.

Can I count that one since she didn't die? Well, I bashed her head in and torched her store, so that's close enough. My grandfather hasn't croaked from the poison yet, but I don't have to see him any more, so that worked too. My father is in jail forever for some shit he never even did. Then there's Barb, my half-solved problem. Next time I burn down my problem, I'll wait until I'm sure she's dead before I do my victory dance. I remember Barb's terrified eyes staring at me from the crack in her doorway and hide my smile from Nina. I don't want her to think I'm not taking her daddy issue seriously.

"It's just that sometimes..." she trails off.

Someone has dropped a ballpoint pen in the grass and I reach out for it with newly trimmed toes. "Here, give me your arm." I grab her by the elbow and draw a line of skulls that look more like black spiders. She twitches when I get past her elbow but I hold firm until the line snakes from wrist to armpit. "There."

She holds it out to examine my work and the corner of her mouth curves up. She has been sitting in the sun too long and her nose is pink under her freckles. I don't know if she likes it or if she has heatstroke.

"Let me do you." She whips the pen from my fingers before I can protest and draws a stylized sunburst with squiggly rays on the inside of my wrist.

She doesn't let go and I don't want a line of stupid sunbursts all the way up my arm. I'll go insane before she's done. "Where's Beth?"

I say. I can't take any more of this touching shit today.

Her head pops up like an alarmed deer and she runs off to retrieve her sister. Beth is over by the picnic tables again, coaxing the birds with someone's discarded french fry. Disgusting. Nina gets her to drop it and hauls her by one hand over to the shade. The kid wiggles like a minnow on a hook.

Redheads are not like me. I tan eventually but they keep on burning all summer long. Nina and her sister are sun-fried and that's going to be their mom's first clue that they snuck out today.

I'm doodling on the sole of Beth's shoe when a white cruiser with lights on top and a long black stripe marked Police rolls past. It's at the alley where I parked the car when the brake lamps glow. It backs up and the cop inside holds a microphone to his mouth. *Damn.* Our ride home is gone. Watching intently while I draw swirls joined to squares, Beth doesn't see it, but Nina does.

"We have to run for it!" She jumps to her feet, dragging Beth along.

I take Beth's other hand and pull them both back down to the grass. "Relax. They don't know we have anything to do with it." I roll to my side and prop my head on my hand, giving me a clear view of the action.

Beth imitates me and I'm annoyed so I change position and sit up. She does too. "Why is the policeman looking at your car, Lily?" She pokes me on the back of the hand with a chubby finger.

"Well, it wasn't really my car."

Nina draws in her breath and holds it. Her eyes go from me to the police car, and back again.

"It was my friend's car and I'm done borrowing it so he is going to return it for me." All true, except the friend part.

"Oh." She pokes me again and I give her an elbow. She thinks I'm playing with her, but I'm just annoyed. I shove her hard and she topples onto her back. She comes up laughing, like Nina did when I shoved her in the pool. Two of a kind, they like it rough.

"It's getting late. We'd better go." Nina yanks Beth up so quickly her feet leave the ground. It's probably a good thing she stops this shoving game now before the kid ends up crying. She's no match for me. "We have to get home."

"I'm telling mom you and Lily drank beer." I thought the brat would have forgotten about that by now, but here she is, threatening me.

"No, you won't," I counter, and she puts her hands on her hips in a repeat of her earlier standoff at the picnic table. "I'll hold you under the waterfall bucket with your mouth open."

Nina's round eyes stare at me as if I'm an alien.

"J.k!" I say quickly. "I'm *just kidding*." I extract the roll of candy I swiped from the store and wave it in front of the brat's face. Her eyes light up. I snatch it back before she tries to grab it. "Nah-ah! Only girls who can keep secrets get candy."

"I really like candy." Her stubborn duck feet point sideways.

"You have to promise not to tell or I'll cut your eye out."

"Lily!" Nina's steps between us.

"I mean, cross your heart and hope to die." I laugh like I was kidding the whole time.

"Huh?" Beth looks utterly perplexed and afraid to take anything from me. "I don't wanna die!"

"She means pinkie swear." Good old Nina, translating into four year old lingo. She hooks Beth's pinkie with hers and they exchange a serious nod.

"Fine." I mimic the serious face and hand over the candy. "Are you gonna share?"

"Nope." The little shit skips away from me, smug in her knowledge that I won't strangle her in front of Nina.

"We need to get home before mom wakes up for her night shift." She's too young for the worry lines that crease her forehead.

As far as I'm concerned, their mom is the least of their worries. It's the dad, Mister A-1 Electrical, who needs to be taken care of. I trace the outline of the knife I carry in my pocket. I'm pretty sure I can distract him.

CHAPTER 13

"How was your meeting?" Erin was waiting on the back step for Allie when she got back. Wrong-Way Rachel glowered beside her, miserable in her kitty harness. Allie picked up the cat and ruffled the hair behind her ears.

"It went well." Allie gave her a modest smile. She'd had a poor night's sleep and woke with a punishing headache this morning. It had taken effort to clear her mind and focus. When she'd started her presentation, she'd sensed a room full of closed minds. Many businesses were resistant to change, especially when they didn't understand the benefits.

She had taken her time and was thorough in explaining the technical side, using layman's terms whenever she could. In the end, their energy changed as their minds opened to the new possibilities and she knew they were on board. This was a big contract and would be a jumpstart for her new business. She promised to outsource some of the work to local contractors, and that was the piece that had turned the presentation around.

After a catered lunch and rounds of smiles and handshakes, she tucked the signed papers into her case. She presented Erin with the bottle of de-alcoholized wine she'd bought. They could celebrate with a nice dinner later.

"I was sure you'd nail it." Erin took the bottle. "Let's put this in the fridge."

She released the cat from her harness and brought her inside. Rachel disappeared immediately.

"I'm glad you feel better. I was worried this morning." Erin pulled her into her arms and two-stepped across the kitchen. She kissed Allie on the corner of her eyebrow. "You barely slept. Did you have nightmares all night?"

"I had nightmares? I don't remember." Hazy images filed by in a macabre slide show. A knife. Stabbing. Slashing. Blood running dark and red across pale skin. Seagulls. Were these things in the past? A possible future? Were they happening now? She had no idea and they made no sense. Perhaps they were simply someone's random thoughts. She had fought to push them from her mind all the way to her meeting. Now Erin was bringing them back.

"You said Lily's name."

"Oh?" Memories solidified. The dreams *were* about Lily. She was sure of it. Erin deserved to know. "I do remember something. I think Lily has a new underling. I feel hate. Fear. I see a knife, blood, awful things."

"Has she hurt someone?" Erin snatched the truck keys from Allie's hand. "Do we need to go?"

"No," Allie laid a calming hand on her arm. "There is nothing we can do right now. I think these might be Lily's thoughts I feel, not her actions."

Erin sat at the table and arched her neck back. "I can't find that evil monster. After you left for your meeting, I went to the motel Barb told me about. I circled the entire neighborhood and kept an eye on the place but she's never there."

"But I had your truck."

"She looked so desperate that I lent her my bike." Leaning on the doorway, Ciara's grin told Allie everything. She'd probably gotten fed up with Erin pacing the kitchen and told her to take the bicycle to do whatever it was she so badly needed. Allie could imagine Erin pedaling Ciara's hipster bike as fast as it would go, her binoculars and notepad bouncing in the flower basket. Surveillance on a bicycle, despite the amusing visual image, was probably more covert than in Erin's big truck. Erin was fit. She could ride for miles.

"You'll find her," Allie said. "But not today."

Erin put a hand on her shoulder. "I understand that you don't want to intrude, but you can't work from the kitchen table any more. You need a real office."

Allie nodded. "And a faster internet connection." She turned to Ciara. "Do you mind if I have a couple of techs install fiber optic cable?"

"Yay, new holes in the wall for mice."

"Rachel is an excellent hunter."

Ciara's mouth twisted sideways and she laughed. "Fine, darling. Whatever you need. The storage room across from the bathroom could be an office." Ciara patted Allie's hand. "It's bigger than it looks. You'll see, once we move that junk to the shed."

"I'll carry junk," Erin volunteered. "Let's start tomorrow."

"It sounds like we all had busy mornings. I know *I* need to unwind. Why don't we go for a walk and you two can get to know each other better?" Allie glanced from Erin to Ciara.

Fifteen minutes later, the two women nearly jogged to maintain Allie's brutal pace. "We should go this way." Allie marched off the paved walkway and along a narrow trail through the brush at the water's edge.

On the other side of the murky Red River, Winnipeg's bland offices and apartment buildings crowded together in vanilla and chocolate blocks. She lengthened her stride. The only way to decrease the pressure in her head was to follow the course set out before her. The pervasive thought was simply to *go this way*. She wasn't sure what they'd find, but judging from the pain in her temples, it was urgent. "Hurry."

Erin followed without question.

"I'm not familiar with this path." Thistles clung to Ciara's dress and scratched her bare legs. "Are you sure you aren't getting us lost?"

Allie broke into a jog and Erin and Ciara plowed through the bushes to keep up. This was supposed to be a group walk, a chance for everyone to bond, but they'd barely been able to talk before Allie had felt a familiar pull. The sensation that something needed her attention *right now*. Then it had become another of her weird adventures.

God knows Erin should be used to this by now, and even though they'd never directly spoken about it, the strange escapades of their university days were probably surfacing in Ciara's memory.

"Allie! Where…?"

Beside her Ciara stumbled and wrenched the edge of her dress away from a bramble. "Aw, bloody hell!" She snatched a torn piece of her hem from the prickles. "My favorite dress, again." She folded the ripped fabric and stuffed it in her pocket.

"Just a bit further," Allie urged. She glanced at Erin who tilted her head to the trail. Branches whipping behind her, Allie took off again, faster than before. When they neared a bridge, Allie stopped and turned. "Not here." She looked up at the traffic crossing above. "There."

"We need to go up on the bridge?" Erin raised to her toes, ready to run wherever Allie indicated.

"Come on." Allie swatted at the brush and lead them up the incline. Cars whipped past. She took a step onto the road and a motorcycle swerved, horn beeping long after he was gone.

"Baby!" Erin caught her by the elbow and pulled her back. "You need to pay attention."

Allie pointed to the opposite side of the bridge. A delivery van zoomed by and her hair fluttered in the sucking wind.

"I don't see anything." Ciara brushed dark bangs from her face.

"Listen!" Erin cocked her head and the others fell silent. In between passing vehicles, they heard it. A high-pitched whine.

Ciara stared at Allie. "You *heard* that? From down there?"

"Uh, more like I felt it." Allie looked to Erin, back to the other side of the road. *Hurry.*

Erin shot forward after the next car passed.

"Left!" Allie called.

Erin turned and followed the edge of the bridge's concrete barrier.

"No, your other left!" Allie pointed.

Erin pivoted the other way. Suddenly, she perked up and dashed forward.

Allie waited for a series of trucks and spotted a break in traffic. She sprinted across, Ciara close behind. By the time they reached the other side, Erin had already lifted an iron grate that covered the entrance to the bridge's drainage system. Underground, something wailed for help.

Erin knelt and thrust her arm inside. "It's deep but it's down there." She poked her head through the hole and came back up. Wrenching the heavy grate aside, she slid her upper body into the drain. With bent knees acting as anchors above ground, she grunted and twisted through.

"Honey, do you see him?" Allie peered into the dark hole. A small animal thrashed in neck-deep muck. His distress sent spikes of pain to her temples.

Erin scooped up a brown lump and held the struggling armful tight. He peered at her with startled brown eyes and sneezed. His skinny legs dangled.

"What is it?" Ciara leaned in.

"I'm not sure. It's too dirty to tell. Maybe a baby muskrat."

"You did it again Pet Detective." Ciara slapped Allie on the back. "You found a lost animal. God, how I miss our university days! Remember that skunk you thought was the neighbor's cat? You should hang up a shingle, really."

Allie rolled her eyes. They had learned the hard way that tomato juice didn't work as well as people said. She reached out to touch the quivering lump. Static electricity stung her fingertips and she flinched away.

"You weren't kidding. Erin really is a superhero," Ciara stage-whispered.

Erin's ears turned pink.

"Is he hurt?" Allie bent for a closer look. What creature exuded such energy?

Ciara tore the rest of the tattered hem from her dress and handed it to Erin. "Here. Unless it's a cat, you're probably better with animals."

Allie shook her head. Ciara had not changed a bit.

"Besides, muskrats have sharp teeth. It's likely to bite off my fingers." Ciara folded her arms.

Erin took the cloth and cleaned dirt from the animal's face.

His energy was weak, an intermittent glow, yet there were sparks. One pink triangular ear appeared from the filth and she leaned close to examine him. "Hmm."

Erin cleaned the other ear and they stuck out like large pointed flags on either side of its head. "You're definitely not a muskrat."

"It has a bat face," Ciara volunteered.

"It's cute, whatever it is." Erin hugged it gently while she wiped down its body and paws. When she was done, she held it out for everyone to see. The color of a fawn, with white markings across its chest and underbelly, the animal's tiny body shook violently. Unusually large ears were now pinned back to its head.

"It's a chihuahua!" Erin exclaimed. "And it's a boy."

"With a bat face." Ciara reclaimed her soggy mud-covered scrap of cloth. "I can sew that back on."

"He has certainly had the adventure of his lifetime today," Allie said. He looked so exhausted. Helpless.

"You should hold him." Erin frowned when Allie took a step back. "Animals love you. He might stop shaking."

Allie pursed her lips.

"He needs you," Ciara offered.

Allie let out the breath she hadn't realized she was holding and reached for the dog. She ignored the static shock when she touched the soft fur. Warmth enveloped her and she closed her eyes. Her lungs filled with sweet air. Fiona felt like this. Fiona, the *best dog ever.* She was gone too soon. The warmth intensified and Allie gasped. It was hot. Too hot. The sensation intoxicated her.

"I can't." She backed away, hyper-aware of Ciara and Erin's eyes on her.

As usual, Erin came to her rescue. "Don't worry, I've got this." She folded the dog into the front of her shirt, exposing her toned midriff, and crossed the road. She looked taller, more confident. Immensely competent.

Allie watched her well-defined calf muscles flex and release with each step. How had she managed to find this woman, this rescuer of animals and people? This woman who had her eye as well as her heart?

Ciara elbowed her in the ribs. She had noticed too. The two women followed Erin back to the house, giggling like teenagers.

Erin handed the dog to Ciara when they reached the back yard and stripped off muddy clothing. Undressed to her skivvies, she balled up her clothes and wrung out the water.

"I think you need to get rid of those too." Ciara pointed to her bra and panties, lips squeezed tight to keep from laughing. "You don't want to track mud through the nice clean house."

"Cut it out, you old lecher!" Allie punched her on the shoulder. She had a point. They had spent hours cleaning everything until it was spotless. Livable.

Erin hung her wet socks side by side on the handrail, and then straightened them so they were exactly parallel. She frowned at the two giggling friends.

"She's so dirty." Ciara caught Allie's glare. "I won't look, honest." She held the sad-eyed dog up and imitated its forlorn expression.

Erin solved the faux dispute. She wiped her feet on the doormat and stalked past them to the bathroom. "You get to clean the muskrat."

Allie handed Erin a towel when she emerged from the shower, skin scrubbed pink. "Ciara is just kidding."

"It's not the first time I've been teased." Erin rubbed her hair until it stood up in spikes. "It's no big deal." She dried behind her ears and finished.

"I guess we just get a bit silly together. It's been so long since we've seen each other, and university was a crazy time."

"I get it. Hanging out with Z-man is like that." Erin slipped into the clean clothes Allie had brought.

"Yeah, Chris is a funny guy. Once you get to know Ciara, you'll love her just as much."

Erin glanced at her out of the corner of her eye. "What's up with the dog? You love dogs. Are you missing Fiona?"

"Maybe." A vision of Fiona's happy tongue dangling from the side of her mouth accompanied an ache in her chest. "I don't know."

"Let's go see what he looks like."

Allie nodded.

Erin carefully arranged her towel on the rack and followed her downstairs.

"Here he is, the pooch of the hour, freshly washed." Ciara handed the dog to Erin. "So handsome."

"Come here, little guy." Erin picked him up and snuggled onto the sofa. The dog curled into a tight ball on her lap. His tawny coat, still fluffy from the vigorous rubdown, shone. Oversize pink ears moved like satellite dishes at every sound. "He has no marks or tattoos, but he looks healthy, except for the shaking." She checked his body, ears, belly and inside his mouth while she talked.

Allie brought a small bowl. "I know he drank his fill of mud today, but he might need water to wash it down." She held it in front of the dog and his pink tongue extended to lap up half the dish.

"He won't stop shaking." Erin held the dog up and light shone through his semi translucent ears. "Somewhere inside, his internal engine must be off-kilter."

"He has an adorable bat face." Ciara leaned between them to scratch the dog's chin.

Allie took a step back with her water dish. "He seems like a perfectly nice dog, for a chihuahua."

"Auntie Agnes always said it's not a real dog if you can kick it thirty feet." Erin crooned and gently massaged the dog's ears so they unfolded and stuck straight out. He snuggled against her cheek.

"Your auntie Agnes adores animals as much as you do."

"She knows I'm kidding," she whispered to the dog.

"Is the superhero scaring the puppy?" Ciara's laugh rang like a silver spoon against crystal.

"I know he's cute, but he needs to find his owners." Allie resisted the pull she felt toward this needy creature. "While we make dinner, why don't you take him to the animal shelter?"

Erin's eyebrows shot up. "But I thought you were led to find him."

"That doesn't mean we keep someone else's dog. He just needed our help." Even as she said the words, she knew that's not what she felt. "I already programmed your phone with the address. It's not more than ten minutes away."

Erin got to her feet, dog clasped to her heart.

"He's not ours, Honey." Allie shook her head gently.

"We're making vegan stuffed seitan roast!" Ciara called out on her way to the kitchen. Erin wrinkled her nose and Allie gave her a stern look.

Ciara was removing a gray oblong-shaped loaf from the oven when Erin shuffled back in the door carrying a plastic bag emblazoned with the animal shelter logo.

Allie frowned at the suspicious bulge under her T-shirt. "Did you forget your mission, soldier?"

Erin shook her head. "The animal shelter was a zoo, literally." She lifted the front of her shirt, where the chihuahua shivered against her warm skin. "They are over capacity, with five million cats and pet rabbits. They can't accept any more animals."

Allie placed a hand on her hip. "*Five million*, really?"

"Honestly, I'm not making this up so we can keep the muskrat." She made a kissy-face at the dog. "They suggested I try another shelter in Brandon, but all the shelters are overcrowded right now due to the flooding. So many misplaced people make for a lot of misplaced animals."

"Shall I set one more plate for dinner?" Ciara teased.

Allie sighed.

"The good news is that our waterlogged canine friend does not have a microchip." Erin tilted her head at Allie. "Or bad news, depending on how you want to take it."

"Well, it sounds like we have no choice." Allie sighed. "For now. Please tell me you have dog food in this bag." Erin handed it over and Allie lined up the contents on the counter. "A month's worth of premium puppy food—"

"Nothing but the best for our muddy buddy." Erin interrupted.

"A brand new collar—"

"Rainbow-colored, of course." Erin's grin was irresistible.

"A matching leash, a food dish and a half-dozen dog toys." Allie raised an eyebrow. "Should I believe this story about the overcrowded shelter?"

"Cross my heart." Erin held up the tag on one of the toys. There was conviction in her eyes.

It was inevitable. Tension formed a knot between Allie's shoulder blades. "Promise me one thing before you send the new baby announcements to the relatives."

"Anything."

"Place an ad online and check social media to make sure no one is looking for him."

"Done!" Erin filled the dog's new dish and placed it beside Ciara's water bowl. "Rachel is going to love her new brother."

"I wouldn't hold my breath on that one." The cat was skulking somewhere and hadn't yet met the intruder.

Erin set the dog on the floor to explore and joined them at the table. He immediately lifted a hind leg and peed a stream of yellow onto the corner of the cabinet. "I got it!" She leapt up and blotted the tiny puddle with a paper towel.

"I'm so glad you didn't rescue a Saint Bernard." Ciara placed a white ceramic baking dish on the table and followed it with a salad bowl brimming with leafy greens and cherry tomatoes. The salad looked tasty enough, but the gray loaf had an oddly suspicious texture.

Erin shot a glance at Allie.

"So pick them off," Allie mouthed when Ciara looked away. Despite their vivid color and versatility, she'd never seen Erin choke down a fresh tomato. Chop and simmer it into a sauce, smother it with cheese, obliterate it with seasoning, but never would she eat an actual tomato. Allie even made a point of grinding their extra chunky salsa.

"Look at us all having a civilized dinner." Ciara smirked. "We're like the United Nations. We have our pale-skinned Swedish American representative," she nodded to Erin who rolled her eyes. "Allie gets to represent Ireland, Canada *and* the Ojibwe people. I am English and, of course we have our nameless Mexican representative chewing the corner of my grandmother's chair." She scooted the dog away from it with her foot. "And the wine is French. Bon appétit!"

"Did you drink it all while you were cooking?" Erin quipped and Ciara laughed. She poured her a glass.

Allie rested her chin on her palm and watched Erin stoically fish around the tomatoes with the salad tongs. The knot between her shoulder blades unwound. Everyone was allowed a quirk or two. She raised her hand to hide her smile when Erin picked up the spatula to address the issue of the vegan mystery loaf. They definitely would have to sneak out for burgers later.

CHAPTER 14

"What the fuck? Goddammit! Motherf—!" There is a long pause, then "Awwwww," followed by a rustle of clothing as Nina's dad slumps to the porch steps.

Take that you bastard!

Step one of my plan is complete. He'll need some help and four new tires to get that van back on the road. Behind the neighbor's hedge, I crouch like a panther and find a break in the foliage where I can watch. He's sitting there, staring at the van and scratching his head.

With one hand tight to my mouth, I squeeze fingers hard into my jawbones to keep my laugh in. My other hand clutches the lock blade knife I liberated from Albert and Barb's house. It was my first best friend when I got to Winnipeg and never disappoints me. Squeaks of air escape my nose, but he's too busy talking on his cell phone to hear me. Yes, he will be very late to work today.

Step two is where he goes into the van and reads my note. I rock back and forth on my heels. I can hardly wait for his reaction. He gets up and I move to a better spot where I can see through the van's windows. I want to see his expression when he reads it.

He's still not there. I move back to my first spot just in time to see the side door slam. He hasn't seen my note at all. He's gone back into the house! He was supposed to go to the van. Now he's messed it up.

The kitchen window is half open and I hear shouts. He's yelling at Nina's mom. Her mom yells back.

"Who did this? Is this your boyfriend?"

"I don't know what you're talking about."

"My van! That's what I'm talking about. Did you tell your boyfriend to do this?"

"What boyfriend? There is no one else."

"Someone slashed my tires!"

"I don't—"

There is a wet smack, like something dropped in mud.

"Leave her alone!" Nina's shrill voice. Something breaks and someone screams.

I crawl out from behind the hedge and select a rock, the biggest one I can throw, and aim for the front window. With a windup that would put a major leaguer to shame, I pitch it and it ricochets off the frame. I'm disappointed but the noise is loud enough to distract Nina's dad.

"Is he out there right now?" He sounds angry, really angry. Soon he'll be back here to search for the nonexistent boyfriend. I don't want him to find me stunned like a rutabaga in the middle of the driveway so I slip back behind the bushes and wait. My heart pounds in my ears but my nerves harden. This guy has got nothing on me.

The screen door bangs shut and I flatten to the ground, watching his work boots stomp from one end of the drive to the other. He's too chicken-shit to go much farther. His boots pause and then I hear the van's door creak open. I get to my knees and find another spot to peek through.

Yes. He's sitting inside and his reaction is priceless. He looks at my note, crumples it in his fist, and then flattens it out. It's like his entire face melted, cheeks drooping, jaw slack. His eyes flick from the paper to the street and back again, fingers shaking while he carefully folds the paper. He slips it into his breast pocket and looks over his shoulder before he slides out. When he closes the door, it doesn't make a sound. One eye on the street, he punches numbers into his cell phone.

"Brad. Are you screwin' with me?" You can tell he's trying to act tough, like a mobster, but his voice quavers more like a pussy. His eyes narrow while he listens to the answer. "You really don't know what I'm talking about, do ya?" As if Brad can see him, he nods. "Okay then. Come pick me up at the beer store. You know the one, off St Mary's." He straightens his shoulders and walks out the driveway. "Right now."

Ha, what a loser. As soon as he's gone, I get to my feet and saunter up to the door like I've just arrived. *Ding dong,* I push the doorbell and put on my innocent face. I practice my expression in the glass reflection while I wait. Eyebrows up, mouth open in a round oh. No, that might be too much. I try it again without the mouth and Nina opens the door while I'm standing there with my eyebrows up.

"Oh, what a surprise." I had to make up something fast but it came out weird.

"Well, you rang the doorbell, why were you surprised that I answered?" Nina's face is red, and she looks like her sense of humor was flushed down the toilet. I hate it when she's no fun. I took care of her problem, what more could she want?

"Never mind." I put on my happy face. "Are you comin' out, or what?"

She sees me looking past her. "My mom is resting. I don't want to disturb…" One eye puckers at the corner. She's lying. "How long have you been out there?"

I try the eyebrows up expression.

She tilts her head.

"I just got here. I saw your dad take off."

She puckers her brows. Is she suspicious?

"Swear on a stack of bibles, I didn't see a thing." I hold out my little finger, like she did the pinkie swear thing with her sister.

"You're acting weird." Her voice lowers. "Did you pop my dad's tires?"

"Maybe." I do a victory gangsta strut on the step. "Don't worry, he won't bother you again."

"Are you kidding?" I don't have to guess at Nina's expression this time. She looks pissed off. "He came straight in and punched my mom in the face. I think he might have broken her nose but she won't go to the hospital." She pokes the middle of my chest with her finger. "You caused that!"

Don't touch me. "But now he's read my note. He's not coming back."

"What else did you do?" Nina's whisper rises to a squeal and she shoots a glance over her shoulder.

"Two words, black and mail." I treat her to my most dazzling smile. "He ran out the driveway scared shitless."

"Whaaat?" Nina reels back. "I thought you were kidding!" She clunks down in a kitchen chair. "Oh, my God. What have you done?"

She's left the door wide open, an invitation. I step over the threshold. This is my first time actually being invited in but not my first time in the house. Once they left the door unlocked and I gave myself a tour. I know the layout and I know where Nina keeps her diary. I'm a superstar in it by the way, but I don't think my eyes look like *glimmering emerald pools*.

"You got any beer?" I open the fridge door far enough to see the lonely carton of milk in the middle of the center row. Aside from the milk, some ketchup and a half jar of jam, it's empty.

Nina jumps up and slams it shut.

"You have to go!"

Gawd. Her sense of humor really was flushed down the pisser.

"Who is this?" While she was making a huge deal out of me looking in the fridge, her mom appeared from her bedroom. Her sister is holding the tail of her mom's shirt.

"Hi Lily." Beth seems happy enough to see me. She drops the tail and does her cutesy pose. "Do you have any candy?"

"Is this your friend?" With a washcloth pressed to her cheek, Nina's mom acts like there's nothing weird about having half her face swollen up like a pumpkin but I can't help staring. "I bumped into the door. It's fine." Everyone in the room knows it's a lie, but nobody blurts the truth. She extends her free hand to shake mine and we squeeze like anacondas. She's trying entirely too hard.

"I'll go to the store and buy you a bag of ice, mom." Nina looks at me pointedly. "We're out of milk. I'll pick some up for Beth and we'll be back in a few minutes." Sometimes the corner of Nina's eye twitches when she lies. Today, it's the whole side of her face.

Her mom studies me, and then goes to find her purse. She hands Nina a twenty. "Pick up something for lunch too."

"But you said we could—"

Her mom gives her the look every kid knows. *Don't even start.*

Nina looks down and her jaw tightens. She heads for the door.

Beth pats my pocket before we leave. I guess that's her four-year-old hint for me to buy candy. *Fat chance, brat.*

All the way there, Nina walks ahead of me, her feet stomping in her sandals. Is it possible that she's still mad at me? "Hey, what's wrong with you?" I break a twig off someone's hedge and toss it at her back. She ignores me and keeps walking.

At the store she bypasses the milk and stands in the aisle forever before she finally grabs two boxes of macaroni dinner off the shelf. Mac and cheese is good, why did she act like it was such a hard decision? She loads a big bag of ice cubes into my arms.

"Carry this." Those are the first words she's said since we left the house. She turns her back and leads the way to the cash register.

As soon as we leave the store, she ambushes me.

"What do you think you're doing?" Her face squinches up like she ate a sour berry and doesn't want to spit it out.

"It's a little thing called revenge." I jut out my chin but she's as tall as me so it doesn't work as well as I'd hoped. "You can't let him get away with it. You need to get him back for what he did to you."

She turns away and then swivels back to me. The squinchy face is gone but her eyebrows are still down. If I had to guess, I'd say she was confused.

"He needs to pay."

"How are you planning to blackmail him?" One hand creeps to her hip. She's coming around.

"Already taken care of." I do a smaller version of my gangsta strut but she's not impressed. "All we have to do is wait for him to pay up."

"Tell me what you did." The hand on her hip clenches into a fist but her feet stay planted on the sidewalk.

"Fine." I stop my foot shuffle and meet her eye. With one hand, I pull my knife from my pocket and flick open the blade. She should be impressed by my obvious skill but her eyes widen. Her pupils shrink to tiny dots. I close it and slide it back out of sight.

"He punched my mom in the face for what you did." She's still angry but it's not my fault he didn't read my note when he was supposed to. There is no way I'll convince her of that, so I go on to step two. The note.

"He's gonna pay me— us, and he's gonna leave you alone." It's a brilliant plan. I hold my hands out, palms up. If it works for the guy on the commercial for Honest Jim's pre-owned Cadillacs, it'll work for me. Nina looks at my hands and wrinkles her nose.

"What are you doing? You look like a traffic cop giving directions."

She made me feel stupid. And I *hate* feeling stupid. Why is she doing this to me? I put my hands down. I should practice that before

I try it again. "I wrote him a letter to tell him I knew what he did to you and that he would have to pay or I would turn him in to the cops."

"You told him you'd report him?" Nina drops her grocery bag and the macaroni lands with a clunk on the sidewalk. "He's going to kill you. And then he will kill us."

I hold my hands out again and this time it seems to work. "Whoa, whoa. I didn't sign my own name for frig's sake. I wrote it like it was from someone else, maybe a guy from work. I cut out the words from different magazines so it can never be matched to my handwriting." I didn't tell her that creating an entire blackmail letter with words cut from different magazines was a total pain in the ass. I gave up halfway through and printed the rest of it with Albert's pen. I disguised my writing of course. He'll believe it.

"You cut pictures out of magazines?"

Her face has that look again and I'm tired of her attitude. "Hey, I'm trying to help you out here. Maybe I should go."

"I'm sorry."

I didn't see that coming.

She reaches for my hand. "Don't leave me... um, don't leave."

That's better. I let her look in my *glimmering emerald pools* and she calms. "He'll pay. I promise you. And when he does, you'll have enough money to take your sister and get away."

"What did your note say?"

"Trust me. I know what I'm doing." This is not my first experience with blackmail. My grade six teacher Ms. Barker will never forget the fifty bucks she paid to keep me from telling. Seriously, it was disgusting what she was doing with the principal when I walked into his office that day. She made sure I passed her grade so she would never have to see me again.

"What did it say?" Nina is like a dog with a bone.

"Pretty much what I already told you. I know what you do to your kid. I'm going to turn you in if you ever do it again." I recite like a shopping list. "If you pay me six hundred bucks, I'll keep my mouth shut, blah blah you get the picture." I don't mention the part where I threatened to do to him what I did to his tires.

"Six hundred dollars?"

That's the first number that popped into my head. "Don't be greedy!" Why hadn't I thought of asking for more?

She shrinks back from me. "I need to get home." She grabs the ice from my arms and hurries away.

Well, shit. Be like that. I turn on my heel. I have no idea what the hell is wrong with her. I should keep the blackmail money for myself.

It's time to get paid. I suck in my gut and hide behind the utility shed at the park. Daylight is fading and all the brats went home hours ago. It's deserted. It's not long before a white van pulls in and headlamps round the corner, splashing light where I had just been standing. I tuck my feet sideways so they don't stick out. I am invisible.

When he gets to the trashcan shaped like a rocket ship, he stops and sits in his van with the engine running. I keep still but nothing happens. The minutes pass and my legs shake from the effort to keep my body sucked to the wall. Is that why he's stalling? Is he trying to wait me out?

I'm a panther in stealth mode. My taut muscles uncoil, controlling my slow-motion descent to the ground. Finally, I'm flat on the grass, the earthy smell of the recently mowed lawn in my nostrils. On my belly, I become a soldier wriggling under barbed wire.

I get to the edge of the grass, right behind the van and shimmy sideways until I can see his face in the side-view mirror. At the wheel, his expression is bland, a zombie waiting for the apocalypse. Is he afraid? Planning something? Has he called the cops?

The possibility hits me like the cold water bucket at the splash park, sucking the air from my lungs. Is there a S.W.A.T. team out there right now? I swivel my head slowly, very slowly, and check the shadows. Nothing moves out there. No men surround me. Maybe there is a sniper five hundred yards out, the crosshairs of his scope trained between my eyes, waiting for me to make a move.

I hold my hand out but there is no red dot. I check if there is a telltale laser beam pointed at my body. Nothing. I ease sideways and check again.

I'm clear. You're clear. We're all clear.

No, that's not commando lingo. That's from the hospital show I saw last night. *What the hell?* My mind is playing tricks on me and I'm confused. Am I overexcited? *Dammit!* Why is Nina's dad sitting there?

He's not stupid enough to call the cops. They would find out what he did to Nina, and to his wife. Anger boils in my guts and growls up my throat. I slide my hand into my pocket, fingers searching for my knife. *Get out of the goddamn van and give me my money!*

The thought has scarcely entered my mind when the backup lights blaze into my eyes and he hits the gas. I blend my body with the nearest fence, my head vulnerably exposed. The van careens toward me and the back bumper crashes into the post.

I'm buffeted like the wind shakes a caterpillar on a blade of grass. The shock rattles my bones as if I've been hit by lightning. The treads of a brand new rear tire miss my face by inches before he slams it into drive and pulls forward. The van races to the other end of the parking lot and stops with a squelch of rubber. My brain screams at the red brake lights.

I'm stunned and my limbs won't obey. The view under the streetlight blurs and I can't keep my head up. I rest my cheek flat on the ground and a puddle of drool drips from the corner of my mouth. Is he going to back up and kill me now? Is this how it ends?

Through the blur, I'm aware of his door opening. One foot hits the ground and then the other, like he's testing the water. He's in motion, heading for the trashcan. He drops a plastic bag inside. He doesn't glance right or left, just keeps his head down and hurries. Back in his van, the shifter grinds into gear and his brand new tires squeal when he drives away.

It occurs to me that he didn't see me at all. He panicked and his collision with my fence post was a coincidence. He did it. He delivered my money. I won. A lazy smile creeps to my lips and my returning confidence helps me ignore the saliva drizzling down my face.

I lay there for five minutes, maybe five hours. I can't be sure. I might have slept. It's dark when I open my eyes, and mosquitoes are feeding on my exposed skin. The parking lot is empty.

I roll over and pull myself up using the busted post. My feet swim beneath me and I drop to my knees. *Holy shit.* I have a headache from hell. I pat down my limbs but I'm pretty sure that nothing is broken. I just need a second and I'll be okay.

When my head clears, I step from the shadows and stick my arm into the trashcan. On top of a mound of garbage is the white plastic bag. I grab it in my fist, the square corners of the bills inside reassuring. There is money in it, lots of money. I grab it and run, my steps weaving for the first block. I don't stop to catch my breath until

I reach the street where I parked my car.

I freeze in the middle of the road. I'm sure this is the right street, but where is my blue car? The only one here is a black Mustang, but it's parked in my spot. It's a sweet ride. I peer through the window at the keys dangling from the ignition. I definitely didn't hallucinate the lucky rabbit's foot key chain. This is the same car I stole. How could I have made such a mistake?

Another image seeps into my head. Me, moments after I stole the car. I was adjusting my seat so I could reach the pedals and looked up to see someone jumping out of my way. I give my head a shake because my memory must be jolted, and the memory, or hallucination, or whatever, wavers in my brain.

Damn if it didn't look like that bitch cop from Morley Falls. There she is, not six feet from the hood of my car. Her eyes are wide and her mouth is open as she leaps sideways, dragging a bicycle - a pink girlie bike with a flowered basket mounted on the handlebars. As she turns, I catch a glimpse of an equally startled little dog peeping out of her backpack.

Bizarre. The mixed-up memory prances like a circus elephant and fades. *Gawd, that is enough to give me nightmares.*

With one hand to my throbbing head, I swing the door open and get in. I shake off my dizziness and turn the key. The engine catches right away and transitions to a throaty rumble. Now I remember. This is the right car.

I turn off the interior lights before I open the bag and there it is. My headache evaporates. Six hundred bucks, in twenties. It's a good size stack and looking at it makes my stomach tickle. The tickle ebbs and flows with the pounding in my chest.

In the movies they always smell the money, so I do too. It smells like freedom. I feel good. I feel powerful.

CHAPTER 15

Allie brushed the kitchen curtains aside and peered out at the street. She'd finished her meeting and returned to an empty house. Worry had ratcheted up when her calls had gone directly to voicemail. It would be dark in a few hours. Something had happened.

At the end of the driveway, Erin dragged Ciara's bicycle, its front fork twisted sideways. She breathed in relief. Blood streaked her shin from a skinned knee and her shoulder hadn't fared much better.

She put down her cell phone and threw open the door. "Are you okay? Where have you been? I tried to call you." She must have dialed Erin's number twelve times with no answer. The shiver in her spine told her that something was wrong. If she hadn't been so distracted by her meeting, she would have noticed sooner. She might have been able to warn Erin and keep her safe. Thank God it was nothing worse than scratches and a wrecked bike.

"I'm fine. No big deal. Lily almost ran over me. All I need is a wrench and I can straighten the forks." Erin leaned the bike against the steps and plucked the pup from her backpack. She placed him on the ground and he immediately lifted his hind leg to pee into the air. Then he scurried after her to the garden shed.

"Wait. What?" Allie followed her across the driveway. "You found Lily? How? Where?" She skipped around the dog at their feet. He was like an oversize rat but she didn't want to stomp on him.

"I followed her from the motel." Erin ducked into the shed and returned with a crescent wrench. Pinning the front tire between her knees, she loosened the nut securing the handlebars.

"Why didn't you call me, leave a message, or something?"

Erin regarded her as if surprised. "I didn't want to interrupt your important meeting. Then after all this," she swept a hand in the direction of the crooked tire, "I tried to call, but my phone was out of juice. Were you worried? I thought you would just *know...*"

"I'm not psychic, for Pete's sake," Allie huffed. "There's no crystal ball."

"I'm sorry. I guess I never realized you would worry." Erin looked down.

"I'm sorry too. Maybe I worry too much." Allie laid a hand on her arm. "How did you find Lily?"

"That kid is a real prowler." Erin aligned the forks, tightened the nut and lifted the wheel off the ground. She gave it a spin and the tire wobbled. She set it back down. "I wrecked the rim. I guess I'll be buying Ciara a new wheel. Do you think it comes in pink?"

"Oh fer geez, Erin!" Allie exploded. "Would ya tell me what happened?"

Erin's face broke into a wide grin. "I knew you had it in you." She chucked Allie on the shoulder with a grease-smeared knuckle. "I guess you *can* speak Minnesotan if you try hard enough."

She followed Allie into the kitchen and told her story while Allie cleaned her scrapes.

"I've been trying to locate Lily but I kept missing her at the motel. Turns out that the kid sleeps during the day and prowls the city at night. I wanted to go out and you took my... uh, *our* truck to your meeting, so I had no choice."

"Don't worry, Honey, it's still *your* truck." Was Erin deliberately trying to frustrate her? "So, you were forced to take Ciara's chick-magnet-bicycle on surveillance, with a chihuahua in your backpack. That must have been a sight. I'm truly sorry I missed it." Allie smirked. "What happened when you found Lily?"

"I spotted her leaving the motel and she skulked down the alley like she was up to something. I followed her to the mall. It was almost six o'clock, closing time, and there was a fair amount of activity in the parking lot. She's one sneaky girl. One minute she's ahead of me, and the next she's three rows over. Somehow I lost her."

"I was at the end of the lot when suddenly this car came speeding toward me with no one at the wheel. I jumped out of the way and pulled the bike with me, but I crashed it into the pavement on the way down. Before I hit the ground, I thought I saw Lily's head pop up. God knows she could barely see over the wheel. Her eyes bugged out when I dove for it so I'm sure she recognized me." Erin made a face when Allie cleaned the scrape on her shoulder. "I can't believe she stole that car!"

"I'm so glad you're okay." Allie applied a large bandage.

"I only skinned my knee and the bike will be okay when I get a new wheel. I'm glad Arthur wasn't hurt."

"I imagine you did your famous special agent dive roll." Allie had seen Erin in action.

"I imagine so." Erin chuckled.

"So… Arthur? You named your muskrat?" The chihuahua peered up when she spoke and his tail wagged tentatively. The warm orange glow surrounding him pulled at her like a tiny beacon of light at the end of a dark hallway. She bent to pat him.

A knot of pain seared her belly. Pain like the anguish of losing her loyal canine friend. Deep in her soul, she knew Fiona was at peace. No longer blind, she frolicked in doggy afterlife. Allie snapped upright. This creature that Erin called a dog looked more like a rat.

"I can't decide what to call him." Erin stroked his soft ears. He cuddled into her but kept his adoring gaze on Allie. "I'm going to try a new name each day until one sticks."

"Sounds reasonable." Allie scowled. Not really. She should find his real owners who would already know his name.

"Speaking of names," Erin smoothed the dog's ears back like a rabbit's, "have you ever had a pet named Ciara?" She avoided eye contact.

Allie exhaled through her nose. "Is this your way of asking if Ciara and I were lovers?" She might as well say it out loud. "You crashed into the pavement, dragged a twisted bicycle for miles, and you're still oozing blood on the floor. You pick *now* to be worried about Ciara?" She could see that Erin was serious. The ever-confident Erin Ericsson was jealous. Jealous of what Ciara and Allie might have shared. "Let me assure you that we're only friends."

"Yeah, well, you're just friends *now*, but were you ever *not* just friends?"

Allie, hands on hips, faced her girlfriend. "That's icky. That would be like kissing a relative."

Erin squinted and adjusted the dog's new collar.

Allie frowned. The pup's energy was bright, but Erin's was blurry. A cocoon of warmth usually surrounded Erin. A cocoon that drew Allie in. Not now. It was as if the warmth was sucked into a shell of insecurity and fear. Allie didn't have romantic feelings for Ciara, but how could she explain their past? This void between them made her uncomfortable. She needed to try. "Ciara and I were roommates in university—"

"Yeah, skinny-dipping sexy roommates!"

Allie startled at Ciara's voice. It was rare when anyone got the jump on her. She'd been distracted.

Eyes alight with mischief, Ciara leaned against the door frame. Her old roommate had no boundaries and certainly didn't respect personal space. They were exciting qualities in a party environment, but not so endearing in adulthood. And her timing couldn't have been worse. How much had she overheard?

"Why don't we all get drunk and I'll tell you about our crazy escapades?" Ciara held out a bottle of wine, lips curved into a mischievous grin.

"Ciara!" Allie sputtered. "This is not a good time."

"I've gotta go." Erin stepped between them, pup still in her arms. "I have things to do."

"Honey…" Allie watched the energy between them wane with the increased distance. When Erin shut the door, what remained of her warmth fizzled out.

"Is now a good time?" Ciara waggled the wine bottle in front of her face.

Allie brushed it aside and plopped into a chair. "You know I don't drink any more." The dark energy that had taken over Erin's space in the home brought anger with it. She reached for the cat, who turned instead toward Ciara. Allie furrowed her brows. "And I'm sure you remember why."

"Oh right, that weird headache thing." Ciara slid the bottle back into its brown paper bag. "You still zone out, don't you?" Rachel circled her legs and she picked up the cat.

Allie sank her forehead into her hands. "Your timing always sucked, girl."

"I've got to come home sometime, don't I?" Ciara stroked Rachel's fur and the cat chirped. "Lovers' quarrel?"

"We hadn't even got that far. But we needed to talk about some things."

"Is it about the dog?" Ciara held her hands out and Rachel climbed onto Allie's shoulder.

The cat draped herself behind Allie's neck and tickled her nose with her fluffy tail. Rachel had not forsaken her after all. Allie closed her eyes and breathed. In and out. In and out.

Ciara waited silently until Allie opened them again. "One cat, five minutes, and... you're back." Ciara looked at an imaginary watch on her bare wrist and gave her a tentative smile. "Are you back?"

"Was it really five minutes?" Did Ciara know her that well? Better than Erin did?

"More like a minute and a half, but you know how I like my drama." Ciara retrieved the cat from Allie's shoulder and made kissing noises. Rachel sniffed at the air and Ciara flipped her upside down to rub her belly. The cat flopped bonelessly.

"Well, since you've single-handedly driven off my girlfriend and stolen my cat, you owe me." Allie pulled her by the hand to the back room, piled high with boxes, cables and computer equipment. "The fiber optic connection was installed today. Erin cleared out the storage room so you are the lucky one who gets to help me set up my temporary office."

"Look at me." Ciara gestured with sweeping hands to her hipster attire, her ink-stained fingers. "I'm low-tech. I write. With an actual pen. On paper."

Allie laughed. She didn't intend for Ciara to touch a single piece of technical equipment. "You're going to assemble the desk."

Ciara regarded the large rectangular box leaning against the back wall. "Aw, you bought it from that Swedish place. There are a million parts, and such teeny tiny tools. Look at my big ole fingers!" She held up her hands, each finger festooned with an ornate ring.

"That's why I bought you real tools." Allie handed her a set of T-handled hex keys.

"You've been plotting this." Ciara over-enunciated each word like a Shakespearean actor.

"I'll pay you." She had been hoping to hire her old roomie to assist with the business setup. Part of her contract stipulated that she hire local talent. "Real Canadian cash." Ciara could use the money. A Masters degree was expensive.

"Smashing. Fetch me a wine glass and I'll drink the whole bloody bottle myself while I put it together."

"I can't wait to see how it turns out." Allie ripped open the first box of electronics. "There's my new server." She cradled it in her hands and her mood lifted. The disjointed mental images bombarded her and generated headaches almost every day. Images and thoughts of people she knew were not as distressing as those of the knife, running feet, smoke and fire, all crisscrossed and colliding with each other in her mind. She couldn't make sense of any of it. Her morning walks helped, but it was getting progressively more difficult to stay focused on her work. Her senses had been way off lately and this would be a good distraction.

"Your mother was a hamster and your father smelt of elderberries!" On the floor, Ciara took a sip straight from the bottle and turned a page on the hefty booklet of instructions.

"What?" Had she zoned out? She put down the computer equipment.

"It's a quote from Monty Python. Don't you remember?" Ciara held up the bottle. "I was so obsessed with the Holy Grail when we were at U of T." It was true. She was quite entertaining when she drank.

A slow smile reached Allie's lips before she responded. "I'll tell you what's wrong with you... your head's addled with novels and poems. You come home every evening reeling of Chateau le Tour."

"Atta-girl." Ciara smiled. "I know you preferred the old classic movies but I'm pleased that I influenced you during my Monty Python phase."

"Katharine Hepburn's 1930s movies were way better than Monty Python."

"Bollocks."

"You can't dispute the fact that she was lovely to watch."

"She was exquisite." Ciara expertly twisted a hex key and attached the back of the desk to one side. She was good at deciphering intricate instructions and skilled at manual tasks. They continued their friendly banter while they worked and Ciara had half the desk built before the wine was drunk.

Allie checked that the phone and internet connection were working before she assembled and connected the electronics. This type of work kept her mind occupied, nearly invulnerable to distraction or intrusive thoughts. They might have the office together by the time Erin got back. Then there would be time for a real talk.

CHAPTER 16

Erin pressed her foot on the gas pedal and rolled down her window. She plugged her phone into the charger and the screen instantly glowed. Chris Zimmerman must be working the night shift.

"Z-man. What's up?" Erin put the call on speaker and kept her eyes on the road.

"Hey love bunny! How's the Canadian honeymoon?"

"Don't even start." Her fingers tensed on the steering wheel.

"It's too quiet around here without you and your drama. When are you coming back?"

"I'm working on it. We're here for the summer, at least. Allie's business is doing really well."

"You're not thinking of staying there for good? Is this because you didn't get the promotion to Forensics?"

She clenched her jaw.

"There's a position in Traffic coming up. You love all those intricate formulas and measurements. You'd do great."

The last thing she wanted was a transfer to the traffic section. "Uh, it's all kind of up in the air right now."

"Will you be back by fall?"

"As soon as Allie gets her business stabilized. Another month or two."

"Well, talk to your wife and get back here pronto, girl. I miss my favorite sidekick." A tinny radio played in the background. He was probably sitting in his cruiser.

"You mean talk to *my girlfriend*. I can't picture Allie as anybody's *wife,*" she snapped. Wife. The word conjured a mental image of a round-bodied old fishwife in kerchief and frumpy dress. That was certainly not who Allie was. Why did the marriage issue keep coming up? Had he spoken to Allie about this?

She realized how irritable she sounded. "I'm sorry. It's been a long day." Tailing Lily around town had taken more out of her than she'd realized. Not to mention the bicycle crash.

"Whoa girl. Tell it to the Z-man." Sometimes Zimmerman flamed like a drag queen but he was undoubtably masculine, and one hundred percent heterosexual. If she could talk to anyone, it would be him, but right now she didn't feel like it.

"How's Picasso?" she asked innocently. His beloved lizard collection was a reliable distraction. "Has he escaped into your mother's pantry lately?"

"My chameleon has been a good boy, but I can't say as much for Merlin." He chuckled.

"Is Merlin your Komodo dragon?" It was working.

He sighed at the old joke. "You know Merlin is a spotted gecko. He's harmless, but he's a rascal. He got out of his cage last week and almost gave my mother a coronary."

Erin laughed out loud. She imagined the portly Mrs. Zimmerman standing on a kitchen chair, shrieking at the top of her lungs. The visual image came complete with fuzzy housecoat and slippers.

"Mom phoned police emergency but I was tied up. Dispatch called Gina to rescue her."

"No more secret affair?"

"Nope, mom met Gina and they got along great." He paused. "Last night they stayed up late swapping stories about the old days. Mom heard all about the legendary Gunther Schmidt, whiskey runner, veteran, and trapper extraordinaire. Finally, I just went to bed and left them to it."

"Gunther? How is he?" Erin had seriously misjudged the man and it was clear that Gina adored him as a second grandfather.

"The old crocodile is indestructible. He's getting out of the hospital soon and says he *wants* to go to a senior's residence. No one ever figured he'd sell his place by the river."

"Gunther is selling?" Erin rubbed the corner of a tired eye. *Inconceivable.*

"Gina thinks he likes all the nurse ladies. He's as happy as a newly-hatched chickadee."

Erin remembered how he'd looked in the underground cellar after Lily had poisoned him. It was hard to imagine that he'd survived.

She scratched the dog's ears. "I have to say that I'm pleasantly surprised that your mom is okay with your girlfriend."

"You know how moms are. She's always wanted to be a grandma."

"Gina's pregnant?" Erin pounded the steering wheel and the dog skittered off her lap.

"Five and a half months."

"Five and a half months! How is she already that far along? Why didn't you tell me?"

"We were keeping it under wraps because there were medical concerns. You know…" His voice caught.

"Is the baby okay?" Erin sat upright.

"The baby seems fine *now*. I can't explain all the medical stuff. Babies are an alien species."

"But Gina didn't even look pregnant."

"It wasn't noticeable until recently because she's carrying the baby high. I don't know what that means but that's what my mom says."

"Now that I think about it, she did look unusually *content*."

"Yeah, she's happy. We're happy." He sounded more than happy. He sounded delirious.

"Well, I'm delighted for you, big guy. I just hope the baby takes after Gina. Can you imagine a toddler with your feet?"

"What's wrong with my feet?" As if he didn't know. Size fourteen police boots were special order.

"They're like a pair of canoes." Erin snorted. She could imagine him right now, staring at his oversize feet with his forehead puckered. The police radio squawked with a series of numbers followed by an address.

"Duty calls. Give my best to Allie."

"Sure thing," Erin said automatically, but Zimmerman had already disconnected. The screen glowed for a few seconds before it faded to black. She rubbed her tense jaw.

Icky, Allie had said, yet the two ex-roommates seemed awfully close. Were they really just friends? Ciara's comments had not made it seem that way. Was this jealousy or did Allie's statuesque best friend intimidate her? She opened the window and shivered with the sudden temperature drop.

Beside her, the chihuahua flattened himself to the seat, ears down. She patted his trembling back. "Come on Arthur, it's only the wind." The dog peered up at her with glossy brown eyes and she rolled up the window. "You're the saddest looking little dude I've ever met. Don't you like your new name?"

The dog's tail twitched.

"How about Lucifer? There's a big scary name for you. Maybe you'll grow into it." She scooped the pup into her lap but he continued to shiver. "Shaky Pete? You're right, that's stupid."

He snuggled against her belly.

"Rover?" Erin grinned to herself. "That's a good one. With those huge ears, you could track the Mars Rover. Tonight I'll call you Rover."

Rover calmed as Erin drove. All she knew was that she needed to be near water. She headed onto the northbound highway. A big green sign flashed by. Lockport. There was a river and a dam and there must be fish. She hadn't held a fishing rod in weeks and the unyielding sensation of concrete beneath her feet made her agitated. Lockport sounded good.

Daylight waned by the time she found a parking spot near the river's edge and settled the dog into her backpack. "Ciara keeps reminding me that you have four good legs but it's faster this way." He wiggled his head out the open zipper like an infant in a baby carrier. "Ciara's so great. She's so funny. Blah, blah, Ciara." The dog's ears flattened. "I'm sorry, buddy. I sound like a jealous teenage girl."

"Rover, you and I are going to find us a fishing hole." The dog blinked and his tail thumped inside the pack. She slung it over her shoulders. "We'd better get a move on before it's too dark."

This was a challenge and Erin loved a challenge. She studied the stars popping up along the horizon to calculate her time. Summer days were getting longer but, in fifteen or twenty minutes, what was left of the light would be gone. If she didn't hurry, she would have to rely on the moon to navigate. No big deal. It was only a city path after all, not the Minnesota woods.

She trotted, one step ahead of the hungry cloud of mosquitoes tracking her human scent. Half an hour's brisk walk upstream brought her to the Lockport Dam. Rover perked up at the noise and Erin risked a moment to stand still.

A cascade of water sparkled in the moonlight and she gaped at the sheer force roaring over the massive structure. When the insects homed in on her, she sprinted to evade them. Below the dam, the river was deeper. She could almost see the walleye thrashing at the end of her line. Her mouth watered. She would come back with her rod.

She released Rover from her pack and he shook his tiny body, legs shuddering with the force.

"Are you still sleepy? Well, go do your business before the skeeters eat you alive."

The dog skittered into the brush. Erin smiled. He was hot on the trail of something and she'd better catch up before he disappeared in the dark. She followed him, amused at the seriousness with which he undertook his task. She'd always considered small dogs mostly ornamental, meaning they had no real dog skills. Rover might prove her wrong.

Nose to ground, he scampered through the bushes and across the field. He was quicker than she thought and she jogged to keep up. It wouldn't do to lose this dog after she'd rescued him once. When he reached a fallen log, he nosed it and his ears stiffened like triangular sails. His body stiffened and his raised his hind leg backwards.

"Oh, you think you're a hunting dog, do you?" Erin sank to one knee and patted his head. "But you're pointing backwards. Did you find a mouse?"

A deep-throated chatter emanated from behind the log and Erin leapt to her feet. The pup barked, a gleeful pronouncement of his canine ability. Erin snatched him up and retreated a few steps. Many animals foraged at night. If this is what she thought it was, it would be a very bad idea to confront it.

The dog quieted in her arms and together they waited. Insects attacked her bare skin in droves but curiosity demanded she catch a glimpse. The chattering stopped. She circled the log, making sure she gave it a wide berth.

A growl vibrated in Rover's throat, and she patted his head like a proud parent. "Shhh." He was tenacious, but severely outmatched.

Behind a screen of brush, she squatted and made a low profile. Soon, she was rewarded when a bristly shadow eased away from the protection of the rotted wood. The near-sighted porcupine ambled out to strip berries from a currant bush.

"Seriously?" she whispered to the dog. "You're not that tough." She tucked him under her arm and retreated.

When they arrived at the truck, Erin loaded the dog into the front seat and swatted the majority of mosquitoes out the door before slamming it. She ignored the itch of insect bites across her shins. The walk had cleared her mind. She had been petty and juvenile. There really was no reason for jealousy.

Was it Ciara's overt sexual energy that made her feel ill at ease? It was true that Ciara's approach was unabashedly full-force, no holds barred. In contrast, Erin shared the understated subtlety of her Nordic heritage. Different personality styles, that's all it was. She should call Allie. Erin checked her iPhone, but the dreaded No Service notice was displayed in the top corner of the screen. She should drive home and talk to her in person.

She started the engine and drove out of the parking lot onto the main highway. Streetlights blazed past as she neared the city. Puppy cuddled on her lap, she realized how tired she was when the yellow line down the middle of the road blurred. She jerked upright. Did her head bob? Was she at risk of falling asleep at the wheel?

She tried all her night shift tricks, blinking her eyes hard, stretching her jaw, and tickling the roof of her mouth with her tongue. If she had a package of sunflower seeds, she could stay awake all night but right now she didn't have any. She couldn't shake the fatigue.

A brighter residential area lit up the sky and she turned off the highway. The streetlights might keep her alert. Maybe she could stretch her legs for a minute and get her blood pumping. She parked on the side of the road and rubbed her eyes until they burned.

Now her phone's screen showed full bars and she picked it up. There must be a cellular tower nearby but it was after ten. Should she call Allie? She nearly dropped it when it rang in her hand. Call display read Chris Zimmerman. She exhaled in relief.

"Dude, it's late." She idly scratched a mosquito bite on the back of her neck.

Erin eased open her window and swatted out a squadron of mosquitoes. Not that it would make a difference. She turned on the air conditioning and cranked the fan on high. The wind might keep them down. "Dang skeeters are eating me alive."

"A-hem." Zimmerman cleared his throat like an old man.

"Seriously Z. Twice in one night?"

Erin yelped when a dozen blood-sucking insects simultaneously drilled into her shin. She vaulted out the door, slapping at her legs. The dog stared at her from the seat. Not a single mosquito bothered him. She was the delicacy of the evening.

"I forgot to tell you something earlier." Zimmerman tapped his knuckles, or was it his boot?

Erin stopped scratching and listened. The dog crawled back into her lap and closed his eyes. Why was he not scratching from insect bites?

"You know I always try to help you out, right?"

Erin grimaced. Even the squeaky clean Officer Zimmerman had been tainted by the media frenzy she'd created in Morley Falls. It was a stench that would have to dissipate over time and left other departments reluctant to soil their hands by association.

"Well, I finally managed to contact a friend whose husband is with Winnipeg PD. She says she'll ask him to keep an eye out for Lily. I'll let you know if I hear anything."

"Thanks Z." She was lucky that he was resourceful, and connected. He'd always been on her side and she sure as hell would move heaven and earth to be there for him on his wedding day.

"Hang on! Who's—?" Zimmerman's normally low voice raised a couple of octaves. "Aw, never mind. It's nothing."

"You're edgy tonight. Too much coffee?" She scratched welts on her ankle. Would Ciara have anti-itch ointment at her house? "Now get off the phone and get your paperwork done."

"I'm not doing paperwork." He lowered his voice to a whisper, as if it suddenly mattered. "I'm doing surveillance."

"Let me guess. You're sitting in a marked patrol car, directly underneath a streetlight, across the road from your target."

"Uh, I'm not under a streetlight."

She smiled to herself. He probably was. "Whatcha working on?"

"Trying to catch the suspicious character who's been stalking my mom."

"I told you Allie said not to worry—"

"Shhh!" Zimmerman's hoarse whisper stopped Erin's words. "There the bugger is! He's been circling my mom's block when he thinks I'm at work. Same red sports car, same bald guy hunkered down in his seat. I gotta go!"

The siren blasted, scrambling the phone's sound into alternating static and squeals. Zimmerman must have dropped the phone and forgotten to disconnect their call. Between the garbled sounds and the real life chase happening on the other end, Erin's pulse raced. What if Allie was wrong? Was the mysterious man in the red car dangerous?

Tires squealed and the siren distorted something Zimmerman shouted. Was he calling for help?

"Z-man! Talk to me!" Erin's fingers dug into her steering wheel. She pressed the phone hard to her ear and thumbed up the volume.

The squealing halted. A moment of silence was followed by a terrible thump. A gunshot? The eerie silence was filled by a tinny voice on the AM radio. She held her breath.

"Dang!" Another thump.

"Z-man!" Erin shouted as loud as she could. "Are you okay?"

There were rustling noises and then Zimmerman was back on the line. "Erin? Are you still there?"

"What the heck just happened? Are you okay?"

"The phone rolled under the seat."

That explained the thumps, but what about the siren and the squealing tires?"

"I lost him," he groaned. "Two blocks into it, all I see is dust. That car is fast."

"Oh my God. I thought you were in a shootout or something."

He chuckled hollowly. "I wish I could get that guy in my sights."

Erin shook her head. Her heart rate had settled back to normal but her nerve endings were still firing. "You nearly gave me a heart attack, buddy." There was something strange going on, but she had to trust that Allie was right. "It's probably some poor vacuum cleaner salesman trying to make a living."

"He can explain that to me when we meet face-to-face," he harrumphed. "Sorry, I didn't mean to worry you."

"I'll let you get back to your *surveillance* then." She hung up and leaned her head back. The events of the day hit her squarely between her exhausted shoulder blades. She was reluctant to go home and face Allie after her childish jealousy. Maybe she could stall until Allie was asleep. Tomorrow she needed to apologize. Tonight, she was tired. Maybe she could close her eyes for a moment. Only a moment.

Her lids drooped. Was she reliving Zimmerman's pursuit or did a black car race into an alley just at the edge of her peripheral vision? The hood bounced when it vaulted over asphalt and back onto gravel. Erin's brain processed the information as if she were relaying it over the police radio: newer model Mustang, black in color, driving erratically, southbound. That was the same make of car she saw Lily steal. Her finger twitched to activate the overhead light bar as she fell into the dream.

CHAPTER 17

It takes only a few minutes to drive to Nina's house in my shiny black Mustang. I'm satisfied when the only car in the driveway is her mom's red van. No more dad. Easy as that.

Nina's bedroom light is off, but it comes on in an instant when I toss a pebble at the window. By now she knows the drill and slides it open. She knows I'll keep throwing rocks until she does.

"Pull out the screen," I whisper.

"What happened to your face?"

I put a hand to my cheek and it comes away red. The skin is rough. I never noticed that before now.

"It's a scratch. No big deal."

"You're going to have a nasty scab." She sucks in her bottom lip.

"The screen." I almost got my head run over for her tonight. The least she can do is stay on track.

She pulls the plastic tabs and the screen falls inside. I toss the bag up to her and it takes her about three seconds to count the bills.

"This is only two hundred."

"That's your share." This was my idea and she can't possibly imagine that I would give it *all* to her. I did the work. The other four hundred is tucked into my pocket in a tight roll of twenties. "Don't be greedy."

"I'm sorry."

That's more like it. "Sneak out."

"Right now?" She glances over her shoulder. "It's almost eleven"

Wow, that means I was passed out at the parking lot for hours.

133

Well, I deserve a beer. "Yeah, right now. Just come for a while. I have a car." Nina won't admit it, but she really likes when we drive around. "You can be back before anyone notices."

Fire dances in her eyes and she shoves the screen back into place. She's coming.

I wait in the car, engine running, and she slides in beside me a few minutes later. As usual, she buckles up and then stares at my seatbelt. She never lets me get away with it. I sigh and snap it on. What's the point, really? We're in a stolen car. It's not like a seatbelt violation is the first thing a cop will nail us for.

"Where are we going?" Nina smoothes the wrinkles on her lap and adjusts her shirt collar. The corner of her lips curve up. She's too restrained to allow herself to actually smile but I know she's excited.

I shift into drive and slouch in my seat so I can jam the gas pedal to the floor. The tires squawk and we rock back in our seats. Nina's grin widens. Tonight I'm driving the car I was always meant to drive. The Mustang's black paint gleams like the shiny coat of a panther and Nina has to be impressed. The steering is responsive as I veer down the first alley we come to and the speedometer hits sixty before we reach a crossroad. Sixty kilometers is not as fast as sixty miles, but it sure looks kick-ass when the dial zips past.

There is no limit to the stupidity of car owners. This sucker is worth forty grand easy. Who would leave forty grand cash sitting in a mall parking lot? Leaving the keys in the car is just the same. Stupid people deserve to have their cars stolen, just like my stupid uncle deserves it when I drink his beer.

I park a half block from my motel and tiptoe in. Uncle Albert works nights a lot, sometimes double shifts, and I never know when he's going to be here. His snores shake the bedroom door. I ease open the fridge door and take out the six-pack he bought on his way home. He'll be scratching his head in the morning, wondering if he actually put that beer in there or not. Within a couple of minutes, I'm back in the car and we take off again.

In the next alley, I push it and the car hits eighty before I have to slow for the crossroad. I gulp a mouthful of beer and place one hand in the twelve o'clock position on the steering wheel. I'm slouched so low I have to peek between my knuckles to see over the dash.

Nina is not as cool as me. Like on a midway ride, she curls one hand around the door handle and clenches the front of her seat with the other. Her face is frozen. I can't tell if the half-grin is from excitement or fear. She squeezes the beer I gave her, unopened, between her knees. She's on the best ride of her life.

"Did you seriously blackmail my dad?"

"Damn right." I can't believe she doubted me. "The bastard deserved it."

"He did." Her eyes narrow and she gives a single nod. "He really did."

I suck the last of my first beer and twist open a second. Maybe it's the time I spent conked out in the park, or the thrill of the fat roll of twenties in my pocket, but my head floats. I'm on cloud nine.

Nina fiddles with the buttons and the sunroof slides open, giving us a view of the streetlights flashing past. This night is perfect and nothing can go wrong. By the time I flick the cap from my third beer out the window, the excitement bubbling up from my belly overwhelms me.

Like a wild animal, I whoop to the sky. It feels good to let it out. I do it again. This time, Nina whoops with me, hers a tiny baby noise, but a holler all the same. She turns the radio up and surprises me with her choice of heavy metal. I roar out the sunroof while she accompanies me with drumbeats on her thighs. Her head bobs, whipping her hair back and forth. It looks cool. We look cool. We *are* cool.

When we pass a sign directing traffic to the highway bypass, I instantly make my decision. Tonight we're going to see how fast this car will go. I jerk the wheel to the right, throwing Nina against her seatbelt. With a little luck, and only a few cars around, no one will notice us. I steer the Mustang to the on-ramp and twist the cap off my fourth beer. Nina still holds her unopened bottle between her knees. She would have so much more fun if she drank it.

"Come on, don't be a pussy." I point the neck of my bottle to hers. There is a ninety-nine percent chance she'll do what I want if I call her a pussy.

"I'm not thirsty." She shifts in her seat. "And I don't really like beer."

"Pussy."

"Don't call me that. I'm not a—"

"Pussy. Pussy. *Pussy!*"

"Stop it! You're as mean as my dad!"

I almost pull the car over to the side of the road to slap her mouth. "I'm nothing like that bastard."

"Oh, I didn't mean that." Nina's face blanches, eyes round as marbles. "You're not... I'm so sorry." She twists the cap off her beer and swallows half of it without taking a breath in a show of good faith. One eye squints with the effort. She takes another sip. "I'm sorry, Lily."

"Fuck that!" It's over and I can't stay mad, not on this perfect night. My fourth beer sloshes in my gut, giving me the gift of forgiveness. This must be how the church people do it. Enough of that holy wine and they're so happy they'll forgive anyone. I stomp on the gas pedal and the car zooms onto the highway. I watch the speedometer shoot over a hundred.

Always sticking to side roads, I've never driven at highway speed before. Everything seems so fast. The dotted yellow line morphs solid and road signs flash by, barely giving me time to read them before they're gone. My pulse pounds in my throat and my entire body vibrates. With the sunroof open, the roar inside the car is deafening and the wind twists Nina's hair upright like the Tilt-A-Whirl at the summer carnival.

"You're going too fast!" Nina's face is pink and her knuckles are white against the armrest, but she still has a smile on her lips. Her empty beer bottle rolls across the floor.

Nausea hits me with dizzy force and I slow to a crawl. Cars honk their horns and swerve around us. "I feel sick."

Nina touches my head. "Maybe it's the excitement. Maybe you're hungry. Did you eat today?"

I can't remember what car I'm driving or how I got onto the highway. I can't remember what I did a half hour ago. "I dunno."

"Let's get food." A wrinkle appears in the seamless skin above her eyebrows.

"Okay." The next thing I know I'm sitting in a car that says Ford on the brand new steering wheel. My foot is planted on the brake pedal and I notice that the engine has a nice rumble when it idles.

An orange truck stop light shines down on a couple with a young child. The man is wearing sweat pants, a baggy T-shirt and ball cap. So is the woman. They walk past to the diner. I look back at their beat-up blue truck. The one with the smashed headlight and dented bumper. My stomach rolls and my head throbs.

"Trailer park trash."

"What?" Nina looks out the window.

"That's what my father would call them. Trailer park trash are people who dress like that and take their kids out for dinner when they should be in bed." My dad, my old man, my minion who is in jail because he was stupid.

"Oh." Nina's gaze comes back to me. "Let's get you something to eat." She reaches across, pushes the shifter into park and unclips my seat belt. I lurch onto the pavement and almost puke right there.

I take my knife from my pocket and thumb the blade open in one flick of my wrist. *Practice makes perfect.* As I walk past, I jam it into the side of trailer park trash's front tire. *Pssht!* Ah, that feels better. The sheer sensation of blade piercing rubber gives me an energy boost. The tire is flat before my knife is back in my pocket and I keep walking.

Nina hasn't noticed what I've done. She takes my arm and leads me to the gas bar where rows of junk food greet us. All I see are the colors of the packages. They're so blurry that I can't read a single one.

She picks me out a pizza sandwich and a small carton of chocolate milk. She gets a bottle of coconut water for herself. At the checkout, she takes out the wad of money I gave her and the attendant gets up from his stool behind the counter. Slow as a garden slug, he tallies up her purchase. Before he's finished, I add a bottle of orange soda, three popsicles, and two blue bingo daubers.

Nina looks sideways at me but doesn't say a word. She peels a twenty off her wad. Nina is *very* good at math. She's probably already got everything totaled in her head.

"Nineteen sixty-five." He stares at me as he stuffs the items into a plastic bag. I remember the bloody scrape on my face. *Shit, get over it. It's no big deal.* I rise up on my toes.

Nina hands over the twenty.

"Wait." I try on aviator sunglasses from the counter display and give him my stink eye from behind the mirror lenses. His expression doesn't change. I add two pairs to the pile.

She peels off two more twenties and I grab a lighter and a couple of Mardi Gras bead necklaces at the last second. Nina gawks at me and I shrug. *I want them.*

"A pack of Marlboros too," I demand.

The slug shakes his head. "Don't carry that brand."

"The blue and white pack, then."

"You got ID?"

Fucker. He knows I don't. "Forget it." I toss the lighter on the counter. "I don't need this, then."

The Slug adds the new items to the total. I reach for a roll of duct tape with mustaches printed on it and Nina finally shakes her head. Like a child, I put it back. She pays for it all out of her share of the blackmail money.

"Let's blow this popsicle stand." I snort through my nose. I just got Nina to buy me three popsicles. *I'm not drunk, I swear.*

The cashier glances from my face to the Mustang outside the door. When he looks back, I'm ready. I've practiced for moments like this. I look him straight in the face, squeeze the corner of one eyelid and twitch. Nobody messes with that glare. He looks down and crams the new items into a second plastic bag. I grab it and shove the door open.

"Thank you, come again," he recites in a monotone. He couldn't give a shit if he ever sees us again.

Nina leads me by the hand to the rear of the truck stop. I don't have the energy to protest that she's touching me when she makes me sit at a picnic table. Mosquitoes swarm around the streetlight. I wolf down half the pizza sandwich and push the rest away. It suddenly looks disgusting. I lean my elbows on the table and my head droops on my neck.

Do I hear flies buzzing or is the noise inside my head? It's like that time I had the flu and my grandfather tucked me into bed like a baby. I hated it but I couldn't stop him from swabbing my forehead and spooning chicken soup down my craw.

"Tell me what happened to your face." Nina pours some of her coconut water onto a napkin and swabs my head like my grandpa did. The napkin comes away red.

"Nooo…" My legs don't cooperate and neither does my brain. I lay my head on the picnic table and saliva dribbles from the corner of my mouth. I don't give a crap about the ooze right now.

"Were you in an accident? Do you have a concussion or something?"

"…Consuction?" That didn't come out the way it sounded in my head. "Ungh…"

"Stay here." Nina gallops back to the store and returns with a cup full of ice. She pours it into the plastic bag and presses it to my head.

"Owww." Why am I letting her do this to me? I'm slipping. Losing my way. I'm going to slide right into a black hole under the table. Somehow I crawl on top and flip on my back. Flying bugs whirl around the light above me.

Is the table spinning, or am I?

I'm a shipwrecked sailor clinging to a piece of driftwood. In the middle of the heaving ocean waves I roll over and vomit. Again and again until the pizza sandwich has emptied from my gut.

Out of the corner of my eye Nina's sandals skip away from multicolored splashes on asphalt. I feel hollow. My wet cheek dissolves into the picnic table. The blurry image of a big eighteen-wheeler rolls by, its black exhaust enveloping and cleansing me. My head clears. I twist my body to dangle my legs over the side.

"Do you feel better?" The wrinkle on her forehead wavers and then locks in a straight line. She hands me a napkin.

"That was disgusting." I scrub my mouth, shredding the napkin, and toss it onto the lumpy puddle of vomit.

"You look better." She sits beside me and tries to brush my hair from my face. I push her away.

"I'm fine." There are chunks in my hair but I don't care. I yank it behind my ears and wipe my hands on my thighs. My stomach turns inside out. *Am I sick? Am I hungry after all?*

I unwrap one melting Popsicle, chomp it down and then attack the other. They cool my raw throat. I drop the wrappers onto the puke pile and follow the popsicles with gulps of orange soda. I aim the empty bottle at the pile and it sticks on top to garnish the whole heap. It's a sloppy mess for the lazy gas station man to clean.

"If you say so." Nina's shoulders scrunch to her neck. She's timid like she's been beaten. She cautiously slides beside me on the table and regards the mess. Her nose crinkles.

"Hand me that bingo dauber." My voice is scratchy from barfing.

She flinches and hurries to hand it over. When I drew on her at the water park, she liked it. If I do it again, it'll make everything better.

"Gimme your foot." I strip off the plastic wrap and it makes a satisfying noise, like torn duct tape. There's a flash of memory. One year ago. Me. Taping Gina's mouth shut before I lit her store on fire.

139

My heart thuds with excitement.

Nina removes her sandal, presents her foot like an offering, sole out. On impulse, I doodle on her toes. It looks like shit. A curled shred of plastic on the edge of the dauber catches my eye and I grip it with trembling fingers.

Rip.

The tearing sound makes me wish I had insisted on getting that mustache duct tape at the store. What would it feel like to tear it off Nina's pink mouth? But I don't want to touch her.

She stares at me like one of those white baby seals. Innocent.

Nobody is innocent. I smash the end of the dauber on the picnic table and scribble until her entire foot is blue. "Congratulations, you're a goddamn Smurf!"

She giggles, the sound burbling through her freckled nose. "Um, Smurfs are blue with *white* feet."

"Whatever. Let's go." I hop off the table and head for the car. Stars explode behind my eyeballs and the parking lot tilts sideways. Somehow, I keep my feet under me. *I am fine.*

Nina scoops up her sandals and grabs the shopping bag with my last-minute items.

A cop car exits the highway and circles the lot. It stops directly behind my Mustang. Inside the gas bar, the slug gets his lazy ass up from the stool. His head swivels toward us.

CHAPTER 18

"That shithead ratted us out!" I grab Nina's arm and yank her down behind a minivan. She clutches her plastic bag like a granny with a purse. At the truck stop's gas bar, the slug attendant puffs his chest out when he talks to the cop. The slug gestures in the air and points to the picnic table.

With the police car's steel crash bars not two feet from the Mustang's bumper, that option is gone. I narrow my eyes and commit the attendant's face to memory. When this is all over, I'll be back.

There are always other options. I make a quick check of the other cars in the parking lot. It doesn't look good. On our heels, we shuffle away, closer to the diner. We slip inside the glass door, right beside the restrooms.

Still licking gravy from his lips, a fat loser nudges past us on his way to take a crap. He's perfect and I step right in front of him.

"Excuse me, kind sir." I tilt my eyebrows and make the sad face that works so well on stupid grownups. "I wonder if you might be so kind as to give a pair of lost girls a ride."

He stops dead in his tracks and stares down at me like my face is made of hamburger. *What's the big fucking deal with a scratch? Seriously, get over it.* Maybe it'll help if I tilt my eyebrows some more and stick out my bottom lip. I can't read his expression, but I don't think this is working.

Nina shoots me a strange look and surprises me by taking over. When she steps forward, he turns his eyes on her. His pupils dilate and I know what that means. I deliberately bump into him like I lost my balance. He's an idiot if he thinks she's a ho. She wouldn't get naked with him for a million dollars.

The pink glow is sucked out of Nina's cheeks. She understands what this guy wants. "Wanna party?" I know where she learned that line. It was in the movie we watched last week. Her eyelid twitches.

He licks his lips and looks her up and down. "Do I have to take your friend too?"

As if I ever would. I show my teeth and stare out the window. The cop is gone from the gas bar. Is he looking for us by the picnic table? I stand on tippy-toes but there is a red truck in the way. I nudge Nina. *Hurry up.*

She opens her mouth and a tiny squeak comes out. Her skin looks like death. She swallows and tries again. "Whatever you want."

I tug at her arm. *Get rid of him. We don't need him.*

Nina forces a smile but her face might crack in half. The corner of her mouth twitches and it spreads to her cheek.

"If you give me your keys, I'll wait for you in your truck."

I tug at her arm again, harder this time, but she spreads her feet and stands her ground.

"You think I'll fall for that one?" He runs his tongue over his lips. "If you're still here when I come out, I'll give you the ride of your life."

Nina's shiver travels from her neck to her spine and leaves her trembling. She looks like she will pass out right there. He brushes her aside in pursuit of the toilet. As soon as he's gone, she bends double and gags. Saliva drips from her mouth but she doesn't barf. She's tough.

"Come on!" I grab her sleeve and pull her out the door. "I got his keys."

"How?"

I open my hand to show her the Ford logo. Her eyes widen when it dawns on her. I picked that loser's pocket when I bumped into him. Besides my Mustang, there are only two Fords in the parking lot and my first guess is right. His truck is the jacked up red one with the huge tires. The kind they say men with small dicks like to drive. We both climb up into the passenger side, out of sight of the gas bar, and I jam the key in the ignition. I slink low in my seat and twist my neck in all directions. I still can't see that cop anywhere.

I grit my teeth when I see the shifter. This is a standard transmission. Not my fave. Of course I can drive a standard. It's just that, in a truck this size, it's pretty damn hard to put enough pressure on the clutch and still see over the steering wheel. Especially when you're less than six feet tall. I reach for the lever and inch the seat forward as far as it will go.

Nina is already buckled up and I dutifully pull out my safety belt. Safety first when you're jacking cars. Will she never let up? When she hears the click, she nods. The stick is in first gear and I stomp the clutch to the floor before I turn the key. The radio blasts country music. As soon as the engine rumbles, I ease my foot off and we roll forward.

There is no sign of the cop and excitement rises in my chest. The fat loser in the bathroom looked like he would be there a while. He should have brought a Playboy magazine because he's not getting any real girls tonight.

"Ha ha! See ya later suckers!" I check the rear-view mirror. No one can stop us now.

Nina sits stiffly in her seat, her face turned to the window. I wrench the wheel sideways when I see what she's looking at.

The cop is running beside us. He's lost his hat and his mouth is open. I can't hear a damn thing he's yelling over the wailing radio. He can't keep up when I grind the shifter into second gear and we pick up speed. Directly ahead is the Mustang, and the cop car.

"Lily, no!" Nina yells.

Sometimes she knows me better than I know myself. I laugh and swerve to the right. The truck's front bumper smashes through the back of the police car like it's made of aluminum foil. The metal folds sideways into the back tire. Nina's head snaps forward with the impact but I don't feel a thing.

"Fuck you!" I yell at the top of my lungs. The engine sputters and I stomp my foot on the clutch but it's too late. *Shit, I've stalled it.*

Nina curls into a ball on her seat. She holds her plastic bag in a death grip. In the side mirror, I see the cop catching up. *Objects in mirror are closer than they appear.* That is definitely true.

I restart the engine and slam the truck into gear. We jerk forward.

Face red as a tomato, the cop jumps onto Nina's door, arms wide. His hands slide across the glass and onto the frame. He must be hanging by his fingertips. "Pull over!" Steam from his breath fogs

Nina's window. She's terrified.

The cop grabs at the handle and wrenches open the door. He hangs on when it swings out on its hinges and returns. He comes back boots first and manages to get one foot inside. "Pull over *now!*" He grabs Nina's arm like a big gorilla.

Nina screams. "Lily! Please stop." Her voice is as high as a little kid's.

The cop hauls her toward the open door. I swerve to throw him off and he loses his grip. He's going to fall.

"Push him out!" I yell at Nina.

She looks back at me. Tears run down her cheeks. I swerve harder and she lurches face-first toward the cop. I swerve again and he grabs at her, fingers searching for anything to hang on to. Nina jerks her head back and there's a trickle of blood on her cheek. The cop's watch dangles from his wrist. The only thing keeping her inside is her seat belt.

"Kick him!" If I was over there, I'd kick him right between his eyes.

She shakes her head. I'm disappointed.

"Stop!" The cop retreats to the door and struggles to hang on.

There is no way he can run this fast. He must look like a trout on a stringer. I push the truck faster before we hit the highway ramp and finally the cop loses his grip. In the rear-view mirror, I watch him tumble onto the shoulder, his shirt torn open and legs tangled. He disappears into the weeds.

That was funny. I laugh like a maniac inside my head.

The open door howls and Nina pulls it shut. Chest heaving, she twists to look behind us. She wipes her eyes with the back of her hand. There are no red and blue lights. No one is going to catch us.

Slouching in my seat to put all my weight on the gas pedal, I push the speedometer until it reads triple digits. At least five minutes pass before I say anything. "That was close." I show my teeth when I smile. It's a real smile if you show your teeth. I punch her shoulder.

Nina jumps and puts a hand to her cheek. It comes away with a red smear. The cop's watch scratched her. Now I'm not the only one with a messed up face.

"Hand me the bag." I don't want her getting all depressed about this. It's over. We won.

Stunned, she looks at her hands and seems surprised to find that she's still holding the bag. Her fingers tremble when she puts it on the seat between us.

I take out a pair of sunglasses, slide them on and check myself in the mirror. They are too big, but the effect is good. "I'm a secret agent."

Her mouth twitches. Did she try to smile? I hand her the other pair.

She gives her head a shake and turns away. "I don't feel like it."

"Pussy." It worked before. It will work again.

"Stop calling me that. I don't like it." She leans forward to check the side mirror.

"Fine, then don't *be* one." I wait for it. Finally the silence gets to her.

She jams the glasses on and turns her face to me. "Happy?"

I reach over and help her adjust them. "You look exactly like Lara Croft from Tomb Raider."

"Yeah, right. A red-haired, freckle-faced ugly Lara Croft." She rips the glasses off.

I push them back on. "You're *not* ugly." That part is true. Every guy she passes turns to stare at her. She just doesn't notice. I poke her cheek and she blushes. She'd do anything I asked her. I turn off the highway and drive her home. The truck is loud so I switch off the engine. I don't want to wake her parents.

"Did you have fun?" She always ends the night by telling me she had fun. Not tonight.

"My arm hurts." One shirtsleeve is stretched past her hand. She pushes it back and rubs her shoulder.

"Your face is scratched," I add. As if she didn't know. "Blame it on your dad if you really want to get rid of him."

Nina tilts her head and the oversize sunglasses fall to the end of her nose. She doesn't really look like Lara Croft but she liked that I said so. I can tell.

"Blame your dad. It's a good idea." Sometimes fate hands you gifts and you have to know how to cash them in.

"I'm not sure."

"Whatever." I shrug. "Come here."

She catches her breath. "Why?"

"Trust me. Come here."

She leans toward me, eyes closed, lips tense.

I dump the Mardi Gras necklaces out of the bag and startle her when I drape one around her neck. She pulls back and fingers the shiny plastic beads.

I put on the second necklace. "In New Orleans, girls have to flash their titties to get one of these."

"That's not true."

"Uh huh." Of course it is.

Her nostrils flare. "I'm not going to…"

"Fuck, no. That's not what I meant. I was just saying." I give her a shove, a hint to get out. I've got shit to do.

I'm going to find Barb. I'll finish what I started.

CHAPTER 19

Allie woke with a start. After hours of office setup and reminiscing, she'd fallen asleep in her chair, cheek plastered to the newly assembled desktop. Her nerve endings still sizzled with the sensory overload, images as vivid as an IMAX screen with the speakers blasting. She remembered her dreams. She didn't always understand them, but she remembered.

She'd dozed off to the rumbling of the cat's purr in her ear and the tickle of whiskers on her cheek. Rachel must have kept her company for a while but at some point, the cat had gotten up and abandoned her.

She saw an image of Erin and the puppy hiking down a trail in the moonlight. The dog was bright, excited. Erin's conflicted energy pulsed. Had she already come home? Had she gone to bed without waking Allie?

Other images filed past. Diving into cold, murky water. Surfacing with a small boy strapped in his car seat. She held him close and he morphed into an infant. The tiny baby's lips were blue, lungs unable to breathe. His stillness pierced her heart. She searched for Erin but another woman, face darkened by grief, stepped forward. Allie shook her head.

The image faded and was replaced by a green-eyed panther. Lily prowled tonight. Allie shivered at the dark predator in her dream, its black coat gleaming with intensity. Right now, Lily was persistent, disoriented and dangerous. She manipulated someone. A young female, naive, and compliant.

Oily smoke constricted Allie's chest. She held her breath when powerful claws closed around the girl's throat. Was this girl a willing partner, or the next victim?

She jumped to her feet, sweat beading the back of her neck. The office was empty. Ciara was gone to bed, probably hours ago. She'd last been aware of her crazy friend curled up on the carpet, singing a silly song from the Rocky Horror Picture Show. How she'd hated that movie. The crowd was too frenetic and it hurt her head. Ciara must have done the Time Warp for the last time and gone to bed.

Allie rubbed her cheekbone where it had pressed on the hard desk. Hands trembling, she fought for control of her thoughts. There was too much information coming at her. It was too fast. Everything was scrambled.

Relax. Meditate.

She took in a deep breath and stretched her spine. Her eyes focused on a patch of morning light peeping through the blinds and she let all else slide. She had not done this as often as she should. Busy was not an excuse when it made her suffer so. Her talent, if this was the proper name for her burden, needed regular maintenance and she had been neglecting it.

She breathed again and the whims of her dreams fled as her strength returned. Gradually, the kaleidoscope of color splashing through her mind dulled to its customary monochromatic blur. She rolled her shoulders and her muscles loosened. That was better. She needed coffee. And she needed Erin.

Allie found Erin asleep on the couch, her neck crooked at an uncomfortable angle. Cuddled to her belly, the chihuahua perked its ears at her arrival. A twinge of guilt pinched the skin at the corners of her eyes. When had their relationship been reduced to sleeping apart? She held out her hand and then pulled it back. Erin had come in late. She probably needed sleep more than she needed to be woken.

Allie backed away and went to the kitchen. The puppy hopped off the end of the couch and waddled directly on her heels. He stood at the door and pressed his nose to it, as if there was an exit button. She grinned. He looked ridiculous.

"What do you want, Gizmo?" With those ears, he resembled a gremlin. Should that be his name? No, he was Erin's dog. Erin's responsibility. She opened the back door and let him into the yard.

Her head was clearer than when she'd first woken but a dull buzz still vibrated at the base of her skull. Menacing images writhed and spit venom, pushed to be released. Lily's laugh. A low growl. The two blended into one.

Allie filled her lungs, imagined the air became pure light. It trickled through her body, banishing the darkness. The awful images retreated. Exercise would help too. She hoped there was an early morning Tai Chi class at the park.

Ciara's cheap coffee maker stared at her from the kitchen counter and she regarded it with trepidation. This was her next challenge. Why had she shamed Erin into leaving her fancy cappuccino machine behind in Morley Falls?

She flipped open the top of the coffee maker and grimaced. Just as she'd feared. This plastic contraption had not been cleaned since it was last used. With her fingertips, she pinched the edges of the crusty filter and folded them over its heap of grounds. The whole mess went into the trash. She could just imagine Erin's face if she had been the one to find it.

Wait, Erin had probably already seen this. That was why she insisted on driving out to buy coffee. This was the first morning Allie had not awoken to a hand-delivered steaming café latte.

Allie looked at the kitty footprints on the counter. She really needed a hug but both Erin and the cat were unavailable. She opened the blinds and set to work scrubbing out the inside of the coffee maker.

In the driveway, a pair of crows pried at a trashcan. A third joined and they took turns, swooping and snatching at the lid. If more birds arrived, it might be like the old Hitchcock movie. She avoided horror films but that one about the crows was a classic, and totally worth it.

The squawking became ominous.

She opened the door to the broom closet. Where was Rachel? She never missed morning cuddles on the kitchen counter. A ripple of apprehension traveled across the back of her neck. The squawks and caws of the birds increased in volume and she glanced out the window. They had abandoned the garbage and were onto other pursuits. The neighbor's trash must be more tantalizing.

After a thorough wipe-down, she deemed the coffee maker usable and opened cupboards one by one until she located a grocery store brand tin of medium roast. It wasn't premium java but the aroma should rouse Erin. She dumped a scoop into a fresh filter and thumbed the power button. Nothing happened.

After a moment's investigation she discovered the disconnected electrical cord. She shoved the plug into the closest outlet and jumped when a spark arced between the two. The machine sputtered to life. That's why it was unplugged. The power button was jammed in the on position.

Was Ciara so financially distressed that she couldn't afford to replace her bargain brand coffee maker? She made a mental note to gift her a new one before they left. Coffee dribbled through the filter, missed the pot and splashed a puddle on the counter. Maybe she'd do it today.

The shape of the puddle grew. It mimicked the dark shadows that crept from the corners of her mind. It spread into wings, talons forward, yellow eyes intense with pursuit. Nausea clutched at her gut.

She tore her eyes away and focused on the coffee maker. In her peripheral vision, the puddle spread to the edge of the counter. Something was wrong. She gritted her teeth and her head throbbed. Worry gnawed at her nerve endings. She sensed fear.

The majority of coffee made it into the pot but the puddle threatened to breach the counter's edge. Allie created a makeshift dam with the dishcloth and pushed it against the vile spill. She forced herself to breathe normally. She needed to work today. How could she, if she couldn't even concentrate enough to make coffee? She clutched the back of the chair until her knuckles blanched.

Erin could ground her. She peeked into the living room but her girlfriend still slept, although she had roused enough to turn over and relieve her neck's awkward angle. The coffee maker steamed and bubbled, aroma filling the air. If that didn't wake Erin, she didn't know what would. And where was her darned cat?

"Rachel?" she crooned. "Kitty kitty."

There was an answering meow from the window overlooking the yard.

Allie brushed aside the curtain. "Why are you hiding?"

The cat's bottlebrush tail stood straight, her posture tense.

"Are you excited about the birds?" Allie smoothed the cat's fur but the hairs sprang back to attention. She followed Rachel's gaze and her heart twisted. "Omigod! The puppy!"

She grabbed the broom, flung open the door and raced across the gravel in her socked feet. Rachel barreled out the door and headed for the shed, her missing foreleg not the slightest encumbrance. Allie arrived moments after the cat.

Wedged between the spokes of Ciara's front bike tire and the side of the shed, the puppy hunkered, ears back, lip curled from bared teeth. Trembling, he projected all the ferocity of a field mouse. The birds swooped, touched down and snapped sharp beaks through the spokes. He yipped and snapped back.

"Shoo! Go on!" Allie swiped at the air. The crows scattered. They circled above and one by one hurtled past, wings slicing air with razor-sharp precision. The last broke formation and the momentary lapse allowed Rachel an opportunity to snatch a tail feather. The bird screeched at the indignity and the cat launched herself onto the fence in pursuit. She hissed at the departing marauders and arched her back, excessively pleased with herself.

"Are you okay, little guy?" Allie fell to her knees and reached behind the bicycle where the dog still cowered. "I'm sorry. Come here." She softened her voice and edged forward until she could hook two fingers through his collar.

In her arms, his entire body shook. His heart hammered and she clutched him to her chest. His shaking ceased and an intense surge coursed through her, rattling her vertebrae. Colors saturated and sounds amplified until they were agonizingly acute. It was as if she peered through a magnifying glass, one that clarified and honed her senses. Stunned, she held him away from her skin.

He perked his oversize ears and winked a shiny brown eye. She shook her head. He packed too much energy in that tiny bundle. It was like touching a live wire and she wasn't ready. She placed the dog on his feet and he followed her into the house. His tail whipped back and forth as he dashed to his food dish. The winged menace retreated from her thoughts, but the troubling dark shadows still skulked at the corners.

Lily was out there.

The coffee puddle had long since breached her dishcloth barricade and she shifted her bare feet around the spill. She dropped a wad of paper towels onto the floor and stepped on it. Her right eye throbbed and she rubbed her temple. She poured herself a cup of coffee, added milk and sugar, and took a sip. It tasted awful, but it *smelled* like coffee. With the mug between her palms, she inhaled the steam. It was nearly nine o'clock. She should wake Erin.

Beside her, the pup had arranged mouthfuls of kibble on the tile and was busy sorting the four different shapes into separate piles. Rachel watched the process with interest and then leapt forward to scatter the piles with one swipe. She swatted a couple of round kibbles, chased them across the floor. The pup stared after her and methodically set to work separating the piles again.

Allie stifled a giggle. What a quirky fellow. He reminded her of Erin's six-year-old nephew Jimmy. If Jimmy was a dog.

"Ow! Hey!" Erin's grumpy outburst signaled that the cat had woken her first. Moments later she appeared in the kitchen doorway, one hand rubbing her neck. She lifted her foot to dislodge something from between her toes. "Damn cat tried to kill me again."

"I guess you got in late." Allie decided not to comment on the marks left on Erin's face by pillow seams.

"I feel like I stepped on a Lego." Erin rubbed the bottom of her foot.

That's where the stolen kibble ended up.

"You made coffee?" Rumpled clothing, puffy eyes, hair twisted into uneven tufts, Erin looked as if she'd slept in the alley. She raised her eyebrows at the mess leaking onto the floor. "Sort of."

"Some might call it coffee." Allie poured the contents of her mug down the drain. "*You* would not."

"I'm sorry." Erin teased fingers through her matted hair. "I don't know what was wrong with me last night. I'm just frustrated. I don't have my badge. I don't have my gun. I feel like I'm outside the circle trying to prove something to everyone. Lily is stealing cars. So what? It doesn't mean she's plotting murder. What am I even doing here?"

"You know she won't stop. I feel it too. You aren't on your own." Allie held out her arms and Erin sank into them, the warmth between them a protective shield. Allie's fiery nerve endings cooled. Weight lifted from her bones. They were fine. Everything would be okay.

Beside them, the dog crunched down the kibble in the first pile and attacked the second. Erin tilted her head. "My nephew does that. He can't allow different foods to touch." She leaned over to pat the dog. "He's sure hungry."

"He's had a tough morning." A prickle of guilt made her squint. The pup was so young and vulnerable. She should have kept a better eye on him. She changed the subject before Erin could inquire. "Does he have a name yet?"

"Um, I tried Rover last night when I took him with me to find a fishing spot."

Allie had sensed that Erin was hiking. She should also have guessed that Erin would go straight to the river. "Lockport Dam!" she blurted without thinking.

Erin nodded. She didn't look surprised that Allie had guessed. "I'm going to give it a try tomorrow morning. I'll catch us a trout for supper."

"Trout. That sounds nice."

The dog spat out a square kibble that had mistakenly made it into his triangular pile. "Somehow Rover doesn't suit him today," Erin said. "You should have seen him track down a porcupine. He's a tenacious little dude."

"That he is." He'd just fended off a murder of crows. Allie dumped the coffee maker into the waste bin and wiped down the counter. Things felt normal. Her head was clear, her mind her own. "Let me tell you about the skinny-dipping incident."

"You don't need to…"

Allie shrugged. "We did a lot of crazy things in University. After a concert one night, a group of us climbed the fence at the YMCA and went skinny-dipping in their pool. We were stupid. The security guard caught us. He wouldn't give us our clothes back until he finished his big lecture. Ciara was having none of it and walked all the way home stark naked."

"In the middle of Toronto?"

"She said people honked their horns but no one bothered her."

"That's it?"

"Yes. Ciara has a flair for the dramatic. I'm sure she would have told you a much more entertaining version." Allie slipped her feet into shoes. "I have a meeting in a few hours and I admit you've spoiled me for coffee. Can we go out for a latte?"

"I'll get my keys." Erin frowned at the table, and then checked the floor. "I swear I left them here." She patted the pocket of her jeans and then slowly swiveled her head to the living room. "Rachel!"

"I know her latest hiding spot." On hands and knees, Allie slid her arm under the sofa, pulled it out and jangled the set of stolen keys in her hand. "Coffee," she announced.

Erin picked up the pup and dangled his legs over her arm. "I can't leave you alone with that pesky cat." She padded out to the truck in her bare feet.

Allie drove. "When are Chris and Gina getting married? A fall wedding would be nice, don't you think?"

Erin gaped at her. "How did you know? I just found out last night."

"They're perfect together. It's logical, isn't it?"

"Maybe for you." Erin directed Allie to the coffee shop and they pulled up beside the folding chalkboard sign.

Erin's cell phone bleated a series of piercing tones and she wiggled it out of her pocket. "Hello?" She made a face as she listened to the voice. "I don't think that's—" She plucked at the corner of her lip. "It might be a good idea to—" She sighed and rolled her eyes. "Perhaps you should—" She winced and pulled the phone away from her ear as a woman's voice rose in pitch. She turned to Allie and mouthed the word *paranoid*.

Allie caught the gist of the conversation. Barb Schmidt, who had narrowly escaped being burned to death, was freaking out. She thought Lily was stalking her. She was convinced that the girl was plotting to kill her.

"Have you reported this to the police?" Finally, Erin had the opportunity to speak a full sentence. "I see." She paused and listened. "Maybe a counselor is not such a bad idea. After all, you've been through a great deal." The dog prodded her arm with his nose and she stroked his ears. "Of course. I promise. I *will* stop her." Erin disconnected the call, the tension in her jaw muscles visible.

Allie reached over and squeezed her hand. "You have no shoes. I'll get the coffee."

"I guess we're not in Morley Falls any more." Erin addressed the pup. "No dogs allowed. No bare feet allowed." She held up his tiny paws in surrender. "You'll love it there. I'll teach you to swim." She lowered her voice to a stage whisper. "I'll let you chase the cat all you want."

Allie swatted her shoulder before she exited.

Ciara's bicycle was gone by the time they returned with two extra large coffees and a brand new coffee maker. This machine was many steps up from the one Allie had thrown out. Easy to clean, it had no tedious filters to dispose of. It wouldn't electrocute anyone or drip half its contents on the counter. Ciara should be pleased.

Erin sent the dog to explore the yard and went to shower.

Allie kept a strict eye on him out the window. He circled the yard and sniffed at the spot where he'd hidden behind the bicycle. Then he lifted his hind leg and marked it. A smile spread across her lips and she let him in. He looked up at her, wagged his tail expectantly. She didn't dare touch him again but the little guy was growing on her. He was not bad for a chihuahua. He wagged his tail once more and headed off in search of the cat. She had to admire his resilience. And he was entertaining.

"Have you seen the critters?" Dripping water, Erin shook her head until it stood up in uniform spikes. "Come see."

Allie followed her to the living room where the cat was asleep on the largest sofa cushion. Snuggled into her fluffy underbelly, the pup rested his head on her single front paw. She curled her tail around him. Allie's eyes widened. "Rachel has a maternal side?" Not once had the cat deigned to cuddle with her golden retriever.

Erin laid a hand on her arm. "He's part of the family now."

Allie opened her mouth but her voice stuck in her throat. She turned away. Once vivid, her image of Fiona was fading. She was not ready to replace her.

"I know, Baby. You need time."

Allie gulped back a tear.

Erin stroked her shoulder. "I need to get out of your hair today. I'll see if I can figure out what Lily's up to. You'll have the whole afternoon to yourself."

Allie remembered the dream she'd had about Erin walking the river trail at night with the dog peeping from her backpack. "Did you really stuff the dog in your bag last night?"

Erin's blue eyes twinkled. "Yeah, that's me, a spoiled rich girl with a chihuahua in my purse. I'd never stoop to that, would I?" She raised an eyebrow, tempting Allie to taunt her.

Allie smiled. She didn't need to shatter Erin's tough facade. She was strong, and she was adorable.

"Oh yeah, I fixed the darn back door so it locks now. You just got your office set up and we can't have someone walking off with all those tantalizing electronics."

Allie's eyebrows shot up. Last night she'd struggled to get the door to close but this morning she'd been so wrapped up in herself that she hadn't noticed how smoothly it opened and closed - until now. Erin must have worked on it after she'd come home late. That was the beginning of her apology.

Erin gave her a wink and Allie's chest warmed.

CHAPTER 20

After I drop off Nina, I sleep on the bench in the park until it's time. With one last glance down the road, I stretch my legs and walk to the truck. No one has paid it any attention since I parked it there. It's invisible, like me.

I hop in and turn the key. I know exactly where I'm going and what time to be there because it pays to listen in on other people's conversations. Other people like Albert, on the phone with Barb. You never know when the stuff you hear might come in handy. Like now.

In fifteen minutes, Barb will be finished her burn treatment at the university hospital. She will drive straight to her secret home and I'll be right behind her. How could she think she'd be able to hide from me?

Yup, there's her car. *I'm a genius.*

I park and wait, engine running. There is a dirty blue and gold ball cap with a big W on it wedged in the seat. I put it on. It's friggin' huge. There isn't an adjustment small enough but I do my best to stop it from sliding over my eyes. That loser at the truck stop sure had a big noggin.

I hunch behind the wheel and a few minutes later I'm rewarded. A lady with a scarf scurries out the main door and heads straight for Barb's green car. It's her. She gets in and drives like an old grandma, honking her horn before backing out of her parking spot. It's not hard to follow her but I keep a car between us so she doesn't recognize me.

In front of a two-story house, she parks and gets out. I'm smart enough to stay back and she doesn't even know I'm here. When she's inside, I drive by slow so I can remember this place. I reach the end of the block and hit the gas.

It's only a few minutes to Nina's. She promised to come to the movie marathon at the Cineplex. We're gonna movie hop all day.

My head pounds and my back is stiff. Nina and I watched five hours of monster movies today. I'm sure she hated every single one but she didn't dare complain. Not when I got her in for free. I even smuggled in the snacks and hid a dozen beers in the washroom. Nina ate so many Twizzlers that I thought she was gonna puke, but she still had room for Milk Duds. She went back and forth to the washroom to sneak the beers in and even drank two herself. She did me proud.

Nina's mom was busy making up with her stupid dad so nobody noticed when she went out with me. As long as she was home by nine to babysit. I left her brat sister a bag of candy and Nina gave her strict instructions to hide if daddy came looking for her.

I manage to drop Nina off at home afterward without her getting weird on me. She's good at following instructions but I can't really trust her with the important stuff. Not yet. She's too straight arrow and she's not ready. She'd spoil the whole damn thing.

I watch movies and drink Albert's beer at the motel until I'm ready. It's the perfect time. Everyone's tucked in their beds and it's still too early for the working people to be awake. I feel good and I've got a buzz on from the Coors. First things first. I need to find something to start a fire. A nice can of gas, or a box of dynamite. Yeah, dynamite would be perfect. I've never tried that. Someday I hope I will.

I stash the noisy red truck on a side street and sneak through the neighborhood on foot, trying each place as I go. Something's off. Maybe between the movies and the motel, I drank too much. Maybe it's the excitement. My hands are shaking. I can usually jimmy the latch with my knife but right now I just can't get my shit together. I boot the second door in and my foot hurts like a son of a bitch. It's not as easy in real life as in the movies.

Finally, in an unlocked garden shed, there's a red jerry can and a quart of oil beside a lawnmower. I was starting to think my plan would fail but now I'm back on track. Between these two, I can destroy anything.

Oh, look. There's a bonus. A half bottle of whiskey winks at me from the top shelf. I twist off the cap and park my butt on the engine of the lawnmower. Rest is all I need. The whiskey goes down easy and a few swallows calm my trembling fingers. My foot feels better. My headache eases. I lean back with the whiskey bottle. There's no hurry. I can savor this moment. The moment before the kill.

My lips feel numb and my vision blurs. The bottle is empty. When did that happen? I don't remember drinking it all. I drop it to the ground and look at the plastic container in my other hand. One litre of oil. The letters swim in front of me. It says litre instead of quart. Why the hell can't Canadians just *say* quart when they *mean* quart? I grab the jerry can and stumble out of the shed. There's a light glow on the horizon. It's almost dawn! Did I park this way, or that?

Finally, I find the truck and toss the containers in the back. I'm still pissy about the way this country makes math so hard. Don't even get me started on why only half the signs around here are in American. The rest are in a friggin' foreign language.

I jump into the driver's seat and start the truck. The streets are still empty and it doesn't take long to get to the two-story house by the Esplanade Bridge. Barb's stupid green car is parked right out front like a sign. She deserves what she gets.

I park across the street after I circle the block three times. The house is dark and all the blinds are closed. Barb is sleeping like a baby. She doesn't know I'm coming. I turn the headlights off but keep the engine running. With the gas can in one hand and the friggin' *quart* of oil in the other, I sneak into the back yard. There are no dog toys or water dishes. That's a good sign.

I try the doorknob. It's locked so I force the tip of my knife between the door and jam. With pressure in the right direction, I ease the latch until it pops open. I'm that good.

The house smells weird. With my feet on the entry mat, I try to figure out what that stink is. Boiled cabbage. Barb must have cooked dinner last night. I always hated when she cooked that. She is definitely in here. My heart speeds up and there's a growl in my throat that I'm not sure I'm making on purpose. It sounds like a panther. If I was crazy, I might think I really *was* a panther. But I'm not crazy.

I drop the gas can on the carpet and twist the cap off the oil. Then it hits me. I didn't get the lighter. I check my pockets to make sure. How could I have forgotten something so goddamn essential? I want to kick the can clear across the room but that might wake her. My fingernails dig into my palms. There has got to be a box of matches in the kitchen.

I try not to sound like a raccoon on steroids when I root through the drawers. Nothing. I check by the fireplace. It's one of those new gas ones you flick on with a switch.

Fuck. What am I gonna do?

I'm frozen. Like a pussy.

Make a decision. Don't be a pussy.

I leave the gas right where I dropped it and sprint out the door. I'll be back in two minutes.

At the truck, I fumble with the door handle. My hands slip and I try again, yanking it open wide. I jump in and almost pull my seatbelt across. Damn Nina and her bad habits. I let it snick back into its sheath and slam my foot down on the gas pedal. There was a store nearby.

Anger burns my throat like battery acid. My hands shake like Doctor Jekyll's. I wish I could put them around Barb's throat and squeeze until I feel better. I think about my skin touching her skin and the battery acid turns to molten lava. My head swims. I need to kill her with fire. Fire is my friend.

I don't bother to hide the truck this time. I skid to a stop in front of the store and leave the door wide open when I run inside. I grab the closest lighter from a counter display and bail out.

"Hey!" is all the night cashier has time to say before I'm out the door and back in the truck. I jam it into reverse.

For the six blocks return trip, I push the truck as fast as I can. One hand in my pocket, I trace the shape of my knife. This time, I'll make sure. Barb's gonna die.

CHAPTER 21

Allie drained the rest of the latte in her coffee mug. Erin had been sweet enough to make it for her this morning before she went fishing. She'd been determined to arrive at the Lockport Dam before the first hint of dawn and had taken the excited dog with her. He probably spent more time in Erin's backpack than on his own two feet, but he loved the adventure.

It wasn't yet five in the morning, and still dark, when she'd waved goodbye and headed for her office. Nightmares had plagued her all night and she couldn't sleep anyway. If she was up early, she might as well make good use of her time. Mornings were her favorite. There was a period of stillness between the time the late people went to bed and the morning people arose. Less energy circulated in the atmosphere or something. Her mind was calm and she could focus without interruption.

This morning was unusual. Instead of the calm, she was agitated. The pain in her head spiked when Erin's phone rang for the third time in a row. She must have forgotten it. With her foot, Allie pushed the office door shut but the shrill tones pierced the wall. It irritated Allie like nails on a chalkboard. At the edge of the desk, even the cat grumbled and swished her tail.

Some night owl, like Erin's buddy Chris Zimmerman, was persistent. Sure, he was excited about getting married, but really, he should wait until it was a decent hour. Not everyone worked night shift.

Each time the phone rang, her headache ratcheted up a notch. She couldn't concentrate. This was useless. She pushed the keyboard away. She would have to find that darn phone and shut off the ringer. Her bare feet thumped on the floor as she stalked down the hall. Where in the world was it?

It rang again and she stared at the sofa. Rachel. How had the cat carried the cell phone? That cat was turning into a real kleptomaniac with Erin as her primary target. If Allie's head didn't hurt so much, this might be funny. She slid her arm underneath and located the phone, along with Erin's missing sock, in the back corner.

Caller ID displayed a blocked number and she tapped the icon on the screen. "Chris, really—"

"Officer Ericsson! Help me! She's found me!"

Not Chris.

Breathless, the woman's voice bordered on hysteria.

Allie sat and pressed the phone to her ear. Black clouds rolled from the back of her brain and thundered behind her eyes. She tasted gasoline. Smoke gagged her throat. She squeezed her eyes shut. "Is this Mrs. Schmidt?"

"I called 9-1-1 but they won't listen. Lily's outside in a red truck. As soon as I told them my name, they gave me the number for the mental health department. They told me to call them first thing in the morning!" Barbara Schmidt's voice squealed from the phone's tinny speaker.

"I believe you." A shadow detached itself from the corner of Allie's mind and surged forward. Its oily black trail filled her head with noxious fog. Claws pierced her chest. She gasped.

"I hear her downstairs right now." Barb whispered. "I'm in my closet."

"I don't know what to—"

"She's going to kill me. I'm going to die!"

"Erin's not home—"

"Please help me!"

One hand to her temple, Allie fought for focus. Blood roared in her ears. The fog enveloped and threatened to suffocate her. The cat's whiskers tickled her cheek and she grabbed her like a life preserver until warm energy trickled between them. Rachel purred and her body relaxed, limp as a dishtowel. Allie breathed in, breathed out, and the clouds parted. She knew what to do.

"Mrs. Schmidt," she said calmly. "Listen carefully."

Barb's breathing was ragged but she waited for instructions.

"When I tell you, I want you to get your keys and run as fast as you can to your car."

There was a frantic scrabbling noise.

"Wait," Allie urged. "Stay perfectly still and don't move until I tell you."

The phone went silent, save for Barb's terrified breathing.

"You need to drive out of town before you call your husband."

Minutes ticked by.

"Wait," Allie whispered again. *Soon.*

Lily's sharp-edged anger split her thoughts and her stomach nearly emptied its contents.

"Go now!" Allie ordered. There was a loud crack as the phone hit the floor and then the sound of running feet. The pain receded as if it had never been. Slumped against the cushion, she exhaled and released her hold on the cat. Her eyes closed. Barb would be safe.

When she opened her eyes, it seemed lighter in the room. Fur rumpled, Rachel hopped off the couch. She climbed onto the windowsill and pushed her wet nose against the glass.

"Yeah, I feel the same way."

The cat looked at her, as if listening, and turned her face back to the window. The morning sun had broken free of the horizon and it promised to be a lovely day. Already two crows perched on the roof of the shed. Their beady eyes trained on the trashcan, they wouldn't miss an opportunity today. The cat's spine arched when she chattered at them.

Allie turned away. "You're right. I need coffee." She sniffed the air. It smelled like coffee. Was Erin home? She rushed to the kitchen where Ciara leaned against the counter.

"You're back." Ciara raised her coffee mug in salute.

"Back?" How long had she been sitting on the sofa with Erin's silent phone? Had she zoned out? She pursed her lips at Ciara's Bat Girl pajamas. She looked like a teenager in the black top and shorts. "You'd get along well with our friend Chris."

"It's hard to find a man with good taste. And you're changing the subject, as usual."

Allie didn't respond.

Ciara took the hint. "Well, then. Is Chris available?"

"Sorry, he's getting married."

"Lucky wench." Ciara held out a clean mug. "Have some. It's good." She winked. "The coffee fairies brought me a present while I was away."

Allie poured herself a cup and added milk and sugar.

"Are you sure you're okay? You didn't even notice when I got up. I thought caffeine might help." She indicated the machine with a flourish. "Thank you. This is absolutely smashing!"

"How long was I out?"

"Not that long." Ciara concentrated on the bottom of her mug. That could mean anything from a few minutes to an hour.

Allie checked her watch. It hadn't been as long as she feared. "I answered a phone call for Erin and helped out her friend. No big deal," she fibbed.

"It sounded, um, intense." Ciara tilted her head.

So, she had overheard at least part of the call. "Everything is fine now." Allie couldn't quite meet her eye. Rachel landed on delicate feet beside her and rubbed her cheek against the warm coffee machine.

"Is the resident superhero sleeping in?"

"Fishing with the dog."

Ciara nodded. "That explains why the little rascal is not following you around with his puppy dog eyes. He has a serious crush on you. Does he have a name yet, or will you insist on calling him *the dog* for the rest of his life?"

Allie shrugged, more from guilt than indecision.

"Well then." Ciara picked up the cat and stroked her ears. "What have you planned for today?"

"Honestly, I'm struggling with all the paperwork involved in setting up this project. I should splice myself in two just to keep my head above water. I need to liaise with local groups and writing proposals was never my forte." Allie's headache had eased but she was so far behind that she might never catch up. And lately, she'd been no help to Erin. They were supposed to be a team. She'd promised.

"I have some extra time."

Allie gave her a tentative smile.

"I'm really good at schmoozing officials. How do you think someone with my crappy grades made it into graduate school? I bullshit very well."

"That you certainly do." Allie laughed. One of Ciara's redeeming qualities was that she never took herself too seriously.

"I'll pay you."

"I was hoping you'd say that." Ciara winked. She hoisted the cat and Rachel draped over her neck like lingerie on a clothesline.

"Come, I'll show you what I'm working on."

"Okay, but I'm not using that damn computer. I'll do it old school, on paper."

"Fine with me."

CHAPTER 22

Erin parked her Toyota Tacoma in the driveway of the decrepit bungalow that was home for the summer. Ciara's pink bicycle, with its brand new front tire, leaned against the shed at the end of the driveway. Snuggled into her windbreaker, the pup perked up his ears and oriented them like satellite dishes.

"Well, Billy Bass, fun time is over."

The dog's ears drooped.

"We caught a small mouth bass. The name sort of makes sense."

His ears flattened to his skull.

"You're right. You weren't much help." It was the dog's fault there was only one fish, and not two. After she'd removed the hook, he'd chased the first one back into the river. She picked the dog up and tucked him under her arm. "I can't decide what to call you."

She retrieved the cooler from the back of the truck and set the dog on the grass. He toddled over to the shed and lifted his leg on Ciara's tire. Whether or not the bike was there, he peed in the same spot. He finished and wagged his tail at her.

"Feel better?" The agonizingly delicious aroma of fresh coffee greeted her as soon as she entered the house. She'd made sure to pick up some decent dark roast, and it smelled like someone had found it. She poured herself a cup, removed the bass from the cooler and headed to Allie's office.

"I'm making dinner tonight!" Erin announced as she leapt through the doorway, fish held up by the gills.

Phone in hand, clad in Bat Girl pajamas, Ciara leaned back in

166

Allie's chair. Her bare ankles were crossed on the desk. She held a finger to her lips and wrinkled her nose at the fish. "Good morning, Alyssa Brody Consulting." Accent sharpened to finely clipped points, she sounded like the Duchess of York. The cat swished her tail between Ciara's feet and glowered at Erin.

Erin dropped the fish to her side. Alyssa Brody Consulting. Was the new business name Ciara's idea? It had always been Allie's Consulting before today.

"Of course, Mr. Vargas. I assure you our qualified technicians are fully aware. We will ensure the work is done to your specifications. Yes, sir. Why, thank you... Pardon me?" She twirled a lock of hair around an index finger and the corners of her mouth lifted. "I prefer vegan fare, but I regret that I have a prior lunch engagement. Perhaps another time. Have a pleasant day, Mr. Vargas." She hung up the phone and pulled her feet from the desk. The cat sniffed the air and sat upright. Eyes bright, she jumped to the back of Ciara's chair and took a swipe in Erin's direction.

Erin swung the fish out of range. "Did Allie's client just hit on you?"

"Um... yup." Ciara's duchess accent evaporated. "Happens all the time."

"I hope he didn't ask what you were wearing."

Ciara laughed. She pointed at Erin's prize. "That's cat food."

"No, this is dinner. Do you know where your boss is?"

"She had a strange morning and went for a run to clear her head." Ciara held up a finger when the phone rang again. "Good morning, Alyssa Brody Consulting." Her accent was as refined as before.

Erin exited when Ciara turned to write longhand on a pad of legal paper. Both dog and cat followed her to the kitchen where she noticed, for the first time, her cell phone on the table beside Allie's bag.

"There you are!" She hadn't been able to find it this morning and had finally left without it. She eyed the cat and checked her call log. Underneath a list of missed calls was one she didn't recognize. Caller ID was blocked. Probably Z-man. He often called too early or too late. She might give him a watch for a wedding present.

She wrapped the fish in foil and reached for the fridge door. Her phone rang and the display read Caller ID Blocked. She plopped the fish on the counter. "Hey Z."

"Officer Ericsson?"

"Barb? Uh... Mrs. Schmidt? Why are you whispering?" The cat and dog were playing noisily behind her and she pressed the phone to her ear.

"I did what you told me and I wanted to tell you that I made it."

"You made it?" Erin repeated. The woman sounded nuttier than the last time they'd spoken.

"I did exactly as you said. I ran as fast as I could, got in my car and drove out of town. I won't say where, but I'm safe."

Erin pressed her lips together. "You did what *I* told you? When?"

"When? Why, I've been driving ever since. I've only just arrived."

"No, I meant, when—"

"Thank you for saving my life."

Allie must have taken Barb's call. Is that what Ciara meant about Allie having a strange morning? What in the world had happened while she was fishing? "You called about Lily?"

"I knew it was her in that strange truck. When she came in the house, I hid in my closet and called you right away. I knew what she was up to and I was right. There was a gas can by the door when I ran out."

"Gas! Did you call the police?" The hair stood up on Erin's forearms. Between a persistent background buzz on the connection and the noisy pets, she could barely hear. She thumbed the call volume to maximum.

"I told you. They didn't do a darn thing the first time I called. I'm not calling again. I'm just happy to be alive."

"I'm relieved that you're okay. Is your husband with you?"

"He finally believes me. He's coming and we're both moving far away."

"Is Lily still staying at the motel?" Erin needed to find that kid.

"Albert said he hasn't seen her in days. He checked out and left her things with the desk."

She wouldn't care enough to go back for it. With no home base, how would Erin find the girl now? "Does Lily have any friends?

Barb snorted. "She's a monster. Who would be her friend?" She was quiet for a moment. "Albert once mentioned that he dropped her off at the housing complex by the mall. You know, the one with all those cheap gray townhouses. She might be staying there."

Erin *didn't* know, but maybe Ciara would. She'd probably ridden her bike all over the city. "Is there anything else you can tell me?"

"Good luck. You'll need a lot of good luck."

"Can you ask your husband if he mentioned a friend's na—?" The call disconnected and Erin stared at the screen until it went black. A name would have been helpful. What the *hell* had happened last night?

She walked to the office to ask Ciara but the phone was ringing again. No wonder Allie had asked her friend for help. Erin's questions would have to wait.

The fish should go in the fridge before it started to smell. Back in the kitchen, she gaped at the counter. Save for the shiny new coffee maker, it was bare. She opened the fridge. Nope, she hadn't subconsciously put the bass in there. The noisy pets. Rachel. The puppy, always underfoot, was also notably absent. Erin clenched her jaw. If that evil cat was capable of stealing her phone, a mere fish would have been child's play.

She dropped to her haunches and looked under the table. No. She checked the windowsill behind the curtain. How would the dog get up there anyway? He wasn't Spiderman. He was just a pup. A pup with an invisibility cloak. Erin checked both bedrooms, and then went back to the office.

With a look of utter amusement on her face, Ciara pushed her chair out and allowed Erin to check underneath the desk. She still held the phone's receiver to her ear with one hand and took meticulous notes with the other. Color-coded file folders now fanned in front of Ciara, each precisely equidistant from the other.

If she was so damn organized, why was her house a wreck? Erin couldn't figure some people out. And there was no cat in here. She stomped out.

She'd fixed the back door so Rachel couldn't have escaped unless she'd learned to open knobs. She wouldn't put it past her, but what about the dog? He hadn't *seemed* devious.

Coffee. She needed more coffee. She made a fresh pot and poured herself another cup. Her cell phone rang. Caller ID was blocked.

"Barb. Did Albert remember something?"

"Barb? Nope, not the last time I checked."

"Z-man."

"Hey girl, I have news!" Zimmerman sounded excited.

A woman's muffled voice scolded him in the background.

"Mom. Seriously?" He must have his hand over the microphone.

Erin stifled a laugh. Zimmerman should have moved out of his mom's house a decade ago. Falling for Gina was the best thing that had ever happened to him.

"I've finally got news about Lily for you," he announced.

Erin perked up. Rachel and her stolen fish could wait.

"I got a call from my buddy, you know the one who's married to—"

"I remember." Now his mom would think *she* was being rude for cutting *him* off, but he really needed to spit it out.

"A Winnipeg police officer was injured while trying to stop a vehicle theft. There were two suspects in the stolen truck, two girls, one blonde and one with red hair. Get this, the red-head called the blonde Lily."

"Lily." Erin's heart hammered in her ears. She'd injured a policeman. *Holy crap!*

"My buddy's husband was working that shift. He remembered we were trying to locate a girl named Lily. He called me an hour ago."

"Did they arrest her?"

"They found the truck wrapped around a telephone pole. The kids were gone."

Lily must have wrecked the truck after she'd left Barb's house. Barb hadn't mentioned another girl. Had Lily been on her own by then? She'd had a busy night.

Erin filled him in on the details of her initially confusing phone call from Mrs. Schmidt, and the fact that she'd as yet been unable to hear the rest of the story from Allie.

"You need to talk to your wife, Erin." Zimmerman urged.

"She's not my wife—"

"Might as well be," he said dismissively. "Maybe she can use her woo woo mojo to find Lily, and that other kid too. Those two are out of control."

Besides Allie's foster parents, Zimmerman and Gina were the only other people who knew about Allie's gift. Unfortunately it didn't work that way. She couldn't just program in the coordinates and follow the directions to her destination. Sometimes she sensed things, sometimes she didn't. Since she'd lost Fiona, she couldn't focus her intuition very well at all. She didn't have the words to explain all that to him. "I'll ask her."

"Oh, I almost forgot to tell you. Gina is going to have a boy. She told the ultrasound tech that she didn't want to know, but the assistant spilled the beans."

A boy. Allie had been talking about a baby boy in her sleep. Was this the child?

"She's due three weeks after the wedding. You gotta be here!"

She could hear the smile in his voice and she smiled back. "Don't worry, I'll be there."

"I gotta go. Mom needs me to take her to aqua therapy class."

"Say hi to Gina and your ma for me."

"Right." The call disconnected.

There was a muted shuffle in the bottom cabinet. The cat. Erin slid her phone onto the counter and flung open the bottom door. "Gotcha! You evil thief…" Alone in the middle of the cupboard, the puppy blinked. There was no cat. And no fish. Well, no fish *any more*. Shredded bits of aluminum foil and a trail of fish bones led to the hole in the wall behind the cabinets.

She held dog in front of her face. "Fess up, Clyde. Where's Bonnie?" He wagged his tail and blinked shiny brown eyes. She instantly forgave him. "Aw, I know it wasn't your idea. That cat's a seasoned criminal. You didn't have a chance." She smooched him on the end of his black nose.

Ciara sauntered into the room, now changed into camouflage skirt and form-fitting pink T-shirt. "You and Allie are perfect for each other." She filled her paisley-patterned water bottle at the sink and pulled on her boots.

Erin felt her ears grow hot. Puppies and babies always made her silly. She couldn't help it. "Have you heard of a mall with a crappy gray housing complex nearby?"

"You must be talking about Beverly Hills."

"You're pulling my leg." Erin couldn't tell if Ciara was kidding.

"That's what they call it. I don't know its real name because the sign's covered with graffiti. It's about a block from the Triple X strip mall by the airport."

"Can you be more specific? An address maybe?"

"You can't miss it. It's the one with triple X on almost every business listed. Triple X liquor, Triple X videos, Triple X… you get the idea." Ciara shook her head. "Are you sure you need to go there?"

"I need to find someone."

"I guess you can take care of yourself." She looked Erin up and down. "Good luck."

"Thanks, Ciara."

"Can you tell my boss that I had to go to the university? I'll be back later and play secretary again." She opened the door.

A flash of overhead activity rained shreds of foil down on Erin and the cat streaked down from the top cabinet. She flew out the open door, fish tail clutched in her sharp teeth.

"That's my bass." Erin growled. "I hope she chokes on a bone."

"Good kitty." Ciara's evil grin glittered like the cat's. "Sorry about your fish, superhero. I'll bring home a vegetarian pizza."

"Put bacon on it," Erin quipped.

Ciara mounted her hipster bike and waved the pinkie on a multi-ringed hand. The scales of a Japanese koi tattoo glittered down her calf as she pedaled. She had to admit, Ciara was like an edgy supermodel, but she wasn't as bad as Erin had feared. And she *was* funny.

From the back step, Erin supervised the dog when he urinated on his favorite spot. By the time Allie came running up the driveway, she still hadn't seen hide nor hair of the cat, or of her bass. There was a pair of crows arguing over something behind the fence. Maybe the cat had eaten her fill and the birds were taking care of the rest. She didn't have the heart to look. *Let the scavengers have it.*

Allie collapsed onto the step beside her, sweat streaming down her brow. She wiped her forehead with the back of her hand. Erin checked her watch. She'd been home for over an hour and Allie had gone out before that. How far had she needed to run to calm herself? She reached out for Allie's hand and entwined their fingers.

"I talked to Barb." Erin was the first to speak.

"Is she okay?"

"She thinks Lily tried to kill her." Erin looked at her pointedly. "She thinks *I* saved her life."

Allie nodded.

"You answered my phone."

"I had to. My head was going to explode."

"I'm glad you did. Barb said there was a gas can at the door when she ran out."

"And oil. There was oil."

A shiver traveled up Erin's spine. She could just imagine the images Allie had been forced to see. It was not like she had a choice. They assaulted her.

"Lily forgot something. I told Barb to run when Lily left."

"You saw all that?"

Allie's nostrils flared. "Not exactly, but I just knew."

"She's safe, thanks to you." The dog returned from his exploration and hopped onto Erin's lap. She stroked his ears.

Allie's eyes widened, and she dropped Erin's hand.

"What's wrong?" Erin reached for her but Allie pulled back.

"The dog. He's on your lap. He has too much energy."

"What are you talking about? Has Clyde done something?"

"Clyde? Is that what you're calling him today?"

"Wrong-Way *Bonnie* is on the lam. She tried to pin the fish caper on poor little Clyde." Erin held the dog up and waggled his paws.

"I know he amuses you, but please keep him away."

"Tell me what's going on." Erin put the dog on her lap.

"That dog is a fireball. He's too intense. I'm afraid I'll burn to ash."

"I thought this was about Fiona."

"It was… at first. I miss Fiona every day." The corner of Allie's mouth turned down. "Then I touched him and it was as if I'd been struck by lightning. Light and color and sound became so intense…"

Erin looked at Clyde. He was a furry little chihuahua with big ears, beady eyes and a wet nose. He was energetic, yes, but powerful? The puppy tried to wiggle free of her arms to go to Allie and she clamped down. "Sensory overload?"

Allie's eyes flicked to hers.

Erin smiled. *Bingo.* Too much energy all at once.

Allie nodded uncertainly. She backed away. "I need to change and get ready for my video conference."

Erin shrugged. Later. She would try out her idea later.

With Allie holed up in her office for the day, Erin spent her time on the phone trying to wheedle information from the local police about Barb's call last night. She was transferred from the Information Processing Unit to the desk sergeant and back. It was useless. Erin didn't even have the street address. They couldn't send anyone to a break and enter with no complainant and no address.

She'd ended up leaving a message for Zimmerman's Winnipeg

contact but she didn't have high hopes. There was nothing to go on. The complainant had fled. Lily had probably removed the evidence. What was left? A hysterical phone call from a crazy woman.

Why was this kid always out of reach? Erin tossed the phone on the sofa. What could she do now? She went to the shed to retrieve the toolkit and the puppy padded along behind her. There was always something around here that needed fixing.

It was mid-afternoon by the time Allie emerged from her office. She carried the plate from the sandwich Erin had made her for lunch and plunked it onto the kitchen counter. "It turned out to be a good day," she sighed. "Thanks for lunch. I was so busy that I would have forgotten to eat."

Erin picked up the puppy and cradled him in her arms. She led Allie to the sofa and they sat side-by-side. "Will you try something with me?"

The corners of Allie's eyes puckered. "Is this like the time you said we should jump into the river holding hands? It's warm, you said."

"Nothing like that." Erin gripped her hand and held tight.

Allie's head snapped back. Her pupils dilated.

* * *

The panther paces behind a wall of flames. Head low, ears back, the beast glares through green eyes. Oily black smoke rises.

Claws tear at my throat.

Behind the panther, a girl. Skin like alabaster, hair like fire, and eyes like the beast. No, not the same.

The panther watches a man play with a small girl. His heart is black. The girl is innocent. He laughs only with his mouth.

Pressure squeezes my chest.

The beast prowls. Dirty money. Flashing lights. A man in uniform falls like tumbleweed. Oil and gasoline. The blade of a knife. Blood red anger. So much hate.

I cannot breathe.

The panther stalks a woman. Dirty buildings all in a row. A flowered basket on a pink bicycle.

Stop! No!

* * *

Allie's pupils reduced to pinpricks. She ripped her hand from Erin's and held it to her throat.

"Did I hurt you?" Erin's voice caught. What had she done?

Allie took a deep breath. "I'm okay."

The dog stood at attention on Erin's lap, his tail straight up like a flag on a rural mailbox. He slowly lowered one hind paw until he was on all fours.

"The dog is acting strange. Is something wrong with him?" Allie asked.

Erin put the pup on the floor. "As far as I can tell, Clyde's in good company." She offered her lopsided grin in apology.

The dog plunked his rear end directly in front of Allie and whipped his tail back and forth. His brown eyes shone. She inched away.

"I haven't seen him act like that before." Erin drew him onto her lap and petted his ears. "His body went rigid, and he stuck his leg straight out behind him as soon as I held your hand. He looked like a hunting dog indicating prey, only in reverse. You connected with him, didn't you?"

Allie breathed out her nostrils. "Yes. It's hard to describe. It was like driving very fast on a motorcycle with no helmet."

"I sure hope you haven't actually done that." Erin kicked herself. This was no time for a traffic enforcement lecture. "I wanted to try acting as a buffer between you two." According to Allie, massive amounts of energy had flowed through them but Erin hadn't felt a thing. "What did you see?"

Allie gulped and rubbed her throat. "A black panther. Lily. A girl with red hair and green eyes. A man who wants to hurt a little girl. Money. A policeman falling. The images were mixed up. The panther stalking a woman. A pink bike. Ciara!"

CHAPTER 23

I turn over on the park bench and straighten my spine. The hide-a-bed in the motel would have been so much more comfy but I'm locked out. I couldn't see anything of mine through the window and it wasn't worth my time to jimmy the lock for an empty room.

I bet Albert has finally taken off with Barb, poor lovesick old bastard. He'll be stuck with her for the rest of his life and here I am. Abandoned again. This is the story of my life. Nobody sticks around for me. My mom left. My grandfather left. My father left. Now them.

Fuck 'em all. I have Nina.

My knuckles are scraped bloody. When did that happen? Was it when I tried to roll the truck off the bridge? I never figured the wheels would straighten out like that. I barely had time to jump out before it went clean across and smashed into a light post. It's not what I planned but it was still funny. Almost as funny as watching the cop fall off the side and crash into the ditch. The memory makes me smile.

When I push my hoodie back from my face, the late afternoon sun burns my eyes like a vampire's. But I'm not a vampire. I've been here since dawn. Where did the day go? The panther in my stomach growls and it foams the back of my throat. I feel bruised from the inside out. My head feels like a friggin' watermelon. Where the fuck is Nina?

My stomach turns over again. I need milk. I could drink a gallon of it right now without stopping. I roll off the bench and my legs wobble beneath me. Don't mistake that for weakness. I'll cut your eye out if you piss me off. At least that's what I told the guys who tried to mess with me an hour ago. They took one look at my blade and ran like pussies.

I stare down the road to Nina's house. She knows I'm here but she won't come out. Irritation fizzes in my mouth and it tastes like puke. I need milk now.

A lady with a baby in a stroller hurries past without looking at me. She knows better. I smooth my hair behind my ears. I can't do a damn thing about the bloody scrapes right now but there's one thing I know about this neighborhood. Everyone will pretend not to notice.

With my back stiff as a soldier, I walk to the QuikStop and right back to the cooler. I take a quart, yes a goddamn *quart*, of milk from the shelf and crack open the top to take a long swallow. Ooh, there's chocolate milk. My stomach flops over. I put the first carton back, tear open the chocolate milk and down half of it in a few gulps. It gushes over my chin and down my shirt.

"You gonna pay for all that?" The lady at the counter doesn't look much older than me. She won't even come out from behind the counter to challenge me. I pick a bag of chips off a display, take my milk and give her a zombie stink eye. She takes in my bloody face and knuckles, and her mouth drops open. I walk right out the door when she reaches for the phone.

My stomach settles by the time I return to the bench. I dump the rest of the chocolate milk and dig into the chips. I'm satisfied and not so pissed with Nina any more. She's been holed up in her house since I dropped her off but maybe it's not her fault. What if she can't get out? It's time I go see what's up. I rock to my feet and stumble forward.

"Bloody hell!" A lady on a bike scrapes her boot on the ground to steer around me. "Mind the road!"

With my hood up and head down, I didn't even see her until she almost flattened me. Pedaling like a maniac, she looks like a punk Barbie doll. Tattoo Barbie on a pink hipster bike with a woven basket on the front. When she passes I get a flash of fuzzy memories.

I'm in the mall parking lot. I jack the Mustang. It's black as a panther. I smile at the thought, and then frown. The seat's too far back and I can't reach the pedals. I'm adjusting it and when I look up, I see the cop's surprised face. She's on that same stupid pink bike and she hits the pavement before I hit her. When she goes down there's a dog in her backpack. That part *can't* be real.

I scratch the scab on my face. Nina thinks I had a concussion. Could any of it be true? The screaming at the back of my brain tells me it was real.

Fuckin' Officer Ericsson is in Winnipeg. She was riding that goddamn bike. That flower basket clinches it. There can't be another one like it in this whole city. Was she following me? The anger in my gut says she was. I need to follow Punk Barbie. I have to find that cop before she finds me.

Punk Barbie is headed down a route I know and I dog trot behind her. There is a shortcut that catches me up when I fall behind. I had a rough night and it's not long before my ass is wiped.

There's my solution. Someone left a BMX bike by a fence and I grab it at a run. I swing one leg over and that's when I realize that the seat is as low as it can go on the frame. If I sit, my knees would be higher than my chin so I stand to ride. It sucks but it's better than running. Someone yells in the distance. I pedal fast until I'm out of range.

I crunch down the gravel alley, searching for Punk Barbie between the houses. After a mile she stops at a restaurant with a neon sign in the window that says VEGAN. That's nasty. I tried something vegan once and it tasted like grass. Besides, everyone who goes in is a loser. I'm not a loser.

Punk Barbie doesn't lock her bike. She rolls it into a rack that looks like rainbow hula-hoops and goes in. I'm tempted to take it just to see the look on her face. Nah, I wouldn't be caught dead riding that piece of shit. I lean against a brick planter and wait.

My head is clear like it hasn't been in days. I'm close. I feel it. Barb's gone, but now I can find the cop.

Twenty minutes later she comes out with a cardboard box and tilts it into her stupid basket. Her skirt flutters up when she hops back on and we're off. A half block behind, I tail her across the bridge and down by the river. She coasts into the driveway of an old house with a busted front step.

With my hood low, I watch from the other side of the road. Punk Barbie steers around a truck and I'll be jiggered if it isn't that bitch cop's Toyota. I've seen her in it a million times back in Morley Falls and the Minnesota license plate is like a friggin' flag.

I should run up and stick my knife right between Punk Barbie's shoulder blades. I drop the BMX and duck across the road behind the truck. What will the cop do when she finds her friend's corpse?

The blinds flicker open and I melt into the tire well. Is someone watching? No, it's only a cat. Like a spider, I inch around and crouch by the bumper. I'm behind her when Punk Barbie steps off her bike and leans it against a garden shed. She slides the box from the basket and takes a step toward the house.

Now. I can do it now.

My growl scrapes metal shavings into my belly and my blade flashes open in my hand. My knife and me, we think the same. In my mind, the blade sinks into her neck. I tear it out, and the serrated spine separates flesh from bone. Like in the movies, blood spurts everywhere. The world turns red.

My hand shakes with excitement. I always wanted to know what that felt like. I tense my muscles and transfer my weight to pounce.

CHAPTER 24

Allie's throat was raw, her skin bruised. She pointed to the window, lifted her dry tongue and choked out one word. "Ciara!" It stuck to the roof of her mouth. Sweat dripped from her brow and burned her eyes.

Without hesitation, Erin leapt onto the back of the sofa and wrenched open the blinds. Settled on the windowsill, Wrong-Way Rachel squawked in protest. "I don't see Ciara."

On the floor, the puppy nosed Allie's pant leg. He stood and, like a compass, rotated to face the front of the house. One leg extended awkwardly behind him, and his energy sparkled like sunlight.

Erin tilted her head and followed his sight line. "It's just a kid on a bike." Her eyebrows formed a wavy line and she shrugged.

Allie shifted away from the dog. Perfectly upright, his tail quivered and he twitched his nose as if scenting the air. The intense pictures she'd been bombarded with had faded when she had dropped Erin's hand but they increased when he was near. She bent forward and held her knees. Dark after-images swirled.

Stomach acid rose, burning its way up until she tasted it. She hurried to the washroom and closed the door. Bent over the toilet, she retched but her throat remained dry. She sank to her knees, her cheek against the cool porcelain bowl. She could hug Erin for doing such a good job of cleaning it.

"Baby! Are you okay?" Erin's warm energy radiated through the door.

"Okay," she croaked. "I'm okay."

Erin pushed the door open and knelt beside her, holding her hair back. She touched Allie's cheek with the back of her hand. "You're sweating. You're hot."

Images spun in Allie's mind. Red. Blood. Sharp teeth sink into her friend's neck.

"Ciara. Go help Ciara."

Erin jumped up and ran.

* * *

The back door springs open and I freeze, halfway to my feet. *It's her. The bitch.*

I flatten myself behind the truck. I am invisible. Even the best soldier knows when it's time to retreat. I shove my blade into the tire's sidewall, slow and easy so the air leaks quietly. It's my calling card.

Like a phantom, I sneak back to the path and reclaim the bike. I spit a stream of saliva across the road when I ride away.

I found you first, bitch. You are going down.

* * *

"Ciara!" Erin tore the door open and faced the yard, the handle from the mop like a sword in her hands.

Ciara startled backward and the pizza crashed to the ground. "What's going on?" She picked the box up and eased open the lid. "You broke my pizza."

"Who is out here?" Erin circled the truck, mop handle raised to attack.

Ciara's grin wilted. She stared at Erin, mouth open. "Is everything all right?"

"You're in danger. Did you see anyone?"

"The only danger I see is a superhero in my driveway."

Erin wrenched open the shed to check hiding spots. She vaulted the fence and checked along the property line. There was not a single place of concealment she didn't search.

Back in the driveway, she swiveled to focus on the path across the road. When she'd looked out the blinds, there'd been someone on a bike. A kid. She'd assumed it was a boy. Could it have been Lily? A prickle traveled the base of her skull. Did Lily follow Ciara? Was it possible?

"Is this still about the cat stealing your fish?" Ciara joined Erin at the end of the drive. "Are you pissing about?"

"This is no joke." Erin kept her eyes on the shrubs that bordered the path. Was Lily watching?

"You're officially freaking me out."

"Allie said you were in danger." Erin backed down the driveway to her truck and stopped. One tire was flat. She slid her fingers over the slit in the sidewall and the hair on the back of her arms prickled. A two-inch blade. Just like when her tires had been slashed in the police parking lot back in Morley Falls.

She turned and considered Ciara's pink bicycle. Had Lily noticed the bike when she'd spotted Erin? With its homemade basket, it was unique.

"See? I'm fine. I don't wear a helmet, but I don't know what—"

"Where were you today?" Erin noticed Ciara's eyes on the mop handle. She set it against the step. "Please."

Ciara counted rings on her fingers. "I was at the university. I worked on my paper in the library. I went to the phone booth and made some calls. After that, I met Mr. Vargas, *Raphael*, for lunch." She held a finger to her lips "Don't tell Allie I'm dating her client, but he's really hot." She counted the last ring. "Then I picked up pizza on the way home."

"Did you go anywhere else?" There must be something. Erin didn't believe in mere coincidence.

"Lunch went *a bit* longer than I planned. I didn't get back to the library." She pursed her lips to suppress a sly grin. "I rode my bike the long way home afterward."

"Why did you go the long way?" Erin's interest piqued.

"To help you out."

"To help me?"

"You wanted to know where Beverly Hills was. I rode by to get you the address." Ciara rifled through the contents of her bag and produced a shred of paper. "It's actually called Northview Estates, and it looks worse than the last time I was out there."

That was it! Erin took the paper from her fingers. Lily had been there. She'd spotted the bike and put two and two together.

"You were followed home."

Ciara's eyebrows shot up. "Who? Why?"

Erin sighed. She might as well tell her why she had come to Winnipeg with Allie. This was no laid-back vacation. "There's a criminal from Morley Falls who moved here."

"A criminal!" Ciara scooped up her pizza box and headed into the house.

Erin followed her. "I came to stop her. You're involved now, so you need to know."

"Her? She? A woman criminal?"

"A girl."

"A child? You're talking about a child?" One of Ciara's eyebrows slanted outward.

"She's no average child. She's killed. And she'll kill again."

"A murderess!" Ciara frowned. "There was a boy on a bike. At least I thought it was a boy. He was by the park... and the bridge. Maybe..."

"She's sneaky. And dangerous. She's older than she looks." Erin remembered the kid across the road. Hunched over, the kid had looked smaller. If he had stood up straight. If there was no hood. Erin closed her eyes with the realization. Lily's stalking experience was evident.

"When you met me in the driveway, I thought you were wound a bit too tightly, sweetie." Ciara put her pizza on the table and eyed Erin. "But if Allie was worried, I'm worried. Allie knows things. I trust her." She looked around. "Where is she? Does she have a headache?"

Erin nodded. Ciara certainly knew her well enough. She turned to check on Allie but Ciara shouldered through the door first. They found her on the sofa, arms wrapped around the cat. Rachel's yellow eyes gloated at Erin from the safety of Allie's shirtsleeves.

"I see that you're fine." Ciara picked up the dog from his spot by Allie's feet. Even in Ciara's arms, the dog watched Allie.

"I'm glad that you're okay too." Allie scooted the cat from her lap and Rachel resumed her vigil at the window. "I sent Erin to help you."

Ciara tilted her head. "Superhero saved the day."

Allie nodded and took Erin's hands. "Thank you. Lily's gone."

"I wish one of you had told me you were tracking a mini serial killer." Ciara's words were flippant but her brow crinkled with

183

concern. She looked from Allie to Erin and sighed. "Life's never boring when Allie is around. Squashed veggie pizza in the kitchen when you're ready." She took the dog with her. "You're dishy enough to be a cat." He perked up his ears. "Fancy some road pizza?"

Erin knelt beside Allie. "Are you sure you're okay? I'm sorry. I took a chance."

"If you hadn't, Ciara might have been hurt. Lily followed her home."

"I figured. She must have recognized the bike. I was riding it when she spotted me at the mall." Erin stood up and clenched her fists. Muscles tensed between her shoulder blades.

"Lily." Allie stared at the ceiling. "So much hate. It hurts to think about her."

"Are you angry with me?"

"No, I'm not angry." Allie met Erin's eyes. "It was terrifying and exciting, but everything was out of control." She sucked in her breath. "I need to stay in control."

"Control." Erin repeated.

"How did you figure out what to do?"

I have no idea. I took a crazy risk without regard for your safety. "Well, you and the dog seem to have a connection but you're too sensitive. You're like the ten amp fuse in our old house that gets tripped by the five hundred watt blow dryer. You needed a buffer. By now I realize that I have about as much psychic sensitivity as a stump. I'm the perfect buffer, Baby."

"A buffer!"

"You say energy flows through everything. I just held the dog and then you."

"I'm not sure I'd claim success quite yet but at least I didn't actually vomit." Allie rose to her feet.

"Maybe you can get used to Clyde, and we can—"

"He needs a better name." Allie put a hand on her hip.

"You're trying to distract me. I think you could get used to the dog if you tried. How about Gino?"

"After Gina, your first crush? Naming pets after old girlfriends is *my* thing." Allie's sense of humor was coming back. "This dog is yours and you should name him your way."

"What about Sonar? Radar? Barack? He's got those big ears."

"I don't think any of those work." Allie got to her feet and headed to the kitchen. The dog met her in the doorway and she sidestepped. He followed, his tail like a helicopter.

"Are you trying to choose a name for Mr. Picky Eater?" Ciara had divided the squashed pizza onto three plates. She sat at the table and blotted the corner of her mouth with an organic napkin that looked like burlap. With dainty fingers, she slid the napkin onto her lap. "I was absolutely gob-smacked when the dog turned up his nose at my pizza. Do you suppose he's a carnivore?"

Allie gave a tiny smile and allowed him to sniff her sock.

"He's probably still full." Erin crammed a handful of crust into her mouth. She'd start with the easy part and make her way to the purple spongy stuff.

Allie looked at the dog's full dish on the floor. "But he hasn't eaten much at all."

"That dog is my hero. He was in on Erin's great fish caper today." Ciara laughed, her open palm colliding with her thigh at the same moment. "And you should have seen Rachel escape out the door. If it hadn't been for those two, we would be looking at dead fish right now." She leaned down and patted the dog.

Erin frowned and separated a tomato from the vegan cheese. She nibbled around an unidentified object embedded in the pizza wreckage.

Ciara retrieved three cans of raspberry-flavored beer from the fridge and passed them around. "I found these at the market."

Erin stared at the stylized fish on the label and popped it open. Apparently Ciara's aversion to fish didn't extend to alcoholic beverages. She took a swallow and shrugged. It tasted just like beer, with raspberries.

Ciara considered Allie's untouched bottle for a moment, then picked it up and put it back in the fridge. "Sorry, love. I forgot about the no drinking thing. Are you feeling better?"

"I'm fine." The skin at Allie's jawline rippled.

Erin's teeth had been on edge since their safe haven was violated. Allie needed to rest but Erin had to get out. To move around and check out the neighborhood. "I'm taking the munchkin for a walk."

"She's gone for now, Honey, but be careful." Allie squinted as if concentrating.

"I have cheesecake." Ciara offered. "Are you sure you want to miss it?"

Erin envisioned a slab of tofu swathed in sauce that tasted like alfalfa. "Thank you, but I'll pass."

"I'll take you up on dessert." Allie got up for plates.

Erin headed out the door. Even though Lily was gone, she'd feel a lot better if the nameless dog watched her back while she changed the slashed tire. Afterward, they could scout the neighborhood together. He was small but his canine instincts appeared intact.

The last of the daylight had fallen over the horizon when Erin propped her mini flashlight against the porch step and pumped the jack under the frame of her truck. In the dark, she swore when she rapped knuckles against steel and sat back to rub her fist.

Rachel glowered down at her from the window, keeping silent watch on her folly. Yes, she could have waited until daylight to change the tire, but what if something happened in the meantime? Off-guard was never a comfortable place to be. It took her longer than anticipated but finally she stowed the jack and tossed the damaged tire in the back. First thing in the morning, she'd find a tire shop and get it replaced.

"Come on dog. Let's run!" The chihuahua hopped on his hind legs, excited by her tone. Pulling hard against the leash, he led the way for the first block. He walked behind Erin for the second. Tongue hanging out, his little legs draped over her forearm as she carried him the rest of the way. She jogged down each alley and street in a methodical pattern until she'd covered a five-block radius.

Satisfied, she returned home. The kitchen light was out. Thank God. She'd missed the mystery cheesecake.

She found Allie and Ciara snuggled in front of the TV watching a black and white movie. Ciara was back in her Bat Girl pajamas, the cat stretched across her shoulders like a disheveled mink stole. Ciara had already braided one side of Allie's hair and was working on the other.

Erin felt an ache in her gut. She could tie any number of fishing knots, even a Bimini twist, but braiding hair was one thing she'd never mastered. "Well, ladies, I'm headed to bed." She picked the dog up and patted his head. His ears sprang up.

"I'm coming too." Allie untangled her braids.

"After all my hard work." Ciara protested.

"You know I don't really like braids. I just let you talk me into it because you enjoy messing with other people's hair. You should have been a stylist."

"There's still time for beauty school." Ciara quipped.

Allie waggled her fingers and followed Erin.

"Fine." Ciara dragged the placid cat to her lap. "Wrong-Way Rachel will finish the movie with me."

Erin placed a hand on Allie's waist. Allie was coming to bed early. That could mean only one thing. By the time Allie closed the bedroom door, Erin could no longer suppress her smile. She needed the comfort of their intimacy too.

* * *

Allie turns in her sleep. Darkness suffocates her.

The panther stalks.

Obsession. Contempt. Revenge. Power.

No! Wake up. Wake up.

The girl with hair like fire obeys the panther.

Fear. Anger.

A little one cries.

Weak. Trusting. Naive.

Hide. He's coming!

A baby. A boy, curls soft as down, skin ashen, waxy.

Death.

Nooo!

CHAPTER 25

At the end of Nina's block I dump the BMX bike into the bushes. The whole street is deserted. Nobody stays out at night around here. Nina's mom's van is parked in the driveway and her dad's work van right behind it. The guy doesn't like to take advice, does he? From two houses away I can hear the screaming. No one will call the cops to complain. Not in this neighborhood.

"I told you not to come back!" Nina's mom's voice is high and shrill. "What have you done? Look at her!"

"She's making it up. I never laid a finger on her." Her dad's voice is harsh as gravel under my heel. Bastard. Nina blamed him for the cut on her face. Serves him right. Now maybe her mom will kick him out for good.

"How could you do this?" Something crashes and somebody screams.

I slink behind the house when a car comes. Gang-bangers looking for some fun. Shiny rims spin past and speakers thump long after it's out of sight. The vibration pulses in my chest. We're in sync.

On an empty paper bag from a trash bin, I scribble a new blackmail note.

Hey Loser. You didn't listen. Now you have to pay $1000. You know where. Bring it at midnight tomorrow or go to jail.

I wedge it under his van's wiper blade.

"Not my baby!"

Wait. Are they even talking about Nina? I slip around to Nina's window. It's dark and someone's crying. I toss a rock. No one comes.

The trashcan is empty. I drag it to the window and tip it over so I can climb on top. There's a faint whine so I shove in the screen. Beth crawls out from under the bed and her eyes bug out when she sees me.

"Lily! Why are you in my window?" She stands on the mattress and stares at the bent screen. "Daddy's going to be mad."

"Where is Nina?" I don't give a crap about her dad. "She was supposed to meet me at the park. What happened?"

"Nina lied. She said Daddy scratched her face, but I told mommy it wasn't true. She came home like that. When she was with you." She points a fat finger at me.

"You little shit." I take a swipe at her through the open window and nearly lose my balance.

"You're mean." She retreats to the carpet where I can't reach her.

"Go get Nina."

"Daddy said to stay in my room. He said to be good and he would give me a present later."

I don't have time to explain to her that she won't like what her daddy wants to give her. She'll figure that out for herself when he comes back. "Go get Nina."

"No." She crosses her arms and her bottom lip puffs out. "Daddy said."

I've figured out where Nina is. She's in the middle of the screaming match with her parents, trying to protect Beth and her useless mom. I jump down from the window and slither around to the driveway.

Through the kitchen window, there's Nina standing with her skinny fists up. Her mom's hiding behind her. I don't see her dad until he takes a step forward and smacks Nina square on the mouth with the back of his hand. She bends over and covers her face.

Hey! Stop it. She's mine.

I yank the wiper blade up and grab my note. With my pen I scribble lines across the part where it says *$1000* and replace it with *a million*. For this, he can pay me a million fucking dollars.

From my spot behind the bushes, I watch the house until they stop screaming and the kitchen goes dark. The light comes on in Nina's mom's bedroom a few seconds later. She'll never kick him out.

A million dollars. One million dollars. I'll be a millionaire. The smile spreads across my face. The tickle in my belly makes me fidgety. I'll buy a jet ski. No, I'll buy a yacht *and* a jet ski. Maybe I'll buy a helicopter and park it on my yacht. Nina can come hang with me.

"Lily!"

I bolt upright. Nina is whispering too loud. Her dad's gonna hear and smash her in the mouth again. I zip to the backyard and up onto the pail again.

"Hey." I'm cool like I just arrived.

"What are you doing here?" Her lips are fat but there's no blood. Her dad is good. That won't leave a mark.

"You didn't come to the park. I waited all day."

"My dad… He's mad." She looks at me with red eyes.

"Yeah, I heard."

"How long have you been out there?"

"Don't blame me for what he did. I just got here." It's not my friggin' fault she wasn't smart enough to duck.

"I'm not… I don't know. My mom saw the scratch and asked me what happened. I told her what you said."

"Why didn't she kick his ass out?" I know why. She's useless.

"Mom didn't believe me. She believed him. And Beth squealed." There was a thump under the bed. The kid was hiding.

"That brat needs a slap in the head."

"Lily! I know you don't mean that." Nina looks me in the eye.

I stare back. *The hell I don't.* "Of course not. I'm only joking."

"She heard you." The corner of her eye twitches when Beth crawls out.

"Hey Beth. Want some candy?" The kid goes for it as usual.

"I like candy." Beth climbs up onto the mattress beside Nina and I fake smile at her. She smiles back and holds out her hand. "Are you nice today?"

"Are *you* gonna be nice and not rat us out?" I turn it back around to her. I learned to do that when I was seven and my mom was worried that I couldn't tell right from wrong. She got my grandfather to take me to a head shrinker. That was a waste of money.

"I pinkie swear."

I got no problem telling right from wrong. I just pick whatever is easiest. I wipe the lint off a naked stick of gum in the bottom of my pocket and she takes it.

"Thank you," Nina prompts her through swollen lips.

"Thank you," the kid says like a polite robot.

"Let's get the f—" I notice Nina's crinkled up eyebrows. She's ready to give me a lecture about swearing in front of Beth. "Let's get the *flippity dippity* outta here."

Beth giggles around her gum. "You're funny."

"Hurry up," I tell Nina. "Your parents are f—" Nina still has that look. "Your parents are *busy*. Let's go. They'll never notice. Beth won't tell, will you?" I stare hard at the brat. "Cuz if you do, you don't get candy."

Beth folds her arms.

Nina puts a leg up on the window, her face toward her sister. "If Dad comes in here, you hide under your bed and don't come out, okay?"

"But Daddy said…" Beth looks at the door, looks at Nina. "Okay." She scoots back under.

"Good girl. I'll be back for you as soon as I can." Nina climbs out. I'm hanging on as hard as I can but both of us on the trashcan is too much. The side folds in and it crumples sideways, spilling us onto the grass.

I land on top of Nina, my forehead crashing into her cheek. She sucks in her breath and holds it until I get off. Her shirt is up, showing her bra. Her cheeks are pink. This is the first time I've noticed that her belly button is an outie. *Weird.* She sees my eyes on her bare skin and her face burns red as fire.

"Are you sick?" I don't want to be around her if she's sick. *Don't friggin' give it to me.*

"Um… no." She gets up and quickly straightens her clothes.

"Your plan to blame it on your dad didn't work, eh?" *Stupid.* How was she gonna prove that anyhow?

"What? My plan? It was your…" She stomps ahead of me. "Never mind."

"You ready for some fun tonight?" I'm hungry. My head hurts, my knuckles are sore and I really need a beer. I ran more in the last twenty-four hours than I have in the last month. "Let's go get wasted."

"I don't want to get chased by the cops again."

"That was no big deal." It *was* a big deal. It was a rush.

"And I don't want to proposition any men." Nina's face pinches, like she smells sour milk.

"What are you talking about? That was hilarious." I clap her on the shoulder and stand like she did at the truck stop. "Wanna party?" I mimic.

Her eyes turn into snake slits. "What about you? You sounded like Oliver Twist. *Excuse me, kind sir. Can you give a poor girl a ride?*" She laughs and slaps me back. "He thought you were nuts. It was never going to work."

I look away. *Don't laugh at me.* Right now I could wrap my fingers around her throat and squeeze until her eyes go blank. "Piss off. It always works."

Her smile droops and we walk in silence for a minute.

She's making me angry. Is she gonna wreck my entire night? "Let's go get a car."

"What if we get caught?"

"I never get caught." Well, almost never.

Forty-five minutes later I'm behind the wheel of a blue car with a half tank of gas. Nina has her window rolled down and her hair whips in the breeze. She has a smile on her face when she sucks on her Slurpee.

"Your mouth doesn't look stupid any more." It's true. Her lips aren't puffy.

Her smile turns down. She tosses the rest of her drink out the window. The old Nina would have made me drive around to find a trashcan. I glance sideways at her. Is she ready?

"My dad's in jail so he can't hurt me any more."

Nina's eyes snap over to me, but I'm cool. I keep mine on the road. "He did this to you?" she asks.

"Worse." It's not really the same, but he wouldn't give me money when I asked, and he tried to tell me what to do. That's just as bad. I twist my mouth and do the eyebrow thing to make my face look upset. My practice paid off because she believes me.

"I hate my dad." She punches the dashboard and snatches her fist back. "I wish he was in prison too." She folds her fist inside the palm of her other hand and rubs it. Her eyebrow flinches. "I wish he was dead."

There, she said it. The magic words. "Fuck him!" I pound my fist on the steering wheel and pretend I'm angry.

"Fuck him!" she shouts and punches the dash again.

Inside, my heart flutters in my chest. This time it will be perfect. This time I have a new minion. "I'll help you kill him."

Her eyes widen but she doesn't speak. Her pupils are tiny pinpricks. She doesn't say no.

"First, let's find beer."

I drop her off at her house before the sun rises. She drank more tonight than ever before and she's having trouble balancing on the bent trash pail. I hold her by the waist so she can get through the window. She teeters and falls off, taking me down with her. I'm flat on my back and she reaches over to wipe the hair from my face.

"You're beautiful."

She's had way too much to drink. I swore to myself I wouldn't let that happen again. She gets weird. Before I can react, she grabs me by the shoulders and kisses me halfway between my mouth and nose.

"I love you." Her cheeks are red, her lips quiver, but her gaze doesn't waver when she says it.

What the hell was that? I've got no words for her so I keep my mouth shut. She intruded on my personal space, but it was so quick I barely noticed. All that's left is the wet ooze on my upper lip, like the trail a slug leaves in the garden. As fast as she violated me, she jumps back onto the pail and heads through the window on her own.

My ass is still on the ground when she crashes to the other side. I'm in a daze. The only other person stupid enough to try to kiss me ended up with a black eye, face down in a mud puddle. Grade three was a tough year for Ronnie Andrews. He should have known better when I told him to get lost.

I scrub the wet spot on my face with my torn knuckles. They burn. Nina's head hasn't come back up so I climb onto the pail to see what's going on. Someone whimpers and Nina pulls her little sister out from under the bed.

"What's up, Beth buttercup?" Is she upset that we didn't bring her candy? Did she lose her teddy bear?

The brat crouches on the floor and Nina winds her arms around her. Beth stares up at me with round watery eyes. Both of them cry but neither one makes a sound.

"Daddy." Beth hiccups. "Daddy was mean. He came in my room and he hurt me."

Nina holds her hand over her sister's mouth and Beth's eyes bulge. "Shhh." She rocks her and hums a tune I don't recognize. Nina's face goes blank. Her cheeks sag and she squeezes Beth until she squirms. Nina's whole body goes stiff like she wants to kill her dad with her bare hands.

Let's kill him. Kill him. Kill him!

Nina's face is hard as gravestone. "Let's do it."

My heart pounds like a wild animal in my chest. It might tear right through. I give a single nod. *Message received.* Before I leave, I prop the bent window screen back into place as best I can. This is no time to raise suspicion.

I'm dancing inside when I run back to the car. It'll be so easy. He has to give me the money tonight. After he pays the million dollars, he can pay with his life.

There's just one other thing I want to take care of before then. I'll need to be fully awake for it, though. I let the car idle while I catch a quick nap. I wind myself in a cocoon with the blanket in the back. Sleep comes fast and there are no dreams.

An anaconda is squeezing me and, when I jolt awake, my mouth tastes like rotten eggs. I kick my legs out from the blanket. My knuckles feel raw. A new scrape crisscrosses the old ones. That is a mystery. It must have been a helluva night.

There is liquid in a vodka bottle on the seat. I don't even remember where we got that. There's a fuzzy memory of passing it back and forth with Nina. Her giggling. Me telling funny jokes. I strain it between my teeth and gargle before I spit onto the floor. It's an improvement. The sun is above the horizon so it must be almost nine o'clock.

Scheisse! It's later than I thought. I scramble into the driver's seat. They'll be up and moving around by now. I don't want to miss an opportunity.

On the road by the river, I park a half block from the bitch's house and slouch in my seat. The truck sits in the same spot in the driveway but a fresh tire replaces the one I slashed. Bitch cop didn't waste any time.

It doesn't take long, less than half an hour before Punk Barbie comes out. Today she's dressed like a goth princess and her pink skirt matches her bicycle. I can't wait until she's on the road. I'll run her down like a white-tailed deer. I'll follow her and—

It's the bitch, Officer Erin Ericsson. The screen door slams as she sprints to the driveway. She's trying to get Barbie in the truck but Barbie won't go. She's feisty, that one. *Let her go, bitch. I'll take care of her.*

CHAPTER 26

"Hop in." Erin opened the passenger door for Ciara. Halfway down the block she noted a blue car that wasn't there when she'd mentally cataloged the neighborhood last night. Had someone new moved in? Was someone having an overnight guest? She'd check that out later.

"Gallant, but unnecessary." Already astride her bicycle, Ciara tried to squeeze past.

"We'll drop you off on our way to Windy City Alarms." Erin blocked her path.

"I'm going to feel like I'm living in Fort Knox." She flicked the handlebar bell with her thumb.

"The new alarm will be temporary. Just basic surveillance equipment. Allie's business insurance requires it." That part wasn't exactly true. There was no insurance. Not yet anyway.

"It's only a twenty minute ride to the university and I promise not to go anywhere near Beverly Hills." Ciara backed up and steered to the other side of the driveway.

"You forget that Lily knows where you live." Erin swooped her hand toward the passenger seat. "Come on. It's safer. I promise to pick you up at noon. You won't have to wait."

* * *

Someone else is coming out of the house. She's tall. When she leans over the step, I see her long brown hair. *Holy shit.* I didn't know *she* was here. It's the bitch cop's zombie girlfriend. She was there on

196

the river when my dad was caught. She saw me. Not like other people see me. She looked right inside me. She was the first one who ever did. This can't be a coincidence. Are they all here for me?

Shit. Barbie is putting her bike away. What's my next move? Follow them?

No. This is the perfect chance to get inside that house. I slide my hand into my pocket and caress my knife. All I need is a lighter and a tinder-dry old house.

* * *

Erin held the door wider. Ciara scowled and her shoulders slumped. "All right. Don't get your knickers in a twist." She rolled her bike to the shed. "This is a one off, and I'm only doing it because I trust Allie."

"Thank you," Allie breathed. She pulled the seat forward and slid into the front after Ciara squeezed herself into the back. "I think it's best that you're not on your own right now." She rubbed her temple with taut fingers.

"Headache?" Erin kept one eye on Allie while she backed out the driveway. Allie's attention lingered on the same blue car she'd noticed. She would *definitely* check that out later. "What's going on?"

"I'm not sure. Something feels wrong. I've been thinking about Lily, a lot, but I'm also worried about the other girl. And there's a man. Just when I try to focus on one, the others intrude."

"And you still talk about a baby boy in your dreams." Erin shrugged when Allie shot her a look. She'd hoped that their romantic interlude might help Allie sleep, but it didn't happen. Erin had awoken to her crying out more than once. She'd curled herself around Allie and gone back to sleep.

"I'm confused." Allie tilted her head back and exhaled. "The only thing I was really sure about this morning was that Ciara shouldn't ride her bike."

"This is what your headaches are about?" Ciara piped up from the back. "You're psychic. I often wondered."

"Well, I'm not sure I'd use that word. I don't see dead people or anything." Allie turned to face her friend. "It's just intuition. That's all."

"Uh huh. I was your roommate long enough to know it's more

than intuition but I got the impression you didn't want to talk about it."

"You were right. It's hard for me to understand what it all means." Allie flipped her hair over her shoulders and wrapped it into a ponytail. "And it's even harder to explain to someone else."

"She wouldn't even talk to me about it for the longest time." Erin pulled up in front of the university and let Ciara out.

"Don't worry about picking me up. I can catch a ride with Raphael." Ciara slung her army surplus messenger bag over her shoulder. "I'll take care of the office this afternoon."

"Raphael? Isn't that Mr. Vargas' first name?" Allie's eyes widened. "Are you dating my client?"

"We'll talk later." Ciara winked.

Allie opened her mouth to speak and closed it. She shook her head as her friend strode away in her pink taffeta skirt and combat boots.

"She's growing on me." Erin grinned. "Anyone with the nerve to dress like that deserves my respect. Or the attention of the men with the really long-sleeved white coats." Erin mimicked a struggle with a straitjacket.

Allie pinched her arm. "You like Ciara, admit it."

"She's a bit radical," Erin began, and Allie pinched her again. "But yeah, I like her. Mostly because she's nice to you. You would have figured out what was going on between those two if you hadn't been so distracted by Lily. Now let's go get that surveillance equipment you said we needed."

"I don't think I worded it quite like that. I think I said that Ciara's home was vulnerable."

Erin tallied up the items they'd need to buy. Allie wouldn't want her to overdo it, but they needed cameras, indoor and outdoor sensors, a wireless control panel, and a better lock for the door. Maybe even security lighting. She could monitor and control it all from her smartphone. If Ciara didn't want to keep it, they could take it back to Morley Falls with them. It was long past time to replace their decrepit home alarm.

"Huh?" Erin was vaguely aware that Allie had said something.

"Are you planning all the equipment you'll buy, that we don't really need?" Allie's mouth twisted sideways in a wry grin.

"Maybe." And maybe she could keep it under five hundred dollars. "Let's make it quick. The critters were cuddled up on my pillow when we left but I don't want to leave them alone too long. I'm not confident that the dog's house-trained."

"He still needs a name." Allie's brow puckered. "The dog. The cat. There's something happening."

"Are you having a vision of the dog peeing on my sandals?" Erin snorted. What could the two rascals possibly do that would top the great fish caper?

"I don't know." Allie massaged the back of her neck. "Every time I try to divert my attention, it all snaps back to Lily. I don't understand what she's up to but I sure feel a lot of strong energy surrounding her."

"Let's stop at the alarm store and then take a drive over to Beverly Hills. If she's around, you're bound to pick up some vibes or something."

"Vibes." Allie blinked hard. "You make it sound like feel-good hippie vibes. Believe me, it does not feel good."

"I'm sorry Baby." Erin reached out for her hand.

She gripped it and took a deep breath.

* * *

Allie hurried to the passenger side. "I'm proud of you, Honey. You didn't break your five hundred dollar limit." Pressure made her head throb. Some people's knees ached before a rainstorm. She got an aching head before an energy storm. Something was brewing. It was big, and Lily was at the center.

Erin loaded the boxes of electronic equipment behind the seat of her truck. "Five hundred Canadian dollars. That's what, sixteen bucks U.S.?" She smirked and got behind the wheel.

"Very funny. The value of our currency is not really that different." Allie gave a half-hearted grin. It was hard to make jokes while your skull imploded.

"You look really stressed. Is your headache getting worse?"

Erin's blue eyes reflected the sky, the opposite color of the cloud in Allie's brain. The disjoint was disconcerting. Here they were, together on a beautiful summer day. Birds sang, kids played in the streets, but a dark tempest threatened. "Every day it seems worse. I can't shake it. I can't concentrate on anything. Everything is about Lily. She's up to something right now, and I get the feeling that she's watching us."

Erin's head swiveled to the side window. "I'll set up the alarm system today. If you help me program the electronics, it'll be done in a fraction of the time." She turned the truck onto the perimeter highway and headed toward the airport. "Let's check out this infamous Beverly Hills."

"That's where Lily's friend lives," Allie blurted. The name wavered on the edge of her mind and came to her like individual letters reconstituting one by one.

Erin peeked at her out of the corner of her eye. "You know, I saw this documentary on TV once where a psychic just drove around until he eventually ended up at the location where a lost child could be found."

"I'm not psychic." Allie leaned back in her seat. Why was Erin trying to make her gift into more than it was? "I just feel things sometimes. It's totally random. I'm not a tracking dog that can find missing people by sniffing their underwear."

"So you say." Erin arched an eyebrow. The corner of her mouth lifted in amusement.

"Fine. You drive and I'll tell you if I *smell* anything." This was never going to work. "Oh, there it is. It's not Beverly Hills. The sign says North-something Estates. You can't tell from all the spray paint."

"It's Northview. Barb said that Albert dropped Lily off here once. She didn't say which house."

"Oh my gosh. Look at that park." Allie pointed to a grassy area with couple of deformed bushes and a bench. Multi-colored graffiti covered every square inch of it. "She's been there. A lot." Plastic bags trapped in the chain link fence fluttered in the breeze. Ahead, the entire building complex consumed a couple of blocks of high-density, low-rent, housing.

"Wow, I'd hate to take all the vandalism complaints in this neighborhood. Every second car has some sort of body damage or a taped-up window." Erin pointed to a car on blocks in a driveway. All four tires were missing.

"There is so much negative energy here. How will I ever be able to tell?" It was like the time she went scuba diving in Mexico, trapped inside a foggy mask, ninety feet down. The pressure of nearly three atmospheres compressed her lungs. She was acutely aware of the effort it took for every single breath.

"Did you forget? You've done this before. You weren't even trying. Remember the boy you saved from the van? You led the way. Don't try to think. Just feel."

The boy in the submerged van. He'd nearly died. Her dream from the previous night surfaced. Death loomed. Was she simply remembering that event, or was there another child?

Allie inhaled enough air to fill her lungs. Something changed her vision, or did Erin slow down? Concentrating on one side of the road, she focused on the energy radiating from each house as they passed.

Sadness, boredom, grief, fear. Dark whirlwinds in various shades of gray assailed her. A cat slunk along a fence line and disappeared into the yard. This was not a happy neighborhood.

A block from the park, a half-dozen boys took turns practicing bicycle tricks. They stopped and stared when the truck passed. One of the smaller boys grabbed his crotch and shouted something.

"Nice neighborhood." Erin hit the brakes when he tried to hang onto the bumper for a free ride.

"Chicken!" He let go and slapped the tailgate with his hand.

"Future inmate." Erin hit the gas for space between them before she slowed again. She drove down the block and doubled back on a parallel street. "So… talk to me."

"One of those boys is hanging out on the street because he's afraid to go home." Allie had seen the fear, bright jagged colors surrounding the boy who'd grabbed the bumper. A cloud of utter despondency shrouded a home with aluminum foil covering the windows.

"Depressing neighborhood."

Allie pointed to a house with an upside down number. "There's something bad going on there." The huddled image of a child flashed on her retina, then faded.

Erin stomped on the brake.

"It's not the one we're looking for, and no we can't help."

Erin eased her foot back onto the gas pedal. "Is it like this in your head all the time? How do you function?"

"As you know, I've gotten very good at blocking things out.

Strong emotions leak through, but this is different. I'm *trying* to focus but I've spent so much time blocking things that it's hard to let them in. I feel like I'm on a horrible amusement park ride, underwater. And it hurts. How many more streets are there?"

"This is the last one. I'd hate to have your gift."

A corner unit with a dented red van in the driveway emanated gloom. Despondence. Fear. Anger. Like a living organism, it throbbed with pure hatred. "Stop!" Allie closed her eyes and wrapped her arms around her chest. "The darkness here is more familiar than the rest."

"Is she here?"

"She was. But not now."

Erin grabbed a pen from the console and rifled through the glove box. She finally scribbled down the address and license plate number on the inside of her wrist.

"Your notebook is at home on the dresser."

"I'll bet you've never lost anything in your life."

"Aside from my mother and my dog? No, I haven't lost a thing." Why had she said that? She wasn't prone to hurtful sarcasm. Was the horrible atmosphere getting to her? She'd had enough. She needed to shut it down. Block it out.

"I didn't mean..." Erin's eyes puckered at the corners.

"I'm sorry." Allie said. "I think this place is getting to me. I'm not used to so much negativity coming from so many directions. It's worse than sitting in the parking lot of the prison waiting for you to talk to Derek Peterson."

Erin nodded.

"At least then I could distract myself with a good lezzie book on my computer tablet."

"You can download another one to *cleanse* your mind when we get back. I hear your favorite author has published a new one. Something about two musicians falling in love."

"Nothing can top the pirate wench in the novel I read outside the prison." Allie felt the heavy weight on her body begin to lift. Distraction was always effective. "Keep talking and maybe I'll get rid of this headache."

"And what about the pirate captain? She was hot." The corner of Erin's eyebrow lifted.

"You read it too!" Allie allowed herself to smile. "I thought you said, and I quote, *lesbian romances are mindless drivel.*"

"Well, it was there, and I had time, and I kind of got into the story…"

Allie patted her knee. "Admit it."

"Okay, I liked it," Erin grumbled.

"Don't worry, I won't tell a soul." An image of her cat flashed through her mind. Rachel was up to something, and the dog was fully complicit. A dark shadow sliced through the images. "We need to get home. Now."

CHAPTER 27

Derek rubbed his jaw. The spot where he'd bit down on the rusty nail in his sandwich still hurt. His tongue constantly caught on a jagged edge in the middle of his molar. He'd probably cracked it.

It wasn't as if he could just pop over and see his regular dentist. He was in prison. In prison, you had to file a request and wait. And wait some more.

What difference did it make anyhow? He couldn't eat much. Since he'd mangled his tooth, he'd discovered worse things in his food. A rat's tail, a shred of what looked like someone's underwear, and so many fingernail clippings he'd lost count. He didn't want to imagine what was in his soup.

He stood to pace and tucked his thumb through a belt loop. He'd lost so much weight that his pants hung from his hips but the guards wouldn't give him a goddamn belt. *You might hang yourself*, they said. As if he needed to do *that* to end his life. If he wanted to commit suicide, all he had to do was eat what was on his plate.

There were two things that encouraged him to live. The hope that he could somehow be with his wife and daughter, and breakfast. Badger, a.k.a. Ethan Lewis, didn't have any buddies on breakfast detail. No one to piss in his soup, no one to contaminate his food, and no one to threaten him when they brought his meals.

Derek waited like a kid at Christmas for that blessed sound in the morning. Santa and his sleigh. The uncontaminated food cart rattling from cell to cell. Steve, the breakfast guy, actually said hello when he dropped off his scrambled eggs. He didn't shove his tray through the slot so everything spilled on the floor. He delivered the coffee still hot. If Derek ever got out of this place, he would send Steve a carton of cigarettes.

"Inmate Peterson."

Derek froze mid-stride when his name boomed through the cell's intercom. He looked at the camera mounted on the wall. Had he done something wrong?

"Prepare for transport."

Transport. What did that mean? Was he going back into general population? *What the hell was going on?* Was he coming back? He grabbed the photo of Lily and the drawing she'd made for him, shoved them in his sagging shirt pocket and stood by the door. With his wrists through the slot, he waited.

A guard sauntered down the hall. He spun a set of handcuffs on his fingers. "It's your lucky day." He snapped them around Derek's wrists.

Lucky? How?

"Yeah, usually it takes a lot longer to get into the dentist but there's a new doc and he's chomping at the bit to pull some teeth." He smirked at Derek. "You ready for that?"

Was he? He'd pull out the damn tooth himself if he had a pair of pliers. The dentist. Derek's tooth throbbed at the welcome news. He practically skipped on his way to the medical wing.

He didn't even turn his head when some dirt bag mopping the floor hissed at him. Today, he didn't care what *Badger gonna do.* He was getting this tooth pulled. No more cutting his tongue. No more jaw pain.

He still had his breakfasts. He would survive. Badger could go to hell.

The dental suite was quiet. Goosebumps rose on Derek's skin when the guard slammed the door behind him. There was no dentist. He was still handcuffed. Something was wrong.

"Hey!" He called out but the guard was gone. He pressed his cheek to the glass window in the reinforced door. "Where's the dentist?"

He whirled at the scraping of steel behind him. Ethan Lewis. In one hand Badger held something shiny, a dental tool of some kind. All that mattered was the point at the end.

"Ethan." Derek deliberately used the inmate's real name. There was no sense in stroking his ego. He backed off and the other inmate sneered.

Which knee was the damaged one? He couldn't remember. Maybe if Ethan took a step, he'd be able to tell.

"Don't fucking call me that. My name's Badger."

Derek sidestepped when the weapon buzzed the air beside his ear. He backed off another step and circled to the right.

Ethan hopped to close the distance. *Right.* It was the right knee. He held the tool in front of him like a knife.

"You want to do a remake of West Side Story, right here?" Derek circled again. Maybe there was another tool where Ethan had gotten that one. He chanced a quick look at the instrument tray beside the dentist's chair. Empty. Only one had been left out, just for Ethan.

Derek had been so excited about seeing the dentist, he didn't pay attention to the guard that brought him. Was it the same one who'd trapped him in the stairwell? How much did an inmate pay to buy a guard? Probably a lot. On the streets, he never forgot a face. In here, his instincts were shot.

"I don't know what movie you're talking about." Ethan tossed the weapon to his other hand and took a swipe at Derek.

"It's not a movie, you uncultured loser."

"Whatever." Ethan spit on the floor. "How about we make our own movie right here? Pig dies in Oak Park Heights."

Derek clenched his fists. This dirt bag sure liked the sound of his own voice. He needed to shut up.

Ethan tossed the weapon back to the first hand and bared his teeth. "You're gonna die."

He sounded just like the asshole that had delivered his sandwich with metal shavings yesterday. Derek turned sideways and kicked out as hard as he could. This time he wasn't aiming for Ethan's knee, but Ethan hopped to protect it anyways.

The sole of Derek's running shoe connected with Ethan's right hand and the weapon clattered to the floor. Ethan dove for it but Derek was ready. He leapt on him and wrapped his cuffed wrists around Ethan's neck. They tumbled to the floor and Derek increased the pressure until Ethan whimpered like a child.

Keys rattled in the door behind him. *Guards.*

"Stop. Don't make me hurt you." Derek eased off.

Ethan twisted from his arms and reached for the weapon. His

fingers were inches away.

Derek kicked him in the head and wrapped his thighs around his chest. He squeezed until Ethan's face was purple.

The lock turned and the door swung open.

Two new guards stood open-mouthed. "What the hell?" They backed away and one thumbed the mike on his radio.

In twenty seconds, the room would be crawling with the Emergency Response Team.

Derek would be boarded again. He let go and rolled over.

Ethan gasped for air, his hands to his throat where the cuffs had abraded his skin. He glanced at the open doorway and back at Derek.

They could both hear the call for E.R.T. They both knew it was a matter of seconds. Derek shook his head. *Don't.*

Ethan snarled and came at him one last time. His fingers clawed Derek's vulnerable eyes. Derek clenched them tight and whipped his head away. Pain tore at the side of his head. He kicked out blindly. His elbows skidded on something warm and slippery. Something wet. He opened his eyes.

Ethan leaned over him and spit out a chunk of bloody tissue. His eyes were as wild as a lunatic's.

Blood poured down the side of Derek's neck. His ear. The insane bastard had bitten his ear. He aimed his heel at Ethan's face and made sure it connected dead center.

Ethan's nose twisted sideways and he crashed backward, motionless.

An army of boots thundered in the hall. The cavalry was here. Derek pressed his hand to his head and slumped to the floor. If he didn't get out of here soon, there was no question. He'd be dead.

CHAPTER 28

My shoulders are square, my back straight, and I have a smile on my face. I'm just here to visit my friend. At least that's what it'll look like if a nosy neighbor spies me from their window. I saunter into the bitch cop's back yard and up onto the step. I rap my knuckles on the screen door, but I don't expect an answer. All the while, I take in everything around me. The step's busted, the house looks like shit, but whoa, what do we have here?

I back off the step and inspect the electric meter. A wire feeds over to a gray plastic box screwed into the siding. Wires snake out the bottom, form a perfect loop and continue to a second box. What the hell is that? I'm always watching for security systems but I've never seen one like this before. It's not like they would be nice enough to put a label on it.

I can't get into the box without a screwdriver but I can fuck it up. With the tip of my knife, I pry one of the staples from the siding and tug on the wire. It holds firm. Beside the step is a wooden handle from a broom or a mop. That will work. I insert it through the loop and twist it like a garrote around the cop's throat. In three turns, the wires tear loose from the bottom of the panel and the red light goes out. My heart skips a beat every time something dies. This counts.

With one ear to the wall, I hold my breath and listen. No alarm bells clang. The house is silent as death. I toss the handle into the grass on my way back up the step and shove my knife through the space between the latch and the striker plate. With my skill, it's open in seconds. I step in and close the door behind me.

This is only a crappy old house. How could it be the command center for a police operation? A shiny coffee machine on the kitchen counter looks like a friggin' space ship. Who likes coffee that much? Cops do. Officer Erin Ericsson lives here.

My gut tilts sideways. I stab my knife into the table, scraping the finish all the way to the edge. I kick a chair over for good measure and stomp it until leg cracks. *Sit on that, bitch.*

Something skitters across the hallway and I hug the wall in the corner. Is someone else in here? I hadn't considered that. I grip the handle of my knife and peek around the doorframe. There's a gray flash at the end of the hall. A cat. Or a rabbit. It's moving so fast it's hard to tell.

I step out and squat, knife held loosely in my hand. I never skinned a cat before. My grandfather knew better than to let me have a pet, no matter how many times I asked.

"Here kitty."

Toenails scrabble across hardwood and a black nose peeps out from the doorway. What happened to the gray flash? Is it a dog? I try again.

"Here doggie."

The corner of an ear twitches above the nose.

"Come and get some candy." I hold my hand out but he knows as well as I do that there's nothing in it. The nose disappears back into the room.

"Fe Fi Fo Fum."

In five giant steps, I'm down the hallway and pounce into the bedroom. Nothing. On my knees, I check under the bed. Where the hell did he go? I crawl over and yank open the closet. Clothes hang in perfect military lines but there is no stupid dog. No longer a giant, now I feel like Elmer Fudd looking for Bugs Bunny. I don't like being made fun of. Toenails scamper across hardwood. He's a wascally wabbit, but I'll catch him.

Back on my feet, I'm ready to leave when I spot it. A notebook with Morley Falls PD embossed on the front cover. It's hers. *She* had it on her the last time I saw her. Making friggin' notes about my life. It's none of her business. What did she write about me? I flip through pages but it's like she writes in Egyptian and I can't read more than two or three words at a time. It's worse than a doctor's handwriting. I don't even see my name anywhere. There's a lot of initials and numbers and dates and times. How is anyone supposed to read this?

I rip out a fistful of pages and throw them into the air like snowflakes. I slice through the bedspread and stab the pillow until I'm exhausted. It's more work than you'd think, and not really worth the effort. I empty the dresser drawers instead. Ain't nothing here I want.

I step to the bathroom and check the medicine cabinet. On the corner by Nina's house, there's always someone looking for drugs. Maybe there's something I can sell. I dump everything from the shelves into the sink and sift through the containers. There are things for chapped lips and removing nail polish. Another bottle holds headache pills. The same crap you can pick up in any convenience store. Useless. I plug the drain with toilet paper and leave the water running. That's the penalty.

The bedroom upstairs is worse than the first. Clothes are jumbled into a laundry basket and the closet is a mess. There is no dog, cat or rabbit in here either.

The last room has the door closed. That must mean something. *Bonus.* The command center. Computer equipment clutters one whole end of an L-shaped desk with three big monitors lined up. Coils of cable tangle behind half a dozen towers in a row. Red and green lights flash randomly from everything. This setup could land the space shuttle.

I shove a monitor and it dangles off the edge of the desk, saved by its safety net of attached wires. One shoe in the air, I aim a kick at the screen but the room's too small for acrobatics.

I've got one foot in the air and don't even see it coming. The gray furry flash zips past and my pant leg twists like I've been hit by the Tasmanian Devil. It's enough to screw with my balance and I land on the floor by the office chair, left arm crumpled beneath me.

"Son of a bitch!"

Did I bust my goddamn shoulder? I use up every single cuss word I know by the time I wrestle my way back to my feet. It's a good thing I'm right-handed. I'll make him pay.

"Here wabbit." There's an answering thump in the kitchen. "Gotcha." There is no way I'm letting him past me. He's trapped. I cartoon strut to the entrance, knife gripped hard in my good hand. The kitchen is empty. How can that be? Over my shoulder the hallway is silent. I swivel back. I'm sure he's in here. In the middle of the room, I turn in a circle, knife held out. "Come out. I want to make myself a pair of slippers."

The house is so quiet I can hear the water running in the bathroom sink. I'll stand stock-still to wait him out. The digital clock on the stove changes. One minute. Two. There is the slightest sound from below, like an animal shifting its weight. Without making a sound, I reach for the handle.

Ping!

I jump like a scared deer and instantly hate myself. On the floor at my feet a metal screw rolls to a stop. I look around, look up. Who threw that? I spin around to the hallway. A puddle of water has already spread across from the bathroom. There are no wet tracks running through it. I circle to the back door. It's still closed.

Plunk!

Something bounces off my head and I whirl around. Who is messing with me? Where are they hiding? I look back at the bottom cabinet. Someone small. I kick the door and am rewarded with the shuffling of tiny feet.

Found you.

I flick the door open with my knife and it bounces back on its hinges. I bat aside a box of cereal, two jars of peanut butter.

Scheisse!

Sharp spikes pierce my skin and I snatch my hand back. Droplets of blood ooze from two punctures and I stare like a thirsty vampire. My heart pounds in my ears. The color is darker than I remembered. I imagine it sprayed across the wall. Flooding from the bathroom sink like a gushing wound.

My stomach gurgles and there's a low hum in my throat. How long have I been crouched here staring at the blood? I wipe my hand on the cereal box and dump it on its side. What the hell hit me? The cabinet is empty. A ragged hole in the back is not big enough for a dog. Was it a rattler? I saw that movie about snakes. I'm not sticking my fingers in there.

Two more drops of blood seep through the cut and drizzle down the side of my hand. Did something really bite me? A snake? *Ridiculous.* Could I have just scratched myself on a nail? I'm losing my mind. My throat's dry. My shoulder aches. The lack of sleep for the past few days has caught up with me. I need a drink.

Bloody thumb in my mouth, I open the fridge. On the middle shelf are three bottles that might be beer. I slide my knife onto the counter and pick one up. On the label, above a picture of a fish, it says *Raspberry Cream Ale*. The alcohol content is a whopping seven percent. Raspberry fish beer sounds weird but seven percent alcohol sounds great.

My left shoulder is gorked so I sandwich the bottle between the countertop and my belly to twist off the cap. It does taste like raspberry. I was hoping it would taste like Budweiser. This is pussy beer, but it's pussy beer with a kick. One by one, I place the other two bottles by the door. Nina will like them if they taste fruity.

I consider the fact that I'm hung over and I haven't slept much lately, but I'm sure I didn't dream the friggin' Tasmanian Devil. My messed up shoulder is proof. And what about the creature with the big ears? Did I hallucinate that? Maybe I did. It's obvious there is no dog here. Just me and the devil.

The clock says I've already been in here three quarters of an hour. I haven't done half of what I wanted. I wanted to burn this shit down, but it's time to get out. Who knows when the bitch cop will be back? With my good arm, I scoop my beer off the floor and tuck it close.

Thump! Screeek!

The noise shoots spikes of excitement through my system. The devil is back. *I'll kill him.* I leap around, ready to stomp the life out of whatever awaits me. The kitchen is empty.

What the fuck is going on? Is this place haunted by a freakin' ghost? Are those bitches witches? Prickles run up my backbone and I feel cold. This is like that movie where the guy gets ripped to bloody shreds by a poltergeist.

Who haunts me? I'll torch this whole goddamn place. I reach into my pocket for my lighter. The one I stole from the gas station to finish Barb. My hand shakes when I realize that it's the same. This is exactly the same as the lighter I took from my mother's purse that day. The day she fell…

Just say it.

I shake my head. She left me.

You did it.

Eyes squeezed tight, I shout the words. "I killed her!"

Spit flecks my lips with the force of my words. I pushed her fat ass into the swamp and smashed the life from her skull. She'll stay in her mucky grave until the end of time.

Or will she? I turn slowly, ever so slowly to look behind me. Everything is the same as it was a minute ago. There are no chairs floating in the air, no rattling chains. I snort through my nose. My mother's ghost is not here. I adjust the weight of the beer bottles tucked into my elbow and jut out my jaw.

On the fence outside the window, two crows squawk. Their beaks point right at me. Everyone knows what that means.

I stare at my mother's lighter in my trembling hand. Is this what remorse feels like? Or fear? Whatever it is, I'm not used to it, and I don't like it. I imagine my breath steams in the suddenly icy air. Claws scratch against wood somewhere inside the walls and my backbone stiffens.

Fuck this. I'm getting the hell out.

I drop the lighter back into my pocket and reach for my knife. The counter is empty but I run my hand across it anyway. I swear to God I put it there. Before I opened the fridge. I'm positive. Do ghosts steal knives? What about the Tasmanian Devil? Was that even real?

Right on cue, there's an eerie thump inside the cabinet. I ain't looking in there again. From the drawer, I grab a paring knife and slide it into my sleeve.

My grandfather would never have approved of this cheap piece of crap. He would have said, *If you're gonna use a knife, use a good one.* One with a tang that goes all the way through the handle. Well, he's not here right now is he? He left me too…

Say it. Say it Say it!

He didn't leave me. I poisoned him. Is he dead? Are they both haunting me?

Holy shit! Is this what it feels like to go insane?

Knife in my sleeve, arm wrapped around my precious beer, I back toward the door. One foot behind the other I shove it open with my ass. I'm not taking my eyes off this freakin' kitchen. If something comes for me, I wanna see it.

I jump when the door slams shut behind me and the crows take flight. Their black wings create air currents and a single tainted feather falls to the ground at my feet.

I sprint for the car as if the Tasmanian Devil himself is on my tail.

CHAPTER 29

"Did you forget to lock the door?" Arms full of electronic equipment, Erin toed the back door. With no resistance, it thudded open. She frowned her annoyance at Allie. "You were the last one out..."

"I locked it. You have me trained." Beside her, Allie laid her boxes down and stepped back. "Something happened."

"So, the dog *did* pee on my sandals while we were out?"

"No, it's not the dog," Allie whispered.

"Rachel." Erin stalked into the kitchen and slid her armload to the table. Beside an overturned chair, the cat peered up at her. "Is that your innocent face?" She righted the chair and it yawed to the left.

The cat mewed and settled to her haunches. She twitched smug whiskers, claiming the tiles in front of the cabinet. She was hunkered down for the long haul. Erin cracked the door open behind the cat. The peanut butter was still there, the box of cereal on its side. She narrowed her eyes.

"I'm not buying it. What else have you done?" One glance down the hallway confirmed Erin's suspicion. She splashed through a pool of water coming from the bathroom. "Rachel! How did you...?" Medicine bottles bobbed in the sink. She plunged her hand through ice-cold water to clear the drain. "Damn feline..." she muttered through gritted teeth.

Across the hall, the office door yawned open. Erin went rigid. Allie kept that door closed. It was a habit, and everyone in the house respected it as business space. Unless Rachel had grown opposable thumbs, she couldn't be responsible.

"Allie!" she called out. "Stay where you are. I think someone—"

"Lily."

The mere word reverberated all the way to Erin's clenched jaw. She crept to the office and peeked around the frame. The computer monitor twisted in its cables off the edge of the desk raised the hair on the back of her forearms. Add that to the overturned chair behind the desk. There had been a struggle.

She straightened the monitor and backed out the door. What about the bedrooms? The shredded comforter was crumpled on the bed she shared with Allie. Pillows were slashed and stuffing spewed like dandelion fluff.

Her stomach plummeted at the sight of her notebook, half its pages torn out and shredded. She exhaled. It had taken years to modify her neat high school handwriting into the indecipherable scrawl of a police officer. It was the next best thing to locking things up, and it saved time.

The cat had gleefully greeted her in the kitchen, but she hadn't yet found the puppy. He was so young and vulnerable. *Did Lily…?*

"Allie, where's the dog?" Erin's voice rose to panic.

The silence from the kitchen was deafening. Two at a time, she vaulted the stairs to check Ciara's room. It was in its normal state of disarray and she couldn't tell if it was better or worse than when she'd last been up here. But there was no dog.

"Allie!" She tore down the stairs and into the kitchen.

Feet splayed wide, Allie lay flat on her stomach with her head inside the bottom cabinet. Tucked beside her, Rachel's fluffy tail swished with delight.

"What are you doing?" Erin squatted behind her. "Is he in there?"

"Well, sort of." Allie wiggled out enough to let her see, and aimed the LED light from her cell phone at the back of the cabinet. "He's in the wall. Stuck." A shiny black eye and one oversize ear peeped through a jagged cutout in the drywall. Vigorous thrumming on metal pipes suggested the dog happily wagged his tail.

"How did you find him in there? Did he bark?"

"Rachel told me."

"The cat *talks* to you?" Erin had witnessed Allie's intuitive ability first-hand so many times that this didn't seem outside the realm of possibility.

"No, silly." Allie's nose crinkled in amusement. "I just meant that she showed me with her body language."

"Oh." It was not some sort of magic after all.

"You saw her when we came in, didn't you? Rachel was trying to tell us to look in the cabinet." Allie pointed to the square of tiles the cat had been guarding. Was there really a method to the cat's mischief? "It was obvious, wasn't it?"

"Uh, yeah," Erin fibbed. The whole truth was that she'd been blind-sided by the break-in and the flood of water in the hall. She'd missed it.

"And his energy is in there." Allie shrugged.

"Maybe you're not such a bad kitty." Erin stroked Rachel's head and the cat chirped. "Did you hide your little brother in the hole?"

Rachel twitched her tail into Erin's face, the tickling hair less annoying than usual.

"Rachel, you're an angel." Allie slid out and gathered the cat in her arms.

"More like a ninja. That cat knows the inside of that wall like the back of her lonely front paw."

"I wonder how the dog got wedged between the drywall and the abandoned ductwork." Allie scraped out shreds of twisted aluminum foil. "It smells fishy in here."

"Remember the great fish caper? I told you these two critters are in cahoots." Erin pursed her lips to keep from grinning. She retrieved each shred of foil with her fingertips and placed them in the trash.

"Aw come on, Honey. He must have been scared and followed her to hide."

"Look, there's blood." Erin pointed to the overturned cereal box. "And human finger marks. I think it's Lily's blood, not the dog's." She poked at it with the tip of her truck key until it slid onto the floor. She brushed it to the side. "Good boy. Did you get a piece of her?"

"Do you really think he bit Lily?" Allie's eyebrows shot up. "He's just a puppy."

"He's young but he's got canine instincts. If he felt threatened, he might have tried to protect himself."

"Such a tough guy." Allie slowly shook her head. "He's a dog after my own heart. If only he wasn't—"

"Zapping your nervous system every time you touched him?" Erin tilted her head.

"Yes, that." Allie squeezed back in beside Erin. "How in the world do you suppose he got wedged in there?" She shone her light inside and one beady black eye glinted at them.

"I imagine his tail sticking out when the cat cruelly shoved him in from behind." Erin dodged a swipe from Allie.

"Well, he's not too distressed but we need to get him out." Allie opened the drawer and poised her fingers above it. "I don't suppose Ciara would be impressed if I used her bread knife on the wall."

"Would she even notice?" One more bent or abused household item didn't seem a big deal.

Allie withdrew her hand and closed the drawer.

Erin got to her feet. "I'll look for something in the shed." She halted at the sight of the cat tending to a new spot in front of the refrigerator. There were no more pets to be found, so what in the world was that wacky feline doing now? She opened her mouth to tell Allie and closed it. She was no kitty whisperer. If the cat was trying to tell them something, Allie would figure it out. "I'll be back in a minute."

Fifteen minutes and a few scraped knuckles later, they had enlarged the hole using hedge clippers and a small pruning saw. Erin coaxed the excited dog from his hiding place and snuggled him into her chest. As she stroked his hair, her fingers explored for injuries. "You sure have a way of getting yourself into fixes you can't get out of."

"You might consider naming him Murphy. As in Murphy's Law."

"Do you look like a Murphy?" Erin held up the dog. His big ears drooped. "He doesn't like it."

"Who's talking to animals now?" Allie playfully prodded Erin's shoulder and immediately jerked back. "Wow, I almost forgot about that shock. He doesn't look like much, but he's got powerful energy."

"I wish I could see the world as you do, if only for a moment."

"No, you don't." Allie turned away.

"I guess I'd better report this break and enter." Erin set the puppy down and found her cell phone. As in all big cities, the call went directly into the hold queue. She put it on speaker and busied herself examining the bottom cupboard.

Ciara stored little in here. She placed the two jars of peanut butter up onto the counter. She squinted at the smear on the bloodied cereal box. Was that the hint of a ridge pattern? It sure looked like it. From her introductory forensics course she couldn't quite tell if it would be enough for an identification but she could pick out a half dozen points right away. A closer inspection might reveal more. How many points did it take to make a criminal identification in Canada?

She put down the box. Why bother? Lily's prints weren't in the system.

Winnipeg was a big city. Would they send a forensics officer to a break and enter where nothing was stolen and damage was minimal? In a city sometimes known as murder capital of Canada, they might not have the resources.

* * *

Allie kept perfectly still while the dog sniffed around her foot. Could she do it? Was she strong enough? Hand quivering, she reached toward his plaster-dusted muzzle. Energy lapped at her like waves in the ocean. *I'll be burnt to ashes.* "It's like trying to touch the sun." She dropped her hand.

"Maybe I can help. Let's do what we did before. I'll be the buffer in the electrical circuit." Erin slid the phone out of the way. "Are you ready?"

She hesitated and finally nodded back.

Erin scooped the pup into her lap and covered her girlfriend's hand with her own.

Allie jolted upright and stared at the dog. He peered back with iridescent eyes. His fur emanated a radiant glow that intensified the longer she looked at him. Her foster mom had always reminded her to breathe.

She inhaled.

Exhaled.

Just as she'd learned to block out mental intrusions as a child, she melded emotion with thought. Her mind cleared and her muscles relaxed. Like sunshine through a prism, the glow separated into rainbow colors and encircled the three of them. Pure light surrounded them as a single unit. The very air shimmered. Her body was weightless. She squeezed Erin's fingers, not so much for comfort as to keep her feet tethered to the earth.

Allie turned her face to the door. Lily had entered through there. Energy, dark and oily, permeated the house as she explored, ransacked, raged. Her trail lingered like smoke, clung to the spot where they now sat. A dark shadow accompanied the girl, like a separate entity. Was it a disembodied conscience? If so, it was blackened to its core.

There was suddenly not enough air. Her lungs burned. She squeezed her eyes shut.

Gasp!

She fought panic, struggled to keep hold of Erin's hand. The dog whined softly.

Somewhere outside herself were fragments of sound. Erin's voice. It was too far away to understand, but the message came through loud and clear. I'm here. Right beside you.

Colors swirled, broke apart, melded together once more.

Breathe. Concentrate.

Her thoughts snapped into sharp focus. Emotions separated from actions. Allie saw with clarity. Lily had come in while they were gone. She had a knife, a lighter, and a plan to wreak revenge on the police officer who'd come after her. She desperately wanted to kill.

She'd been angry, confused, vengeful, afraid. Afraid? Lily had left before destroying the house because she was afraid. Of what? The puppy had bitten her, the cat had tormented her, but that was not the source of her fear. She had been haunted by thoughts of her grandfather. Thoughts of her mother.

The sound of Lily's panicked voice still echoed against the walls. *I killed her.*

Two black crows witnessed her confession. When she bolted out the door, they took their knowledge to the skies.

Allie opened her eyes, stroked the dog on her lap.

Erin's face was pinched, worried.

She smiled and released the death grip she'd held. Erin's hand must feel—

Wait! The dog? The dog. On her lap. She glanced down and froze.

She filled her lungs. Exhaled. She wanted to inspect her hands to see if her fingers had been burned to stubs, but she knew. Somehow, everything was fine.

"When did this happen?" She jutted her chin at the dog, curled contentedly between her crossed legs. "How?" She hadn't even been aware of him.

"Uh, I couldn't hold him." Erin scratched her eyebrow. "He started whining when your breathing changed and wiggled right out of my arms. Once he was in your lap he settled down. You've been petting him with your free hand for a while."

"Really?" The mental change from panic to clarity. That was the dog. They'd connected. She'd been right. It was powerful. Her heart plummeted when she remembered Lily. Now she understood why thoughts of her had intruded every time she'd tried to focus on the disappearance of her mother. The girl's energy was intertwined because she'd been responsible.

"Lily killed her mother." Allie whispered.

"What?" Erin sat upright.

"I can't explain how I know. Not in a way that wouldn't sound completely insane. I'm convinced that Lily murdered her own mother."

"Holy moly."

"She's been drinking alcohol. She hasn't been sleeping. She's not thinking clearly and she wants to kill."

"What happened in here?"

"She came to destroy the house but the pets distracted her. One minute they were there, the next they weren't."

"Ha. Rachel." Erin chuffed.

"She got confused and then afraid her mother was out to get her. Well, the *ghost* of her mother."

"I swear to God I'll never malign that cat again." Erin crossed her finger over her heart.

"Lily ran out of here like she was being chased by demons."

"Unfortunately, I don't think that will keep her down for long. She's relentless. If she can't get at me, she'll go after someone else. We need to find that person before she hatches a plan."

"I feel that too." Allie gingerly set the dog on the floor. He wagged his tail and circled her. "I also feel that the dog and I have been able to connect."

"You called a truce? He agrees not to incinerate you and you agree to give him attention?" Erin paused. "I'm glad you came to terms. I was concerned."

"I'll always miss Fiona," Allie said hastily, "but I might be ready for a new dog."

Erin scowled at the cell phone on the floor. Its screen no longer glowed but the tinny musical sound coming from the speaker confirmed that she was still on hold. "I think there's an online report form we can fill out." She picked up the phone and disconnected the call.

Out of habit, Allie inched her toes away as the dog trooped past to join the cat. Whiskers almost touching, the animals stared together at the dark space under the fridge.

"This is definitely animal body language. Are you not seeing this?" Erin rocked up to her feet. "Are they trying to *tell* us something?"

So wrapped up in herself, it took Allie a second to reorient to the world outside her mind. "They are. Let's move the fridge."

"The pets are guiding us in home decorating now?" Erin's smart-ass comment wilted on her lips. "Okay, Baby. If you say so." She gripped the ridge around the door and the cat sprang onto the counter to watch. Erin heaved, wrenching the heavy unit back and forth until its electrical cord was taut against the outlet.

The dog's tail beat rapidly with each inch gained. Rachel placed her front paw over the edge and prepared to jump into the void. When their quarry was exposed, both animals exuded delight. Spikes of excited energy flitted from one to the other.

Allie clicked her phone and LED light beamed into the dark space. "This is the most useful app I've ever downloaded—"

"Whoa, what have we got here?" Erin reached behind the back wheel. Half concealed behind a clump of dust, she nudged a black object.

"What is it?" Allie held the light steady and kept her elbow up to ward off the cat. Rachel's whiskers twitched with anticipation. She was seconds away from launching herself down there and messing up everything.

"Hand me something to fish it out with." Between the tight space and the intruding pets, the drawer was out of reach.

Allie contorted herself to block the puppy and hold back the cat. She handed down the first thing she touched. "Here."

"What the fork?" Erin snickered and poked the dessert fork at the clump.

"There's a knife." Not a kitchen knife, this was a hunter's folding knife, meant for serious destruction. Silver recessed screws secured the black molded handle to an exposed four-inch blade. Polished steel glinted to a wicked point. The serrated backside threatened vicious injury.

Erin turned it over with the fork. "Where did this come from?"

"It's Lily's." Allie's brain crackled with the knowledge that this blade had been intended for Ciara. The girl had fantasized about plunging it into her friend's neck, stabbing her to death. Blood spattered the image.

"Why is it here?" Erin hooked a tine through a hole in the butt of the handle and suspended the knife between them.

Allie closed her eyes. "It's the knife Lily had last night. The one she wanted to stab Ciara with."

"Holy crap." Erin dropped the knife to the floor and the dog sniffed it. She pushed it out of reach.

A sour taste rose from Allie's stomach. She swallowed against it. "Today, she would have hurt Rachel. Would have hurt the dog." She wrapped her arms around herself. "I can't bear to think about what might have happened."

Erin speared the knife again and hoisted it to the top of the fridge. "Ciara is safe, and the animals are safe. It sounds like they gave Lily a run for her money." She reached over to pat the cat's head. "Nobody messes with *my* cat."

Allie nodded slowly. "Rachel had swatted the knife under the fridge. Lily was afraid it was the ghost." She frowned. "The ghost of her mother." She paused. "Lily hasn't shown fear of anything else, and we can use this knowledge against her."

"How? Invite her for a séance?" The corner of Erin's mouth twitched.

"I'm not sure, but it's important that we remember." The atmosphere compressed in a micro shockwave and she turned to the open door a moment before Ciara stepped through.

"A séance?" Ciara shook off her denim jacket. "You're not planning some wacky theme party, are you?" The dog raced to tug at her bootlaces and the cat mewed from the edge of the counter. "Count me in." She picked the puppy up and stood close to the counter so Rachel could climb up to her shoulders.

Allie flew at her and hugged the three of them together. "I'm so glad you're okay."

"Quite a greeting." Ciara eyed her.

"For your safety, we need to ask if you can stay with a friend."

Erin's posture straightened as if she wore an invisible uniform. She was in work mode.

"You're having the party without me?" Ciara tucked a lock of red hair behind her ear. Last week it had been black. "If I can come, I'll make the hors d'oeuvres." Could she never be serious? "We could have those teeny tiny— What happened to the fridge?"

"There's been a break-in." Erin described the damage.

Ciara's jaw slackened at the mention of the chair. "It was my grandmother's. It was the only possession I cared about." She sighed. "Maybe I can find some proper glue to fix it."

"I'll help you." Erin touched her shoulder. "And I'll mop up the water in the hall. We'll put the fan on for a few days."

Ciara expressed a complete lack of concern over the hole they'd hacked into the wall behind the bottom cupboard. "Was it your child murderess?"

"I'm afraid so." Erin could have been standing on any street in Morley Falls, breaking the news to a victim of crime.

"I understand your concerns, but I'm not leaving my home."

Erin turned to Allie, her puckered eyebrows begging for backup.

"You're in danger." Allie gripped Ciara by the shoulders. "Lily came after you the other night. She knows who you are now. She might try again."

"I'm not leaving." Ciara shook her head. "But I'll make you a deal." She crossed her tattooed arms.

Erin's shoulders slumped.

"I'll have a friend come stay with me. We can babysit Rachel, and the dog-who-needs-a-name, until you two are done whatever you're doing."

"Do you have someone in mind?" Erin reached for the pocket where she normally kept her police notebook. She dropped her hand.

"Are you sure you want to get this involved with my client?" Allie knew it was inevitable, but she had to ask.

"Raphael is adorable. I just can't keep my hands off him." A sly grin overtook Ciara's mouth. "Besides, he fights MMA on weekends. No child would try messing with him."

"Deal," Allie said. Lily wouldn't come back here. "I'm glad you have a bodyguard tonight, even though he poses a conflict of interest for my company."

"Fine, but I'm still going to install the new security system." Erin indicated the stack of boxes on the scratched table.

"Maybe you can fix the fiber optic connection too." Allie volunteered. "Lily broke it."

"I don't think you need to worry about the handsome Mr. Vargas." Ciara said. "We're working on a proposition for you."

Allie arched an eyebrow.

"He wants us all to get into bed together." Ciara's lips curved into a suggestive bow.

"I sure hope you're speaking figuratively and not literally," Erin said.

"Of course. It's business." Ciara's smirk remained.

Allie shook her head. "We'll talk about this later. Right now, Erin and I have to take care of something, and we're taking the dog."

"Allie, love, you lead the strangest life." She nudged past Erin and opened the fridge. "Aw, my raspberry ale's been nicked." She put a hand on her taffeta-skirted hip. "This is the last straw, I'm calling Raphael to come over straightaway."

CHAPTER 30

As soon as Nina comes to her window, I open my fist and let the rest of the rocks spill to the ground.

"Shhh," she whispers, careful not to touch the bent screen. Since we wrecked it the last time, it's held in place by two wobbly corners. "Can you come back when Beth is asleep?" Her little sister's messy hair bobs up beside her and the kid pushes her wet mouth against the screen. It topples out onto the ground.

I'm balanced on the battered trashcan, trying hard not to tumble off. I'm so goddamned tired and I ain't got time for this. "Are we gonna do this, or what?"

"I have to wait..."

"Get the fuck out here and let's do this."

She narrows her eyes at me.

"If he touches your sister again, it'll be your fault."

Beth starts to cry and both their faces disappear. Nina's comes back a moment later. "I don't like when you swear in front of my sister." She hikes one foot out the window.

"So, don't *make* me." I jump off the pail and a whiff of raspberry fish beer bubbles up from my stomach. Like the ghost, the strange beer haunts me.

Nina hops down, and when I catch her, my sore shoulder feels like it's tearing from its socket. The kitchen knife in my sleeve presses its point into my skin. Do I tell her the Tasmanian Devil attacked me?

She freezes and meets my eyes. She's too busy dealing with her hormones to notice my arm. I stare back without blinking. Like I practiced in the mirror, I squint one eye, just a little, and let her go. She releases her breath.

I need her to follow through with my plan so I'll play along, for a while. With my hand around her sweaty paw, we run to the park where I've been waiting. By the time we get there, her cheeks are pink and her eyes shine with excitement.

I drank another beer on the way, so this is the last. Solemnly, I twist the cap off and hand it over. A gift. To show how much I care. "It's the only one I could get. You can have it all."

She takes a sip. "What are you going to do?"

She stands close. Too close. I edge away and finger the lighter in my pocket. I imagine spurting blood, the sound of shrieking flames, the stink of burning flesh. "We."

"We," she repeats obediently and leans closer.

"Kill him."

She catches her breath and looks at her beer. "I'm not sure."

I give her a shove and she almost falls off the end of the picnic bench. "Don't be a fucking pussy." I hold my palm up like I don't even want to hear her goddamn excuses. "Are you telling me you'll let him keep messing with your baby sister because you're too scared to stop him?"

She eases back over until I feel the heat from her thigh against mine. "I'm sorry." She gulps beer and it gurgles down her throat.

"You know what he's doing to her. He did it to you."

She folds in half, chest on her thighs and wraps her arms around her knees. "He's awful."

"He's a bastard."

"Yes, he's a bastard." She repeats.

"Your mom will never get rid of him. You need to do it."

She sits back up and her eyes burn with anger. She tilts her head back and finishes the bottle. I've seen what one bottle of regular beer will do to her. What will seven percent alcohol raspberry fish beer do?

"Do it for your sister." One final push.

"I wish he was dead."

She said it. She's mine.

Her chest heaves in and out like she's running, but she's sitting still. Her face is so smooth it's scary. A doll in a horror movie.

A quarter moon is up and, from its position, it's almost time. "I have a plan. Come on."

"Are we going to steal a car?"

"What day of the week is it?" Since I bailed out of the motel, my head is scrambled. I've been sleeping in the park in the daytime and hanging out with Nina at night. She babysits her sister too so I don't know when *she* finds time to sleep. She doesn't look tired. She looks like she wants to go ride roller coasters. Or help me steal a car.

"Sunday. Today is Sunday." Her eyebrows tilt into question marks and she puts a hand on my arm. "Are you okay?"

I flinch away like my jacket's on fire. She's not supposed to touch me. "I *know* what friggin' day it is. I was checking to see if *you* knew."

She puts her head down and tucks her hand into her front pocket.

"Sunday is the best day of the week to steal a car." Six blocks from here is a huge Catholic church. The sign out front advertises Sunday night mass at nine. They'll be in there praying and blabbing for hours.

"Why are you taking me to a Spanish language Catholic mass?" Nina slits her eyes.

I waggle my fingers in front of her like a magician. "This is the easiest place I know to find car keys. Maybe we can score ourselves a pimped-out El Camino."

"That's racist." She pauses so I prod her forward, up the wide concrete steps. She stops again at the huge rounded wooden door.

"Come on, don't be a pussy." I pull the handle and shove her inside ahead of me. "All you gotta do is stand there and look pretty. If anyone comes, distract them. I'll find the keys."

"Pretty?" Her face flushes pink and she stands at attention beside the coat racks in the lobby.

One by one, and quick as a professional pickpocket, I check the first row of jackets. A whole shitload of snotty tissues, a couple of cell phones and a gross, disgusting baby soother. I wipe my hand on my pants and hit the next row, pocketing two sets of car keys. Should I find one more?

There's a commotion at the door and I stop dead. A dark-haired man in a suit is talking to Nina. He smiles too much and I can't understand a single word he says. I bet Nina can't either.

"Busco a mi abuela," she blurts, surprising the hell out of me.

He nods his head and rattles off another long string of words that seem to have too many vowels.

"Lo siento." Nina shakes her head.

I pocket a tiny scarf wrapped around a hanger. It has ducks on it so maybe it's a baby cloth. I don't care. As long as it burns. Through a gap in the coats, I watch Nina back toward the door. She shoots a look over at me and the man's head swivels to follow. He reaches out as if he wants to fetch her coat for her and I slither to the end of the row. I'm ready to spring out of hiding and escape.

"Está bien." She pulls open the door. "Me voy."

The door closes behind her and she's gone. She's abandoned me. The man who smiles too much shrugs and goes back inside.

I wait to the count of five and slip out the door after her. She's at the end of the parking lot, sitting by the trunk of a massive poplar tree.

"You chickenshit!" I slug her in the shoulder and she curls into a ball. "You left me!"

"I'm sorry." Her eyes shine with tears. "It was a church. He was so nice. I was afraid God would be angry. I had to get out."

"God?" I never saw that coming. "There is no God. There is just us. And them." I put my hand on her shoulder, like the TV preachers do. If it works for them, it'll work for me.

She straightens up and looks at me.

I pat her on the head. "I didn't know you could speak Spanish."

"I learned it from Dora the Explorer."

That's right. That's the show she was watching with her little sister the first time *I* watched *her*.

A shy smile curves her lips when I laugh.

"I'll take care of you." I pull the two jumbles of keys from my pocket and thumb the unlock buttons on both fobs at the same time. Lights flash on two cars in the lot. "You get to pick."

It ain't no El Camino, but this white Audi is a sight to behold. *Hallelujah for church people.* They got some nice wheels. Nina settles into her cream-colored leather seat and fiddles with the radio controls. Legs crossed, face serious, she looks like she could get used to a ride like this.

"I can imagine you on Wall Street in ten years, wearing one of those stripy power suits. You're so smart, you'll probably be a millionaire."

She looks over at me and I have no idea what that expression on her face means. Either she's flattered, or she thinks I'm crazy. Either way, I don't care. She probably will be a millionaire, but I'll be a billionaire. If you combine Bruce Willis, the girl from Kill Bill, and that girl with the dragon tattoo, that'd be me. I'm going to kick serious ass. No one can stop me. Not even that bitch cop and her crazy girlfriend.

"Will you teach me to drive?"

"No."

She turns away.

"Fine. But you don't start on a car like this."

Her face comes back around.

"I'll take you to Emerald Links and we can race golf carts around all night."

"It's not the same."

"It's all you can handle."

She snorts through her nose but keeps her mouth shut.

The clock on the dash says it's time. Time to get my— *our* money. Time to get rid of Nina's dad. I shut off the radio and turn down the road to the park. The post Nina's dad hit last time, the one I was hiding behind, still dangles from the steel cable that connects it to the next. I rub my head where the scab isn't fully healed. *Fucker.*

At the end of the turnaround, under a burnt-out streetlight, is his van. With no headlights on, it's too dark to see if he's even in it. Something about this whole situation feels creepy. I glance in the rear-view mirror. Is there someone behind that tree, or is it a shadow?

"That's my dad's van," Nina announces. As if she didn't know he'd be here. I told her, didn't I? *Well, fuck it.* She knows now.

"He's going to pay the ultimate price." I shut the headlights off and coast to a stop at the corner. I fiddle with the dash to turn off the interior lights so they won't betray us. He'll never know what hit him.

The van sits there. Silent. Dark. Spiders crawl up my back and I shake the knife out of my sleeve. I double-check for my lighter. I don't want to look at it. It's *not* hers. Not my mother's.

"I don't see him." Leaned forward in her seat, Nina unsnaps her safety belt.

She's ready. I hand her the knife and she holds it like she's going to slice a tomato. Well, she's kinda right. "Wait here. I'll be right back."

I slip out of the car and shut the door without a sound. Nina waits obediently, just like I taught her. I sneak up beside the van and peek through the passenger window.

Is he already dead?

In the driver's seat, Nina's dad is sitting upright in his seat with his neck twisted at an odd angle. I'm wondering if his neck is broken when he coughs and straightens. That's when I notice the half-empty bottle of vodka on the seat, the trail of vomit down his checkered shirt. He's passed out drunk.

There is a white plastic bag on the floor with a note attached. My blackmail money. What a loser. He can't even deliver it without screwing it up. He deserves what he gets.

I ease open the door and pour the rest of the vodka on his shirt. He doesn't even stir. Dead drunk is what he is. He might as well smell as bad as he looks. The cops will think he did this to himself.

I snatch up the bag with a pang of regret that it'll be my last payment. It doesn't feel heavy enough, or the correct shape. It had better be right. The note tears off and flies to the ground. There's no time and I don't care what he had to say, anyway. All I want is the money. I run on panther's feet to a row of bushes and stash it inside.

A moment later, I spring up beside Nina's window and scare the crap out of her. She didn't even see me coming. I'm that good.

She creaks the door open, eyes wide, face pale as the moon, knife in her hand. "Where is he?"

"He's hammered. Totally passed out."

She nods her head like she's not at all surprised that her father is drunk.

"Come on." I hold the door and she hops along behind me in a crouch. At the van, I pop the gas hatch open and unscrew the lid. I stuff the ducky cloth into the hole with my fingers and leave the tail hanging out. I point to the driver's door and give her a shove. "Go kill him."

She stares at me, eyes ready to pop out of their sockets. "Wha... How?"

With one arm around her waist, I steer her to the door and open it, letting it swing wide. I hold my hand like I've got a huge butcher knife and mimic overhand thrusting motions.

She draws in a sharp breath and her whole body trembles. She better not turn pussy now.

"Do it!" I hiss through my teeth, although an atomic bomb wouldn't wake him now. I jab her in the ribs. "Hurry up!"

She opens her mouth and sucks in another breath. "I—"

"Do it!" I close my hand around hers and thrust the knife toward her dad's throat.

She pulls away but it nicks the skin near the collar of his shirt. A drop of blood appears and she rears back. "I changed my—"

With my arm around her waist and my hand wrapped around hers, I push forward again. The knife tears a hole in his breast pocket.

"Nooo!" This time she fights me. Even with my sore shoulder, I'm stronger. I put my weight into it and the knife plunges into his chest.

He groans. There's blood. Lots of it. Just like I hoped.

"Look what you did!" Excitement like I never thought possible sears my veins and my throat opens to howl.

"Stop!" She twists in my arms and pain shoots through my injured shoulder. "You're crazy."

"What did you say?" I slap her in the back of the head.

The knife falls but she doesn't even apologize. She presses her hands to the hole in his shirt. "No! Daddy." Blood gushes between her fingers. She's not supposed to do this. Why isn't she happy?

This is not part of my plan. I slap her again. "Let go. I'm going to torch this."

"Daddy. Daddy. Daddy." She crawls halfway over him, one hand on his chest and one reaching for the seatbelt.

"Let's get out of here." I tug at her ankle but she won't listen. What is wrong with her? We got what we came for. "Let's go!"

I release her leg. She's not who I thought she was. She's a loser. Just like him. I can't believe I fell for it.

I've already got my money. What am I waiting for? I snatch up the knife and wipe the blood on his shirt. My grandfather said you must always keep the blade clean. I shove it into the front of my pants, between the belt and buckle.

I don't need her. I don't need anyone.

I reach into my pocket for the lighter and flick it.

CHAPTER 31

"Turn left, no right." Allie clutched the dog to her chest. He nosed the air and his tail stood straight up.

Halfway into a turn, Erin wrenched the wheel the opposite direction and made the corner, tires bumping over the curb. "I called Zimmerman before we left. He gave me the mobile number of his Winnipeg Police contact, in case…"

The image of a laughing, curly-haired baby boy materialized in Allie's mind. The baby suddenly turned blue. "Is Gina okay?" she blurted. Where had that thought come from? Why was she thinking of Gina at a time like this?

"Uh, he *did* mention Gina. She's had premature contractions. Nothing to worry about, the doctor said." Erin frowned. "Can we stay on task and worry about your baby fixation later?"

"I'm sorry. It just popped into my mind. I'm having trouble focusing. I'll try harder." She hugged the dog and he peered left. Allie pointed in that direction. "Go over the bridge and take the first left."

"Attagirl. That dog's like a cross between my dad's fish finder and the radar I use to catch speeders."

"I hope he's as accurate." Allie stroked a velvety ear.

"Actually, I don't think he's the one locating Lily at all. You're doing all the work. All he's doing is reading you."

"Do you imagine that's how it works?" Allie didn't fully understand how her gift worked. It just was.

"You know how dogs can sense things people can't?"

"Of course. Dogs have a keen sense of smell. Some can detect cancer, or even if their owner is about to have a seizure."

"Well, I think this is like that." Erin shrugged.

Was it that simple?

"I think the dog is reading you. He can sense some sort of energy or scent, or whatever you give off, long before you're aware."

"Really?" Pressure in her skull increased and Allie massaged a temple. "Drive faster."

Stopped at a red light, Erin looked both ways and then snuck through. "Your foster parents used to joke about your two-second warning for trouble." She pressed the gas pedal and the truck grumbled with the increased speed. "Maybe the dog can give you more time."

Allie stared at her. More time. That could change everything.

Frown lines marred Erin's smooth forehead. "Should I be turning or something? We're almost at the park."

On Allie's lap, the dog whined and climbed on the door to see out the window. "The park. Yes. That's where we need to go." They left the residential area behind and now trees dotted both sides of the road. With streetlights spread further apart, it appeared dark, ominous.

"Are you ready for this?" Erin reached over to touch Allie's hand and drew in a breath. "Your hand is hot." She laid her fingers against Allie's cheek. "Your face is flushed. You're burning up. Do you feel it?"

"Fire." Allie saw orange flames licking, black smoke curling into the air. "Hurry, we must stop her."

Erin put her hand back on the steering wheel and rounded the last corner. She braked behind a white luxury car and pulled the door latch to get out.

Allie laid a hand on her thigh. "No, leave this one." She pointed ahead to where the truck's headlamps splashed light on a dirty work van.

Figures silhouetted in the driver's open doorway. The girl with hair like fire. Her father.

Lily overpowered the whole scene with the stench of her hate. She separated from the others and flitted into the darkness.

Erin slammed the shifter into park and wrenched her door open.

"Catch her." Allie urged.

Erin sprinted as soon as her runners hit the pavement.

* * *

I hold the flame to the cloth stuffed in the gas tank and the tip glows red. Lights from a truck expose me. Someone's coming.

Vaulting over the fence, I make for the bushes where I've stashed the money and grab the bag. Excitement bubbles in my veins. I'll sit on the hill and watch the fire as I count my million dollars. That's what I'll do.

I find a spot with a good view of the parking lot and settle down. Something rustles in the leaves and I freeze but it's only a rabbit. At least it's not a bird. I hate birds. There's just something about them that freaks me out.

I settle in a new spot. Nina is still trying to stop the bleeding, trying to pull her dad out. Two losers, together.

Sparks spurt from the back of the van where the rag is smoldering. Why does it take so long? Is it because I stole it from a church? Is God angry? Is the ghost of my mother out there, working against me? Nah, there's no such thing as ghosts.

I force a smile to my face and untie the knot in the top of the bag. This is the big time. I never imagined a million dollars would feel like this. It's so light. Maybe it's all hundreds. Or thousand dollar bills. I saw one once on TV. It was sweet.

What's this? I rip the folded up newspaper from the bag and tear it apart. Horrible smelling goo is at the center. There is no money. Wrapped inside is a pile of dog shit! This is like Nina's dad sticking his middle finger up at me. He was never going to pay. I jump to my feet. I hate him so much. I want to run back down this hill right now and stab him in the neck a million times. Once for every dollar he owes me.

My body shakes but I don't move a muscle. There are people down there. One of them turns and starts toward me.

It's her.

* * *

Allie shifted the dog from her lap and locked the door behind her. She ran to the figures in the van. Light spilled from the open doorway onto a gruesome scene. A young girl with red hair worked frantically to stem the flow of blood from a man's chest. He batted her with a dazed fist. The stench of liquor stung her nostrils.

This was the girl she had dreamt of. The name that had been on the tip of her tongue formed in her mind. *Could it be Nina?* The man inside was her father, and he was dying. Nina tugged at his shoulders and his head bobbed forward. Foam flecked with pink spewed from his mouth to his chin. Already he was taking his last breaths. His energy waned to a pinprick and folded into itself. There was a disturbance in the atmosphere and then a moment of stillness. It was as if time stopped.

Allie held her breath. She had never before witnessed death. Never at the point where life left the body, yet she knew it had happened. There were no angels with trumpets here to claim his soul. No demons rising up to claw him home. Just the snuffing of his energy, like a match that has burned and fizzles out. He was gone.

"Daddy!" Nina screamed. The color in the girl's skin blanched and pale interior light cast angular shadows to the ground. Her tangled red hair bobbed when she spotted Allie. "Help me." Her panicked energy was a solar flare in the dark.

"Run!" Allie shouted. She wanted to hold up her arm to shield her eyes. "Run now." She grabbed the girl around the waist and tugged. There was no hope for the man and there was no time. They must get away.

"No."

Ephemeral colors swirled around her in a haze of greasy black smoke. Allie bit down hard, trapping her tongue between her teeth. She tasted blood. They were in danger.

She wrapped her arms around the girl and tore her away from the van, from her father. The girl screamed and flailed against her but Allie didn't stop until they were safely behind Erin's truck.

Inside, the little dog pressed his nose against the glass. His inquisitive energy soothed her. Her breath was ragged, adrenaline surged, and every nerve ending tingled, yet she felt strong.

"Nina. We must stay here."

The girl's head jerked upright at the sound of her name, eyes wide with the shock.

"There is danger." Allie held her when she struggled. "Your father is gone."

Tears streaked the girl's freckled cheeks. "It's my fault."

We'll be safe here. Allie nodded at the thought and sank down, taking the girl with her.

Nina melted into her arms.

* * *

Gravel spun from Erin's runners. Damn, what she wouldn't do to have her pistol with her right now. There was a spark, a flash, and the shadowy figure ducked behind the van. She could hear Allie's raised voice, and she almost turned back. Did her girlfriend need help? Should she abandon pursuit? No, her directions had been loud and clear.

Stop her.

Erin circled the van. Flames spurted from the gas tank. In moments, they would reach the fuel.

"Allie! It's going to burn! Get away!" Could she hear? Was she listening? Did she already know?

On the other side of the van, there was a commotion as Allie struggled with someone. She took a step toward her and stopped.

Catch her.

She had to trust Allie's intuition. She turned and ran to the last spot she'd seen the escaping shadow.

Away from the streetlights, the trees stood in darkness. Erin hurdled the steel cable joining the posts that served as the perimeter of the parking lot.

"Holy shit!" Lily's voice came from up the hill to the right. A grouse sheltered for the night startled into flight, breaking out of a thicket where the girl must be hiding.

Erin stood still and tracked the origin of the sound. The bird's wings beat in a particular thrum that she knew well. Lily was not the only one who had grown up in the woods. Erin raced for the thicket but Lily was gone. She squatted, slid her cell phone from her pocket and dialed the number Zimmerman had given her.

"Constable Audette." His greeting was instantaneous, and brief.

"This is Erin Ericsson, from—"

"I know who you are."

"I got your number—"

"What can I do for you?" His question was polite, the tone abrupt.

"I'm at Riverbank Park. The one past the bridge—"

"I know where it is. What's the problem?"

Erin took a breath. Wherever Lily was, she wasn't making a sound. She had gone to ground. "There is a van on fire here. People are in danger. I'm in foot pursuit of the suspect—"

"Are you serious?"

"Yes! We need backup." Would her tainted reputation get her any help? Had he even listened to what she'd said? "Hurry." She pressed the icon to disconnect and put the phone away. She breathed in and held it. In the distance, a branch creaked. Lily had surfaced and was on the move.

Erin rose to her feet and wove her way through the trees. She heard the soft whip of a conifer branch and changed direction. Brush divided ahead and dark branches jittered against the night sky. Even with a partial moon, her vision adjusted to the dark. She bounded over a fallen tree to soft earth.

Something skittered to her left. A rodent. Or a rabbit. Not a girl. She ignored it and kept true to her course. Near the rise, a twig snapped and then there was silence. The river was not far away now. If Lily made it there, she could escape, carried downstream by the current faster than Erin could follow. If the kid was a good swimmer.

Ahead another twig snapped. Erin broke into a gallop. Lily had the same idea.

At the top of the rise, Erin stumbled and fell to her knees. Over the riverbank, black water rippled. Eddies curled and vanished. Crests in the shallow rapids glittered. The water was fast, and it was high. The bank would be unstable.

Lily was not at the river's edge. A movement in Erin's peripheral vision caught her attention, and she blocked with her forearm. Pain shot to her elbow like an electric bolt. She bent double, cradling her arm.

Lily stepped from her hiding spot, holding a crooked stick. The cold-eyed glare reminded Erin of Derek Peterson, back on the Morley Falls River. He'd attacked her the same way. Like father, like daughter.

"Want more?" Lily swung again, but pulled the strike at the last second.

Erin blocked air.

"Ha." Lily assumed a predator's stance, eerily pale eyes intense in the moonlight. The knees of her dirty jeans were torn and mud smeared her face. Disheveled hair stuck out from her hood. Was she trying to camouflage herself? Had she been sleeping on the street? The smell of liquor wafted between them. She'd been drinking.

Lily circled and Erin pivoted to keep her in front. She jabbed with the end of the stick and Erin dodged. Lily seemed to be favoring one arm. She was injured. Did this teenager believe she could fight a police officer and win? With a stick?

Erin waited. The girl jabbed once more and Erin sidestepped to come in on her left. With one hand on her shoulder and the other on the hem of her hoodie, Erin whirled and threw her into the dirt. A classic judo hip throw. The stick careened into the air, out of reach.

"Fuck!" Beneath her weight, Lily squirmed. She thrashed her legs. She spat. She screamed.

"Stop it."

"I'll kill you, you witch! I'll kill you."

"Hold still. You're hurting yourself," Erin ordered. She adjusted her position and pinned the girl's arms to her body.

A rumble shook the ground, and they both looked to the rise where a black cloud smeared the sky. The burning wick had finally ignited the tank. Sirens wailed. Were they coming? Or going somewhere else?

The girl laughed. "It worked."

Where was Allie? Was she safe?

Lily twisted under her and freed an arm. She raked at Erin's face, nails gouging the skin under her eye.

Close. Erin turned her head.

Lily bared her teeth and bit down on Erin's arm, jaw clamped like a dog. She'd learned that from her Dad too. Her teeth shredded fabric, missing Erin's flesh.

Erin opened her hand and drove her palm into Lily's temple. A stun. The girl's head sank and her eyes rolled back. There would be mere seconds to gain control. Erin flipped her over and brought her to her knees. She wished she had time to search her but Lily was coming around. What she wouldn't give for a set of handcuffs. Zip ties would work too. Why hadn't Allie told her to bring zip ties?

With Lily's arm behind her back, wrist locked for control, Erin waited for the girl to get her bearings and hauled her to her feet. Lily came to her senses, growling like an animal. The hair on the back of

Erin's neck prickled. She steered her toward the approaching sirens. They were coming. Thank God for Constable Audette.

Red and blue lights bounced off trees and Erin picked up the pace. They stumbled over a rock and Lily drove her skull backward. Erin evaded the head butt. The kid was relentless. Being this close made her uncomfortable, and it wasn't just the mud Lily had slathered over her face. Was it her vile body odor or her vicious personality? Erin needed a shower. She couldn't wait to turn her over to the local PD.

More emergency lights joined the ones that had already arrived. The parking lot buzzed with activity when they topped the rise. Plumes of thick smoke rose from the blackened van, its driver's door still hanging open. Behind the wheel, a charred figure leaned sideways, as if his lifeless body sought to escape his scorched coffin.

Lily laughed. "Got you!"

"Shut up." Erin fought the impulse to stun her again.

A single figure slumped in the back of a police cruiser, its dome light flashing. Beside the emergency vehicles, a firefighter rolled up a long hose. Where was Allie? She couldn't see her truck.

"I'm going to fucking kill you." Lily hissed through her teeth. She struggled and Erin put pressure on her arm. "Ow! My shoulder."

"Stop fighting. You're hurting yourself." Erin growled.

"Hey there!" Someone shouted and a man in uniform loped toward them from the parking lot. He shone his flashlight into Erin's face. "Are you Erin?"

"Yes. You must be Constable Audette." She squinted, her night vision ruined. "I've apprehended the suspect I witnessed lighting the fire in that van."

"You weren't exaggerating. We've got another kid in custody and a body in the van. Burnt to a crisp."

A smile touched Lily's lips and faded. She snorted. "Crisp."

Constable Audette shot her a dark look. "The kid we arrested says she's responsible. We found a note near the edge of the park. Looks like it implicates that kid too." He turned his flashlight on Lily and Erin blinked hard in the sudden darkness. He reached for his handcuffs.

"My shoulder is injured. Please, sir. Not too tight." Arms tensed, Lily kept perfectly still while he cuffed her skinny wrists in front of her. A defiant smirk twisted her lips.

Erin frowned. Why was Lily holding her arms like that? Did she think she was Houdini or something? Erin would never handcuff a suspect in front. It was not protocol. She reluctantly let him take custody.

"Allie. Where's Allie?" White spots still danced across Erin's vision and she couldn't see her anywhere. What had happened while she was chasing Lily?

"There's another lady down there. She's talking to the Sergeant. What did you see this kid do?"

"I saw her approach the rear gas tank area, lean over and then there was a spark. She ran and I chased her down."

That was all she could actually testify to. What else could she say? *Lily is the one responsible for the death of that man down there, no matter what the other girl says. She also broke in and trashed Ciara's house and harassed my pets. She ran away because she thought there was a ghost. No, officer, I didn't witness it, but my girlfriend saw it in her mind. She's gifted, or something.*

She backed away from Lily. It repulsed her to be so near the girl. Was this how Allie felt all the time?

"What happened to your shirt?" The Constable pointed to Erin's torn sleeve. "Did this little girl put up a fight?"

Erin grimaced. "Hit me with a stick. Tried to bite me. She still needs to be searched."

"Don't worry, I've got custody now." Constable Audette didn't understand what Lily was capable of. His dark mustache curled up when he scrutinized the girl's face. "What's up with the mud? You go all commando on this lady, did ya?"

Lily narrowed her eyes and stared back. Her eyes flicked to the semiautomatic pistol at his hip.

"Think you're tough, do ya? We'll see about that." He gave her a nudge toward the flashing lights. She resisted but he clucked his tongue and held her arm tight. She lowered her head and plodded forward. A prisoner to the gallows.

In the parking lot, an unmarked car partially blocked their view of the burnt van. A reporter with a camera ducked past and was blocked by a stout firefighter. He pointed a stern finger and the reporter withdrew. His camera strobe flashed from a safe distance.

With professionals monitoring emergency scanners twenty-four hours a day, media response was fast in this city. Erin was glad they didn't have to parade the suspect past the corpse. That's the sort of picture that would hit the front page. She turned her face away. The last thing she wanted was more media attention.

The firefighter circled, spritzing hot spots. Smoke trailed into the sky and an objectionable odor filled the air. Plastic, upholstery, and burning flesh. Erin coughed. She breathed through her mouth but could still taste it.

A detective was arriving and Forensic Identification wouldn't be far behind. Erin wondered if Nina's dad had died by fire, or something prior. Her home study forensics courses had covered multiple scenarios, none of them pleasant. Suddenly Erin didn't feel so bad about being passed over for the Forensics Unit back home. Her sinuses clogged with soot, her skin crawled. Everything associated to Lily was poisoned.

They passed the first police cruiser. Seated behind a Plexiglas shield a girl bowed her head. Red hair drooped over her face. From Allie's description, that must be Lily's friend, Nina. Lily didn't even turn her head when they passed. It was as if she walked by a stranger. Was this some new game?

A crew cut officer up front scrawled notes in his notebook. He wouldn't be able to interview Nina until she had a parent or advocate, but he would note everything at the scene.

Erin followed a pace behind Constable Audette. Lily was Winnipeg PD's responsibility now. They skirted the fire truck where two men were stowing equipment. There it was. Her Toyota parked by the abandoned white Audi. The puppy bounced up and down on the seat, paws scratching at the glass. He looked excited. Happy to see her. Had Allie locked the door?

Behind the truck was a police SUV, its emergency lights still activated. An older officer sat at the wheel, with Allie on the passenger side, a clipboard in her hand. The officer was taking her witness statement.

Erin exhaled. Her shoulders unwound with the immense relief of seeing Allie unharmed. Safe.

Allie's head swiveled toward them and her eyes locked on Lily.

Constable Audette knocked on the window and the older officer rolled it down. Erin noted the stars on his lapel, the softness of his jawline, the Sergeant designation on the vehicle. This was the man in charge. His nametag read Paswan.

"You got the other kid?" Sergeant Paswan asked. His eyes flitted to Lily, to Erin. "Who's this?"

"This is the officer I told you about. Ericsson, from Minnesota. My wife took that course with her boyfriend."

The Sergeant grunted.

"Z-man's just a friend." Erin clarified.

The Sergeant tilted his head. He had recognized her name. "The Raging Ranger from Morley Falls, eh?"

"I'm not a ranger." Goddamn the reporter who'd come up with that inane moniker.

He gave his head a sideways bob and Constable Audette nodded. Erin's gut roiled. She hoped to hell Allie hadn't been entirely forthcoming in her statement. *I don't know, officer. I just felt the pull to come here. You see, I had these visions, and...* The Sergeant would write them both off as nut jobs.

Inside the SUV, the senior officer retrieved the clipboard from Allie and jerked his chin toward the door. She climbed out, took a step toward Erin, and stopped to look at the puppy in the truck.

"Stay here." The Constable prodded Lily against the side of the SUV. "I gotta talk to Sarge."

Erin kept a polite distance when he leaned through the open window. The two men talked in low tones.

Lily raised her head and a tiny glint ignited her pale green eyes. One side of her lip lifted. She gave her shoulders a shake and her handcuffs rattled.

Erin took a step forward. There was something furtive in the way Lily angled her wrists. Behind her, Erin could hear the dog's nails scratching the window of her truck. He really wanted out. Did he need to pee? Something else?

Allie joined Erin. Her entire body trembled. She took in a deep breath, held it and let it out. She was trying to maintain control. The puppy yowled. Erin reached into her pocket for her keys and thumbed the unlock button on the fob. The lock shushed open.

The color drained from Allie's face. She turned to the dog again.

Erin put her hand on her arm. "Baby, why don't you wait in—?"

* * *

Pain seared Allie's abdomen, white hot in its fury. Simultaneously, there was a metallic clunk as an ill-fitted set of handcuffs hit the ground.

"Die, witch." Lily twisted her fist and blood dripped from the blade between her knuckles. Her eyes widened, pupils dilated, mouth opened. Jagged energy drowned out the light.

"No!" Erin's voice.

Allie doubled over. Her vision funneled to a point. She stared at the knife in her gut. Ciara's knife. The one she'd peeled vegetables with last week. Blood spilled through her shirt.

She should have paid attention to the dog. He'd warned her but she hadn't listened until it was too late. Her foster mother told her that she couldn't change fate. If only there had been more time. She fell to her knees.

She remembered her mama's tousled red hair, like angel wings, as the world spun.

On the pavement beside her, Erin straddled the girl and twisted her arm. Doors slammed. Boots pounded the ground.

Lily turned her face to Allie, pale eyes furious. "How did you find me? Tell me!"

"Your mother sent me." The earth wavered and rose to meet her.

CHAPTER 32

Erin packed the last of Allie's belongings into a cardboard box. A long row of computer monitors still dotted the L-shaped desk. A new motion sensor, linked to a central monitoring system, oversaw it all.

"Raphael, sweetie." Ciara called. "One more." A muscular, olive-skinned man smiled shyly and carried the box outside. On the floor beside her, Rachel sulked in her kitty crate. Ciara squatted and stuck two fingers through the wire mesh. "I'm going to miss you." The cat's whiskers twitched. She turned her back and swished her tail.

Erin picked up the last box and Ciara hefted the crate. They stacked them on the front step.

Erin grabbed her in a bear hug and squeezed until Ciara squirmed in her arms. "I'm so sorry about how everything turned out."

"I'll miss you, superhero. And I'll miss your quirky need to clean my house."

"We'll miss you too." Erin picked up the crate and the cat grumbled. She loaded it into the cab.

Raphael slid the last box into the back and closed the tailgate with a thump. Ciara winked at him and he blushed.

"You need to name that dog." Ciara reminded Erin. As if she hadn't already hinted a thousand times.

"We will." Erin got behind the wheel.

Ciara walked around and opened the passenger door. "No more crime-fighting shenanigans, okay?" She reached out and placed her hand on Allie's pale cheek. The puppy leapt from her lap and she winced. Ciara scooted him over to Erin's side. "Remember what the doctor said. You're lucky to be alive. It's going to take a while for that wound to get better."

"Good thing she didn't steal your carving knife." The circles under Allie's eyes were dark but the light in her eyes was bright as always. She would heal.

"Thanks for the guilt trip." Ciara kissed her on the cheek. "I don't ever want to spend another night in the hospital I.C.U. to find out if my best friend will make it." She glanced at Erin and back. "Your wife never sat down once. She paced a groove in that horrid brown tile."

"My wife." Allie said to Erin.

Erin's head tilted. "Maybe."

"Take care of yourself and I hope you're well enough to enjoy your friend's wedding." Ciara closed the door and Allie immediately rolled down the window.

"You be careful. Remember to lock your door." Erin started the engine. "Set the alarm. You can monitor it from your smartphone."

Ciara stared at the shiny new phone Allie's business had purchased for her. No more living off the grid.

"Don't worry. No one will ever break into this place again." Solid muscle on Raphael's forearms bulged when he crossed them over his chest.

"Between you and Erin's Fort Knox security system, we're safe as houses." Ciara smiled when he blushed again.

"I like the idea of you and Raphael teaming up to run my office here." Allie put a hand on Ciara's shoulder and whispered. "Are you going to make an honest man of him, or is he your toy du jour?"

"I think he might be a keeper," Ciara whispered back.

"About time. We'll talk business when I get back to Morley Falls. A partnership sounds like it a good plan. This business is already too much work for one."

"A three-way," Ciara said too loudly and Raphael's face flushed to his ears. "Fabulous."

They waved as Erin backed out the driveway. The puppy bounced up and put his paws on the back window. His black nose pressed against the glass.

Ciara grabbed Raphael's hand and dragged him up the steps.

CHAPTER 33: TWO MONTHS LATER

Derek Peterson picked up the plastic bag and ripped off the seal. Some asshole had written *van Gogh* on the tag and he threw it on the floor. It wasn't the worst prison nickname he'd heard of, but he sure didn't want it to stick. Inside were the belongings he had surrendered when he was booked into Oak Park Heights Prison. It was all that remained of his previous life, and it was surprisingly light.

One hand holding up his baggy pants, he dumped the contents onto the waiting room floor. His loafers were stained and misshapen from the river water, but he kicked off his inmate's sneakers and shoved his feet into them anyway. He pulled out his leather belt. Oh how he had missed this simple luxury. He eagerly slid it around his lean hips but it hung on him like it was made for another man. A man in his past.

The door opened and with the sudden draft came a small man with a large briefcase.

"You're late." Derek got to his feet and his old shoes pressed uncomfortably on his toes. "I don't want to spend another goddamn second in this place."

"Sorry, sorry," the small man said. "I had trouble at home. My wife—"

"Stop whining," Derek snapped. "I told you I'd help you with that." If there was anything Derek hated more, it was an ex-wife who thought she was entitled to every last shred of a man's dignity.

"Just get me the hell out of here."

"Done. Already done." The lawyer glanced nervously at Derek's missing earlobe. "No one will call you van Gogh again."

Derek glared down at him. "Don't ever call me that."

"Sorry. Uh, as your solicitor, I'm happy to inform you that you're free to walk out that door any time you want."

"That should have been the first fucking thing out of your mouth." Derek grabbed his bag and shoved the door open. Cool air chilled his lungs. As if tentacles reached out to snatch him back to confinement, he hurried down the steps and away from the building. The sky was spectacular from outside the prison walls. Magnificent.

The lawyer opened the door of a black sports car and he slid into the butter soft seats. He had his freedom and he was never going back.

"A free man, yes you are. Free to live your life."

Derek squinted out the side window. The sun was brighter than he remembered. Had he been looking at it through tinted windows all this time? "You sound like fucking bad song lyrics, man."

The man's hands trembled on the wheel. "Please don't use that language. I'm trying to help."

"You. Don't be a pussy," Derek barked. "Remember where I've been for the last year. You want me to say please and thank you? To get on my knees and beg you to get me a P.I. license? You've got your head up your ass."

The lawyer's neck shrank into his shoulders. "Sorry, sorry."

"Listen, Dick. Your name's Dick, right?"

"R— Richard, actually."

"Well, I'm gonna call you Dick." Derek smirked when Richard's face flushed. "I'll help you get evidence on your cheating whore of a wife as soon as you get me my license. You'll be a fucking free man too."

"It will take time," Richard complained. "Your felony conviction was reduced to a gross misdemeanor. You can qualify for your license, but paperwork always takes time. I assure you I am pressing forward on this."

"Dick, listen to me. I need cash, and I need to earn it legally. I've got a kid who needs me and too many eyes are watching me now."

"A couple of weeks, a month. No more than three..." Richard pulled up in front of a dilapidated motel with a neon sign in the window.

Derek held out his hand. "Gimme a fucking advance."

Richard winced. "I thought this was a trade for services."

"I'm getting that bitch off your back. Isn't that worth more?"

Richard peeled a half dozen bills from a fat wad in his wallet. Derek eyed him sternly and he peeled off a few more.

"You know where to find me, Dick." Derek picked up his bag. "Right here at the finest fucking motel in Morley Falls." He slammed the door and headed to the last place he'd seen Tiffany. He'd find her. They'd build a new family, a new life. And he'd start right here.

CHAPTER 34

Erin started with the wide end of the tie in her right hand and the other in her left. She wrapped the big one over the little one, under, up to the right, to the center, through the loop... *Crap.* She unraveled it and started again. "There are, like, fifteen steps. Are you sure you need an Eldridge Knot?"

Chris Zimmerman rose to his feet. The tails of his tuxedo lodged in the crevice between the chair seat and back. He tugged them loose and smoothed the wrinkles. He'd just showered but beads of sweat dotted his forehead. Was he going to make it to his own wedding?

"My bride is perfect," he grumbled. "I need to look presentable. You can't tie it like you're putting on a fishing lure."

"What's wrong with a regular knot, or a bow tie? What in the world is wrong with a good solid bow tie? The kind that's already done and has the clip on the back."

He glowered at Erin. "I think you're tying a Half Windsor. I need an Eldridge Knot. You're my best man. Didn't you practice this?"

"I didn't have time to practice the pretentious Eldridge..." Regret choked the last of her sentence and she dropped her hands.

"It wasn't your fault that Derek Peterson's rotten spawn hurt Allie. Look on the bright side. You got her. The kid's going to jail. Allie will be fine, and if we ever get this figured out, I'll know how to tie an Eldridge Knot at *your* wedding."

"A man died." Erin clenched her jaw. "Lily's friend's father."

"The way I heard it was that it was no big loss to society. He was abusing his kids, beating his wife. He owed money to bad men. It was a matter of time before someone put him in the ground. If it was his own daughter, his victim, so be it."

"I don't think his daughter did it. Not on her own anyways."

Zimmerman squinted at her. "My friend's husband—"

"Constable Audette."

"Yes." He waggled his shoulders the same way he did when he said *whatever*. "Constable Audette found a note in the parking lot from the victim. It sounded like the guy thought his kid was extorting money from him and he refused to pay. That, and the abuse are clear motive. That kid—"

"Nina," Erin prompted.

"Nina," the shoulder waggled again, "is going to juvy until she's an adult. She won't be eligible for day passes for a long time."

"I don't think they call it juvy in Canada, and stop it with the shoulder thing. You're wrinkling your suit." She smoothed his collar. "Hold still." He was handsome, in a big dorky sort of way. She couldn't ask for a better extra-brother.

"I'm sorry about how it went down in the Canadian court system." He put a hand on Erin's arm. "You did good, Erin. How could you possibly fathom that she would be able to plea bargain like that?"

"Unbelievable." Erin whipped the skinnier tail over the wider one and brought it around to the neck loop. "Remember that case up in Canada a while back where that couple, you know the one…"

He nodded. "The serial killers. The guy who raped all those women and the wife who helped him. They killed her own sister."

"That's the one." Erin yanked the tail around again and shoved it through the loop. "She convinced the authorities that she was a poor victim in all of it. Testified against her husband in return for a light sentence in a minimum security facility."

"That's what Lily did." Zimmerman placed two fingers between his exposed Adam's apple and Erin's angry fingers. "The note implicated the other girl, the motive pointed to the other girl, and Lily said she had no idea what the girl was going to do. Claimed she was forced to set fire to the van after Nina murdered her dad. They dropped the fire-setting charge in exchange for her testimony."

"What about her attack on Allie?" Erin clenched her jaw.

"They plea bargained that to aggravated assault."

"It should have been attempted murder." Her teeth gritted against each other. "Why didn't Lily get charged for the theft of the truck? She hurt a police officer."

Zimmerman shook his head. "He could only identify Nina, and Nina wouldn't testify against Lily."

"So, one count of mischief and one of aggravated assault. She has no prior record." He lifted his fingers from his throat to count and Erin cinched the tie tight. He squeaked.

"If Lily hadn't stabbed Allie, she probably wouldn't do any time at all?" Was it fate? Would Lily be walking free right now?

"It looks that way. At least she will be off the street for a while." Sweat dripped down Zimmerman's temple. "Could you go easy on my throat?"

"She'll get day passes after, what, a year? I'll cringe every time I read about her shopping at the mall with her escort." Erin looked at the knot. It was off center.

"Don't be so rough on the Canadian justice system. They didn't match her prints to the break-in at your friend's house until after they'd offered her the deal to testify."

Erin snorted.

"I made sure Morley Falls requested her prints and Bert in Ident tied them to the ones from the Dolores Johnson case. The ones you found. Lily actually bragged about that arson when she got to juvy. Did you know?"

Erin's jaw dropped.

"The prosecutor won't extradite a kid. Not for a half-assed confession and a trifle of circumstantial evidence. But here's the kicker. She recanted her accusation that her father ever touched her. Sexually, I mean. She fabricated the whole thing. Her story changed so many times that it cast doubt on his conviction."

"You're kidding me. So he served a year for assaulting a police officer." Erin touched the scar on her bicep through the sleeve of her tuxedo.

"Yup. My buddy in the parole office says he's applied for a P.I. license."

"Is that even possible?"

"Since the conviction wasn't a felony..." Zimmerman left the rest unsaid. "Did you hear that he earned himself a prison nickname?"

"A nickname?"

"Van Gogh." Zimmerman loved his gossip.

"They named him after a crazy one-eared painter?"

"Yup. Another inmate bit off part of his ear in a fight. He wouldn't file a complaint, said he did it to himself, just like that painter."

"Fitting. Erin gave the knot one last tug and it settled into the spot directly below Zimmerman's Adam's apple, perfectly centered. "Let's get off this topic. I don't want to ruin your big day."

"Yeah, my big day." His huge hands trembled in his lap.

She needed to distract him before he went down in a quivering heap. "How's your mom?" She pursed her lips to keep the snicker in.

"I'll never be able to un-see what I saw." His forehead squeezed together in the middle.

As soon as they'd returned to Morley Falls, she'd discovered why his mom had never seemed too concerned about her back alley stalker. Allie had sensed it long before when she'd said he didn't need that big surveillance system. He got more than he bargained for when he viewed those recordings.

"I assume you've properly met her new boyfriend. Is he nice?" Erin bent to brush an imaginary particle of dust from the toe of her shoe. A gleeful snort escaped.

Zimmerman sighed. "Yes, Henry seems like he treats her okay. I just wish my mom had told me, instead of letting me think she had a stalker."

"With a red sports car." Erin sucked in a guffaw and smoothed the crease she'd made in her trousers.

Zimmerman looked at her and she looked back. His mouth curved into his trademark goofy grin. "I chased that poor man around for a month and a half before I caught him on video. Making out with my mom like a couple of teenagers!"

Erin's laughter exploded from her belly and, this time, he joined in.

"You thought she was afraid to live on her own, but all this time she was just dying for you to move the hell out." Erin clapped him on the shoulder.

There was a knock at the door and a six-year old boy in a tuxedo blustered into the room. His shiny shoes danced beneath him in excitement. "Let's go. Let's go. Let's go."

"Jimmy, you're the most handsome time-keeper, ring-bearer I ever saw."

"You look great in a tuxedo too, Auntie Erin."

She smoothed a tuft of hair on the crown of her nephew's head. "Where are your sisters today? Didn't they come?"

"They are home with the flu. I get to stay at grandma's house for the weekend. Mom said she didn't want three kids sick all at once." He made a face. "I'm glad I'm not sick. I'm glad Z-man is marrying my boss."

"Your boss." Erin laughed. "Don't you sound like a big businessman?"

Jimmy stuck out his chest. "Gina says I'm her best minnow catcher and all the tourists come to the Stop 'N Go to buy them. I'm saving up for a real microscope."

"Why am I not surprised?"

Jimmy tugged down the front of his jacket and hopped up to fist-bump Zimmerman. The two exchanged admiring glances.

"You look like a grown-up," Jimmy said, and the groom blushed.

Erin blotted the sweat on her friend's forehead with her handkerchief and arranged it in her pocket, making sure the corners lined up. She straightened his tails and took a step back. Jimmy was right. "A respectable church wedding. I never would have figured it. I'm so glad Gina talked you out of that fantasy character theme wedding."

"I wasn't really going to…" Above his flushed face, his crew cut was razed with precision. He got to his size fourteen feet and took a great gulp of air.

Erin blotted his brow once more with her handkerchief and stuffed it sideways into her pocket, just in time to steady him. "Come on, buddy. Let's get you hitched before you pass out."

* * *

Allie cracked the door open a sliver to peek down the hall. The prelude song had started. She turned to Gina. "Are you ready?"

"I've been waiting for this man all my life. Of course I'm ready." Hair upswept, one tendril twirling down her temple, Gina was a beautiful bride. The brilliant energy surrounding her was enough for two. She placed a hand over the belly bulge in her wedding dress and stroked the lace with her fingertips. "This baby will love his daddy as much as I do."

"Chris is a lucky man and I'm so proud to be your maid of honor." Allie reached out for her hand and led her to the door.

"You look pretty in that pink satin suit." Gina adjusted her veil and smiled. "Here I go, a-waddlin' down the aisle."

Allie stifled a laugh and opened the door wide.

Waiting with his personal care attendant, Gunther Schmidt straightened from his walker and pushed it aside. His suit was rumpled from where he had been sitting, but he'd showered and shaved today. He waved an impatient hand in the direction of the walker and the attendant rolled it away.

Gina held out her arm and Gunther threaded his through. She would support him, as she always had. His grizzled jaw quivered and then his mouth bent into a satisfied smile.

"I'm so happy you could be here to give me away."

"Ya know I love ya like a daughter." He ground his knurled fist into a watery eye.

"I'm glad you like your new place," Gina whispered.

"Bah, who wants to live all alone in a dang swamp anyways?" He shuffled one foot forward. "Too many skeeters. 'Tween me and dat property developer, I got da better end 'a da stick." He took another step, faltered and met Gina's eyes. He sighed. She nodded and Allie closed in on the other side. Gunther gripped Allie's arm with his free hand and balanced between them.

"Chris and I are happy you're just down the street. The baby will need a grandpa." Gina smiled at him and he dipped his head.

A tear streaked down his cheek. "I never seen two more gorgeous women in my whole sorry life." He shuffled forward, one foot playing catch-up with the other. His attendant shadowed them, ready to produce the walker at a moment's notice. Gunther shot a stern look over and straightened his spine.

By the time they neared the chapel and caught a glimpse of the lightheaded groom, the Wedding March had ended. Across the rows, guests craned their necks and children gawked. Up front, Zimmerman's mother peered back, her brow wrinkled. A balding man next to her put his arm around her shoulder and the wrinkles disappeared. Gamely, the piano player started again. Allie grinned. The song might need to be played a few more times before they reached the front.

The piano player glanced up before starting the song for the third time. Eyes bright, he was clearly enjoying the challenge. Gina stepped across from her future husband and Jimmy hopped on his heels, eager to do his job.

Gunther sank into a chair someone had slipped behind him before he could protest. He leaned forward and gasped for breath.

Zimmerman's face split into a crooked smile when he looked into Gina's eyes. His trembling fingers stilled, his shoulders squared. Beside him, Erin was dashing. She wore a matching tuxedo, fastidious in appearance, except for the scrunched kerchief protruding from her pocket. Erin's energy was anxious, a quarterback who's just thrown the ball and now waits for her star player to catch it.

The officiator stepped forward and began. As he pontificated, Zimmerman's skin paled. His eyes rolled up. Erin squeezed his arm, fingers digging through the fabric until her friend's eyes snapped forward. He gulped air.

The officiator turned to him. "Do you, Christopher Anthony Zimmerman, take this woman to be your lawfully wedded wife, to have and to hold from this day forward, for better or for worse, for richer, for poorer, in sickness and in health, to love and to cherish, from this day forward until death do you part?"

Zimmerman's Adam's apple bobbed but no words came out. He tried again and his voice squealed before reaching its manly tone. "I do."

Jimmy skipped in place and held out the rings before he was asked. The officiator turned to Gina. "Do you—"

Gina's knees buckled and Allie caught her before she went down. "The baby's coming!"

Zimmerman froze. "It's too early. Too early." He tucked Gina, with her big belly, into his chest. "It's too early!" He ran, pregnant almost-wife in his arms, white gown fluttering like a dove in flight. His mother covered her face with her hands.

"What about the rings?" Jimmy shouted.

Erin and Allie raced after Zimmerman and helped him find his truck keys. She opened his door and Zimmerman loaded his bride into the passenger side.

"Call the midwife." Gina squeezed Allie's arm. "Tell her to meet us at the house."

Pain shot through Allie's brain and a baby boy with blue lips whimpered. Her heart squeezed in her chest. All the baby dreams. This is what they were about. "No! You can't have a home birth." She gripped Gina's shoulder.

"But I planned a natural birth. Chris and I wanted..." Gina tilted her head back and groaned. "Tell the midwife to hurry."

Zimmerman shut the door and raced to the driver's side.

Allie blocked him. "Promise me. You must promise." Round-eyed, he prodded her out of the way but she stood firm. "Listen to me! The baby is in danger. Take Gina to the hospital in the city."

"Listen to her, Z-man!" Erin shouted.

He stared at her for a moment and slammed the door. The rear wheels skidded on the road when he put his foot on the gas. He turned to the left. He was going home.

Electricity pounded from one end of Allie's brain to the other. Waves of energy crashed against her skull. Pressure squeezed her throat. She couldn't breathe. She sank to her knees in the parking lot. Erin lifted her to her feet.

"The baby..." Storm clouds gathered in Allie's brain.

"Look." Erin pointed. Zimmerman's truck flashed past, headed the other direction. He had listened. He was taking Gina to the hospital in the city.

Allie wrapped her arms around Erin's neck and sobbed into her tuxedo collar.

"The baby will be fine?" Erin smoothed her hair.

"Yes." Relief flooded every molecule of her body. "A bigger hospital will have what he needs."

"Then don't cry, Baby. We're going to be godparents." Erin held her at arm's length. "You're so hot in that outfit. You should wear that every day." She brushed a tear from Allie's cheek with her thumb. "Let's get our dog to my parents' house and we'll go meet the new kid at the hospital."

Allie motioned to the lawn in front of the church. "I think we've already found a capable dog-sitter."

Jacket off, tie sideways and one pant leg tucked into his sock, Jimmy circled the lawn with the puppy on its leash. His brow furrowed in concentration.

"Thanks for walking our dog." Erin caught up with him when his circles got smaller. "Would you like to dog-sit for us for the rest of the day?" The puppy altered his course and went back. Allie joined in and the boy-dog duo veered around her.

"We're not walking, we're searching." Jimmy followed the dog and Erin trotted to keep pace. "He's helping me."

"How is he helping you?" Allie asked.

"Well, he's a dog. He's got a nose, hasn't he?" Jimmy puffed his cheeks in exasperation.

"What are you searching for?" Allie knew he'd find what he sought, in a minute. In her mind, there was a flash of gold, a brilliant sparkle.

"I was playing and I lost the rings." Jimmy put his head down and tugged the leash. "Go find them Doppler."

"Doppler?" Erin stared at him.

"You named the dog?" Allie asked. The name suited the pup.

"Of course. He wanted a name." Jimmy said matter-of-factly.

"He *told* you that?" Erin shot Allie a look.

Allie shrugged. She hadn't made him say that. She hadn't even been around to influence him. They'd been up north in Winnipeg chasing Lily.

"What do you mean?" Erin quizzed him.

Jimmy sighed. "Well, he didn't exactly talk because everyone knows animals can't talk. I just know that if I was a dog, I'd want a name." He pointed a finger at Erin's chest. "You didn't give him one, so I had to."

Erin exhaled.

Allie smiled at Jimmy's reasoning. "How did you choose the name?"

Jimmy sighed again. "It's obvious. You know what the Doppler effect is, don't you?" He eyed them dubiously. "That's how a police radar works to catch speeders." He tilted his head at Erin when she didn't respond. "Come on, Traffic School 101."

Erin grinned.

"Okay, so here's an easy explanation. You know how the sound a car makes is higher when it's coming toward you than after it has already passed? It's lower after it passes because the sound waves are farther apart. That's the Doppler effect." He pointed to the dog. "That's kind of how his nose works, only with smells instead of sounds. He can track where I was playing. He can even tell from one step to the next which one is more recent so he follows it in the proper direction." Jimmy put a hand on his hip. "That was in the dog book you gave me for Christmas."

Allie nodded. "Doppler. It's perfect." It made sense, but not necessarily for the reasons Jimmy was so meticulously explaining. The pup could read *her* reaction to energy. Her feelings waxed or waned with her proximity to the source. The more intensely she reacted, the more he did. "Good job Jimmy." She stepped in his path and forced the duo to alter course.

"Auntie Allie," he complained. "You're in the way." His eyes popped open and he crouched beside the dog. Doppler sniffed between his fingers when he flattened the grass at his feet. "He found them!" He held up two wedding rings, joined by a pink ribbon.

"Yay." Erin took the rings. "About that dog-sitting job…"

"I'll do it! If you drop me off at grandma and grandpa's, I'll take good care of him until you get back."

"Deal." Erin picked up the puppy and scratched him behind his huge ears. He wagged his tail.

Allie put her hand on the dog's head. "Doppler, you be a good dog for Jimmy."

A YEAR LATER

Allie handed Erin the last bag and she shoved it across the tailgate of her truck. She slammed it shut. They stood close, foreheads touching.

"FBI training is only a few months." Erin kissed her nose. "You can come visit on my breaks."

"Why don't you just marry her and get it over with?" Wiggly one-year-old on his shoulder, Zimmerman wrapped an arm around her in an awkward embrace.

"Maybe I will," Erin quipped and Allie's face flushed.

"You're going to be a G-man… uh, G-woman. That sounds weird." Zimmerman bounced his squirming son. "We'll sure miss you at the station. All the guys will."

"Good luck. Kick some butt." Gina joined in for the group hug, and the baby dropped a soggy cracker down Erin's collar.

"I hope my godson will be able to say my name when I get back." She shook the treat out the bottom of her shirt and wiped the goo from her neck.

"I'll work on that." Allie took the baby and whirled him in a circle. He giggled, his mouth open and curly hair bobbing.

They stood at the end of the driveway while Erin drove away. A solid line. Together.

A USPS letter carrier clanged the mailbox behind them and the baby cried. The mailman continued on his way, but a dark shadow lingered at the edge of Allie's mind. She waited until Erin's truck disappeared before retrieving the mail.

The first item was a brown-wrapped box from her foster mom.

Allie guessed that it contained a brand new Swiss Army knife. Just like the one she'd lost when they'd saved the little boy from the submerged van. Her foster mom had been so proud of her when Erin had told her about the incident. Allie smiled.

She reached into the mailbox for the other item, and cold fingers squeezed her chest. It was a plain rumpled envelope. Allie smoothed the crease over the return address. *Manitoba Department of Justice, Winnipeg Youth Centre.* Erin's name was scrawled in pencil across the front, with an erroneous address that had defied logic when it was delivered here.

Gina and Zimmerman flanked her on the porch step.

She held up the envelope.

"Open it," Gina said.

Allie tore the flap and pulled out a single sheet of folded paper. She read the words and pain seared the jagged scar on her abdomen. The letter, in Lily's teenage scribble, drifted from her fingers to the ground.

I'M COMING BACK

ABOUT THE AUTHOR

Makenzi Fisk grew up in a small town in Northwestern Ontario.
She spent much of her youth outdoors, surrounded by
the rugged landscape of the Canadian Shield.

Moving west, she became a police officer with experience in patrols, covert
operations, plainclothes investigation, communications and forensic
identification. Within the policing environment, she transitioned to internet
and graphic design. She now works for herself.

In her novels, Makenzi draws on her knowledge of the outdoors, policing
and technology to create vivid worlds where crime, untamed wilderness and
intuition blend. Her characters are competent women who solve crime
using skill and a little intuition.

Currently Makenzi resides in Calgary with her partner,
their daughter, and assorted furry companions.

Website: makenzifisk.com

Books in the Intuition series:

Book One: Just Intuition
Book Two: Burning Intuition

Next in the series:

40727753R00152

Made in the USA
Charleston, SC
15 April 2015